THE
LOST
ROYALS
SAGA

DARK SIDE OF THE MOON

RACHEL JONAS

CONTENTS

LOST ROYALS SAGA

COPYRIGHTS

Edited by La Kata E.K.
Cover Design by Christian Bentulan from Covers by Christian
Artworks. All Rights Reserved.
Interior Design and Formatting by Stephany Wallace at @S.W.
Creative Publishing co. All Rights Reserved.

Published December 26th, 2017

WRITTEN AS RACHEL JONAS

THE LOST ROYALS SAGA
The Genesis of Evangeline
Dark Side of the Moon
Heart of the Dragon
Season of the Wolf
Fate of the Fallen

DRAGON FIRE ACADEMY
First Term
Second Term
Third Term

THE VAMPIRE'S MARK
Dark Reign
Hell Storm
Cold Heir
Crimson Mist

WRITTEN AS RACHEL JONAS
& NIKKI THORNE

KINGS OF CYPRESS POINTE

The Golden Boys
Never his Girl
Forever Golden
Pretty Boy D
Mr. Silver
Sexy Beast

SAVAGE KINGS OF BRADWYN U
Break the Girl
Cold as Ice

DESCRIPTION

A supernatural war fast approaching. A young queen who may not live to take the throne.

Evie can't recall her past life, but her quest for answers revealed the truth behind local lore: wolves and dragon shifters *do* exist ... and she's a hybrid descendant of both. Keeping her identity as the returned queen hidden is no small feat. Especially when it's unclear who's friend or foe, who risked it all to bring her back, and why?

It's with Liam's help that she learns to embrace and control her new abilities. Their shared past dates back centuries, an era when Liam was much more to her than just a warrior. She has no memory of their time together; however, traces of a powerful bond linger even now.

But she's torn.

Can the choices she makes in the present override supernatural ties and legends of old? Or is her future already written in stone?

Including signs pointing toward her untimely death at the hands of Nick, the boy who stole her heart the moment she set foot in Seaton Falls?

Evie refuses to be ruled by her past.
Nick's determined to rewrite the future that marks him as her killer.

And as for Liam, her warrior ... he looks forward to stopping him when he fails.

Thank you for your purchase! I would love to get your feedback once you've finished the book!
Please leave a review and let others know what you thought of
"Dark Side of the Moon"
Come hang out in the newly created "Shifter Lounge" on Facebook!
https://www.facebook.com/groups/1416338532435211/
We chat, recommend YA paranormal romances, and engage in other random acts of nerdiness. Once we're fully up and running, there will be tons of giveaways, exclusive ARC offers from me, and guest appearances by some of your favorite YA authors!

For all inquiries, please contact me using my primary email address:
author.racheljonas@gmail.com

CHAPTER I

Liam

Every large clan kept a few witches around. They were pets, mostly, but every now and then they were let loose to torture someone if an Elder deemed them a threat.

Today, I was that someone.

If the three holding me hostage in my own home were any indication, the coven allied with the lycans of Seaton Falls were a nasty bunch.

A small fist slammed the right side of my face, proving my point. I spat blood to the floor and she loved it—the one who looked to be about twelve, although I suspected all three were at least a few hundred years old. Most were. Some were far older.

Their magic paralyzed me, binding me to the chair they dragged in from the kitchen. No rope or chains necessary. The only thing I could do was speak, but that didn't matter much because they weren't here to reason. Their master gave a command and they followed that command blindly.

Like pets.

I first spotted them at this afternoon's meeting—three deceivingly frail figures cloaked in dark garbs, posted beside the Elders. The moment they entered the crowded chamber hidden beneath the library, I knew what purpose they served. They were sort of a supernatural version of the secret service, a failsafe should the assembly between the clan and Council get out of hand. After it was announced that the young shifters of Seaton Falls were being taken against their parents' will, it wasn't hard to understand why the witches' presence was necessary.

Fortunately for the clan, they avoided tasting the wrath these three were capable of raining down.

Too bad I couldn't say the same for myself.

Heavy steps approached from behind and the wood slats creaked with each. So far, all the Elder had done was watch his minions beat me bloody, but now, it appeared he was ready to talk.

A dark shadow blocked light from the window to my left and I peered up, unable to lift my head. I swear, if it hadn't been for the witches holding me hostage in my seat, I would've snapped this guy's neck on sight. He wouldn't be the first Elder I killed. Probably wouldn't be the last. They had a tendency to think they were invincible.

I kinda liked showing them they weren't.

His face was hidden in the shadow of his hood, but I could feel him staring as he came into view. He stopped at my feet. I breathed hard and heavy. I didn't trust him. It seemed he couldn't have cared less about his own clan, so what was to stop him from taking advantage of the paralysis and ending me right now?

"Speak, dragon." The Elder's voice was slow and deep, trembling with the same unearthly vibrato as every other. "What business do you have here in Seaton Falls?"

Before I could answer, another spray of blood left my mouth

when the small one took a second jab. My eyes cut toward her as I panted. I wanted her throat beneath my boot so badly it was almost unbearable.

"Settle down, Scarlet. Let him speak," the Elder commanded.

She, the one I'd let the life out of first chance I got, backed away with a grin.

My eyes went to the Elder again. "Wouldn't it have been more efficient to ask questions *first?*"

Scarlet wound her finger in a slow circle from a few feet away and another jolt of pain ricocheted off my skull. It seemed to irritate her that she couldn't get a reaction out of me other than gritting my teeth.

"Lilith? Marin? Take your sister outside until she learns to behave herself."

The witches responded to the Elder's harshly spoken words without question. The screen door slammed when they were gone, and it was just the two of us now.

"Answer the question, dragon. Why are you here?"

I didn't speak right away. It was important to weigh my words carefully to protect the only person on this planet who mattered to me—*Evangeline*. Not responding at all would have made him end me right here and now. While death had never been something I feared, dying would mean she'd be alone and defenseless. Seeing as how today revealed who and what she needed protection *from*, I had to stay alive.

For her.

"I've only got so much patience," he grumbled, strolling around my chair in a slow circle.

There was only one answer I was willing to give. "I'm here to protect a common interest."

He didn't speak right away and the only sound in the room was his steady ambling behind my seat. I didn't like not having a visual on him.

"A common interest." The phrase seemed to amuse him. "You must mean the girl."

I had to tread lightly. There was a possibility he was unaware of Evangeline's true identity, the reason she was so important to their race and mine. So, the only confirmation I gave was my silence.

"Hm." Linking his hands behind his back, he paced again. "We were told she wouldn't be any trouble." He stopped in front of me, adding, "But you, dragon... you certainly look like trouble."

I didn't reply, only watched the sway of the dark-burgundy robe he hid beneath.

"She was supposed to be the only one," he went on. "And had it not been for her also being half lycan, there would have been no convincing the others to allow it." His steps continued to echo. "The only thing that proved to be a more difficult challenge, was convincing them she even *was* a lycan. It's nearly impossible to trace *our* scent beneath that god-awful smoke."

That'd always been true about her. Yes, she was both—lycan and dragon—but even in the past, her dragon was stronger than her wolf. I believe because she favored the gifts of one over the other.

"Who sent you and what's your mission?" Apparently, he had no plans to let the vague answer I gave slide.

"I have no mission, because no one sent me."

At the sound of my voice, he stopped in his tracks and, while I couldn't see his expression beneath the shadow, I was sure he was furious now.

"I'm supposed to believe it's a coincidence that not one, but *two* bloodthirsty dragons—a species most are fortunate to go centuries without ever crossing *one's* path—just so happened to waltz through Seaton Falls amid such a monumental... *rough patch*... for our people?" He nodded slowly. "Interesting."

This was going nowhere, and I didn't like being stuck here while Evangeline was God-knows-where. Who's to say he hadn't sent someone to interrogate her as well? Yes, she was, technically, a member of his clan, but only by default. Only because she lived here.

But she wasn't like the others who'd been born and raised under their leadership, wasn't regarded as 'one of them'. I knew this because she spoke many times of feeling like an outsider. There was only one she seemed to connect with, but that, like everything else, wasn't quite what it seemed.

"If you tell me who sent her here, I may be able to explain things better," I reasoned.

If I understood how Evangeline ended up in Seaton Falls, alive after dying centuries ago, if I knew whether her regeneration somehow put her in danger, I could better gage who to trust. But until that happened, I wouldn't risk saying too much.

I sighed when he ignored my first inquiry, but didn't let that stop me from making another.

"If this is about me crashing your Council meeting today, I only wanted answers. If I was gonna hurt somebody, I would've done it already. I've been living here for months."

He seemed to only hear one part of my explanation and repeated it as a question. "Answers?"

I was able to nod, which meant the witch's spell was beginning to wear off. "In case you hadn't noticed, a gang of mutts showed up on my property earlier. Seeing as how there's been a problem with them lately, I knew your meeting was where I'd find more information, like why they were sent."

My clothes were still caked with those things' black blood and dark fur. The result of a human bitten by a lycan was a complete and total abomination. No, all didn't turn into these disgusting beasts, but for the majority who did? Ugliest thing you've ever seen.

"And... did you fend off these mutts alone?"

I wasn't sure why that mattered, but shared anyway. Whatever it took to get him to call off his pets so I could check in with Evangeline. "No. There were others here."

I envisioned the four lycans who fought at our side.

"Like whom?" he asked next.

It didn't take long to figure out where his line of questioning was headed or why he was here. It had nothing to do with the Council meeting. Those lycans snitched, the ones who helped with the mutts. I ran their brother, Nick, off my property after discovering he was no ordinary, run-of-the-mill wolf.

His true nature was terrible and sinister regardless of his outer appearance, regardless of whether he realized his purpose. His destiny was to become the *Liberator*... a living, breathing weapon with one mission: to liberate Evangeline's soul from her body.

His ability to hear her heartbeat across a crowded room, his excessive strength, his speed... it all increased his chances of ending her life. It all made him the ultimate predator.

So, why did I let him get away? Why was he still breathing, you ask?

Because the one girl capable of changing my mind insisted on it. As fate would have it, with neither having initial knowledge of how one's future impacted the other's ... they were friends.

Or ... *more* than friends.

He loved her. For all I knew, she felt the same to some degree. Neither spoke of it, but I wasn't blind. And, as someone who's loved her his entire life, I knew the look of a man who'd fallen. It nearly broke him to hear me explain that his assignment was to take her life, but he'd never get the chance on my watch.

One day, his feelings for her wouldn't matter. Eventually, he'd forget all the fond memories and his nature would overtake him. And, because of the handy parlor trick that enabled him to hear her heart, there would be no place she could hide from him. He would seek to carry out the task he was born to fulfill at all costs.

But I'd be there to kill him before he succeeded.

I should have seen this coming—the mess, the fallout. The lycans here had no concept of the big picture, of their past, their legacy. They knew so little of their own history it was almost laughable. Clearly, the Elders didn't trust them with much information, but did they not realize the lack of knowledge would cripple them?

Make them vulnerable?

The oldest wolf I'd sensed in passing, aside from the Elders, couldn't have been more than a hundred. That was still no excuse for the lack of preparation I'd seen here. Most of the kids who turned didn't even have a clue what was happening. In recent years, it wasn't uncommon to hear of clans living in blissful ignorance, pretending to be only human because, sometimes, that was easier. But I couldn't begin to express the negligence of such an oversight. Unfortunately, the residents of this scenic, Michigan town in the hills learned that the hard way a couple days ago. Right before the mutts showed up, many of the teens shifted years before the typical age of transition—twenty.

The end result? A rash of injuries and homes in desperate need of repair after the newly-turned lycans raged out of control. The fiasco had the clan scrambling for a solution. They settled on sending their young shifters to a facility where they'd be trained to defend themselves, their packs, their clan.

Like I said, ignorance is bliss until it isn't.

And it was that same ignorance that brought the three witches and an Elder to my doorstep today.

Evangeline being equal parts dragon and lycan meant they had as much stake in protecting her as I did. Their prejudice for my race—a species they've always revered as unpredictable, dangerous—was apparent. And Evangeline's tendency to present more as a dragon than a lycan didn't help. It made her seem like an outsider to them, but they couldn't have been more wrong about that.

Yes, her mother, a native of a small village in France, was the original dragon. However, Evangeline's father, who ruled a kingdom in the heart of Ethiopia, was one of two original lycans. So, with the death of both her parents... that made her queen.

To their race.

To mine.

A once fallen descendant of two original shifters. And, somehow, she'd shown up right here in this town, and all I wanted to know was:

How?

But I couldn't make it known why I was so curious. Keeping Evangeline's identity secret for now was, perhaps, the only way to keep her safe.

When I decided I wouldn't answer anymore of the Elder's questions, he sighed.

"Very well then." He was calm. A little *too* calm.

Taking slow steps, he pressed the tips of his dry, pale fingers together in the form of a pyramid in front of his chest.

"You leave me no choice but to bring Marin, Scarlet, and Lilith back to join our party, but it would be remiss of me not to give you one last chance to share what you know on your own terms," he added. "Because, once I give them permission to cross-examine you in ... *their own way* ... I can assure you their methods will be most unpleasant."

A flash of Evangeline's face came to me. It was a memory from so long ago I couldn't recall the date. We were in one of many gardens within the walls of her father's kingdom—her favorite because of the large, acacia tree that grew beside the stream. We visited often, but this day was different. It was the day she bound herself to me, and me to her.

For life.

That bond was the reason I could not only find her wherever she was, but ... I could *feel* her. Strongly.

Even now.

Which meant she'd wandered inside my head again—a two-way line of communication that had to be initiated by her for the time being, until she figured out she was capable of allowing me the same privilege.

I wasn't sure when she popped in, but she was supposed to be home getting cleaned up from our ordeal with the mutts. At least that was the plan when I dropped her off a couple hours ago.

And yet, here she was.

She would be speaking soon, but I had a feeling she'd be at a loss for words. With her completely capable of seeing through my eyes whenever she chose to do so, I knew the sight of my present company would be confusing.

"Scarlet," The Elder's gruff voice called out. Right after, three sets of footsteps scurried up the porch and then through my front door. They stood before him, waiting for his next command.

Pets.

"It appears our friend here has decided not to answer any more of my questions, so I was hoping one... or *all* of you, could be of some assistance?"

Having one of them inside my head was bad enough. But all three?

I breathed deep through my mouth, planning to keep them out of my thoughts for as long as I could. If they got in, if they unearthed all my secrets ... I wasn't sure I'd be able to protect Evangeline's identity.

"With pleasure." Scarlet stepped up first, wearing that sadistic grin again. Her hand lifted from beneath the black cloak that matched the others', and her cold, clammy palm pressed to my forehead.

"Brace yourself," the Elder stated. "This *will* be painful."

Painful didn't even begin to describe it. When I yelled out, I felt Evangeline's presence even stronger. I could only hope she didn't decide to be brave again. The last time she sensed I was in danger, she showed up and that couldn't happen today. Not with these four here.

"There, there now, lizard," the Elder said with a laugh, attempting to taunt me with the insult. "This will all be over before you know it. Once you tell me all I need to know, that is."

I couldn't. Not even at the feel of my brain being fried inside my skull.

"He's a tough one to crack," Scarlet smiled.

The Elder stared from beneath his hood, a shadow covering his face. There was a chill to the air when he stepped closer and I knew things were about to go from bad to worse.

"Well, if we can't get him to crack," he fumed, "... I suppose we'll just have to break him."

Marin and Lilith joined in on the fun, placing their hands on me along with Scarlet's. Searing pain shot through my body—all my limbs, scrambling my senses. I was on the cusp of bursting into flames as the dragon within me fought to be set free. However, their magic made that impossible.

They were digging into my psyche, trying to extract everything I knew, my memories, but I fought back. Somehow, through the distracting pain, I kept up the wall between them and my life with Evangeline—the one she lived before this.

"Deeper," the Elder crooned.

And deeper they went.

I yelled out again, fighting as hard as I could, but I felt it the moment one pushed through, piercing the veil, snatching the first morsel I intended to keep hidden.

"What is it, Scarlet?" one of the others asked.

She giggled first, worming her way in just a little further. "How interesting."

"Speak, Scarlet." The Elder didn't sound nearly as amused.

"He's not in here alone," she explained. "There's someone inside his head... *with* him." She paused a moment and then, said the one thing I hoped she wouldn't. A name. "Evangeline."

The room was silent.

"The dragons seem to be ... hmm ... I don't know the word for it, but I might be able to describe it."

My teeth gritted together as I pressed hard to force the witches out, but couldn't. The only thing I *was* strong enough to accomplish was getting rid of Evangeline. There was no telling what was about to be done to me, and I didn't want any gruesome images lingering with her. She'd been through enough. I felt her protesting, but shoved her out of my head anyway.

Scarlet drilled her magic deeper, pealing back the veil,

unearthing my past, all my secrets ... until something jarred her, made her pull away completely. She stared at me with wide eyes like she'd seen a ghost, but said nothing.

"Speak, Scarlet," the Elder boomed again, growing impatient.

With her eyes trained on me, it took a moment to gather her words.

"She's gone," Scarlet began. "I think he pushed her out. Maybe so I wouldn't see more, but ... I don't need her present to feel that they're linked to one another. It's not a familial tie," she tried to explain. "But it's—"

"... a far deeper connection than that."

The Elder finished Scarlet's thought and I took note of the change in his voice. It'd suddenly become lighter, less authoritative. Even more so when he whispered the one thing I was trying to keep him from gathering from this inquisition.

"You're tethered to her."

And there it was.

If he was as old as I sensed, he knew exactly what that meant.

"Back away," he said cautiously, causing his pets to remove their hands and retreat to the nearest corner. "Don't lay another finger on him," was his next command, "but make sure the spell holds."

The natural tremble to his voice was different now, fearful. My guess was, he realized several things in the past few seconds and thought better of his actions.

One: because tethering was an ancient ritual only the original dragon herself—or her descendants—could perform, he knew I was connected to someone very powerful.

Two: Evangeline being a rare hybrid ... he also knew she fit the description of one such descendant, one whose existence was merely legend to most. The reigning king made certain to erase her family's legacy as thoroughly as possible, reducing them to nothing more than a whispered rumor on the lips of the few.

Third: the Elder may have also had knowledge of how deadly she was in her past life, but *didn't* know she hadn't tapped into any of her abilities yet. The mutt she managed to kill when they attacked today was nothing short of a miracle—an echo of her former self bleeding through. If it came down to her and a lycan of the Elder's strength? She'd lose for sure.

But I'd never tell *him* that.

He was silent while weighing his options. "Is it … really her?"

The question made my heart race even more than the torture I just endured. Evangeline's safety was the only thing that mattered to me. I wouldn't jeopardize that for anything.

I sat there half-paralyzed, staring as I struggled to catch my breath. Blood poured from my nose and mouth like a fountain.

"And why... on Earth... would I trust *you*?" I forced out, panting.

There was a long bout of silence that I think weighed heavy on us all. The situation could've taken a turn in the blink of an eye and any one of us could've ended up bleeding out on this floor.

With a sudden shifting of his body, the Elder ordered the witches to leave the house. And, before they were gone, he made a brave move I wasn't quite sure how to read.

"Lift the spell."

"I don't think that's wise." It was Scarlet who'd spoken against him. I wasn't sure what she'd seen during her probe into my psyche, but the blanketed hatred she'd held for me now felt personal.

The Elder wasn't amused by her protest. With one look, his pets scampered away. I smirked at the small one when our eyes locked. Yeah … I was definitely gonna enjoy watching her take her last breath one of these days.

"As you wish," she said softly, keeping her eyes trained on me while she made her way to the door.

As soon as I regained use of my limbs, I was on my feet in a flash, moving toward the Elder.

Wiping blood from my nose with my wrist, I let him know he'd just made a huge mistake setting me free. "Probably shouldn't have done that. Now there's nothing stopping me from ending you. Right here. Right now."

He exhaled before answering. "Yes, I'm aware of that."

"Good." I nodded, watching his feet, noting how every step I took toward him, he took one back. "Then, I'm guessing you *also* know ... I'm going to thoroughly enjoy this."

CHAPTER 2

Liam

My fists tightened.
Heat filled my veins.

All at the thought of how excellent it would feel to crush the Elder's old, brittle skull with one blow. Then, it crossed my mind that I ought to draw this out, so he'd feel it for a while before death came for him. I drew back and rage filled me. Just as I lunged forward to take the first swing, he spoke.

"Wait!"

The fear in his eyes was invigorating, addictive. I wanted nothing more than to draw more of it from him. By any means necessary.

"I ordered the witches to lift the spell in good faith," he reasoned.

It was customary for Elders to stay covered, never revealing their true selves, and to never show weakness. However, before me, this one readied himself to do both. First, he kneeled at my feet without hesitation. Then, to make it clear he'd seen the err of his ways, the dark hood he wore was pushed down to his shoulders, exposing a bald, scaly head. Both hands were locked tight as his weak posture made me sick to my stomach.

"Get up," I growled, barely able to get the words out through clenched teeth. "Don't let what's left of your existence be marked by cowardliness. You *will* die today," I assured him. "But at least do it with dignity."

He lifted his eyes to meet mine, their milky-white centers another indicator of his age. The only other times I'd seen the worn faces of Elders was after I'd taken their lives. This was the first instance one had revealed himself to me while he was yet alive. From the looks of them, you'd think they were more corpse than anything, but their outer appearance was somewhat of a choice. They chose their role and, with their authority and power, came a vow to live a life of solitude without the comfort of a mate, and the curse of *senectute*. Which is, more or less, a complicated way of saying *'old age'*.

Several centuries ago, when Elders were ordained, they opted out of a luxury all other shifters have been afforded. They forfeited the ability to choose when to age outwardly beyond the threshold age of twenty. From the day they took their vow and their role was bestowed upon them, they underwent an irreversible, physical change, becoming what groveled on the floor before me today.

"I need to speak," he stated. "And my posture has nothing to do with wanting you to spare my life."

I was intrigued, so I listened.

"I've lived far too many years to fear death. If my swift end should come at this very moment by your hand, then so be it."

"Get to your point." Intrigue would only hold me off so long.

"I believe I've discovered a few things, dragon. The main revelation being that you were right in regards to our common interest," he explained. "If you're tethered to who I *believe* you're tethered to, then ... we do, indeed, need to reconsider our priorities. For starters, protecting her would instantly become number one."

Some of the tension left my fist at those words and I hated it. The only thing I wanted more than his blood on my hands was Evangeline's safety. With what he said next, I trusted he knew that.

"And I also believe you to be her warrior. One who, like *her,* bears a reputation that precedes you." He fell silent and I imagined he spent that time recalling some of the tales he must have heard long ago. "With how fiercely you protect her, your willingness to lay down your life for hers ... it only makes sense. I've said all of this to acknowledge that, if I'm right about you *both* ... I owe you my sincerest apology."

I didn't speak, only breathed, noting that I didn't detect any fear coming from him.

"While I am not, admittedly, fond of your kind, I respect your service to the royal family," he stated. "God rest their souls."

I stared down on him, finding it hard to do all the skull smashing I had my heart set on with him in such a helpless position. It took a moment to decide how to move forward, but for starters, I was beginning to believe the Elders of Seaton Falls weren't on the wrong side.

"Stand up," I exhaled, keeping my eyes trained on him.

He was on his feet the next instant, but kept his head bowed. Many, many years ago, that would have been the posture of *anyone,* Elders included, in the presence of someone with close ties to the royals. However, time had erased such traditions right along with Evangeline's family. It was strangely nostalgic to be reverenced in the way I was once accustomed to.

"My name is Baz," he shared, another part of themselves an Elder rarely revealed to others. "So ... am I right to assume that our ... *common interest,* if you will ... is a descendant?" He paused and there was hope laced into the syllables when he clarified further. "The queen?"

I stared into his ragged face when he dared to lift his eyes to mine.

"She is," I finally admitted. "And the young lycan you so diligently rushed over to chastise me for running off?" Baz's brow tensed with curiosity when I mentioned Nick. "Yeah ... he just so happens to be the Liberator."

His chest swelled with a deep breath as shock filled his expression. "Are you ... are you sure? What's the likelihood the two would reside so closely to one another?"

I was nodding before he finished. "I'm sure; saw with my own eyes. And, to answer your other question, it's very unlikely, which means it's not a coincidence."

Silence. He now understood why I stepped up to Nick the way I had.

"Tell me who sent her," I demanded, wondering if my newfound leverage would yield the answer I sought.

"You have to believe me, I would if I could," he began, but I could already tell he wasn't going to say the right thing. My fingers wound into his collar and I lifted him into the air, slamming his back to the wall so hard it resonated through the house like thunder. His eyes drifted shut when I came nearly nose-to-nose with him.

"Wrong answer, old-timer."

He covered his face with both arms when I drew my fist back again.

"I'm telling the truth. None of us ever spoke with the courier directly, all we were told was that she's part lycan and was to be taken in as a member. We visited while she slept one night, to confirm she was one of us," he explained, "and once we knew for sure, according to the way we govern ourselves, that made her part of our clan."

I frowned at his mentioning they invaded her home, but didn't veer off topic. "Courier? What courier?"

"The one who delivered the letter," he clarified. "There was an official seal on it so we knew it came from someone much higher in rank than us. A member of the *High* Council," he revealed. "But there was no explanation, no signature."

Anger flowed through me like a life source, but, for the sake of getting answers, I had to stop letting my temper get the best of me.

Slowly, reluctantly, I lowered Baz's feet back to the ground. He straightened his robe and explained further.

"Despite my initial intent when I arrived, you have to understand that we're now on the same side," he reasoned. "We are, after all, discussing the fate of our queen."

A chill made the hair on my arms stand on end. The phrase *'heavy is the crown...'* had never been truer than within the supernatural realm. For Evangeline, because she was a hybrid, the truth was twice as weighty. At the thought of her title making her a target, my heart raced.

"Who else knows?" he asked quietly.

I shook my head. "No one but you, me, and Evangeline."

A distant smile crossed his face before he spoke again. "It is truly a blessed turn of events, having an heir to the Bahir Dar throne arise. With her, the possibility of our dreaded Sovereign no longer having absolute power has arisen as well."

My skin crawled at the mention of him—Sebastian De Vincenzo, the Sovereign who'd ruled the lycans with an iron fist for centuries.

"Her existence gives us something we've long waited for." Baz met my gaze with a sigh before adding, "She is a symbol of hope."

While I understood his optimism regarding Evangeline's lineage ... I wouldn't let her be some pawn in these creatures' ruthless game. If no one *ever* acknowledged her as queen, I'd be perfectly fine with that. Her life was all that mattered—not titles, not some greater objective.

Just her life.

"Any plans or arrangements regarding her go through me. Understood?" My voice was hard and unyielding, but I meant for it to be. "No decisions, no *moves,* under any circumstances, are made without my say-so."

I believe he saw the ferocity behind my eyes because there was now fear behind his.

"Understood."

I moved toward the window, feeling Evangeline's energy pulsing toward me. She was on her way, like I fully expected. Like I feared. Even with the threat of the mutts still lurking about, she was coming to me.

I'm sure this was all very confusing for her—struggling with her attachment to Nick, not being able to deny feeling something for me, too. But our tether was unbreakable. Meaning, it would always only lead her in one direction.

Mine.

Like now, as I sensed her getting closer.

I turned toward Baz again when he spoke. A long breath puffed from his withered lips first.

"Of course, I'll send word ahead for special accommodations to be made for her sleeping quarters," he started. "But, with her and the others leaving for The Damascus Facility in the very near future, how do you propose we manage the situation between our queen and young Nicholas? Assuming we're able to locate him, that is."

I answered without even having to think about it. "I promise to put him down quickly, in the most humane way possible."

When Baz frowned, I guessed he had something else in mind. "I'm afraid I can't let that happen. With the shadow of war looming in the distance, unless he proves to be a problem, it would be in *all* our best interest to have a weapon as strong and savage as the Liberator fighting on our side."

His assumption was steeped in ignorance.

"You say that as if there's a way to control him. If his switch gets flipped, there'd be no such thing as loyalty. He wouldn't be fighting on *anyone's* side. His one and only thought would be to kill Evangeline." I arrived at my original idea once again. "If I end him while he's sleeping, he won't suffer."

"We at least need to speak with whoever sent Evangeline. Maybe they know something we don't. Maybe, since they placed her and Nicholas shoulder-to-shoulder here in Seaton Falls ... they have a plan."

I hated this idea. Being patient was something I'd gotten good at after being alive so many years, but not in situations like this. Not when it came to Evangeline. When I shook my head *'no'*, damning his suggestion, he pleaded with me again.

"I assume you'll be accompanying her. Am I correct?"

I nodded. There was never a question about it. Wherever she went, I'd be there too. I trusted no one but myself to protect her. Mostly because I knew no one else would value her life over their own like I always had.

"I figured as much," Baz replied. "And how, exactly, do you plan to gain access to her? Are you aware of the facility's layout?"

It was a new development, one of many just like it that had been under construction for the better part of a decade. There were rumors, each placed in remote locations, hidden from plain sight. This one was out in the middle of Nowhere-Ville, Louisiana—tens of thousands of square-footage, concealed underground.

Still, regardless of how impenetrable they attempted to make it, I'd find a way inside.

"I'll figure something out," I answered, and trust me, if Evangeline was in danger, I'd move heaven and Earth to get to her.

"What if I make you an offer?" he began. "An offer that would get you inside Damascus where you'll have full access to our queen morning, noon, and night. Would you take it?" He paused before stipulating, "In exchange for patience where the fate of Nicholas Stokes is concerned?"

I stared a moment, considering the proposition. Being close to Evangeline should a situation arise was important and I was sure Baz knew that. Hence the reason he'd chosen to approach from this angle. I weighed my options, never promising I wouldn't, one day, carryout whatever actions I deemed necessary when it came to Nick. But I'd at least wait it out.

For now.

I nodded, which brought a smile to Baz's aged face. Not the sinister one I imagined he donned beneath his shroud while his pets had their way with me. This one conveyed a sense of relief.

"Then I'll see to it that they're expecting you."

"What will I have to do?" I asked. "There has to be a catch."

I was clearly not weak and inexperienced like many of the young shifters being transported to Damascus, so I was sure he didn't intend to have me hide among them.

Baz met my curious expression with another grin. "There will only be two requirements and the first, protecting Evangeline, I have no doubt you'll uphold with honor."

"And the second?"

He took a few steps, but didn't speak right away, clearly stalling.

"The second is that you teach them everything you know," he finally replied. "After all ... our future is now in the hands of the young."

Teach ... I definitely heard him say that.

I hated where this was headed, but if it'd get me closer, I didn't have much choice. So, accepting my fate, I listened as he went on.

"Now, the only thing left to determine is where she'll reside when all is said and done." The elder paced as he spoke. "We don't intend to keep the children at the facility for more than a year, depending on how they progress. That doesn't give us much time to secure a place for her. *Wherever* she settles, I think we'd agree that it has to be remote. A tall, surrounding hedge must be erected and fortified with a spell. A secret, royal militia will need to be drafted and—"

What did he mean we had to '*determine where she'll reside*'?

"Assuming you've figured out a solution for getting rid of the mutts, and assuming we're not at war by the time training is complete, she'll be able to return to her parents," I insisted. This transition was already going to be difficult, I didn't see the sense in it being a point of no return. Evangeline should have been able to return to her old life, as is, once the clan sorted things out.

Baz's expression became solemn. "I believe you're confused."

I turned to face him completely, folding my arms across my chest. "How so?"

He cowered a bit, hesitating before going on. "There's no way we can risk those people putting the clan's identity in jeopardy, regardless of how fond Evangeline might be of them. We'd never be able to extract her without raising questions. They'd demand answers we're not at liberty to give. And, while I understand your affection for our queen ... we can't lose sight of what's at stake for the entire clan if our secret is exposed."

None of the parents seemed to like the idea of their children being taken away, but Evangeline's circumstances were different. The other young lycans didn't face the task of explaining their disappearance to anyone. The Council would deal with questions and suspicions, but, in the very least, the other families would all understand what truly went on in the background; would uphold whatever ruse the Council concocted when their children disappeared.

But not Evangeline's.

All her parents would know is that their daughter was going away in two days without any real explanation. I understood it would take some crafty thinking, but...

"We simply cannot leave loose ends," Baz explained. "And I think you'll agree there's only one way to be thorough."

I shook my head, knowing exactly what he had in mind. "No. There has to be another option."

He took a step closer and his tone was urgent. "I wish there was."

Death ... he and the rest of the Council intended to kill Evangeline's family.

While, if it were anyone else, someone whose story I didn't know so well, I might have agreed. But, as Baz's suggestion rang inside my head, all I could think about was the family she *already* lost, and ... I couldn't let that happen to her again.

"Find another way," I asserted.

He breathed heavily. "There *is* no other way."

A residual twinge of pain from my ordeal with the witches distracted me for a fraction of a second ... but then ... it spurred a thought and I blurted it right away.

"A spell. Something to ... I don't know, make them believe she's someplace else? Make them think she's still there?"

I was grasping at straws, but I had to do something. She couldn't lose her mother and father for a second time. I, too, knew what it was like to be without family and I didn't want that for her.

Baz paced and I hated that I'd run out of suggestions. His withered hand touched his chin when his feet stopped, causing my eyes to shift toward him.

"It's possible that ... maybe—"

"Anything," I interjected. Whatever idea he had, I was open to listen to it.

"A spell might work," he breathed, "but it will have to be one far more drastic than anything you've mentioned."

His drooping eyes lifted to mine again, and from the look behind them, I was sure I wouldn't like this suggestion a whole lot more than the first.

And then, with the words that followed, the Elder proved me right.

"They'll have to forget her. To them, to all humans she's ever encountered," he explained, "it will be as though she never existed."

The small glimmer of hope I held slipped through my fingers in an instant. Baz must've seen it.

"I know this solution is not ideal, specifically for our queen, but if there's anything I can do, anything to atone for the loss, I'm willing to make this right. Consider it an olive branch of sorts." He lowered his gaze to the ground before adding, "Seeing as how our first encounter was rather ... *unpleasant*."

At that word, *unpleasant*, I recalled how much the small witch enjoyed her role as torturer before being called off. I didn't have to think long on how he could make this up to me.

"Deal with your witch," I asserted, adding one final word about it. "Harshly."

Baz inhaled until his chest rose, not seeming elated with the idea, but I was confident he'd comply.

"As you wish."

I was nowhere near satisfied, not in the least, but I'd negotiated all I could for Evangeline. While her parents wouldn't suffer the worst of fates, being forced to forget their daughter was the next worst thing. And because I'd be the one to deliver the news, I prepared myself to do something I vowed I never would ...

I was about to break her heart.

CHAPTER 3

Evie

S taring at the empty stretch of road ahead, I ached with sadness.

All over.

Liam sat silently beside me as we drove, but all I could think about was Nick. He was out there somewhere, alone. My calls and texts all went unanswered, and what made it worse was knowing he'd run off because of me. Because he didn't want to *hurt* me. I was the only one who didn't believe he was capable.

Not today.

Not tomorrow.

Not *ever*.

Granted, I'd only just discovered he was different—that his destiny and mine were set to converge in some tragic way—but the goodness I saw within him gave me hope. Nick was no monster. In fact, if it wasn't for him, I might not even be here today. A monster wouldn't have risked his own life to save mine when I was trapped during the earthquake. It came down to one fact, one aspect of our connection that made me certain I'd always be safe with him.

He loved me.

I zoned out staring at the random scatter of trees along the road's edge as we passed them. This place I once hated, suddenly felt like home and I knew that was partly because I'd have to leave soon, but mostly because of Nick. He made this town come alive for me, taking me under his wing without any knowledge of all I'd been through. He befriended me when no one else had even tried, showed me around and let me into his circle, and that friendship had grown into so much more.

Something so much deeper.

There were several reasons I wasn't ready to leave in forty-eight-hours. At the top of the list was the fact that, if Nick didn't turn up before then, he'd be left behind. And there was also the reality of my family remaining here while *I'd* be hundreds of miles away.

None of this felt right.

Liam's silence only added to my anxiety. He hadn't said much since I showed up at his door hours ago, expecting to find the Elder still torturing him. Instead, he was alone—bruised and wounded, but alone.

Somehow, I managed to convince him to sit still while I tended to the deep gash across his cheek. Of course, he reminded me that it'd heal on its own in a few minutes, but I ignored him and took care of it anyway. Just like I ignored when he insisted he didn't need my help cleaning.

I found rags, filled a bowl with hot water, and we scrubbed his blood from the floor, walls, and furniture together. If he'd been human, the ordeal would've killed him for sure. At the thought of it, I found myself wishing I was stronger as hatred swelled in my gut for those responsible.

Witches—the three girls who attended the Council meeting. I didn't realize who or what they were at the time ... but I knew now.

And I wouldn't forget.

At first, I thought Liam didn't have much to say because I defied him and ran straight into danger, something he very clearly expressed for me *not* to do. But it felt like I had no choice. Not once I realized he was in trouble.

He forewent the lecture I prepared myself to receive, instead choosing to clean beside me without a word. That's how I knew he wasn't angry. It was something else.

This tension was thick and heavy, hanging between us like an ominous cloud. Even now as we drove toward my neighborhood. There was so much to say—about the mutts, the witches, the meeting, Nick, and yet ... nothing.

I was confused and kind of worried, neither emotion outweighing the other. My life was changing, *evolving*, so quickly. As I sat wondering what caused *Liam's* distress, a list of my *own* stress factors wasn't far from thought—finding out I'm a shifter, Nick running away, having to leave Seaton Falls and my parents.

Kissing Liam.

I understood he only did it as a means of triggering me to shift, but that didn't lessen its effect. Technically, he knew me better than I knew myself and I guessed he also knew the rush of emotion was exactly what it would take for me to change. It worked, but ... the feel of his lips against mine was hard to forget even though it'd been hours; even though I had a laundry list of other things to worry about.

There was so much blood—his *and* the mutts'—covering his skin and clothes, he insisted on showering before we left. Now, he smelled like soap and ... man ... and it went straight to my head. Having his scent surround me in the truck only made it harder to forget everything he made me feel.

Beautiful.

Safe.

Content.

Breathless.

Being near him always left me conflicted, wanting to pull away because of Nick, wanting to draw nearer because it felt right. I wasn't obligated to either, but the tug-of-war the two did on my heart was sometimes unbearable.

But I couldn't focus on that right now. I had a plan to devise. One that would ultimately lead to telling my parents I had to leave.

The Elders were likely to concoct a scheme to explain why I, and many others in the community, were being whisked away. Something like a special, once-in-a-lifetime, academic opportunity with limited space. Something that had to be acted upon quickly. Based on the whispers I heard among the clan, the Council had the means and the clout to pull off such a farce. But I didn't want that, not for my parents. Besides, with there being no specified return date, who knew how long the Elders' lie would even hold? I didn't want my mom and dad going to bed at night with no real idea of where I was and why. It just didn't sit well with me.

Which justifies why I was leaning toward telling them the truth.

About everything.

All of it.

Of course, I feared the outcome of such a conversation; it had the potential to end badly. What if they didn't react well? What if they thought I'd lost it and, from this day forward, never believed another word I said? Yes, there was a lot at stake, but I wanted to handle this my way.

Finding out about being adopted a few years ago gave me a different perspective than others. I knew firsthand what it felt like to suddenly come to the realization that your whole life had been a lie. And, although I might have been naïve to think it'd all work out, I wanted to give my mom and dad a chance to know what was really going on. Everyone deserved that.

The truth.

"You're awfully quiet." Liam's voice brought me out of my thoughts and I smiled a bit.

"Right back at ya."

Neither of us looked at the other, just concentrated on the road. Maybe because it was easier.

"What happened to you back there?" I asked, unsure he'd even say.

In my peripheral, I saw the tension in his arm when he gripped the wheel tighter—muscle and veins bulging beneath the sleeve of his t-shirt.

"It started out as one thing and ended as another," was his vague response.

From what I saw, he was being beaten to a bloody pulp by small, childlike beings I was sure were more powerful than their innocent exterior implied. All the while, an Elder stood by, watching. And I felt them, the girls who surrounded Liam. They were inside his head with me before I was forced out.

When he didn't elaborate, I found it hard not to speak my mind. *One* of us had to.

"I need you to be different," I breathed, only worrying a little that I wore my heart on my sleeve.

Hazel eyes met mine for a second before going back to the road. "Different. Different how? What do you mean?"

I looked him over as I decided how to explain, focusing on his long, dark, still-wet hair. We'd only officially met a short time ago, but I soon realized that wasn't true. In another lifetime, he was the closest person to me, and I still felt that now—an invisible, unbreakable thread extending from me, connecting to him.

My trust for him, someone I should have still regarded as a stranger, ran bone-deep. I didn't fully understand it and was to the point I was done trying, but one thing I *did* know was that I needed him to be the one person I could count on to be honest.

I stared out the window again, because looking at him was hard at times. Hard because, whatever this was he made me feel, it was painful trying to control it if I didn't turn away. Yes, I reluctantly admit that he overwhelmed me like the feeling that comes when you stare into the sun too long.

"Seems people have made a game of keeping things from me and I need you to not be one of them." The request wasn't as simple as it sounded, I know, but I hoped he'd consider it. I wasn't a child and the more I knew, the more prepared I could be for whatever came next.

There was no sound other than the old truck bounding over the winding road. We bounced and swayed with it, neither speaking for several seconds, but then the sound of his voice touched my ears.

"You're asking a lot," he exhaled.

"I know."

He fell silent again, thinking.

My parents keeping it from me that I was adopted was only the beginning. There were also secrets between Nick and I that we were *both* guilty of keeping. I understood why he hadn't been forthcoming about what he was. How could I *not* understand? I kept my true identity from him too. It was easier that way, pretending nothing had changed when, in fact, *everything* had changed.

And then there was Liam—*my warrior*. Although that role in my life was a thing of the past, he still thought of himself as my protector. And that didn't end with physical protection. He'd also made it his duty to block me from anything he thought might be too much to handle emotionally as well.

But I needed him to see beyond my almost eighteen-year-old exterior like I saw beyond his of twenty. We were both much older than that in spirit and I needed him to accept that. Just like I was beginning to.

I sat, waiting.

"Okay," he agreed, giving in far easier than I expected, but I didn't gloat.

"Thank you."

Before filling me in on what happened today, he took a deep breath.

"Baz knows who you are," he shared before clarifying who he spoke of. "The Elder."

I turned toward him again. "So, what's that mean for us?"

Us ... Why did that word seem to keep slipping out?

It wasn't like my problems were his, but maybe he made me feel like they were. Like, whatever I went through, he'd be right there on the front-line taking the brunt of it with me.

For me.

"I wasn't sure at first," he started, "but, by the time we finished discussing it, I believe the Elders are now our allies. They understand how important you are, how important it is to keep your identity secret."

It made me nervous that others, *outsiders,* were now aware. Liam, I knew and trusted. The Elders? Not so much.

But I guess this fell under the umbrella of trusting *him.* If he thought things were mostly okay, I'd just have to believe that too.

"When you get there, to the facility, don't be alarmed if you're handled a bit more ... *cautiously* than the others."

"What? Why?"

"I got the feeling the Elder will be seeing to it that you're looked after more closely because we have to be careful."

"But won't giving me special treatment make me stand out even more?"

He shrugged. "Most will just assume you come from money and your parents made special arrangements."

I sat back with a heavy sigh. "I already don't like this."

I was in the middle of feeling *way* sorry for myself when a warm hand engulfed mine, pulsing its heat through my palm and up my arm until it reached my chest, my heart.

"You'll be fine." Liam's words were comforting to a degree, and so was the contact. "I was already planning to be there with you, but the Elder is, supposedly, making that go a little smoother as well."

"Yeah?" I glanced over, very much aware of our hands still linked as our forearms rested on the console between the two seats. I was also aware of a faint smile set on my lips.

Liam nodded and I snorted by accident when a thought came to mind. "What're you gonna do? Teach or something?" My smile broadened and, eventually, a laugh rang out. However, Liam stayed straight-faced.

I leaned forward in my seat to get a good look at him, still grinning. "I was kidding, but ... is that what's happening?"

A heavy sigh puffed from his lips and I couldn't imagine him, a guy who didn't look a whole lot older than me, schooling those of us who'd be attending. He was totally gonna be the facility's version of that hot camp counsellor all the girls secretly crushed on. I was sure of it.

"Now I have something to look forward to. It'll be pure, comic relief watching you stand up there," I smiled, "pretending to be all innocent and wholesome."

Because I had a feeling he was everything *but* that.

A hint of a smile touched his lips too. "This is funny to you?"

I was nodding before he even got the whole sentence out his mouth. "*Oh,* yeah. One-hundred-percent. I can only hope I get to experience it firsthand. What're you gonna be teaching?"

"Can we ... not use that word? Teaching. It won't be like that. I'll just be me, sharing what I know."

"Because you're, technically, kinda old?" I teased.

The corners of his mouth turned up even more and another surge of heat rippled through my fingers when he squeezed them a bit. "Because *we're,* technically, kinda old."

He had a point.

I sat back in my seat and tried to look at the bright side of this. Yeah, I'd be away from my parents, but, during that time, I'd get to learn more about who and what I am. And that's all I ever really wanted.

"I'm gonna tell them the truth. My parents," I blurted, sharing my plan with Liam, secretly hoping he didn't shoot the idea down.

His eyes shifted back and forth between me and the road several times and I had no idea what he was thinking. Maybe that I was insane to even consider it.

"I hate lying to them and I think they should know," I explained, wanting him to understand my rationale.

"How do you think they'll take it?" There was a strange tone to his voice when he asked.

I shrugged. "Beats me, but I've already made up my mind."

He went quiet on me again, but then said something I didn't quite understand.

"Evangeline, we need to talk, but ... I'm not really sure where to start."

There was that tone again. The one that made my stomach do somersaults.

My heart felt heavy all of a sudden too. I breathed deep, preparing for whatever he needed to say that made him so solemn.

"Okay ... what is it?"

It took him way longer to speak than I was comfortable with, and when words finally left his mouth, I wished they hadn't.

"The Council's decided your parents are a liability. One the clan can't afford to pretend doesn't exist."

My hands went numb first, and then everything else. His statement wasn't even registering.

A liability.

He took another breath. "I don't think I have to explain how cutthroat they can be, but I managed to get Baz to compromise," he shared. "Still, I know you won't like the agreement we came to."

Water stung the corners of my eyes when I turned his way, subconsciously squeezing his fingers tighter in mine. It looked like he wanted to stop when he noticed the oncoming tears, but maybe remembered the request I made. The one where I asked him to always tell the truth.

Even when no one else would.

Even when it hurt.

"Their first solution was death." That knocked the wind out of me and I immediately felt lightheaded. Like the world was suddenly spinning ten times faster and I couldn't get my footing.

"Death." I uttered the word with a whisper, unable to even fathom it. "But you said ... you said they'd be okay here when I left. Because they're human," I sputtered, feeling the first hints of wetness on my cheeks. "You *said* that!"

The truck slowed and we moved to the shoulder of the road as heat spread through my limbs. Liam shifted into *'park'* before turning to face me. With his free hand, he cleared my tears away and then let it settle at the nape of my neck.

"We have to stop them."

I was completely irrational as he tried to say more, reaching for the handle to let myself out, planning to walk who-knows-where. I just knew sitting there was not the answer. If I had to go back down into that dark chamber of a basement beneath the library all on my own and face the Elders myself, I'd do it.

"Evangeline," Liam said calmly, taking my waist when I made it halfway out of my seat, feeling gravel beneath one shoe.

"They can't do this!"

"You're right! Which is why I'm telling you I made him come up with something else."

I stopped struggling, but didn't climb all the way back in.

"They weren't willing to just take my word that this wouldn't lead to exposure, but they were willing to compromise."

I had no idea what that meant. Compromise.

"A spell," he sighed. "The witches will have to cast one that will..." When he hesitated again, I knew something terrible would follow. "It'll make them forget you."

A loud ringing in my ears muffled Liam's voice as he explained further, and I zoned out.

They'd have to forget me.

More and more, it felt like the one thing I wanted the most ... was the one thing life kept stealing from me.

Family.

"And I know this is a lot to take in, but I need to tell you the rest," he went on. "Because you wanted honesty." I blinked and more hot tears raced toward my chin. "It won't just be your parents. It's *every-one*. Any human you've ever encountered," he added. "That's the only way to make sure the story holds."

Friends. Teachers. Classmates. Aunts. Uncles. Cousins. Gram.

Everyone.

I nodded as I wiped my face, but it was a forced gesture. Nodding was a sign of understanding, and I didn't understand this. But I knew all too well how powerless I was, and I also knew I'd have to take this lying down. Just like everything else.

"But you have my word that I'll do my best to fix it," Liam promised. "When this is all over, when things have changed, I'll make sure they keep their word and break the spell."

I nodded again. "What if they don't?" It was a grim question, but a necessary one. "After what they did to you, I don't trust them. Can't we find another witch to help break the spell when we get back?"

When Liam shook his head, a wave of frustration washed over me. "Magic doesn't work like that. What one witch does, another can never undo. That's just the way it is."

So, my hope for a future with my parents lie in the hands of the three vicious witches who nearly killed Liam today.

Good to know.

While I didn't share my thoughts with Liam, truth was, I didn't have a ton of hope that things would work out. Not in *my* favor anyway. From where I sat, it seemed like this was my fate. Always had been. I, for whatever reason, wasn't meant to keep anyone close. This universe had gone out of its way to make this abundantly clear.

And now, in a few short days, I'd be erased.

Again.

CHAPTER 4

Evie

D inner had no taste. Well, I'm sure it did, I was just too distracted to notice.

Two pulses from my phone where it sat on the edge of the table made my heart leap. Desperate to hear from Nick, I nearly knocked my fork on the floor trying to get to the message.

'There's a candlelight vigil tomorrow night at 7 for Maddox and his brother. Need a ride?' Beth asked. *'I can have Roz come get you.'*

I typed my answer while my parents chatted. *'Sure.'* But I didn't leave it at that. *'Has anyone heard from Nick?'*

I tapped my foot anxiously beneath the table while I waited. He'd been missing most of the day, but it was likely no one had even noticed yet. Still, it'd ease my mind to know someone reached him.

Even if he wasn't returning *my* calls and texts.

Seemed like it took her forever to answer. *'No one's said anything. Why? Is he okay?"*

I took a deep breath and tried not to let frustration get the best of me. *'Yeah, everything's fine. Just wondering.'*

I set my phone aside and sat staring at the rice, peas, and baked chicken on my plate. My parents carried on with their usual banter, discussing how their day had gone, work stuff. Neither had any clue what was going on in Seaton Falls right beneath their noses. No clue the part I played in all of it. Thinking about it, I was a little jealous they had the luxury of being in the dark. Things would be much simpler that way.

Every now and then, one would glance over at my blank expression, my full plate, and ask if everything was okay. And, every time, I lied and blamed it on being tired.

Was I exhausted? Absolutely. Especially after the day I had— fighting mutts and scrubbing bloody floors—but mostly I was devastated.

Liam's explanation broke down why this spell was necessary, but ... all I kept thinking was how much I'd lost. How, again, I wouldn't belong anywhere, would have no home.

I couldn't imagine not being able to call my mom to share a laugh, my dad to get advice. In two days, they'd look at me and see a stranger. The memories we shared would all be taken away and there was nothing I could do about it.

Because the alternative was death.

That word sat in the pit of my stomach like an anchor. The order of the lycan world was packed with concepts and rules I didn't even come *close* to understanding, but one thing was for sure; Liam and I, as powerful as he was, were outnumbered. I knew he would have fought this with me, but it simply wasn't feasible. We would have to settle for being bullied by the Council right along with the rest of the Seaton Falls clan.

I sat, staring at my fingers as I twisted a ring on the middle one. How was I supposed to do this? Walk away? Pretend not to miss them when they were sure to be *all* I could think about?

Tonight wasn't supposed to go this way. I was supposed to be making the most of these final moments with my parents, but now that felt pointless. Soon, I'd be no one to them. They wouldn't miss me. There wouldn't be any calls checking in. No one would think about me on holidays.

It'd just be me.

Alone.

I stood and their eyes were on me. I pushed my seat in and grabbed my plate to take to the kitchen.

"Headed up to bed already?"

My mother was smiling as she stared, waiting for an answer. I nodded. "Yeah. Not feeling great."

Before I could get past her, she caught my wrist and made me wait while she touched my forehead.

"Hmm... you don't feel warm. Is it your stomach? A headache?"

"No, I think I just need to lie down."

There was concern in her eyes and I wished I could tell her everything. Wished that, if I *did* tell her everything... she would actually remember it beyond tomorrow night. But she wouldn't.

"I'll be fine," I said in a rush, feeling my throat tighten as I fought the inclination to cry again. Felt like I cried way too much lately, and I'd never been that girl. Wouldn't start now.

"Well, just yell if you need us," she added with a smile.

After a brief stop at the sink and an exchanged *'Goodnight'* with my father, I rushed up the steps. I was already nervous about leaving, sad Nick had run off, but now there was *this* tragedy that nearly blotted out all the others.

It took everything in me to keep reminding myself of the alternative to the spell. This option was, by far, the better one. And if Liam was right, their forgetting me would be temporary. However, that was assuming Baz and his witches really did make good on their word. There would have been comfort in knowing we could find another witch to break the magic should it come to that, but it didn't work that way. The witch or witches who cast the spell are the only ones who can break it.

Period.

Not forever, Evie.

I chanted that to myself, hoping it'd stick. I wanted to lie down and hide beneath the covers, pretend none of this was happening, but when I walked into my room, someone had already made themselves at home on my bed.

I gasped so loudly I wasn't sure the sound hadn't carried downstairs.

"How'd you get in here?" I panted, holding my heart while it hammered.

Liam's response was a well-timed glance toward my open window. He made himself at home. Well, about as much as someone his size *could* in my small bed—arms behind his head, one bare foot planted on the floor, the other propped up on my footboard.

I quietly closed the door behind me, locking it right after.

"What're you doing here? It could've easily been one of my parents coming in." I wasn't upset that he dropped by, just confused. With the way my evening was going, having him here to keep me company wasn't the worst thing in the world.

Liam shook his head, dismissing my concern. "I knew it was you; felt you before you even made it up the stairs."

Felt me before I even... Of course he did.

The gentle thrumming inside my chest picked up speed again as I repeated his words in my head. If I hadn't been so preoccupied, I probably would've known he was close too.

My eyes scanned the length of him as I stood there, the way the veins in his arms protruded beneath tanned skin and colorful, inked symbols; the steady rise and fall of his flat stomach as he breathed. He was ... a major distraction, and I don't know, maybe I was kind of in the market for distractions right about now.

When he was around, I almost forgot our lives were in near-constant peril. For example, right now, my thoughts were stuck on how amazing my pillow probably smelled since he'd been resting on it. I fought the pull, though. Just like always. Instead of letting myself get lost in him, I went about shoving things in my closet, things like shoes and books I would've put away if I'd known someone was coming over.

"What made you pop in?" I asked casually, refusing to look at him because my insides would start doing flips if I did.

He'd never been to my house, let alone my room. However, I was sure this was far less inconvenient than having someone *'pop in'* on your thoughts, like I often did to him—by accident, on purpose. It all depended on the day and how strongly the shifter within me longed for him. She, that side of me, had a way of bypassing my conscious mind to go to him. I was starting to get used to it and actively ignored the idea of this being some sort of natural progression.

Hazel eyes were trained on me as Liam explained himself. "There's a chance your friend may come to you tonight. He'll expect you to be alone, unprotected, so I'm staying."

His response made me pause with a notebook in my hand halfway to my desk where I was headed to put it away.

He was planning to stay? As in, all night?

It wasn't until I moved one foot in front of the other again that I responded. "You're both worried for nothing. You *and* Nick. He won't hurt me."

And so what if he *did* try to visit me tonight? It'd be a relief to know he was okay. It wasn't lost on me that Nick had only run off because he thought there was truth to Liam's claim. It wasn't fear of what Liam might do to him—although I had a feeling another run-in between the two wouldn't go well.

I moved to the window to shut it, but paused as I gazed across the yard, toward Nick's house. Most of the lights were on, but there was a dark bedroom that held my attention for a long time—his. I'd gotten used to seeing the dim light behind his blinds while we talked on the phone or texted. He was on his own, probably scared out of his mind, and I couldn't do anything about it.

Standing there, I typed out another message, begging him to let me know he was all right. After hitting send, I locked the window and drew the curtains.

According to the legend, his destiny was to end my life. He was nature's kill-switch because, apparently, a long time ago, I was powerful enough to warrant such a thing. Meanwhile, present-day me had trouble getting more than four bags of groceries inside the house at once, and often had to call on my father to open particularly stubborn jars.

I guess Mother Nature missed the memo. She didn't need to create an entire supernatural being to keep me in check. A flyswatter probably would've done the trick.

"You're too trusting," was Liam's observation. "All it takes is him being triggered."

That word stood out to me and I paused again. "Well, what is it that triggers him?"

Liam let out a long breath. "I wish I knew. Could be random, but if it isn't, if I'd known back then ..."

His voice trailed off, but his words were heavy on my heart. We hadn't discussed the circumstances that led to my death, nor whether the first Liberator actually played a part in it. Hearing the truth today, seeing the heightened emotion brewing inside Liam as he addressed Nick, I assumed so, but hadn't yet asked Liam to confirm. Until now.

I pulled out the chair at my desk and sat backwards with my arms resting across the top, facing him. "Can you tell me what happened?"

There was a chance he'd say he didn't want to discuss it, which would mean I'd have to continue guessing, but he didn't. His eyes closed for a few, and then they opened again, casting a solemn look my way.

"When your father first got word of that thing lurking outside the walls, he consulted Hilda in hopes of finding out what it was," he began, stating a name I'd never heard before.

"Hilda? Who's that?"

"She's part of the coven paired with your father's kingdom. They were some of the most powerful witches in the world, with Hilda being more powerful *still*," Liam added. "She sent him away, told him to return in three days and she'd have an answer for him. All he knew was it *looked* like a lycan, but much bigger. And its silvery fur was like nothing he'd ever seen. Like nothing *any* of us had ever seen."

Liam's retelling reminded me of what I observed in the woods as the six of us fought off the mutts. Nick was significantly larger than his brothers and he, too, had silvery-gray fur that stood out next to the others.

My gaze lowered as I listened.

"He went back in three days, like they discussed, and Hilda explained that she consulted their oracles. That's how we first came to know everything we do about the Liberator. Everything except why he showed up when he did."

I breathed steadily, but my heart raced as vivid images flashed in my head. It felt like I remembered, but couldn't link the pieces together. It was disorienting.

"They attempted to cover you with magic to hide you, but, just like the oracle said, there *was* no hiding," Liam explained. "Because that ... *thing* ... could hear you, your heartbeat, everywhere. Always."

I wasn't sure I wanted the rest of the details, but I asked anyway. "How did it happen?"

There was a long, loaded silence in the room. Liam lie there staring at the ceiling. I couldn't imagine what this felt like for him, reliving something I guessed to be one of the most tragic events of his life. Assuming we truly once loved each other the way I kept feeling we did. Right in the center of my chest. Heavy. Stifling.

"It took you while we were sleeping," he muttered. "Right out of my arms."

A chill ran down my back as his words evoked a sensation I couldn't control, causing my body to remember the way that felt. One second, being locked in the safety of a warm embrace, and then the next, being ripped away from him by a set of dreadful claws.

"I chased it," he sighed, sounding defeated. "For miles, I chased it. You shifted while it carried you away and I could see you fighting, but ... it wasn't enough." His eyes slammed shut and I wondered what he saw behind his closed lids.

"I searched for you until the sun came up, until my voice failed me from yelling your name, until I felt our tie sever. I knew the moment I was no longer searching for *you,* but ... remains," he added somberly. "Something to bring back to your family. Something to make me believe that, after centuries, it was really over." He drifted away then, back to that day, I imagined. "Your necklace and bracelet," he added in a daze. "That was all he left, all he couldn't consume."

My mouth was dry. My throat burned with emotion. I stood from my seat and the room went dark when I flipped the switch. Liam watched me approach the bed and there was a distant look in his eyes. I could see it even with the light off, like he wasn't sure I was real.

I guess I kind of looked at him the same way.

"I'll take the floor," he offered, swinging his long legs over the edge of the mattress.

However, the sound of my voice halted him. "It's fine," I breathed. "...You can stay there."

I had no idea what made me say it. The only explanation I came up with was ... my shifter ... sometimes she had more control over my actions than *I* did. I was beginning to believe she still loved him, remembered all the things about him that I couldn't. It was clear she didn't care that I had only fleeting flashbacks of a life with Liam. Apparently, what we shared in the past had left one heck of a lasting impression.

Something Liam once said was never far from my thoughts. He said I should stop thinking of myself and my shifter as two separate beings. So, I suppose her feelings, whether I understood them or not, were mine too.

Without a word, Liam scooted to the other side of the bed, taking the spot near the window for obvious reasons, being the protector he was. I laid in the warm space he left, easing beneath the comforter while he rested on top of it. My bed was small—bigger than a twin, smaller than a queen. But with him taking up so much space, there wasn't anywhere I could move where some part of me wasn't touching some part of him.

It was comforting for many reasons. Today had brought so much with it, so much loss in many different forms. While I didn't believe I needed him here for protection—from Nick or otherwise—I was grateful not to be alone. My next thought was what it felt like waking up in his bed the first time I shifted. Yes, I was confused and afraid I'd get grounded until the next ice age for being out all night, but I never questioned being well-looked after when he was around.

"Thank you," I said quietly. "For being here tonight."

"Of course."

It meant a lot that he cared enough to show up regardless of his motive, thinking I needed looking after.

Silence hung between us again. He was so, so close. Both our eyes were locked on the ceiling, but I was afraid to move. I needed to say something to break up the heated tension between us, something to take my mind off Nick missing, off the stuff with my parents.

"What about me is different?" I asked. "Do I look and act the same?"

Beside me, Liam turned his head and I felt his stare tracing the side of my face.

"You look exactly like I remember." There was a tone to his voice I couldn't place, but it made me breathe differently. "Except you mostly wear your hair straight now. Back then, it was always curly, of course."

Subconsciously, I reached for the bun on top of my head, feeling the loosely coiled strands. When I did, Liam took my arm, letting his fingertips slowly wander over my skin until he had my wrist.

"I will admit; it's a little strange seeing you without all the tattoos, though."

I turned toward him, confused. "Like, how many?"

"Thirty-seven,"

"You counted?" I asked, laughing a bit. It wasn't lost on me that he still remembered the exact number.

"Didn't *have* to count them," he replied. "I'm the one who *did* them."

The smile on my face faded a bit and I felt my eyes flicker to his mouth, staring as I asked my next question.

"Where'd I have them?"

He wet his lips and I took note of their slight curve. I couldn't blink as he took me on a tour, mapping my skin with his fingertip.

"Here," he breathed, touching the back of my hand. "And here," he went on, turning it over to graze the sensitive flesh beneath my forearm, concluding, "Pretty much ... *everywhere.*"

Heat swept me away, filling me and overflowing until I began to sweat a bit beneath the comforter. Liam said nothing when I slowly pulled my arm from his grasp and kicked the blanket off my legs.

From the corner of my eye, I glanced at the many symbols and words on his arms. "Assuming it's impossible to draw your own, who did yours?"

That distant gaze was back again when Liam answered. "Your brother, Ivan, was the only other person in the kingdom who knew how. We were taught the technique together." That answer enlivened me right away.

Ivan...

He mentioned before that I had brothers, but I never asked about them. Not even their names. Certain aspects of my past seemed more difficult for Liam to discuss than others. Particularly, when it came to my family because, from what he shared, they were his family as well.

The bed shifted and, startled, I held my breath when Liam suddenly sat up. He gathered the back of his t-shirt to the nape of his neck, revealing the moon phase tattoo down his spine. I'd seen it the day before, when I skipped the last half of school in search of refuge from all the confusion. Then, when I noticed the art, I forced myself to look away. Tonight was different, though. I stared unapologetically at both works of art—the tattoo *and* him.

"We all had the same one; you, your brothers and I," he clarified. "I'm not part lycan, of course, so the phases didn't mean to me what they meant to you all, but I was considered part of the pack. So, they insisted I have one too."

I smiled at the memory he shared, secretly wanting to reach out and let my finger run the length of his spine, from waxing crescent to waning.

However, I knew better.

"How many brothers did I have?" I asked out of curiosity, but also as a distraction.

Liam lowered his shirt again and returned to his spot beside me on the mattress.

"Six," he answered. "You were the seventh and last child."

"What were their names?" As soon as the words left my mouth, I remembered that pained look and wished I hadn't been so thoughtless. "I mean ... if you don't mind sharing."

Liam turned his head and I felt the intensity of his stare again. "You can ask me anything. Always," he added. "The oldest was Declan. Then Josiah, Tobias, Ethan, Ivan, and Caleb. And then there was you. Evangeline."

I smiled at the sound of my name leaving his mouth. "You always call me that."

"Because it's your name," he answered with a soft laugh, one that dotted my skin with goosebumps.

"I know that, but ... everyone else calls me Evie. Everyone, but you and maybe a couple teachers." I shrugged. "It's just something I noticed."

He was quiet for a moment while he thought. "Does it bother you? Would you prefer I call you Evie?"

In all other instances, I hated the formal sound of my full name. It seemed like it ought to belong to some old woman who's befriended all the neighborhood squirrels and passes out sugar-free suckers on Halloween. However, when *Liam* said it ... it never made me feel out of place. In a way, it was kind of fitting that only *he* could call me that without it getting under my skin.

"It's fine," I said casually, keeping the rest of my thoughts locked inside. "I don't mind."

He faced the ceiling again and asked a simple question as a smile touched his lips.

"Speaking of the way things were ... still got a sweet tooth?"

I didn't speak, just reached inside my nightstand drawer. When I pulled out three candy bars, the smile turned into a laugh.

"Never leave home without one," I grinned.

"Some things never change, I guess." The sound of his quiet laughter, the depth of his voice, made my stomach twist and turn.

On the other side of my door, my parents thumped up the stairs and I froze, shifting my eyes to the lock. I'd been smart enough to engage it, so my heart settled just a little.

That is, until someone knocked.

I motioned for Liam to stay quiet. With a smile, he pretended to zip his lips as I called out.

"Yes?"

"Just wanted to check on you before we go to bed," Mom replied, trying the knob right after. Another wave of panic washed over me.

"Yeah, I'm good."

"I brought the thermometer up with me just to be sure you don't have a fever."

"You felt my head, remember?" I replied, hoping to keep from having to open the door. She tried the knob again.

"I know, but ... You're being weird now, Evie. You sure you're okay?"

She was right. I *was* being weird, but *everything* was weird. Not just me. All the changes—those that had already taken place, those yet to come—left me feeling undone.

"I'm good. I just don't feel like getting up and unlocking the door."

She laughed a bit. "Which is why you're, generally, not supposed to lock yourself in when you don't feel well, silly."

Liam was still and quiet while my mother and I went back and forth.

"Seriously, I'm okay. If I need anything, I'll just yell."

"Sure ... because *that* won't give me a heart attack in the middle of the night," she said with an air of sarcasm as she walked away.

I could finally breathe once I heard their bedroom door close. I hated lying to them. My hands covered my face and I stayed silent while the curtain I pulled to hide all my stuff behind—the worry, the guilt, the fear, the uncertainty—fell away and I had to acknowledge it all again. Like before, I was aware of everything; how the twenty or so phone calls and text messages to Nick had gone unanswered, how I'd be leaving soon, how I'd be *forgotten* soon. By my parents, my extended family, my friends in Chicago that I'd left behind when we moved away.

"You got quiet on me."

I glanced over at Liam through parted fingers when he spoke, seeing him smile. I must have looked like a child. I pulled my hands away from my face before answering.

"Just ... thinking. About *everything*."

I didn't have to go into detail about that. He already knew. Probably even that Nick missing was a large part of it.

Liam stared at *me* as I stared at the ceiling. "How'd it go tonight? With your parents, I mean."

I breathed deep and shrugged. "For them, it was a normal dinner. But for me, it was ... I don't know ... kind of like the beginning of the end." I placed a hand on my forehead and concentrated on the surge of air that filled my lungs.

"It just feels like I'm destined to be alone," I shared.

Liam said nothing, but he kept his eyes trained on me when I went on.

"Even though I don't remember the past, I'm still aware of it. I think I always was. There were no details, no recollection of having lived before, just this ... hole," I forced out. "This dark void I always felt, but could never place. And I'm starting to believe it's just a part of me. Like, I'm meant to always feel broken."

I was more aware of him beside me now than just a moment ago. It may have been because I was trying to convince myself I had no one, but his presence made that impossible. It was more than him just being here physically. Our link made it so one would never be without the other. Never again. I had no idea how that would play out, nor did I give much thought to it, but, for now, it was nice having a close connection with someone proving himself to be a good friend.

And I needed that right about now.

"I don't want to talk about this anymore," I said, breathing deep when emotion squeezed my throat.

"Then we don't have to," Liam said sweetly. "What do you want to talk about instead?"

"Anything. Tell me what it'll be like at this facility they're shipping us off to."

He shifted a bit, getting comfortable. "It's completely new. In fact, I don't even think the whole thing is finished. Pretty sure they just moved up their grand opening, if that's what you want to call it, because of how things have been going. They're smart enough to realize the young shifters are anyone's greatest resource. And the most important thing is protecting you all, training you to defend yourselves and the clans should it ever come to that."

My brow quirked. "Now ... when you say training, what does that mean exactly?" I pictured myself with sharp weapons, followed by a bloodbath at my feet when I accidentally sliced off my own arm.

"For whatever reason—complacency, convenience, or maybe because they just got too comfortable—a lot of the clans have slacked on prepping the next generation for what's really out there. So, as a result, most don't have a clue how to manage their abilities, no idea how to even tap into them. There are several companion facilities to this one, but they're all hidden."

"Hidden?"

He nodded and put an arm behind his head. "By magic, by decoy houses on the property where the facilities were built underground."

Underground ... they were clearly hiding them well for a reason. My guess was the Sovereign. If he was anything like Liam described, I understood.

"But back to this training thing..."

He smiled and I relaxed a bit in my spot. "Don't sweat it. You'll get the hang of things. And whatever you don't get in class, I'll help you."

I laughed. "I think you forget you're talking to the girl who can't even *shift* on her own."

I felt his eyes on me and caught a glimpse of a smile when he replied. "And, if *I* recall ... I helped with that too."

Heat crept up my legs again as my stomach and head swam at Liam's dizzying words. His not-so-subtle reminder of our kiss was enough to make me burst into flames right here.

"Cute, but, if that's your plan for teaching me, I guess I'm doomed because that can't happen again," I said casually, hoping I pulled off the cool indifference I was going for. However, on the inside, I was anything *but* cool and indifferent. Hot and bothered was more accurate.

"Just sayin'," he mumbled under his breath, still wearing that ghost of a devilish smile.

I was quiet. Thinking about his lips on mine completely wiped away all other thoughts, including our soon-coming journey to The Damascus Facility.

"Get some rest," he breathed. "You'll be fine there. Trust me."

I nodded and didn't question the certainty that came with those words. If Liam said things would be fine, then ... they'd be fine.

He'd make sure of it.

CHAPTER 5

Evie

P eople always say time flies when you're having fun, but I learned something else; time also flies when you're dreading what's to come.

I tried to hold on to my final moments with my parents for dear life, knowing they'd fade in the time between now and whenever they were allowed to remember me again.

If ... they were allowed to remember me again.

"Sweetheart, you're worrying me." My mother's words touched my ears and I knew I shouldn't have held on. It only made this harder on me than it had to be. I'd hugged my father this same way before he left ten minutes before, but I couldn't help it. We'd gone through some things over the last few years, but they still meant the world to me.

"I told you, if you're not feeling great, you can miss school today. I'll call in and we can watch a movie," she offered, moving hair away from my cheek while I clung to her. "I'll even make that soup you like."

This was so hard, letting go. As badly as I wanted to stay, as badly as I wanted to curl up beside her on the couch in PJs while we zoned out in front of the television together ... I couldn't.

A gentle kiss was placed in my hair. "You're not too old to be babied by your mom if you're still under the weather."

What I'd give to let her keep me under her wing forever. Right now, it felt like there was no safer place on the planet. But I knew better than that. If I didn't go willingly, if I didn't let the Elders handle this the way they saw fit, my parents would be anything *but* safe.

At that thought, I willed tears not to fall. If they did, there'd be no getting rid of her and our plan wouldn't work. The Elder, turned ally, plus his witches, were due here at any moment and I didn't want to risk my mother still being here when that happened.

"It's okay. Go," I insisted, forcing a weak smile as I pulled away from the crook of her neck. If I could have, I would have made this moment last forever.

One last glance passed my way and she smiled back, squeezing my hand in hers before letting it go. "Okay, but if you get there and start feeling terrible again, just call me, you hear?"

The corners of my eyes stung as I nodded. And then, just like that, she was gone. A cold chill passed through me and I felt the loss already.

Quiet steps descended the staircase behind me as I watched my mother's car pass the window beside the front door. She was gone, and I couldn't shake the feeling I'd never see her again. Or, if I did, it wouldn't even matter once she'd forgotten me.

A warm arm encircled my shoulder and my throat stung as the stifled emotions began to suffocate me. Again, I found myself grateful for Liam's overprotectiveness. He only left my side these past couple days for two reasons; to shower while my parents weren't home; and when I left my room to interact with them to keep up appearances.

Otherwise, he was right with me, keeping me safe, getting me through this.

It was that same protectiveness that made getting to Maddox's vigil impossible. I would like to have gone, but Liam insisted I stay indoors because of the mutts. It was hard to argue with him on that, seeing as how I believed he was right—they were still out there. I wasn't sure why they were in Seaton Falls, or why *now,* but I'd be happy never seeing another again in my life.

The tears I held back finally slipped down my cheeks—full of hurt, fear, anger. Slowly, one at a time. Not by the bucketsful like I felt they might. I was grateful for this small measure of self-control.

"Why does it feel like I'm always losing everything?"

The question left my lips without expectation that there'd be an answer. I believe Liam knew that, which was why he didn't try reasoning with me. We both knew, to some extent at least, it was the absolute truth. This was just my fate.

I let my hand rest against my thigh, toying with one of my skirt's pleats. I'd gotten dressed and gone through my entire routine to avoid my parents getting suspicious. And, as I stood in the foyer, I now stared through the panes of glass as I thought of Nick. Two nights had come and gone with no word. If nothing had changed, if we were allowed to just be normal teenagers like we once thought, he'd be standing outside near the porch, waiting to walk me to school.

A phantom memory of his hand in mine made my fist clench.

Where was he? Had he made it home and just didn't want to speak to me?

That may have very well been the case, considering. I was sure seeing me with Liam was very confusing for him. No matter how casual I tried to believe our connection was, I was sure Nick could tell there was more. While 'more' was impossible for me to explain, I would certainly try. We vowed not to keep secrets and I fully intended to uphold that.

But ... I couldn't make steps in the right direction if he wasn't around.

"They're here," Liam said flatly, but the undertone of tension in his voice wasn't lost on me. As cool and collected as he pretended to be, I knew better. I felt the shift in his mood immediately.

"How do you know?" I asked.

He breathed deeply. "Because one of Baz's witches has a flare for grandiose entrances. And I'm pretty sure I'm at the top of her crap-list for the punishment she received per my request." As soon as the last word left his mouth, he clutched the side of his head in agony.

"*She's* doing this?"

He couldn't answer, but he didn't have to. A thin trickle of blood dripped from his nose and I felt anger rise in me again. I hadn't had a one-on-one encounter with this girl yet, but I already hated her—for her actions toward Liam *now*, for all she'd done to him days ago.

Liam finally nodded to confirm, standing straighter when the episode seemed to pass as quickly as it came.

"Swear I'm gonna snap her neck one of these days." Something in his tone left me without question that he fully intended to do just that.

The next second, four figures darkened my porch. With the arrival of those who'd come to take everything away from me, my heart leapt.

Liam whispered, getting my attention as our eyes locked. "It'll be fine."

I nodded kind of frantically.

"I'll do all the talking. Just stay close."

As badly as I wanted to be brave, as badly as I wanted to be the fierce Evangeline he knew from before, I simply hadn't tapped into her abilities yet. For now, my greatest defense ... was *him*.

"They believe you're still just as ruthless as you were in your past, so they'll be more fearful of you than you should be of them," he whispered calmly.

He turned to face me. I'm not sure what he saw in my expression, but whatever it was, he said more, an attempt to ease my mind.

"You can be as scared as you want to be on the *inside*, Evangeline." His stare made my breathing slow. "But, on the outside ... I need you brave."

The pressure was on. These powerful beings had to believe I was bigger than them in the supernatural. I knew that, if I spoke, my secret would quickly be revealed. The only way I'd pull this off was to stay mostly silent, observing, passing all my thoughts and questions through Liam to the Elder, giving the impression that I thought too highly of myself to speak to him directly.

When I settled on a plan, I nodded, and Liam proceeded toward the front door. He opened it, allowing Baz and his minions to cross the threshold.

He looked the same as he did at the Council meeting—large, foreboding. In short, I was glad to have Liam guarding me as a tremor ripped through my body. The witches entered in silence and it was then that I noticed the bandage over the small one's left eye. She hadn't been wearing it when I saw her through Liam's vision, but it was clear she'd endured some sort of trauma between then and now. It was brought back to my memory that he mentioned her being punished. Perhaps that's what this was.

Punishment.

The Elder took several steps toward Liam and I held my breath, listening to his heavy steps as he crossed the hard wood. He stopped with a mere two feet between them, and to my surprise, he did something totally unexpected.

He knelt, lowering his head in Liam's presence.

I had no words as I stared at this ancient thing bowing before him. But then, there was yet another shocker when he spoke, addressing *me* instead, using two words that made me swallow so hard my tongue almost went down my throat.

"My Queen."

His gravelly voice was enough to incite a stampede toward the nearest exit, and yet, he referred to me as his queen. I was silent, watching as he proceeded to cast a loaded stare over his shoulder to the three cloaked figures who entered with him. The witches. At his glance, they seemed to come to their senses and lowered with slow curtsies. All four sets of eyes were focused on the ground, but then one's gaze wandered up to meet mine and I knew who she was right away. The small one who tortured Liam.

I'd never forget her face. It was seared into my brain like someone had branded it there with a hot iron. I was almost startled by the strange swell of anger that filled me as we engaged in a stare-down no one else seemed aware of. Within me, from some place so deep I couldn't even identify it, I wanted this girl to suffer. Her mirrored expression made it clear she wasn't fond of me either. Based on the way I witnessed her treating Liam, I could only guess it was a general dislike for our kind—dragons.

I finally focused on Baz again and nodded to acknowledge him. When I did, he stood once more, but kept his head low. He also made no eye contact, which felt intentional.

"Your Highness," he began, catching me off guard with yet another startling reference to my lineage. "My sincerest apologies for the way we must handle this delicate matter."

I breathed deep and felt my heart squeeze at his words, but then I remembered what Liam said. I was allowed to feel whatever I needed to feel on the inside, but on the outside? I had to be a rock.

I wondered if that's how it was before; if these were words he spoke to me often, back when this role I played as queen was my rightful place, not just a farce to keep me protected.

Drawing in air, I exhaled a falsely confident reply. "I understand it needs to be done."

At that, Baz finally met my gaze, his milky-white stare coming before a single nod. "Shall we proceed, then?"

I glanced up the stairs where Liam said this would take place. "Sure."

I led the way and, as expected, Liam acted as a barrier between me and them. My pace slowed as we crept down the hallway with my door at the end of it. Time had run out. The moment I was dreading most had arrived. My feet stopped and the only sound to be heard were the cloaks of Baz and the witches as they dragged the floors. The four closed in on Liam and I.

"Your room?" Baz asked.

I nodded, but said nothing as I stared at the door.

"Scarlet, Marin, Lilith?" At Baz's words, the three stepped up beside me, the small one watching me from the corner of her eye—the one she still had, anyway. Each one placed a hand on my door and then reached for me. However, I snatched my arm away before they had the chance, immediately shifting my gaze toward Liam just as Baz did the same. Liam's eyes were calm and reassuring, but I had no intentions on letting these three lay a hand on me. I'd seen what they'd done to him.

"It's fine, Evangeline," Liam stated calmly. "They need a point contact to cast the spell and to effectively hide your room and belongings with their magic."

He explained that part to me first thing this morning—how they'd make my room appear to be nothing more than a blank section of the wall to the human eye, thus erasing all traces of me from the house. But I didn't want them touching me. *Any* of them.

Especially *her*.

My eyes went to the witches again and I didn't like how hard they were to read. They all had the same smug expression and I hated it. Hated *them* without spending more than five minutes in the same space.

"My Queen, you have my word you're in no danger. Should any harm come to you, these three are well aware of the repercussions." At Baz's words, his witches' faces went blank as if suddenly aware of their place.

"You're perfectly safe," he added.

I watched Liam again and he nodded, agreeing with Baz. I slowly extended my arm. When I did, three small hands pressed into my skin and the witches closed their eyes. Mine, however, were wide open. Afraid didn't even begin to explain how I felt.

Liam's arms were crossed over his chest and I noted the tension in his forearms. While I watched *him*, he watched the witches. The intense expression he wore made my gaze return to them as well. Their chant started as a soft murmur, words I didn't recognize as English. My door began to vibrate. Slowly at first, and then hard and fast. Their mouths continued to move, but the speed at which they uttered these phrases ... it was inconceivable. Their lips were a blur and their sound became one as the frame of my door lit with an ominous glow.

A strange tingling suddenly struck my palms and I knew that, within the clenched fist I squeezed, a flame had ignited. I gave Liam my word I'd keep calm, though, and I was sure shifting right now was the opposite of keeping calm, so I bridled it.

The door continued to shake violently as it rattled against its frame. My heart raced right along with it as the intensity of the witches' chant grew louder, reaching a crescendo. And then, all of a sudden, it all stopped. The witches breathed deeply and slowly released my arm.

I blinked, unsure of whether we were finished or not. "Is ... that it? It's done?"

Scarlet nodded once, wearing a dark smile. "It is. You're as good as forgotten." She made no secret of the joy she got from saying those words.

I meant to look away from her, but couldn't. My shifter had locked in on her, memorizing her features, making sure I never forgot.

"That will be all, Scarlet," Baz said sternly, causing the small witch to cower right away.

"I need to get her out of here," Liam interjected with urgency. "If someone comes back, they'll think we're all intruders. Plus, Evangeline's due at the extraction point soon."

I glanced down at my watch and my heart sank. He was right. My next stop was The Damascus Facility, and... I wasn't ready.

"Very well," Baz replied, gesturing for his minions to head downstairs. They did so right away, but before he followed, he paused to speak again, addressing me directly. There was a sense of humility I didn't miss.

"I hope you'll find the accommodations I arranged to your liking."

His weary eyes rose to meet mine, and I don't know, there was a softness to them I wasn't expecting. Seeing him address the clan at the Council meeting painted him in a frightening light, as did the terror he rained down on Liam before realizing who we were. But now, before me, he was mild and respectful. I hadn't forgotten that his initial solution for dealing with my parents was to kill them. But I was also aware of the fact that he was willing to work with Liam to find a compromise. I didn't trust him yet, but I at least mirrored his respect to a degree.

"I'm sure I will," I replied. "Thank you."

I kept it to myself that I thought these special arrangements were unnecessary. I knew all parties involved in catering to me meant well.

Baz nodded, and then exited with his witches.

A gentle glance passed my way as Liam spoke. "Ready?"

I looked around at the home that hadn't been home for very long, but ... it represented so much more in my heart. This was the place where my parents would live on without me. The place where memories would be made, and the place where ... I'd be forgotten.

A thought fluttered into my head, a fear that, eventually, if I kept being erased from peoples' lives, kept losing those I cared about, I'd eventually just cease to exist. But it was the feel of a strong hand taking mine that brought me back, reminding me there was one who'd *never* forgotten, had never let go.

And he was here now.

Taking a final look around, I nodded, squeezing his fingers tighter. "Ready."

I said nothing as we drove, clutching one of four bags I packed and stashed in Liam's truck before Baz and the witches showed up. I barely even had time to change out of my uniform before rushing out —a very necessary part of our plan to avoid being seen. That home was no longer mine.

Soft music filled the cab of Liam's truck and I was grateful for it. Complete silence would've only allowed my thoughts to grow louder. I couldn't believe we were finally at this moment, my departure.

Our departure.

I don't know that I fully appreciated Liam's willingness to come along until right now, when it counted. Yeah, the few friends I made would be there, too, but it was different. They all had family here in Seaton Falls waiting for them. No one else was alone like me. Now, after the spell, Liam and I had even more in common. Neither one of us had family.

"I'll be there when you arrive," he said, breaking into my thoughts. "I have to hang back from the busses, but if you need anything, you know how to reach me."

I nodded and took a deep breath.

"Also," he went on, "I'll keep my distance while we're at the facility too."

I wasn't sure what that meant.

"You have friends and I get it." There was a solemnness to his tone that wasn't lost on me. "It wouldn't be easy explaining how you know me, so I won't make things harder for you than they already will be."

It was thoughtful of him to say, and I guess on some level, he was right. My friends were Nick's friends. They wouldn't understand my ties to Liam. It was hard enough for *Nick* to grasp. At the thought of him, I shot one last text before officially leaving Seaton Falls.

'I miss you. Please let me know you're all right out there.'

My eyes scanned the endless miles of trees at either side of the road. I had no idea whether he was safe or not, but I had to hold out hope.

"I won't pretend we're strangers," I countered, shooting down

Liam's assumption as to how things would go while we were away. "You don't have to be distant and I won't be either," I assured him.

Explaining things to Beth, or *whoever* noticed the friendship between Liam and I, wouldn't be easy, but I wouldn't make him pretend he didn't know me. I was different, in *many* ways, and my past life was one such example. People would have to accept me as is. And Liam was a big part of that.

He said nothing as my response seemed to resonate with him.

We arrived at the departure point and there were a ton of cars, parents and other young shifters sharing tearful goodbyes. Naturally, my thoughts went back to my *own* parents, and Liam sensed it right away.

His hand came down on mine. "I'm gonna fix this, Evie. I'll do everything I can to make sure you get them back."

I nodded, knowing he meant well, but maintaining a healthy dose of skepticism just in case. In the end, if things never went back to normal, it was that skepticism that would keep me from losing my mind completely. I couldn't afford to be all-in with hope. The potential for disappointment was too great.

I opened the door to Liam's truck, noting how he didn't pull up close—his way of still leaving me the option to deny we knew one another.

"Don't forget; even if you don't see me, I won't be far."

At his words, I nodded. There was a long trip ahead of us— several hours traveling from Michigan to the south.

"Be careful," I called out, closing the door after Liam reminded me I had access to him if anything went wrong.

With my eyes now set on the chartered busses filling with local shifters, I chose to be brave. That's what the *old* me would've done. So, I put one foot in front of the other and made strides to leave Seaton Falls behind.

A new beginning was on the horizon. For *all* of us.

CHAPTER 6

Evie

The screech of the bus's air brakes ricocheted off the large tree trunks that surrounded us. None of the fifty-plus kids on our bus had a thing to say as we stared at the rundown mansion to the right.

The drive was seventeen hours of hell—with frequent stops for bathroom and food breaks, plus one stop to change drivers. Otherwise, this hunk of yellow steel had been our prison.

Beth rose to her knees from her spot beside me in the seat we shared, draping her fingers over the open window just like I did. Chris and Lucas came from their bench across the aisle and crowded us to do the same.

"Where the heck are we?"

Chris's question made the rest of us shrug. No one had any clue. We only knew we were in Louisiana because of a sign we passed a couple hours ago, but ...

"Best guess? Purgatory."

My gaze shifted toward Roz when she spoke for the first time since we pulled off from Seaton Falls. She'd been silent for hours, sitting in the seat ahead of Beth and I—reading, listening to music, sulking.

Like I expected, Beth rolled her eyes at her cousin's response, but I knew it didn't matter much *what* Roz said—good, bad, indifferent—because for whatever reason, Beth couldn't stand her.

"I swear I'm gonna morph out if I have to share a room with that girl." Beth's mumbled statement stole my attention from the failing porch and sagging roof.

"Morph out?"

She nodded. "Shift into a wolf and stay that way until the clan, or whoever-the-heck is in charge here, puts me out of my misery."

I laughed, but she didn't. "Wait... that's actually a thing?"

"Morphing out?" she replied. "Yes. And so is the clan's solution," she added, using her finger to make a slicing motion across the front of her neck.

My mouth closed with a quiet snap and I turned back toward the window with Chris's elbow digging into my shoulder.

There were a total of five busses from Seaton Falls alone, all filled to max capacity, but several others were here when we pulled up and more arrived by the minute. I wasn't sure if anyone else knew the house in the middle of the woods was merely a decoy, but I did, thanks to Liam explaining it before.

At the thought of him, my head swiveled frantically, panning our surroundings. My dragon was seeking him, and I felt how it made my chest tight with worry. Our connection felt more like invisible fibers attached to my core. And when we were separated, they extended outward, trying to link to Liam—those invisible feelers, tethers that kept us in synch.

He was supposed to be here by now. I couldn't ride with him for many reasons. The most pressing one being that the clan wanted to personally see to it that all their young shifters, myself included, made it to The Damascus Facility safely. In many ways, I felt like I belonged to them.

Property.

My breathing was quick and I knew why. Because I still hadn't laid eyes on Liam. A million and five neurotic questions plagued me. *What if he's not really coming and he just said that so I wouldn't protest? What if something happened? What if someone stopped him?*

I hated not having control of these feelings; my attachment to him was not by choice. It was more like a ... need. Something in me *needed* him and often stopped at nothing just to be closer.

But that proved to be quite the inconvenience, considering what I felt for Nick, which *was* by choice. With him being on the run for a few days, with all the time I had to think on this long ride, it put things in perspective. There'd been a knot in the pit of my stomach since the moment he took off and I now knew what that knot meant.

It meant the three little words he said to me not too long ago stayed with me.

It meant I kinda regretted not being able to say them back.

I was desperate to know where he was. The clan wouldn't stand for him not being carted off to this facility with the rest of us, so did that mean he'd be punished for not showing up? I hoped it wouldn't. Especially seeing as how he wasn't even in attendance at the meeting where our fate was announced. According to his friends, they hadn't heard from him. Meaning, he also hadn't shared with them why he ran off. They knew nothing of Liam, nothing of the legend that marked Nick as my killer. If his family still hadn't reached him, he might not even be aware of the recent changes.

I almost went to his door yesterday when I finished packing. All the cars were in the circular drive, but they probably wouldn't have answered anyway. Because they probably hated me. His mom was already president of the *Anti-Evie Club,* but I had the sinking feeling his brothers and father were now honorary members as well. After all, it was my fault Nick took off in the first place.

I just ... really wanted to know he was okay. That was it.

The sound of a roaring engine caused my breath to hitch, and my dragon was at ease before I even laid eyes on the ragged pickup. Liam came to a stop, and once again, the only sound surrounding us was that of cicadas and the occasional squawk of a bird.

Unashamedly, I watched him.

He stepped out of his truck and my eyes were trained on him from the second the first, dark boot pressed down into the grass, right up until his back rested against the driver-side door. Even with the hundreds of tired, irritated, overheated teens hanging from bus windows, he found me easily. There was a ghost of a smile on his lips when we locked eyes.

However, while Liam was noticing *me,* the others were noticing Liam.

"Holy hotness, Batgirl, who-the-heck is that?"

When the off-color question left Beth's mouth, Lucas' head cut toward her quickly. It was no secret he had it bad for her, but, right now, she was too enraptured by the impressive landscape known as Mount Liam to spare Lucas' feelings.

I smiled a bit, but managed to hold in my laugh. "Why are you asking me?"

Beth continued to fan herself with an empty *Lemon Heads* box as she kept her gaze trained on the guy who had a tendency to steal *my* breath away too. She watched him with about as much discretion as a brightly lit billboard against a night sky.

"Well, since I know *I've* never met him, he has to be staring at *you.*"

I nodded when I decided to be honest ... and a little coy. "I know him."

Her eyes found me again. "Old friend from your hometown?"

Liam's gaze finally shifted away, and I nodded to Beth's question. "Something like that."

She tilted her head to the side as if to take Liam in from another angle, zoning out as she ignored Lucas stewing beside us.

"Well, Nick better hurry up and get here sooner rather than later, because that's some crazy-insane competition he's got over there," she joked suggestively. However, if she knew the real reason Nick wasn't here, she wouldn't have found it so funny.

Most thought he was just in a funk and wasn't answering his phone because of it. They were initially concerned when he wasn't at the departure point this morning, but Chris tossed out the idea that maybe his parents made arrangements for him to be brought down later.

Only I knew there was no guarantee.

"Speaking of, have you all checked your phones lately? Any calls or texts from him yet?" All eyes were on Roz when she asked. She looked worried.

The whole crew gave the same answer, but in their own words. The consensus: Nick was still radio silent. Roz sat back in her seat with a sigh before popping her earbuds back in.

"He'll show. I know my boy." The reassuring words came from Chris, but it was hard to tell if he was trying to convince *us* or *himself*.

We all stood there hanging out the windows for any morsel of a breeze to bring us relief in the Louisiana heat. All were quiet; all likely thinking about Nick. The only thing that eventually stole our attention was the sight of bodies filing out of the seemingly abandoned mansion. They wore dark suits despite the heat—the men in pants, the women in skirts—but they were way overdressed for being in the middle of the woods.

We perked up as all eleven stood equal width apart from one another. The woman at the center of their formation smiled as she surveyed us, probably taking in how many of us had arrived. She was beautiful—long, dark hair and features so perfect she was nearly painful to look at. From the corner of my eye, I was also aware of the moment Liam noticed her too. Who could blame him, I guess.

He leaned away from his car as the sight of her seemed to awaken him from mental slumber. The once cool, calm, collected expression that had so many girls on this bus—and probably all the *other* busses

—swooning over him, was gone. He stared at the woman long and hard and I was caught off guard by what felt like a punch to the gut as I watched him watch her.

Why do you even care, Evie? He's just a friend, a non-factor.

I swallowed what I knew to be the first hints of jealousy and forced my eyes away from him. The striking woman raised a megaphone she held at her side and all eyes were on her.

"Young shifters, let me be the first to welcome you to The Damascus Facility."

"Thanks for the intro. Can we get some grub now?" Beth asked under her breath.

I smiled as my stomach growled at the mention of food and turned to listen again.

"We are so excited to have you all here and we hope that, during your time with us, you learn more about who you are, our mission, and forge unbreakable bonds with your peers that time nor circumstance will ever break."

After the woman spoke, Roz let out another of her irritated sighs, prompting a low growl to rumble from Beth's chest. I was sure only the five of us heard it—us girls, Chris, Lucas.

"In just a moment, you'll be released from your busses, shown to your sleeping quarters, and then, once you've had time to get settled, dinner will be served. After you've had the chance to mingle with friends and, who knows, maybe meet a few new ones, you'll have the opportunity to tour our lovely facility if you'd like."

I wasn't sure if I was most excited about getting off this bus or getting a meal.

Our driver stood with lanyards draped through his fingers, and in a painfully slow manner, he checked us off his list and handed over an ID badge as we exited. Each had our name, age, hometown, and species printed on the back with the photos we took when school first started. I eyed mine for a while, noting it specified neither species, but instead read 'hybrid'.

Beth looped her arm through mine as we meandered toward the

old house with our back packs on our shoulders. We were assured that the rest of our things would be brought to our rooms later.

There were so many of us—hundreds if not more than a thousand. We moved in the same direction like a large wave. At the front entrance, the foyer of the dilapidated home was jam-packed with most of us lined up outside, but only for a short time. In two, single-file lines, we were ushered down a staircase hidden behind a heavy, steel double-door. It was beneath the grand staircase I imagined was once the focal point of the house. The fixtures and remnants of expensive fabric suggested that, in times past, this place was beautiful. However, what was left looked like something straight out of a horror movie—tattered drapery hanging from the windows, cracks in the marble tile, webs that looked like spiders the size of cars had spun them.

Liam, of course, wasn't far. I shifted from one foot to the next, able to feel him although I couldn't see him. There couldn't have been more than a few feet between us. That's how strong our link had become. Seemed like it strengthened every day.

Evolved every day.

With Beth suddenly aware of his existence—and his awareness of me—I decided not to search for him. While, no, I wouldn't hide that we were friends, I didn't want Beth to read more into it than necessary.

She and I were still side by side, following Lucas, Chris, and Roz. We descended about three flights of steps before coming to a long, narrow hallway with cinderblock walls and dim lighting. Turning a corner, we realized we were being led to elevators large enough to move cargo. Ten, to be exact—five on either side. We piled into one with about forty or fifty others. Liam was among that number. Whenever possible, he stayed close, ever mindful of his previous role as my warrior.

Even with all the bodies sharing the now cramped space, there were no words spoken. If it weren't for the occasional cough or shuffling of feet, we would have been in complete silence.

During the lengthy ride here, I gathered that I wasn't the only one afraid of what awaited us. Liam was right about so many being clueless concerning the state of things. In some way, it was comforting to know I wasn't the only one petrified about what was to come. Unlike being dropped in a new school all by myself, the Damascus Facility was new to *all* of us.

We couldn't all be fearless and all-knowing like Beth. At the sight of her cool demeanor when the large, metal cube we piled into began to move, I was grateful she was here with me.

My eyes wandered up above the closed doors, expecting to see numbers displayed there, letting us know how many levels we'd been lowered already. But there *were* none. The attendant who stood near the front of the elevator held a tablet in his hand, and from the looks of it, everything was keyed in remotely. Only he knew where we were headed, and judging by the look on Liam's face, he didn't like the secrecy any more than I did.

Being such a large piece of equipment, I expected the elevator to be loud and shake violently when we reached our destination. Instead, the transition from moving to motionlessness was so smooth I barely noticed we stopped. It wasn't until the doors parted to reveal a burst of bright, sterile light that I realized it was time to exit.

We stepped out, Beth and I still linked at the arm, observing our new surroundings. Everything was so ... perfect. It reminded me more of a science facility than a school.

Stainless steel sconces mounted at evenly spaced intervals beamed fluorescent light toward the ceiling. The walls were stark-white, high-gloss. Several sets of double-doors had signs posted beside them—identifiers for rooms that, for now, meant nothing to me and the others. Every so often, there were benches—more glossy white surfaces with stainless steel legs. Beside them, lush, potted plants that reminded me of the ones my Gram used to make me water for her every time I visited.

The soles of our gym-shoe-clad and sandaled feet squeaked against the new tile. This place still smelled like fresh paint and plastic. Too new for anyone to call it home, but home it was. For now, anyway.

"May I have your attention please?" It was the exquisite one again. She hadn't been on the elevator with us, so I guessed there was one specifically for staff.

She tossed her dark mane behind her shoulder while waiting for all eyes to find her. I tried to fight the urge, but glanced over to Liam, hating how it felt when I caught him staring right at her.

Again.

Intense. Thoughtful. Anxious.

Only, this time, I turned quickly enough to catch her gazing right back at him. The hint of a smile ghosting on her mouth as she conveyed something to him with her eyes. I couldn't place it at first, but ... *did she know him? Was that what I was sensing? Familiarity?*

Before I could analyze the two any further, she looked away, focusing on our entire group instead of just one.

"You should have all been given ID tags before exiting your busses. If you'll flip those tags over, you'll find our Damascus Facility logo etched onto the back. Not everyone's logo will be the same color. There are six: black, silver, gold, red, green, and blue."

I flipped mine over—gold. Beth did the same—blue.

"If you look around, you'll find those same logos in their respective colors posted beside each of the six hallways." The woman gestured in a circle from where we stood at the center of a hub of elevators. Surrounding us, six hallways that stretched far like spokes.

"Please form a line in front of whichever hallway matches your badge," she went on. "We'd like to move things along quickly because there are several others waiting to be brought down to get settled."

It sucked Beth and I wouldn't be in the same group. And I'm sure it sucked even more for her because she and Roz were headed for the same line. In fact, just as I thought it, she rolled her eyes when realizing that very thing.

Tucking my thumbs behind the straps of my backpack, I stood near my area, watching as the others filled quickly. But it was only me and two others beside the gold logo. More of that special treatment Liam mentioned the other night, I was sure.

The kid in front of me had his nose so far in the air I was worried a bird might fly up it. The one behind me, a girl, was only concerned with the fact that her phone didn't get service down here in the basement of all basements.

No, seriously. I'm pretty sure Hell was a few floors *up*. That's how deep we were.

That gentle tug in my chest made me aware of Liam again and my eyes went straight to him. To my surprise, he wasn't eyeing the brunette again. This time, he was conversing with one of the suits who'd come out to gather us from the busses. After speaking to Liam, the guy went to two others who weren't students and motioned for all three to follow him. My guess was they were being taken to their quarters as well. The small group walked toward me where I stood at the gold emblem hallway and, when passing, Liam tapped his temple discreetly and I knew right away what he meant.

Our built-in communication system, unlike cell phones, was in full working order even here, in Middle Earth.

The next instant, I was inside his head.

"Yeah?" There was a tone to the question and it caught me off guard even though I was the one who asked. It sounded like I was giving him attitude, and I don't know, maybe I was.

"They're showing us to our spots," Liam informed me. Not out loud of course; just in his thoughts as he disappeared around a corner up ahead.

"Yup. Figured." Ugh ... there it was again. The snark. The attitude.

He didn't respond right away, but when he did, I knew he heard and felt it too. *"...Something bothering you?"*

I had to get it together. Deep down, I knew where all this was coming from. It was the way he looked at the woman. I guessed her to be an instructor or maybe the facility's director, but her position here was irrelevant. They—she and Liam—weren't strangers. I felt it in my gut. And no matter how many times I tried to tell myself not to care; no matter how many times I reminded myself I had no *right* to care, I did.

I cared.

Because I freakin' suck and I couldn't seem to keep my feelings in check when it came to him.

It was, literally, out of my control. The attachment was there, and I could do nothing about it. I suppose, after centuries of existing together, after centuries spent loving one another, the remnants hadn't faded and maybe never would. My body and mind might not have remembered, but my soul certainly did.

Being mindful of how I responded, I tried to smooth things over. I had no right, one way or another, to worry about who caught his attention. In this lifetime, he and I were nothing more than friends. Albeit *close* ones, but friends nonetheless.

"Everything's fine," I lied. *"Just tired from the drive down."* That was kind of true.

He seemed to accept my answer. *"I'll check in later."*

I gave no response, and when I was pushed out of his mind, I knew he wasn't expecting one.

The lines were finally full and mine still had the least—five including me. At the head of our section stood two of the stuffy suits. One guy, one lady. Both wore kind smiles that made me leerier of them than if they'd been scowling. The woman locked gazes with me and I had to smile back. They were all so perfect, like being attractive was a requirement for being hired to work here.

Our female guide and her male counterpart were both of Asian descent. Looking closer at the tag pinned to her jacket, I read her name—Mei. The guy was Randall. Apparently, we were all going to be on a first name basis here, unlike Seaton Prep. Headmaster McNulty had been all about order and knowing our place when it came to being under subjection to the authority figures on campus. It wasn't that easy to convince me this place was cool, though. Only time would tell.

"If you five would follow us, we'll escort you to your quarters," Mei announced, broadening her grin.

We took to the hallway and, veering left, heavy, stainless-steel doors came into view. We stopped at the first and a small piece of paper was taped in the space where a nameplate was meant to go.

"Errol Cohen, this is your stop," Randall said. "The other students will all be four to six to a room, but I think you all will be pleased to know none of you will be sharing your space. You'll each have your own, private sleeping quarters as well as private restroom facilities."

The other kids breathed a sigh of relief after being informed of our isolation, but not me. I was actually hoping I'd have someone else to bunk with, someone to keep me company.

Errol stepped out of our small crowd—a tall kid with a severe case of bed-head. He either didn't care how messy it was, or he'd taken one heck of a nap on the way here and didn't realize it needed combing. He gave a cheeky salute to the rest of us as he shut his door, and when he did, I picked up on his scent when it wafted toward me.

Lycan.

We dropped off two more and then came to the last door where my own name was written on a sheet of paper. When I eyed it, Mei felt the need to explain.

"The paper is temporary. Had we been expecting to open so soon we would've been prepared, but, considering the circumstances, we had to make do."

I laughed a bit because she didn't owe me any kind of explanation whatsoever. I was a nobody. A nobody whose only real requirement was a TV somewhere in my room.

"It's fine," I assured her.

"It's just that ... we know the parents of the kids in *this* area paid a considerable amount to ensure that their children have the best of the best here at Damascus."

"Not mine," I blurted.

At first, both Mei and Randall seemed confused, but it was Mei who recouped and straightened her expression first.

"Oh ... well, we just assumed as much when the director added you to the Gold Sector. That's how the others managed to acquire these rooms. They made it clear you were to be well taken care of," she added. "In fact, I purposely put you in the room near mine so I could listen out for you."

This was all getting out of hand. Everyone had suddenly become members of my own, personal Secret Service. I was glad the other kids were already in their rooms. This was so embarrassing.

"That's really not necessary," I assured them both. "But thank you all the same."

Mei seemed disappointed that I wasn't overly excited about this. Stepping aside, she opened the door to my new room. "The rest of your belongings will be brought down to you shortly. As soon as everyone's been shown to their rooms."

I nodded, but didn't even go in to inspect my new space. Instead, I made a request I hoped my perceived clout would make come true.

"Is there any way I could get a roommate?"

Again, Mei was confused. I was sure most of the other kids would *kill* for a private room, but I had a different perspective, I guess.

"A ... roommate?"

I nodded. "Yeah, and I already have someone in mind. Beth Chadwick. Is that possible?"

She swallowed, glancing toward Randall before meeting my gaze again. "I'll certainly see what I can do."

CHAPTER 7

Evie

I let my backpack slip off my shoulders and onto the floor beside an empty bookcase. The white and stainless-steel décor was carried over into the sleeping quarters as well. Everything from the corridor leading to the elevators, to this very space, was a careful arrangement of clean lines and minimalism. A small bed dressed in white linen was pushed against the far wall beneath what was meant to appear as a window. Frosted glass hid the clever lighting behind it, designed to make it feel like we were above ground. There was even a twinge of coral across the top, simulating the oncoming sunset.

Someone put a lot of thought—and a lot of *money*—into this place.

I walked the perimeter slowly, taking it all in. A sleek dresser with a rectangular pot of faux grass had been placed in the center beside a lamp. Next, a walk-in closet with fresh laundry bags folded on a shelf with instructions on top. Apparently, we weren't expected to do our own washing; there was staff to take care of that on weekends.

Impressive.

Just outside the closet door, a large, complex intercom system with more instructions posted beneath it. Some other time, I'd figure out how to use it, but for now I at least read that we were able to call from room to room, like a hotel.

I moved on, dropping down onto the edge of my bed. This was home. It'd take a bit before that didn't feel so strange.

I took a deep breath, and while wondering how the others were settling in, I also wondered if Nick's family was any closer to finding him. He should have been here, right alongside the rest of us. Having him here would've made things easier for a number of reasons. For one, I missed him. And there was also the fact that I was worried out of my mind; not only about his physical wellbeing, but his state of mind. More than anything right now, I wanted to see him. Unfortunately, even if he *did* attempt to reach one of us, we were in an absolute cell phone dead zone.

A short knock startled me and I hopped up right away. At the door, a small screen had been installed beside it. A blue button labeled *'press before opening'* caught my attention and I did just that. The second my finger mashed it, an image of Beth standing on the other side with her backpack in tow brought a huge grin to my face.

After struggling with the array of locks and deadbolts, I finally got it open and rushed her inside.

"I wasn't sure they'd let you come," I squealed. "I mean, you're cool with being my roomie, right? I guess I should've checked with you first. I just thought—"

"Are you kidding me right now?" she cut in. "If it wasn't for you, I'd be unpacking my things in a room with five other girls, one of which being Roz, so ... I actually owe you a huge thank you."

I smiled. She was just as happy about this as I was.

"Mei ... I think her name was?" I nodded to confirm when Beth made a guess. "She said a second bed would be brought down for me within the hour. They're pretty swamped trying to get everyone settled, so it's not a big deal."

I agreed. For now, we could just chill.

The space was decked out, but sort of empty. Beth set her bag down beside mine and followed the same path I did when first walking in, letting her fingers trace the surfaces she passed.

"Dude, I thought my *first* room was nice," she said with a smile. "But it has *nothing* on this one. Apparently, you saved me from the slums."

I laughed, settling on the edge of the bed again as I watched her explore. "I was afraid it'd get lonely, so I asked if it was okay to bring you in."

Beth shook her head. "I have no clue how much money your parents had to come off of to make this happen, but God bless them." When she smiled again, I looked away. The reference poured salt in a fresh wound.

She stepped into the large closet, skimmed the same letter I had about laundry service, and then ended her tour in front of me where she propped her elbow against the '*window*' sill.

Still scanning our new space, she spoke my very thoughts aloud. "This place is nice, but kinda weird, right?"

I nodded. "Thought it was just me."

She shook her head. "Definitely not. I mean, I'm looking forward to classes and training and stuff, but the whole '*living underground*' thing is what I think is throwing me off. Don't get me wrong, I get that they need to hide us while we learn and all, but ..." she shrugged. "Just seems a bit extreme."

During the bus ride, the rest of us had so many questions. However, every time, it seemed like Beth was the one with all the answers.

"You're probably the most enlightened out of us all."

One corner of her mouth tugged up when she smiled. "I suppose. My parents seem to be the anomaly. They never hid from me what I am, what I'd one day become. And I don't think I fully appreciated that until we all shifted early, and I saw the damage it did to the other kids."

She zoned out for a moment, thinking about one of the many things we discussed while we rode. Apparently, they all shifted the night I did and we *all* had a hard time with it. With twenty being the typical transitioning age, most parents thought they had time to let their kids in on the secret, only to find out otherwise.

"I know most are blaming The Sovereign, but that's only part of the problem. Had the adults taken the approach *my* parents took, we wouldn't be here," she said, not bothering to hide the chill in her tone. "While, yeah, the initial shift might have still been a shocker, we could have at least been learning our limitations, our abilities since childhood." I noted the frustration in her expression. "It's all about control," she added. "If we can master that, that's all we need. The rest will come about naturally."

I let that sink in. Control. I think I was beginning to realize that before she said it, but it stuck with me. I was probably looking at shifting in the wrong way, thinking it controlled *me,* and not the other way around. Like Liam said, our shifted forms were the biggest part of who we were, but it was still us. Not some outside force we needed to bring under subjection. We could control it just like we could control our physical bodies.

I had so much to learn.

A soft growl stole our attention and Beth laughed before I did. It wasn't a warning of impending aggression like when she made the sound at Roz. This came from someplace else.

Her stomach.

She reared her head back. "Come *on!* They know we eat like an army of grown men since we shifted. Why the heck are they making us wait so long to get food?"

I didn't have the answer to her question, but I could help her survive the wait a bit more comfortably. She watched as I stood and walked to my backpack. Unzipping the side, I pulled out two candy bars and tossed her one.

Her eyes lit up and the look of gratitude on her face made me crack up. "Woman, you are like … my godsend today. I swear!"

I pealed back the wrapper as I sat again, taking a bite. The second I did, I was reminded of the conversation I had with Liam. He said that, physically, I was exactly like he remembered, and I still had a thing for sweets. But, other than that, I felt like a completely different person. It was that disconnect that made me question whether I'd ever hone in on whatever abilities I had before.

Beth and I were polar opposites, which I suppose is why we got along so well. She was so strong, and I wanted confidence in my abilities like she had. There was a regality she carried with her, and here I was, supposed to be queen or something.

Oh, the irony.

I was just getting ready to ask what she thought our classes and training would consist of, but another knock interrupted. I stood, hoping it was the rest of our things so we could get unpacked; however, a press of the blue button beside the door made my heart leap.

Liam.

I hesitated. With Beth here, I was nervous to answer because … she might see.

The feelings I try to hide.

The way Liam looks at me, *through* me.

The connection.

All of it.

"You gonna get that or do we have a butler somewhere I haven't seen yet," she joked.

I faked a smile and, realizing there was only one option, I opened the door. Liam stared back and I drew in a deep breath. In his black tee and dark denim, he looked like every girl's dream, every father's nightmare. Right down to the tattoos and that devious look that always lurked beneath the surface of whatever expression he wore. I was almost positive Beth was staring unapologetically from over my shoulder. I imagined it, mouth wide and everything. When Liam's eyes went there, behind me to where she stood, I knew I was right.

I forced a smile and shoved my hands in the back pockets of my jeans. "Hey."

He smiled back—easier, more natural. "Hey. I'm just checking in."

Of course he was. I hadn't been in this room more than twenty minutes and he was already worried. My mouth moved with a smile again, and this time, it was a real one with a quiet laugh trailing behind it.

"I'm good," I answered. "*We're* good," I corrected, gesturing my head toward Beth.

He caught the hint and didn't make moves to come in like I was sure he would have if I'd been alone. Instead, he took a step back. "Well, just ... holler if you need anything. I'm only a couple doors down."

Biting the side of my lip as I scanned him from head to toe, I nodded. "Will do."

When he walked off, I slowly closed the door. Before I could even get it latched, Beth was already starting.

"So, is he an old friend or a bodyguard," she joked, plopping down on the foot of my bed as I turned to face her. She was knee-deep in that chocolate bar, so she didn't bother with eye contact.

"Eh ... old friend," I replied. "*Very* old."

She nodded. "He's an instructor, I'm assuming? I mean, he doesn't look a whole lot older than us, but he definitely doesn't look like a student."

"Yeah, an instructor," I sighed, taking my seat again.

"Cool. Maybe he'll give us both an automatic passing grade because he knows you." She smiled playfully, sucking caramel from her fingers before tossing the wrapper in the trashcan a foot away.

I didn't respond, but perhaps I should have, because my lack of an answer had Beth's attention.

"Uh oh ... did I step on a landmine?" Her shoulders shifted toward me and I didn't necessarily want the attention she was giving.

I had to tread lightly. Beth was my closest friend since moving to Seaton Falls, and even more so now that I was positive all the ones I had before no longer remembered me. However, before she was *my* friend, she was Nick's, and I didn't want to give her the wrong idea about Liam. Like I said, we were nothing more than friends. I wasn't to blame for the connection we had beyond that. That was, apparently, the result of something I'd done to us in my past life. Something that couldn't be undone.

Speaking of landmines, there were so many potential ones moving forward, I wasn't sure of what to say.

Beth's brow lifted as she stared. I had to say something.

"Things with Liam are ... complicated. *Were* complicated," I clarified.

A look of sudden awareness came over her. "Ohhh ... He's an ex."

I cringed a bit at that word because it didn't really fit. "No, not an ex. We've just got a complicated history," I shared. "But all we are is friends. He knows how I feel about Nick."

She nodded then, and I was glad to see she didn't appear to be reading more into it than necessary.

"Understood," she replied. "However, fair warning, friend to friend: I'm not sure how Nick's gonna feel about him dropping in on you like he just did," she added thoughtfully. "Might be a good idea to set some ground rules sooner rather than later."

Ground rules. While, I knew she had a point, it was easier said than done. I didn't like the idea of hurting *either* of the guys' feelings, which was partly the reason I shot down Liam's offer for space when he mentioned it. I meant what I said about us not going out of our way to avoid one another here, but maybe it was equally as important not to go out of our way to be around each other either.

Beth chuckled and I turned toward her again. "So, he knows

about Nick, but does Nick know about him? That's where things could get sticky."

Sticky wasn't even the word for how that first and only meeting between them had gone.

"He does," I shared. "I was honest with him. Honest with both."

She nodded and I could tell she respected that answer. It hadn't been easy being forthcoming with the truth when Nick asked if Liam and I were 'close' in my past, but I didn't want to lie to him. The truth was that Liam and I were close before, but that was then. I wanted to build something new with Nick, and if he'd still have me, I was ready to move forward. No matter how difficult a task, I had every intention to fight the pull toward Liam.

A third knock had me rolling my eyes as I got up again. It was either Beth's bed or our belongings being delivered, I was sure. In the time it took me to walk to the door, I went over new ways we could layout our room to accommodate for the loss of space. I didn't bother with the security screen this time, instead just opening up.

And when I did, shock nearly knocked me right off my feet as I laid eyes on the last person I expected it to be. A blue gaze met mine and I breathed a sigh of relief.

Nick stood there, both hands braced against the doorframe, looking like it'd taken everything in him to come to my room. Or maybe that was wrong. Maybe it was the other way around and this was the look of a guy who'd been fighting himself to stay away.

Where did he come from? Where had he been? Where did his absence leave us?

I almost questioned how he found me, but then remembered. My heart. He probably heard it beating from a mile away. The very aspect of who and what he was that had just led him to me, was the thing about him I was supposed to fear most.

Only, I didn't.

I believed it when he said he loved me. And, from my experience, love was the one thing with the power to change *everything*.

"Nick..." His name tumbled from my lips as I watched him,

wondering if I imagined him standing here. Part of me believed he wouldn't show, or that, when he *did,* he would avoid me completely.

But here he stood.

I still had no idea if we were in the clear, what conclusions he reached while he was away, but ... he was here. That had to count for something, right?

"And that would be my cue to get lost," Beth announced quietly, vacating our room the next second.

When it was just us, Nick's eyes hesitantly landed on mine as he asked, "Can I come in?"

I stepped aside to let him know he was welcome, and then closed the door behind him. For some reason, a chill followed him inside. Not literally. It was more so something I sensed in my heart. This visit hadn't come with a warm greeting—a hug, a smile.

Nothing.

Instead, he stood before me with tension in his shoulders, dark circles beneath his eyes. From the looks of it, he hadn't slept much while he was away. I could only imagine why—the thoughts he must have had while no one was around, the lies I was sure he was beginning to believe about himself.

Despite the uncertainty making my stomach swim, for the first time in days, I had a bit of peace, simply knowing he was safe. But there was everything else to contend with now—how standoffish he was being, how he could hardly look me in my eyes, how he stayed close to the door as though he didn't plan to be here long.

I noticed it all.

He let out a deep breath, and I held mine in when he spoke. "I wasn't sure you'd want to see me," were the words he exhaled, the first he'd uttered to me in days.

My fingers fluttered through the side of my hair and I tried not to seem nervous, but I was.

"Of *course* I wanted to see you. I've been so worried. I called, I texted ... I just wanted to know you were okay."

I wasn't the only one going through a ton of changes. Nick's world had been flipped upside down too, with the explanation of what he was, what it meant for us. I wouldn't hold it against him that he ran off. I might've done the same thing if I were in his shoes. My only concern had been that he came back.

Things got so crazy the other day. Emotions were running high on all fronts with the mutts, with news of Maddox falling victim to one of them, with Liam and Nick meeting for the first time. So many factors were at play and I believed the drama colored all our vision. It made things seem worse than they really were; worse than they had to be. I, for one, had hope that extended beyond some out-of-date myth. I believed in Nick and I. Even if *he* no longer did.

When he ran off, a part of my heart went away with him. I understood and believed the legend of what he was meant to become, respected the weight of the words Liam spoke. However, I knew Nick's heart.

From what I'd been told, the *last* Liberator came out of nowhere. It wasn't someone I knew, wasn't someone close to me. Therefore, circumstances had changed this time around. It was quite possible that what Nick and I shared, what we *felt,* was enough to rewrite our course.

When he finally focused on me, I wanted so badly for him to believe it too. My hand pressed to his cheek and he leaned into it, closing his eyes. He exhaled softly, as though the contact relieved him in some way.

There were still clear signs of resistance—like he wished he'd been strong enough to push me away, but didn't. I wasn't completely sure what fueled the traces of anger I sensed emanating from him toward me, but I could only guess it was because of what he experienced, what he *felt,* when he saw me with Liam. If that was the case, I couldn't fault him for that.

The connection *was* weird. And on top of that, it was powerful. So much so, it didn't surprise me that Nick sensed it too. But I intended to explain it all to him because I wanted to be transparent, wanted him to understand that being tethered to Liam was some-thing out of my control, wasn't something I embraced.

It just was.

"Where have you been?" I finally found the courage to ask.

Nick blinked and lowered his gaze to the floor. "At first? Nowhere," he answered. "In the beginning, I just wandered around. Did that for hours, trying to figure things out, trying to understand how it all got so messed up."

My eyes lowered too, when he said that.

"After a while, I followed my gut and went to my grandfather's place."

My brow twitched. He'd never mentioned a grandparent before now. Especially not one residing in Seaton Falls.

"He passed a long time ago, but we never got rid of his estate," he shared. "He owned quite a bit of property on the other side of the woods, so I holed up at his house while I got my thoughts together."

I chewed the side of my lip, unsure if it was okay to ask this next question. "And ... did you?" I inquired. "Get your thoughts together?"

My heart pounded and I knew he heard it.

It wasn't lost on me how his expression tensed either. "Yes and no."

What did that mean?

"The time alone mostly gave me a chance to let a few things sink in," he explained. "Everything that guy said about me, about what I am ... I believe him."

I wouldn't argue with him about the validity of Liam's accusa-tions, but I would, however, fight Nick tooth and nail if he tried to imply that it doomed us.

"And?"

His eyes lifted to meet mine. "And ... I think we have a lot to figure out." Exasperated, he shared another thought. "For all I know it's not even safe for us to be *here,* in this place, together."

"Nick—"

"Evie, listen," he cut in—stern, cold. He sounded so unlike

himself. "I already know what you're gonna say and, the fact of the matter is, if something happens to you ... If I—"

When his statement ended there, I realized I shouldn't have gotten so excited, thinking his return meant something for us it might not. It all depended on what he said next. There was something behind his eyes that told me he was holding back, and *would* hold back until he trusted himself.

Which might be never.

"If I ever hurt you, even if it was out of my control ... I'd never be able to live with myself."

"But that's the thing; you *won't*."

He shook his head. "You don't know that for sure. None of us do."

I took a step back the moment I felt the disconnection between us. I was foolish for filling my heart with false hope. We weren't okay. It took a minute for me to figure it out, but I knew that now.

Nick watched as I took a seat on the edge of my bed, leaving him where he stood beside the door. I said nothing as I let the reality of our circumstances settle.

He stepped closer, but kept a fair amount of distance between us. My feelings were all out of whack. I went from thinking we still had a chance, to watching our undefined relationship being snuffed out like a smothered flame.

"I think we need time, Evie. Time to sort things out. Time to find ourselves. Time to figure out what we want."

The last portion of his statement felt loaded, but I was too jarred by the rest to cut through the bull and fully grasp what he meant— *'time to figure out what we want'*.

"I did some soul searching," Nick added. "It dawned on me while I was there; I don't know myself anymore. And I think that's part of the problem." He paused to get his thoughts together and I felt a strange stirring of anger swell in my chest. "I've changed so much in such a short time that I look into the mirror some days and ... I have no idea what the person staring back at me is even capable of."

When my head whipped toward him, wetness fell from my eyes, touching my cheeks.

"And you think you're the only one going through things, Nick? You think you're the only one trying to hold on to some semblance of who you were despite your body screaming at you *every day* that you're not who you think you are?"

I didn't expect to sound so angry, but there was no hiding it. "Why the heck do you think they snatched us from our homes and brought us here? *Any* of us?"

He lowered his head and I didn't regret raising my voice. A deep breath puffed from his nostrils and I fought the urge to explode on him again.

"I didn't come here to argue," he said calmly. So calmly it did nothing but piss me off even more. How convenient that he'd had *days* to reach this conclusion, only to dump it on me in the span of five minutes...

"No, you came here to give up on us," I seethed.

I could see in his expression that my words cut deep, but he ignored them, finishing his original thought.

"I came here to tell you I think it'd do us both some good to get to know our new selves better before we try to move forward together. I think we both know we stand to make a huge mess of things if we don't start there."

I felt like there was more he wanted to say, but held back for some reason.

I stood again. "What's this really about, Nick. Because, just a few days ago, you were on board with starting over, taking things slower. Not talking about going our separate ways."

He was absolutely silent.

"I mean, that's what this is, right? You're saying you want to be alone, aren't you?"

"I'm saying I don't know what's best for us right now. And, if that means we back off of ... *whatever* we were ... then I think we owe it to ourselves to have our personal baggage out of the way before we make our next move."

I shook my head at his wording. "We?" I scoffed. "*We ...* didn't make this decision, Nick. *You* did. All by yourself. You disappear on me for days and this is what you come back with?"

His once serene, blue eyes were even cold now as a hard glare settled on me. I'd never seen it there before.

"Doesn't feel great, does it?" His words cut like a knife. "I seem to recall nearly a week of radio silence when *you* decided to run off in the woods not so long ago. But I guess it was okay then, right?"

I said nothing, knowing exactly what scenario he referenced—when I first shifted and went on hiatus because, at the time, I thought I was alone. Thought I was some kind of freak who'd catch fire and hurt someone, hurt *him*. I didn't bother explaining myself to him now, though. His impression of me was already tainted.

Slowly but surely, I was beginning to see our problems were bigger than I realized. And we were both at fault. The secrets between us had become a breeding ground for distrust and doubt. While we held them in, thinking we were protecting the other from our truths, we were mostly protecting ourselves. It'd gotten us nowhere.

Nick took another breath and I knew he was gearing up to say more, something heavier than everything else, so I braced myself.

"And let's be honest, I'm not the only one who has some soul searching to do."

My brow tensed when the accusatory tone of his voice touched my ears. There was a darkness to him that made my skin crawl and, honestly? It made me wish he'd leave.

"I'm not blind, Evie. Or ... *deaf,* for that matter." He paused and, in the time it took him to finish, I didn't breathe. "I saw how you were around Liam; heard every time your heart skipped a beat when he got close to you."

I was shaking my head before he even finished. "That was nerves.

I wasn't sure how it would go with you two meeting for the first time, and—"

"It was nerves, but ... mostly, you were afraid I'd see it." He stopped there and my heart thundered. "You were afraid I'd see what you feel for him."

My stomach twisted in knots and I felt weak in the knees. Being under his heavy stare as I searched my thoughts for a response was reminiscent of being interrogated. And the fact that I knew he heard my heart racing a mile a minute right now wasn't helping my case any.

There was so much he didn't know, so much he didn't understand. But that was my fault too. He didn't understand because I hadn't trusted him enough to share. Now, it seemed like a moot point, but I decided to try anyway. If ever there was a time to grasp at straws, it was now, at the moment I felt Nick slipping away.

I was fidgeting with my nails and I hated how insecure I must've looked, shoving my hands in my back pockets before explaining.

"I told you Liam and I knew each other in my past life, but that was *all* I told you," I began.

Nick stared with no judgement at all behind his eyes. He was simply listening. A good sign.

"He's told me a lot about who I was, or ... *am*. And, part of who I am was tethered to him a long time ago."

Confusion filled Nick's expression. "What's that mean? Tethered?"

I took a deep breath and prayed this wasn't doing more harm than good. What I wanted him to understand was that he wasn't imagining the connection with Liam, but he was, perhaps, misinterpreting it.

"I don't even fully understand it myself, but I know it's something I did to us in the past, linked him to me so we'd never lose one another."

I could see that part was hard for him to hear, so I waited a few seconds before going on.

"It's a dragon thing, and ... it's um ... it's hard to explain." There was more I was going to add, but I felt myself beginning to cower.

"So, you two were together," he said matter-of-factly. "Like ... you loved him?"

A knot in my throat made it difficult to swallow or speak. However, I nodded, confirming what he already suspected. Admitting that was harder than I thought it would be, but I didn't have a choice. Guarding each other's feelings was what had gotten us in this mess to begin with.

Nick nodded too, as this new information sank in.

"And what you sensed with us is nothing more than the residue of what was," I explained. "Not what is."

His eyes narrowed and I wasn't sure what he was thinking. The uncertainty made me sick to my stomach.

"Is there ever really any separating the two?" he asked.

The question hit me right in the gut, knocking the wind out of me.

"Feelings like that don't just ... get erased, Evie."

Based on all I knew, I disagreed with that. I'd seen for myself how easily things could be erased—memories, emotions, pasts, people.

Nick turned away from me and I panicked at the sight of how quickly he lessened the distance between himself and the door. It made me feel like I was out of time, like nothing I said would slow him down. I was right; telling him the truth *did* do more harm than good. But how were we ever supposed to be better if we couldn't be honest?

Maybe that was part of the point he was trying to make, and ... I was just now getting it.

There was something else he needed to know, and I felt obligated to tell him now rather than letting him see for himself. While I fully believed it would hurt my argument, I didn't want to be responsible for him being caught off guard.

"Wait," I called out, feeling my stomach sink when he paused at the sound of my voice. "I just thought you should know, he's ... *here*," I forced out, clarifying right after by stating plainly who I spoke of. "Liam."

The words halted Nick and I breathed harder, watching the back of his head while he stood in silence. The locking mechanism on my door disengaged and I took several steps to follow him. I don't know, maybe I thought there was still something I could say or do to fix it despite knowing it was hopeless.

"Good to know," he concluded, his statement brimming over with dark sarcasm. Before I reached him, the door slammed shut, and just like that, it was over. If I thought we were in the thorns *before*, this was the next worst thing.

Rock bottom.

CHAPTER 8

Nick

There were so many of us here we had to be fed in shifts. From the looks of things, they grouped us by school because there was an equal amount of familiar faces mixed in with the unfamiliar. I believed their goal was to surround us with people we knew so the change would be less jarring.

I was probably the only one wishing they hadn't.

Some new faces would've been a bonus. Especially with my current view across the dining hall being of Evie. I kept catching her eyes and couldn't stop myself. Apparently, she was having the same problem. What I had to do today nearly killed me inside, but if given the chance to take it back, I wouldn't. I walked into her room thinking what I had planned might have been the wrong thing, but, after the explanation about her link to Liam, I walked out positive I made the right decision.

We were no good for each other. At least not right now. For a number of reasons.

Tethered ... that's what she called it. I believed her when she said she didn't understand much about how it worked. Where it got murky was when she tried to convince me that all I sensed between her and Liam were remnants of old feelings. Without question, I knew she cared about me. Whether it was more or less than she cared about *him* I wasn't sure. Either way, I couldn't handle the idea of knowing I didn't have her whole heart.

Couldn't handle the idea of *him* being in the equation.

Yeah, Evie and I had our own issues, but ... Liam was the biggest complication of them all, the one I was least sure we could overcome. The one I couldn't get past. This thing between the three of us was complex, and as much as I wanted to blame *her*, I couldn't. Something in me wouldn't let that happen. As counterintuitive as it seemed, I believed her when she said it was all out of her control. The idea of it wasn't the strangest thing I'd heard lately. Not by far. But this still didn't change the fact that I thought space would be best.

For her.

For me.

At least until we both sorted through our baggage.

From across the table, Roz stared and so did Chris and Lucas. I hadn't given any explanation as to why I'd been incognito for a few days, but I knew they sensed something was up. I didn't intend to share any of it right now, though—not the stuff with Evie, not the stuff about being the Liberator. It all required me to explain things I couldn't, so I looked away from their probing eyes and scanned the dining hall instead.

This place was state of the art. At every turn, there were high-tech gadgets mounted on walls and in the hands of staff members. Several of them monitored us now as we ate. I got the distinct feeling they didn't trust us. I imagined news of how haphazardly most of our first shifts had gone was the reason. It was true that, as a clan, Seaton Falls was a mess—secretive, unprepared, disorganized—but it seemed that was more of a *generational* thing and not a *regional* thing. The few new kids sitting around our table were sharing some of their experiences and they mirrored ours to a tee.

The staff had traded in the skirts and pant suits they wore when I first arrived on a late bus for stragglers. They switched to a more relaxed look—black cargo pants tucked into dark boots, black t-shirts with the facility logo in the center. I showed up later than everyone else, but got the feeling this crew ran a tight ship. Most of the authority figures were lycans but I spotted a few dragons too. Four so far. It was my understanding they were rare to come across these days, so I guessed those who were here took some effort to find and convince to join forces.

Which begged the question: *Why would someone go to the trouble?*

"So, are we just gonna ignore the fact that you've been M.I.A. for days and haven't called or texted *any* of us, or...?" Roz was the one who asked, but I was sure she spoke on behalf of the others.

My shoulders rose and fell with a deep breath. "Leave it alone."

She picked at the roll on her plate and continued to watch me. "Fair enough."

I looked away again, thinking over how the last few days had changed me. It started with the shift when we took on the mutts. More specifically, when I took the life of one. It felt like some of that power, the *rage*, stayed with me long after I was just me again.

I wasn't sure it was supposed to happen that way.

If so, my brothers failed to mention it. But, then again, I was also sure that night was the first *they'd* ever killed too. It left me with a sense of ... darkness. I couldn't quite explain it, but, in short, my fuse was shorter, my thoughts were sometimes too gruesome to share, and I even blacked out a couple times without any recollection of what happened leading up to it.

All I wanted was to feel like me again, but it seemed that was too much to ask.

Scanning the perimeter of the room while my friends' conversation picked back up, I panned past the doorway. The instant I did, the rage I still harbored spread from the center of my chest until it filled me completely. All because of who just strolled in.

On sight, my entire body tensed.

Evie warned me he was here, but I don't think it really sunk in until I saw him. He was dressed in the same gear the *rest* of the staff wore, so I guessed he had some kind of authoritative role. But I couldn't have cared less. I was positive he was here for one reason and one reason only.

Evie.

When I stood and pushed away from the table, mumbling to myself, Roz was up on her feet the next instant, hawking every step I took. From the sound of it, there were several others too, which meant Chris and Lucas had also followed.

Roz grabbed at my arm, but she couldn't slow me down.

"What are you doing?" she asked, clueless as to who I spotted or why he even mattered.

But he did.

Liam was the cement wall between me and Evie, the one factor that wouldn't eventually work itself out with time.

"Nick." Roz's voice was like an echo as I kept my eyes trained across the room on my target.

Liam's steps slowed when he sensed me, and my eyes were already set on his when he turned. Just like before, he seemed unfazed at the sight of me. Like, I was one on a long list of things and people he considered insignificant. Maybe he *did* think that, but a spark within me ignited a thought. One that was heavy and sinister. One I couldn't say out loud.

... I wanted him dead.

Locking both arms over his chest as I drew closer, the smug grin on his face made me charge toward him double-time. I don't know what I planned to do exactly, but I knew it involved my fists being covered in his blood. Just thinking about it, I could feel the warm slickness of it covering my hands and I craved it more and more by the second.

Another surge of rage rolled through me and I felt the muscles in my back thickening with each step. My vision was suddenly clearer, my sense of smell suddenly keener. My body was preparing itself to shift, and I gave little thought for who might notice or what the repercussions might be.

"Nick, stop!"

A small hand pressed firm into the center of my chest. Those seated at the few tables closest to us went completely silent at the sound of Evie's voice. It was hers, but stronger; carrying with it a sharp, brassy undertone when it hit my ears. My guess was, she sensed where this was headed and saw fit to intervene.

To protect him?

The thought of *that* being what drove her to stand in my path made it hard to breathe.

I was aware of her, but only looked at *him*. *He* was what I wanted right now; to tear him limb from limb. More than anything, I wanted to be the one to put him in his place.

The day he broke down what it meant to be the Liberator, he enjoyed it, reveled in what it could potentially do to me and Evie. I could smell the satisfaction on him.

Then.

Now.

I believed he *also* knew it wouldn't be Evie who'd end things. Because I felt something for her, it was only right that I back off rather than put her in danger. And, if you ask me, he expected that.

My fists clinched when he took several steps in my direction— brow tense, shoulders squared, ready. However, a hard glare from Evie stopped him dead in his tracks. They stared at one another for several seconds before his expression softened.

It was almost like … communication? Like, he'd been told to stand down. But I had to have imagined it.

Her warm brown eyes came back to me, sweeping up to meet my

gaze. Her expression was filled with worry and so much more. A few of the monitors watched, but none moved toward me. With them unaware of where or how I'd strike, it would have been so easy to push past Evie's arm and finish the job.

But, for some reason, I didn't, and neither did he. Evie clearly had a hold on us both.

A reality that made heat spike in my veins.

Roz stepped up from behind me and I could tell she had so many questions. Quiet conversation picked up around us again as those who witnessed the brief power struggle lost interest. Liam continued past, and when he came close, I heard the distinct rumble when Chris and Lucas growled, aware of the threat.

Each step Liam took was slow—flared nostrils, eyes hidden beneath hooded lids. He hated me and the feeling was mutual. It was *also* clear he wasn't afraid of me, and that feeling was mutual too. If he was hoping I'd break free from Evie to come after him, he'd get his wish soon enough.

And I'd make sure it was someplace no one could intervene.

"What was that about?" Roz asked with wild eyes.

"Everything cool?" I could hear the concern in Chris's voice, too. I didn't answer either question, just stared down on Evie again.

Did she have any idea how much I hated this—knowing he mattered to her? Any clue how much it broke me up inside having to separate from her despite knowing it was best? I was the one who said the words, but it was *both* of us who ended this.

One secret at a time.

One distraction at a time.

"Can I help you with something?" The question came from a monitor—Mei, the one who'd shown me to my room after all the other students got settled.

I shook my head, feeling the rage subsiding only marginally. "I'm cool. Just need to walk it off," I replied through clenched teeth.

"I'm coming with you," Evie insisted.

"No."

She and Roz both seemed shocked by my tone and how quickly I protested, but being around her was the last thing I needed right now. There was a long stint of silence and a noise sputtered from Roz's throat as she stood with her mouth open, feeling every bit of awkward tension as the three of us stood there.

Water pooled in the corners of Evie's eyes, but her expression was hard when she nodded, swallowing the rejection. "...If that's how you want it."

I was sure my response had put another nail in the coffin of the failed relationship which never even, technically, made it far enough to earn a title. Swiping at the one tear that fell, Evie disappeared in the dark corridor that led back toward the sleeping quarters. Beth was right behind her.

Bewildered, Roz's stare volleyed back and forth between me and Evie until she disappeared around a corner. "I'm ... *clearly* missing something."

I headed for the corridor as well, but not to chase Evie. I just wanted to go back to my room.

"Don't ask," I warned. "I'm not in the mood."

Roz put her hands up in surrender as she took quick steps to match my pace. "Hey, I'm just making sure you're okay."

"I freakin' hate that guy!" My fist slammed into the wall as soon as we were no longer in the presence of the monitors. "I swear he thinks he owns her."

Roz kept her word and didn't ask questions, which I appreciated, although I'm sure my outburst raised more than a few.

We came to the blue hallway, passing beneath equally-spaced, fluorescent lights. My next thought was of how this area was dull and common compared to Evie's, but I quickly dismissed it. I didn't want to think about her right now. When I did, I saw *him*.

The I.D.s we were given also served as keycards. I used mine to open the door to the room I shared with Chris, Lucas, and one other teammate. A lineman, Theo. Inside, the space was riddled with bags of clothes and our personal belongings we'd ransacked before dinner and hadn't yet had a chance to unpack. I pushed everything off my bed and sprawled out on top of it, staring at the ceiling.

Roz leaned against the empty dresser and I could feel her watching me. It was mildly annoying when she did things like this, tagged along at times I felt like being alone, but I knew she was only trying to be a good friend. I knew that was exactly what I needed right now, but it was hard to see the forest for the trees.

I owed her more than my silence. She'd been among the number of people I avoided while I was away. She, honestly, sent just as many texts as Evie—asking if I was okay, if I needed anything, and one was simply a picture of a pizza she ordered with a caption that read, *'this could all be yours if you'd come out of hiding.'*

Thinking about it, it was a little harder to sulk.

"Still can't believe they stuck us here."

Roz shifted from one foot to the other. "You and me both. Feels like we're in *The Twilight Zone*. Makes my skin itch."

Good ol' Roz.

I smiled a bit.

"So, I know you don't want to rehash it all, but can I at least know where you've been?"

The question made me miss the solitude I'd carved out for myself before coming here. "My grandfather's estate."

She nodded. "Weren't you bored?"

Keeping my eyes trained above, I shrugged. "Didn't really get the chance. When I wasn't contemplating the meaning of life," I joked, "I was reading through some of his old journals."

At the mention of the word *'journals',* she perked up. "Find anything interesting in them?"

Truth be told, I didn't understand most of what he rambled about in those things, but reading them made me feel close to him, considering we never had the chance to meet. From what I'd been told, he traveled more than he stayed home and was kind of eccentric, but otherwise, he was a bit of a mystery.

"In the earlier ones, he mostly chronicled his life abroad, places he visited with some woman named Opal. Seemed like he loved her, but I never heard my parents mention her. There's some stuff in there about the adventures he took my dad on back in the day. But in the later volumes, he just went on and on about his quests to find these rings he was kind of obsessed with. Righting wrongs and crap like that."

Roz laughed at my wording. "Wow ... not much for sentiment, are you?"

I shrugged, smiling again. "It's not that, I just think he was losing it. The earlier installments were *definitely* more heartfelt, more coherent. It's the later ones that made it feel like I was reading some crazy old man's memoir."

She pulled a large, plastic container from against the wall and used it as a seat. "Rings, though? Like jewelry or something else?"

Recalling a sketch he'd drawn of one, I nodded. "There were either six or seven. He never seemed sure of the number. They all had dark stones in the middle, but he never says why he wanted them so badly. Just that he needed them in his possession."

"Maybe they were for Opal? The woman you mentioned?"

I rolled over while Roz spoke, bringing the box beside my bed closer. In it, were four leather-bound books. I read the numbers embossed into the spines and pulled the third one out. Untying the strap around it, I turned the yellowing pages to the middle until I found what I was looking for. I handed the sketch I spoke of over to Roz.

"See? This isn't a woman's ring. And I'm guessing the others aren't either."

Roz's eyes lit up. She lived for this kind of thing—the intrigue and mystery always seemed to bring her to life.

"Sweeeeeet."

I smiled and rested against the mattress again while she skimmed the image.

"Pops was quite the artist, I see."

"I guess you have plenty of time to perfect just about *every* craft when you live to be eight-hundred and six years old."

Her eyes nearly bucked out of her head. "Holy cow."

"Indeed," I yawned. "I didn't realize how old he was until I went through his things. He wrote often about letting himself age up, so he could stay put in Seaton Falls. Apparently, that's a thing—getting to choose when to age. He spoke about it like it's a decision people make when they start families, when it becomes more important for their children to have stability and protection within a clan than it is to move around from state to state trying to keep the secret."

Roz zoned out while I spoke, staring at the floor.

"Makes you wonder, doesn't it? How many of the shifters we've encountered in our lifetime—probably even the staff here—have been walking around for *centuries* looking like you and me. Most just probably don't settle down in one spot long enough to care about people noticing they don't age. I mean, technically, we could choose to look like this forever if it suited us."

This was something I had a basic concept of already, but my grandfather's notes helped me grasp a firmer understanding of how it worked. My thoughts went to my own parents, how they had, apparently, allowed themselves to look their ages. I was positive it was only because they fell in love young and started a family right away. They did it so my brothers and I could stay in the town we grew up in. It *also* made sense now that their plan was to relocate to the outskirts of Seaton Falls as soon as I graduated. My guess was, this would afford them the convenience of still being a part of the clan while also having the privacy they sought.

It's amazing the little details that fly over your head when you're blissfully unaware.

Roz nodded. "Ok, so, what if I have kids and then *reverse* the aging process?"

I shook my head. "Nope. Can't. It's a one-way ticket. You can stop whenever you want, but there's no going back."

She frowned. "Well, I guess I've just officially decided I'm never having kids. Not if I have the choice to stay young forever." She laughed and the sound of it lifted my mood a bit. For a second, she actually made me forget about the rage from before.

Her eyes lowered to the page again as she scanned the drawing of the ring.

"You suck," she sighed, which made me smile bigger. "Now that you showed me this stupid thing, *I'll* be obsessing over it like your grandfather used to. Thanks for that." She pulled out her phone and snapped a picture of the ring. She'd use it for research purposes I was sure.

"If you find anything, let me know."

"Will do," she said, standing to rush off to her room, planning a date with her laptop, I assumed. "Anything else I can do before I go?"

It shouldn't have surprised me that she'd ask, but it did. Probably because I was feeling so low today. I gave her question some thought and, while there wasn't a whole lot I *did* have control over at the moment, there was one thing I'd been mulling over and decided to run past her.

"So, this whole Liberator thing has to have a cure ... right? I mean, there has to be a way to reverse it like most curses?"

Roz stared for a moment and I don't think she meant for me to see the skepticism in her eyes, but I did. "It's ... not a curse, though. It's just who you are."

Was that pity I heard in her voice?

"I'll check," she said, quickly amending her original response. "If there is something out there that can be done, I'll find it."

The look on her face didn't give me much hope, but I would settle for her agreeing to help.

She neared the door and it dawned on me that I couldn't just let her go without acknowledging how much I appreciated her coming here to talk me down. More and more, I was beginning to see how she always had my back. As far as friends went, she was one of the best.

"Hey."

At the sound of my voice, she turned to face me again and her brow lifted. "What?"

"Just ... thanks. You know, for everything," I added. "And when I'm ready to talk about it all, I promise I won't keep you in the dark."

A soft smile touched her lips and she nodded before heading to the door again. "Whenever you're ready, Prince Nick. Whenever you're ready."

CHAPTER 9

Liam

Security measures made it impossible to contact members of upper-level staff on my own. So, first thing this morning, I started asking around. My only request was a short conversation with Elise, the director, but no one seemed capable of making that happen. Everyone was either too busy, uninterested in my concerns, or unsure of where her office even was. I was *this* close to making a scene so they'd take me there on their own. However, I was pretty sure that would only get me kicked out, and I couldn't afford for that to happen. This facility was the *only* place I needed to be.

"Can I help you?"

The question made me do an about face when someone finally volunteered to assist me. I turned to find a woman I'd seen once or twice in passing. Her sleeping quarters were in Gold Sector not too far from mine.

I offered a tight smile, one brimming with frustration. "Yeah, actually. I'm trying to find the director. No one seems to know where her office is or how I can arrange a sit-down with her." My brow lifted with a question. "Do you know how I can get in touch with her?"

The woman smiled again and I noticed her name tag, which read Mei. From the looks of it, she considered my request. That meant she must have been one of the few people with access.

"I could help, but there's only one small problem."

The faint smile I managed to fake, faded.

"It's just a matter of security clearance," she replied. "There's a chain of command in place here. Low-level staff bring all questions and concerns to mid-levelers, like myself," she smiled.

I didn't.

"And, from there, if whatever you bring to our attention is out of our jurisdiction, then and only then, would one of *my* team members present your issue to upper-level staff. And, in case you haven't already realized it, the director is one level above uppers, so ... yeah. Your chances of getting to her are slim to none."

Our conversation was interrupted by a static-ridden prompt that came through the walkie-talkie she kept on her hip. She excused herself for a moment and responded to what I assumed to be a lower-level staffer wondering how many monitors were needed in each hall as they prepared for the first day of training to begin.

Another reason I didn't have all day to waste time cutting through red tape. There would be shifters waiting for me in a lecture hall soon.

"Sorry about that," Mei said, apologizing for the interruption. "But it's like I said—"

"Can you reach her *that* way?" I cut in, pointing at the walkie-talkie she clutched.

When Mei didn't immediately respond, I assumed the answer was yes. She struck me as one of those people who takes their job way too seriously, did everything by the book. If I was right about her, it'd take an act of God to get her to budge.

And I didn't have that kind of time.

"I need you to do me a solid and just buzz her. She already knows who I am, and I'm willing to bet she's even expecting me."

And that was true. Seeing Elise yesterday was like looking into the eyes of a ghost. Actually, I was surprised she hadn't sent for *me*.

Mei hesitated, and that hesitation was a sign I could convince her if I just pushed hard enough, pushed the right buttons.

"All I need is two seconds, Mei. Two. It's urgent and it concerns the wellbeing of a student."

When all else fails, play into the vulnerability of a do-gooder's natural inclination to maintain order on the job. All I had to do was make it known that my issue posed a threat to the facility's standard and I was in.

"Give me a moment," she said the next second, eyeing my nametag as she lifted the device to speak into it. It took a moment to weed through the upper-level bureaucracy, but she made it happen. Eventually, the voice of the woman I'd been waiting to speak to since arriving yesterday came through.

"Uh, ma'am?" Mei said, suddenly lacking the confidence she exuded while shooting down all my other requests. It was clear Elise was well-respected by her staff.

"I have a gentleman by the name of Liam here and he's requesting permission to speak with you. It's regarding one of our students," she added.

There was static on the line again and Mei and I both stood in the hall, waiting.

In response to the information Mei passed along, the voice replied, "Naturally." I could tell she was smiling without even seeing her face. "Please, get him to David and have him escorted up."

Mei looked at me with disbelief. "Well, *that's* never happened before."

It was clear that direct access to Elise beyond the welcome she'd given when everyone arrived, was a rare occurrence.

Mei made quick work of swiping her card in the elevator, gaining us access to restricted floors. A tall, wiry guy with bright, red hair stood poised when the doors parted. I picked up right away that he was one of the few dragons on staff. And, from the way it sounded, he was Elise's righthand guy, which made sense seeing as how she, herself, was a dragon. Even for those of us who liked to believe we'd overcome our prejudices, most still preferred to be in the company of their own species when given the choice. It was a matter of trust; the result of a volatile past between lycans and dragons; a past steeped in war and betrayal on both sides, but mostly exaggerations to keep us separated.

From over his shoulder, our new escort glanced back at Mei and I as we power-walked down a dimly-lit, carpeted hallway.

"Morning, newcomer. Name's David," he said, introducing himself.

I gave a quick nod. "Liam."

At my reply, he handed something back, never missing a step. I accepted the keycard from him and eyed it just as intently as Mei did.

"It's to give you access to this floor and many others whenever you should choose to use it," David explained. He glanced back again with a bit of a smirk. "Looks like someone thinks quite highly of you."

Mei frowned and her footing got clumsy when she spoke. Well, more like protested.

"But ... that grants him Executive-level privileges. Only a handful of people in the whole building have these and one of them is *you*."

David shrugged, smirking a bit at how frantic Mei had become. "I don't make the rules. Boss-lady does what she wants and, apparently, what she wants is to make sure Liam here has free reign at the facility."

Mei sputtered again as we came to a stop in front of another elevator. "But he just got here yesterday. Shouldn't there be some type of screening process or ... I don't know, *something* to ensure he can even be trusted?"

I wasn't offended. This was typical behavior of Mei's straitlaced personality type. It made sense that she'd react this way to someone making, what seemed to *her*, a rash decision.

David, however, was growing more and more annoyed by the second. The elevator doors parted and he stepped in. I followed.

"Mei, I don't have any answers. If you'd like to take this up with the director herself, you're fully aware what the process is to file a grievance. However, right now, I have clear orders to deliver this gentleman to Elise before instruction begins. So, if you'd please take two steps back, this is where we part ways," he asserted, rubbing more salt in the wound right after when he added, "Seeing as how you don't have security clearance to accompany us any further."

I was proud of myself for not laughing when Mei was thoroughly put in her place. She closed her mouth with an audible snap and glared at David until the doors closed between us.

"She's a stellar employee," David assured me, "but the woman can be downright insufferable at times."

I smiled at his deduction and was sure it was spot on.

We stepped off and onto yet another restricted floor. One I, apparently, could visit whenever I wanted to. Walls of frosted glass hid expensively-decorated offices that were only visible when we walked past their doorways, all with upper-level staff hard at work inside. Rounding a corner, a familiar face came into view, and at the sight of me, Elise abruptly ended a phone call. She stood, staring with a look that brimmed over with emotion, but she held it in as David delivered me to her door.

It'd been years.

Centuries.

"Thank you, David," she said politely. "I trust that you remembered the keycard?"

He nodded dramatically, making it border on somewhat of a bow. "Yes, ma'am."

Pleased, Elise smiled, dismissing him with the gesture. Alone, I moved closer and that emotion she tried to hide spilled over as we met at the side of her desk.

"It's been so long," she whispered, doing her best not to sob when we embraced. "I thought you'd come yesterday. I couldn't send for you," she rambled. "It would've caused the others to question who *you* are, and then they'd start questioning who *she* is, and—"

"You don't have to explain," I replied, still holding her.

She leaned her face away to get a better look at me, staring with the same adoration and fondness she had in the past. For me, it was like looking into a past I'd long since left behind; like looking into the eyes of the woman who'd been the closest thing I ever had to a mother.

Eyes Evangeline inherited.

"You have no idea how wonderful it is to see you," she breathed, pressing her hand to the side of my face as more water pooled at her lids. "I thought you were ... I thought—" Her voice trailed off, and every so often, I heard faint traces of her native tongue—French.

"I thought the same about you," I admitted.

Her hand pressed to my face again when she smiled. "Did she remember anything when she saw me? Does she know?"

The question struck a chord and I shook my head. "No, but ... she will. She deserves to."

With all the loss Evangeline had experienced, with the feelings of not belonging, she deserved to know who and where she came from. I could only give her so much of that.

She needed Elise—her mother.

Elise became solemn when she nodded, letting her gaze leave my face for the first time since I stepped into her office.

"I hope she understands why I've ... handled things the way I have."

I didn't say it aloud, but I didn't even fully understand her logic *myself*. Now that I realized *she'd* been the one to bring Evangeline back, while I was eternally grateful, I still had no idea why. Or how. Or why, once she *did* bring her into existence again, she handed her over to a human family she must've known wouldn't always be allowed to be in Evangeline's life. Why move her to Seaton Falls? Why so close to the Liberator?

Seeing her, knowing she was behind it all, answered just as many questions as it raised.

A tear slipped down Elise's cheek. "You have no idea how happy I was to get word yesterday that you found her. Once Baz reported the news to the other elders, the information spread through the Council and, eventually, made its way to me. If I'd known you came out of the war alive, I would've brought you in from the beginning," she expressed, remorse filling her eyes. "You have to understand that I didn't know, Liam. I didn't think—"

Emotion overtook her again and I brought her into my arms like she used to do to *me* when I was small. I'd gone over this day in my mind a thousand times, the day I came face-to-face with whoever was responsible for Evangeline's return. There was supposed to be a heavy interrogation, possibly involving torture if necessary, to get the answers I sought, but ... now ... knowing it was *family,* I...

"She'll hate me," Elise breathed against my shoulder.

I was shaking my head as soon as she finished. "She could never. It'll take a while for her to wrap her head around everything, but ... if you want her to trust you, you'll have to be straight with her," I warned. "She's not strong like before. Not yet."

I didn't add that Evangeline was bordering on fragile when it came to her emotions. Nor did I share that a lot of that fragility was the result of severe abandonment and displacement issues since finding out about her adoption. But that was true.

Elise nodded. "I would never dream of lying to her."

She wiped her eyes and I released her.

"That's a good place to start."

"Will you bring her to me this evening?" There was hope in Elise's eyes when I nodded. "I'll arrange for dinner for three to be brought to my quarters around seven and we—"

"I won't stay," I interjected. "You two should have privacy to discuss everything."

My hands were taken the next second and I stopped speaking. "She *needs* you Liam." My gaze lifted to Elise's. "Tonight will be difficult for her and I know she won't turn to me for comfort. She's my Evangeline, yes, but she doesn't remember. However, she's still connected to you. Always has been. Always will be."

I looked away.

"And *you* deserve answers too," she went on. "I've got nothing to hide. Not from you two. My family."

CHAPTER 10

Evie

Beth and I stared at the box that'd been delivered to our room for a solid minute after opening it. Inside, two packages of uniforms. One set of five for her. One set of five for me. And these were so bad, they gave the ones we had from Seaton Prep a run for their money.

She held one up, making a face like someone had hidden week-old cheese somewhere in our room. The entire thing was constructed of a strange material I couldn't quite place—somewhere between leather and spandex. They were mostly black, but dark blue embellishments on the sleeves and down the sides of the legs were, apparently, meant to serve as decoration. And right in the center of the chest, a Damascus Facility emblem in white—the outline of a hexagon with letters and symbols.

"Nope. No way. I'm not doing it," Beth protested.

I laughed, pointing out the word at the top of the letter inside the box.

Mandatory.

She growled—the cranky teenager variety, not that of an angry wolf. The sound was followed by a cyclone of damp, blonde hair when she spun and stormed off to change from her towel, into one of our newly gifted outfits.

I changed too, while she was gone, yawning every step of the way. I hadn't slept well and finally gave up trying around five. Getting to sleep after the conversation with Nick, the explosion between him and Liam that followed, was nearly impossible. It might have helped a little to confide in Beth, but it was never far from my mind that she was Nick's friend before she was mine.

So, I held it in, not knowing when or if it would ever blow over.

While I was up staring at the ceiling, the rest of the world slept. So, I showered to get it out the way, and now I had to shimmy out of the jeans I thought I was wearing today and into one of the suits.

As soon as I got my arms in, Beth stomped out of the bathroom and turned her back to me, pointing at the zipper. "Please?"

I did hers and then turned for her to fix mine too. We stood there, face-to-face, trying not to laugh.

"Evie ... if you're any kind of a friend, you'll kill me now."

I shook her by the shoulders. "Look at the bright side; *everyone's* gonna look like superhero rejects. Not just us."

She smiled again, tugging the shoulder of her suit as she contorted her body in strange ways. "Freakin' thing's riding up already! No *way* I'll make it 'til the end of the day."

I dug down in the box and pulled out two pairs of black shoes and handed her a set with a cheeky grin. "Here, twin."

She stuck her tongue out when she smiled, slipping the shoes on before we stepped out into the hall. I was right; everyone had them on. And we all looked equally pissed about the fashion choice someone made for us. Wetsuits, that's what they looked like.

The entire walk to our first training session, we were serenaded by the lovely sound of grumbling teenagers. I held the map that was given to us with the welcome packages we received when our luggage was delivered last night. We were given our schedules and a directory to help us find our way around. Beth's schedule mirrored mine and I was too happy for words when I realized we'd be together all day.

We followed the designated twists and turns until we reached the main pod hub. It was a large circle with hallways coming off it like spokes, just like the sleeping quarters pod. Each hallway was marked by a shape this time instead of colors. My eyes scanned the wall until I found a large octagon-engraved plate that marked where we needed to go.

"This way," I said, pointing.

Beth was excited about today, but me? Not so much. Nervous was more like it. She was made for this, while I felt like a fish out of water.

The room we approached was huge, about the size of the gym at Seaton Prep. We stepped inside and observed. Large, navy-blue mats lined gray-tiled floors—five to be exact. The outskirts of the room were lined with steel bleachers stacked only three rows high. On them, other kids had found a place to sit while three instructors stood front and center. Each had their hands locked behind their backs and, if I didn't know any better, I'd peg them as military.

Maybe that was *exactly* what they were.

I planted myself right beside Beth and there were fifty or more of us here by the time the steady flow of bodies finally began to slow. At the sound of a three-toned bell, one of the instructors made his way to the door we entered through and shut it. You could have heard a pin drop as he joined the other two in the center of the room once more.

"Good morning, young shifters," boomed a deep, foreboding voice. The one who spoke looked like a living, breathing action figure —complete with arm muscles the size of my head, and a t-shirt so small you couldn't tell me it wasn't made for a toddler.

The other guy wasn't far behind him in size. Even the female instructor—small as she may have been—was clearly in better shape than people I'd seen who practically *lived* in the gym.

Watching them, I wiped sweat from my brow. Beth caught me and had to hold in a laugh.

"Breathe, woman," she whispered before turning back to the instructors.

I missed my cue to respond to the greeting, but I listened intently when the big guy went on.

"All right, name's Dallas, and just as an overview of what we'll be doing here today, let me start by listing all the things this class is *not*."

He paced while explaining in a no-nonsense, southern monotone that reminded me of a drill sergeant. I was now *positive* he had a background in military. Even the way his voice carried across the large room with no need for a mic or megaphone was further proof.

"Number one: this class is not '*What am I? 101*'. While we understand and are sensitive to the fact that most of you are clueless about your abilities, this is not a history class. Blame your moms and dads for your ignorance. *We* certainly do," he said casually. "It's not our job to hold your hand through figuring all this crap out. So, save any questions that fall into this category for another instructor, because I assure you, the three of us don't want to hear it."

Beth and I looked at one another with wide eyes.

"Number two: This class is not your runway. You *will*, I repeat, *will* sweat if I've got anything to do with it. So, ladies, no makeup. There will be no prizes handed out at the end of our sessions for best smoky eye or winged eyeliner or whatever the heck it's called. When you're in this room, we want you focused on honing your physical abilities only," he said with about the most disinterested expression I'd ever seen. "Hair pulled back in ponytails, nails trimmed, mind focused. Understood?"

"Understood," we echoed in response.

"Number three: This class is not a counselling session. Look around you."

At his words, all our heads swiveled.

"And more importantly, take a *whiff* around you. Hopefully, your neighbor has showered this morning, because what you *should* be smelling beneath that *Irish Spring* and *Teen Spirit* is either the scent of a lycan or a dragon. Now, I know I just said this ain't history class, but I'm gonna make an exception for myself this one time. No, our kind have not always gotten along, but we will not tolerate interspecies drama," he said flatly.

"I myself am a dragon," he explained. "But Kas and Martinez here, are lycans. However ... they love and adore me to the moon and back," he joked, actually cracking a smile when he exaggerated a little. "And, as I'm sure you can see, it has very little to do with my soft, chewy exterior. My comrades and I get along because we're civilized. Ain't that right, Kas?"

The brown-skinned man standing in formation beside him gave a quick nod. "Civilized as can be, Sir."

"How bout' you, Martinez. Am I soft and chewy?" Dallas asked.

Martinez's posture didn't shift when she shook her head. "About as soft and chewy as a brick sandwich, Sir."

Dallas liked her answer. The grin he gave made it clear. "But I'm willing to bet money you'll agree that we're civilized."

"Always, Sir." Martinez said back.

I smiled. They were definitely hardnoses, but they didn't seem so bad.

...Yet.

"So, there you have it. If the three of *us* can make this work, you all have no excuse. Which brings us to number four on our list: this class is not the nursery. We will tolerate zero excuses and even less whining. Understood?"

"Understood," we repeated once more.

"And in closing I will add that, when addressing any one of the three of us standing before you today, there is to be a 'Sir' or 'Ma'am' at the end of that statement. Am I understood?"

"Yes, Sir."

The sound of our obedience made him smile again. This time, it was a big one that seemed out of place on such a serious face. "Then I think we'll get along just fine."

Beth leaned in to whisper. "I kind of like this guy."

Of *course* she did. He was tough and a little scary. Just like her.

"On your feet." This time it was Martinez who addressed us.

We rose and filed out of the bleachers, standing where she gestured for us to line up. She walked past each one and her nostrils flared a bit as she identified our species. So far, there was only one other dragon singled out and she was directed toward the last mat to stand alone. Martinez continued down the line and eventually came to Beth. She did the sniffing thing before pointing her toward Dallas. Beth's face lit up right away, seeing as how she now idolized the man.

She ran off with a whispered, "Sweet!"

And then Martinez came to me. She sniffed, narrowed her eyes, then sniffed again. When she backed off, she smiled a bit. "Well aren't *you* interesting."

I wasn't sure what that meant or how to feel about it.

Some of the kids who hadn't been told where to go yet were starting to stare. I felt their eyes on me and I heard a few trying to catch my scent too. One girl down the line seemed particularly annoyed that my being different had slowed things down.

"We've got a hybrid," Martinez yelled out, getting Dallas and Kas's attention. Both walked over and I clasped my hands in front of me. "Her dragon presents much stronger than her wolf, but ... she's definitely both."

"Well, what have we here?" Dallas said with a curious grin.

"Proof that, sometimes, my people can share a bed with yours without being set on fire, I guess," Kas replied suggestively, laughing when Martinez did.

But Dallas didn't join them. As I fidgeted, trying to pretend not to care that they were discussing me like I wasn't even standing here, his eyes softened.

"Lay off. Kid's comin' with me," he decided. Before taking me over to his area, he asked a question. "Can you fight?"

I shook my head. "No, Sir," I said at first, but then remembered that wasn't entirely true. "Well ... not really." Suddenly nervous when I realized how quiet it got, I explained. "Some of us had a run-in with a few mutts not too long ago. Things got crazy, and I ... I had to take one of them down on my own."

That feeling was never far from memory—how powerful I felt for that split second when I ripped that things heart from its chest, still beating. He was huge, twice my size, but I was somehow able to come out on top.

Did I think I could do that again? Absolutely not, but it seemed worth mentioning.

That goofy grin on Dallas' face widened and a heavy hand came down on my shoulder. "You hear that, Kas? Got ourselves a mutt wrangler."

I smiled at his choice of words, and then followed him to a mat. Beth was in his group, too. We stood side by side as the other shifters were assigned an instructor. As luck would have it, the girl who'd given me the stink eye for the holdup was with us too. Even now, she kept giving me attitude with every glance. I noticed one of the kids from the Gold Sector standing nearby—Errol, the one with permanent bedhead. He nodded, acknowledging Beth and I.

With us separated into three groups, Dallas addressed us with that loud, booming voice of his.

"All right, listen up. I need you all to make quick work of finding a partner. And for those already linking elbows with your besties, be aware that this is not a friendly exercise. So, unless you and your buddy have an affinity for punching one another in the face, might I suggest you expand your search."

Beth frowned when Dallas made the announcement and immediately started searching for someone to pair up with other than me. She pointed at Errol.

"You," she said, prompting him to look around, making sure he was the one she spoke to. "Can you take a punch?"

The question made a macho laugh slip from his mouth when

Beth challenged him. "From you? All day. But I'm not gonna hit a girl. It wouldn't be a fair fight."

The back and forth between the two made Dallas stop what he was doing to listen, trying not to smile as Beth stepped up, toe-to-toe with Errol.

Her looks were deceiving. On the outside, she had the appearance of the sweet, innocent girl-next-door. However, I knew for a fact she was a force to be reckoned with.

"You made a *huge* mistake calling attention to yourself," Beth warned, grinning as she perched both hands on her hips.

Errol looked her up and down, partially to size her up as his opponent, partially because I think he liked what he saw. "Oh yeah? Why's that?"

Beth moved in closer, nearly whispering her response. "Because now they're all gonna see you get taken down by a girl."

Poor Errol didn't have time to brace himself before Beth tackled him. Somehow, she swept him right off his feet and before any of us could even flinch, she had him on the ground. She hovered above him with both his wrists pinned to the mat.

"You know, I think you were right about the fight not being fair," she laughed. "Because I'm pretty sure you're about to get your butt handed to you."

Even with the wind knocked out of him, Errol was grinning like someone just told him he didn't have to wear these ridiculous suits. Apparently, he was a glutton for pain and was suddenly smitten by my friend, the blonde brute. And when she offered him a hand to help him up, I wondered if the feeling wasn't mutual.

While watching Beth, I somehow missed my chance to find a decent partner and was left with the attitude on two legs. Her dark, cropped hair was too short for a ponytail, so it was held behind both ears with bobby pins. A neat part right down the middle reminded me of the librarian at my school in Chicago and I was suddenly curious to see how strong she was. I kept thinking she was too neat and tidy for this class. No, she didn't wear any makeup to highlight her green eyes or cheekbones, but she still looked like she'd never broken a sweat a day in her life.

So, was her look deceiving like Beth's? Or was she a 'what you see is what you get' kind of girl, like me? I guess we'd find out soon enough.

She stared down her nose at me and I felt trapped, wavering between ignoring her and introducing myself to see if I was imagining that she had an issue. In the end, I went with introducing myself.

My hand jutted out between us and she eyed it without words. "Hi, I'm Evie," I said with a smile. It seemed like a friendly enough gesture to me, but you'd never guess it looking at her face.

It took a little longer to respond than it should have, but, eventually, she grabbed my hand for a quick second.

"Sasha," she said flatly.

I nodded, committing that to memory before turning my attention toward Dallas again when he spoke.

"Ok, for today, we'll just be going over some basic self-defense maneuvers, so relax and listen closely. There is to be no shifting, no growling, none of that," he enforced. "All I want right at this moment is for you and your partner to decide who's gonna be the attacker this time around and who's gonna be the victim."

My mouth opened, but before I could ask Sasha if she had a preference, she chose her role.

"Attacker," she blurted.

I blinked at her, but said nothing.

"Once you've got that sorted out," Dallas went on, "the attacker is to lunge at the victim full force and I'll be watching both parties to get a baseline reading. The idea is to measure where each of you are offensively and defensively so I know what I'm up against. Is all that clear?" he asked.

"Yes, Sir," our group called out in unison.

He nodded. "Very well then. At the sound of my whistle, attackers attack."

The next second, without any further warning, the whistle blew and my back became one with the matt that was once beneath my feet. Sasha's weight covered me until she could lift herself. And, instead of offering her hand to help me up like Beth had done with Errol, all I got from *my* partner was a cold smile.

"Guess you didn't learn much when you went up against those mutts, huh, Mutt Wrangler?" As she taunted me, the look on her face told me exactly what she was thinking. To her, I was pathetic. I was nothing.

Furious, I pressed my fists into the blue cushion and stood again. Dallas had his whistle in his mouth and held his hand in the air while we all got into position for a second time. Once everyone was ready, he blew it again.

I felt heat coursing through my veins and my limbs filled with electricity as I prepared to withstand the oncoming collision. Sasha lunged just like before. But *unlike* before, I was ready for her. My feet were firmly planted and *nothing* could move me.

Or, at least ... that's what I thought.

Wind burst from my lungs when I hit the mat with a loud thud. Before, I didn't get what people meant when they said they saw stars after a hard collision, but I understood it now.

The ringing in my ears made it impossible to think. The room spun and I thought I'd black out. I was vaguely aware of Sasha lifting her weight off me again before walking away without the customary, sportsmanlike hand I would've offered *her*. Slowly but surely, the swooshing inside my head stopped and a familiar face hovered over me—Beth. She walked all the way over to help me up when my partner failed to do so. Once I was on my feet, she held on to make sure I wouldn't fall again, and before walking away, she whispered a few supportive words.

"If she does it again, we're taking her down after class."

A tuft of blonde hair whisked back to the other side of the room, leaving me to stare at Sasha for the third time as she readied herself for Dallas' whistle. Beth's words tumbled around inside my head and, while I appreciated her having my back, rage began to build in the center of my chest. I could feel it. I'd never been one to tend toward violence, but I wanted to hurt this girl.

Badly.

For some reason, she thought she could push me around. I had no idea what her problem was, but I was done letting her beat me.

That whistle blew and I breathed in deep, letting a little more of my true nature seep into my limbs and then my bones. I felt the second the dragon in me took control and I let her. I had a habit of trying to be *only human'*, but in instances such as this, it paid to let my body respond in ways that felt most natural.

So, that's what I did when Sasha closed the distance between us. I did what felt right, what my shifter wanted.

She came at me fast, but, this time, I was faster. Almost as if she moved in slow motion. I saw her feet pressing deep into the mat for traction, saw the fury behind her eyes when they locked on me. Just as she approached, I raised my arm and pointed my elbow directly at her face.

The room went completely silent for a moment as onlookers suddenly lost interest in their *own* sparring to stare at Sasha and I. That silence was interrupted a few seconds later when she started screaming bloody murder. The sound was awful, ricocheting off the gray, cinderblock walls of the training room. If I had to guess, nearly every shifter in the building heard it, thanks to our keener-than-normal senses, especially the lycans.

"Whoa, whoa, whoa." The frantic words came from Dallas as he jogged to where I stood over my partner's body. By now, she'd gotten a few drops of blood on the mat, making things look a lot worse than I knew they were. She was a shifter, and from what I'd seen with Liam, we healed pretty quickly. Even if her nose *was* broken, it wouldn't be for long.

"She did it on purpose," Sasha yelled out, putting on a show, probably hoping to get me in even more trouble than I was already in.

Dallas knelt beside her, but he watched *me*. "That true?" he asked.

I clenched my fists nervously at my sides when I nodded, admitting this was no accident. From the corner of my eye, I caught Beth doing a discreet fist pump as she stood beside Errol who held a hand over his mouth to keep from laughing. I could see it in his eyes that he wanted to.

"Martinez, see to it that the bleeder gets some ice for that," Dallas called out as he stood upright again. Pinching the material at the shoulder of my suit, He dragged me toward the door.

"You ... come with me."

CHAPTER 11

Evie

Couldn't even make it through the first day without getting into trouble. But whoever would've guessed it'd be for something like *this*.

I didn't hurt people. Like, ever. Not even when they deserved it like Sasha did. Dad taught me to always take the high road, turn the other cheek. However, the more time that passed since transitioning, the more I felt my peaceful resolve beginning to fade away. No, I didn't imagine I'd ever *look* for fights, but I was beginning to think I wouldn't always be inclined to run from them.

Dallas pushed the door open and didn't let go of me until we were standing out in the hallway. His face was red as a beet, and based on the way his tense arms bulged when he locked them across his chest, I gathered that he was frustrated.

"Care to explain?" he sighed, keeping his eyes trained on me.

I chewed my lip, looking at the floor and walls while I searched for an answer that wouldn't land me in even more hot water.

"I um ... I was just defending myself. Like you said, but ..." My voice trailed off because we both knew I'd done more than defend myself.

I hurt that girl.

In hindsight, yeah, I could've just dodged her or knocked *her* to the ground, but something in me wanted to make her feel pain. Kind of like *I* felt pain when she just about knocked me down to the building's foundation every time we collided.

So, did I use excessive force? Yes, but so did she. That made us even.

"We're supposed to be working on self-defense techniques, not MMA fighting."

I managed to make eye contact when I mumbled a timid, "Yes, sir."

At my words, Dallas' expression softened and he exhaled sharply. Unfolding his arms, he shoved both hands in his pockets.

"You've gotta be careful," he began. "I know you're only *part* dragon, but I sense it on you stronger than your lycan side. Dragons have a rep for being barbaric, doing without thinking."

As a novice to all this, I listened intently, ready to absorb any and everything that might help me understand what was happening to me. Dallas was violating his own rule about not turning this class into a history lesson or counselling session, and I had a feeling it was mostly because he wasn't nearly as tough as he put on at the start of class.

"The blind rage ... it'll save your life when it's time for a fight. We go kinda bloodthirsty when we feel threatened and it helps us defend ourselves with clearer heads. Focusing more on taking down an enemy without worrying about being injured or worse," he shared. "But you have to learn not to flip that switch unless it's completely necessary, kid."

He smiled a bit and the sight of it helped me relax.

"In a training session, while sparring with a newly shifted lycan, is *not* the time nor the place to hulk out. Save that for when it really counts."

I nodded. He was stern, but still managed to be understanding. Fair.

Another sharp breath puffed from his thin lips as he mussed the short, dirty-blond hair on his head.

"Unfortunately, whether I get what you're feeling or not, I can't let this slide."

"Yes, sir." I wasn't expecting special treatment.

"She'll be reprimanded, too, since it sounds like she instigated, but you gotta pay for your actions, understood?"

I nodded. "Yes, Sir."

This was the part where I expected to be released, sent to whoever I was being sent to for my punishment, but, instead, Dallas just kinda scanned me for a few seconds before asking a question.

"What's your name again?" he inquired. "It'll take me a bit to memorize them all."

I swallowed hard. "Evangeline, Sir."

He kept his eyes trained on me and didn't blink even once as he stood there, not saying a word.

"Evangeline. From where?" he asked next.

"Seaton Falls, Michigan, Sir."

"And before that?"

"Chicago, Sir."

His eyes narrowed a bit and I wasn't sure why he wanted to know. "Before that?"

I shook my head. "Nowhere, Sir. Just ... Chicago." Of course that wasn't the *full* truth, but it was the only truth I actually remembered. The only truth I felt comfortable sharing.

Silence ricocheted between us as he kept his thoughts to himself. "Only thing rarer than a dragon is a hybrid," he commented.

I wasn't sure what to say to that. Mostly because shifter stats were basically at the bottom of the list of things I wanted to learn. I took his word for it, though.

With a concentrated look, he worked his jaw. "...Hm."

The long stare made me nervous. So much that I was beginning to look forward to being sent to whoever was supposed to deal with me.

"I'll have Kas walk you down," was the last thing Dallas said before stepping back inside the training room.

There was nothing to do but stand there waiting for my escort. However, the silence was disrupted by a question.

"*What's wrong? Where are you?*" The voice inside my head made me push off from the wall I leaned against. I recognized it as Liam's. Before now, only *I* could head-hop, but here he was. Inside mine.

"...How did you?" I started, speaking aloud because I'd been caught off guard.

"*I felt you stressing and then felt the connection strongly enough that I knew I could speak. Can't really explain it.*"

His tone was urgent, which meant he was panicked and would much rather we address *his* question first. However, he obliged when I asked another.

"*Could you do this before? In the past, I mean.*" It probably annoyed him that I had yet to give him the status update he'd been waiting for.

"*It used to go both ways back when the link was first established, but I wasn't sure it'd come back that way this time around. We were ... closer then, so ... the more connected we are, the stronger our tether becomes.*"

When I failed to respond, I think he sensed that I was kind of shying away from what his answer implied, so he downplayed it when he explained further.

"*My guess is it's just because we've been around each other so much lately. But back to my question,*" he said in a rush. "*What's wrong? I felt you all the way from this side of the building.*"

Frustrated, I sighed, leaning against the bricks again. "*Because I may or may not have gotten into an altercation.*"

"*I'm on my way.*" There was absolutely no hesitation, which was strange because I was almost sure he had responsibilities here besides looking after me.

I frowned. "*Don't you have a class to teach or something?*"

"*I do, but they can get along without me.*" I imagined him heading toward the door without any explanation to those seated before him.

"*No, stay. I'm fine. We can talk about everything later.*"

There was a distinct way my soul vibrated with additional energy while he was with me, so I knew he wasn't gone, just quiet.

"*Seriously, my instructor seems pretty cool, so I don't think it'll be too bad,*" I explained, hoping to ease his mind. "*Just go back to what you were doing,*" I added. And then, taking a page from *his* book, I concentrated and forced him out of my head.

The second I was alone again, Kas emerged from the training room and a single nod prompted me to follow him. The halls were completely empty. There were no straggling students or kids wandering around with bathroom passes in hand. No, here there was a rigid sense of structure that I guessed didn't leave much room for such things. And I was also sure it didn't leave room for misconduct. At that thought, I began to worry what would happen when I got wherever Kas and I were headed.

And where was that exactly?

Was there a principal's office or something? I didn't even know the name of the person in charge.

We turned corner after corner and I got more nervous by the minute. Our pace slowed in front of a steel door and Kas glanced over to tell me to wait here before disappearing inside the room. I stood there with my heart racing, pounding against my ribs. It was a small miracle Liam didn't pop in again, but I guessed he knew I'd reach out to him if there was something he could help with.

And there wasn't. I was on my own with this one.

Kas returned and his expression stayed blank from the moment he first met me out in the hall. "Go ahead," he said sternly, causing me to turn toward the door he just emerged from. It was cracked now, so I could see inside a little. Putting one foot in front of the other, I stepped in.

The room was nothing like I imagined. It was warm and inviting compared to the rest of this place. Still-life art hung from tan-painted walls and the carpet here was a medium shade of brown that made it feel like I'd entered a different world.

A head of jet black hair peeked above the top of a high-backed chair and I had yet to see the face of the woman who held my fate in her hands. She shuffled papers around and stuffed them into a folder before speaking.

"Have a seat, please."

Her voice was ... sort of familiar. I recognized it, but couldn't place it right away. It wasn't until she turned to face me that I put two and two together.

"Alice?"

It was like seeing a ghost. The woman had been my first counsellor, the one I began seeing in Chicago. And now she was *here?* That didn't make any sense.

At the sight of my confused expression, she smiled, folding her hands in front of her on the desk. "It's good to see you again, Evangeline."

"You... you, too," I stammered. There was a faint lingering of that same earthy scent I was starting to recognize as lycan. Of course, I wouldn't have noticed it before because I hadn't yet shifted when I used to visit with her, but it was hard to miss now.

"What're you doing here?" I asked distractedly, trying to pull the pieces together. If she was a lycan, that meant she had to have known about *me* all along. And, if so, it meant she let me struggle with my identity issues, all the while secretly holding all the answers.

Or at least some of them.

My fists clenched at my sides as I stiffened in the chair.

"Evangeline, you must have so many questions, but I assure you I can only tell you what I know and that isn't much."

"How ... Why are you ...?" I didn't even know where to begin.

"The High Council assigned me, and several others throughout the years, to keep watch over you. My service began when you turned fourteen, but I was told very little about you. Much like your watchers *before* me and the one who came after."

Watchers?

"I don't understand."

"Neither do I, fully. We're given a command and we follow it per our pledge to the High Council. I suspect the mission was mostly to ensure that you had someone safe to talk to, someone within the realm of the supernatural," she clarified. "It was the only way to make sure pertinent information was never leaked to the outside world."

As if any human would've ever believe the things I've seen and experienced if I told them anyway.

"It was a risk we couldn't take," she added with a smile. But *why* was she smiling? None of this was okay. It was just more lies. Lies on top of lies.

"And Cruz?"

Alice nodded. "Yes. And the two guidance counsellors in your schools before that, although you had a relatively normal childhood and never needed to speak with them," she went on. "They were there for you just in case."

There for me... She was trying to romanticize this, but it didn't work. Not on me. Here I was, thinking no one but me knew I was different growing up, and all along, someone had placed these beings around me who at least knew I wasn't imagining it all.

"So, everything I ever confided in you, you just reported back to whoever appointed you?"

Once, I used to regard this woman as a friend, someone I could talk to about my crazy world. But now, like everything else, I knew that was false.

"No, Evangeline," she said calmly. "It was all still very much shared in confidence. Our mission was never to report anything because you didn't *know* anything. It was merely a precaution should you begin to remember bits and pieces from your past. We needed to be in place as a failsafe should you ever decide to share your experiences. As your guidance counsellors, we were the first line of defense before your parents would decide to seek outside help." The casual manner in which this was all explained made my skin crawl. "And, while I understand you're likely upset right now, the argument is irrefutable because, well, it worked. We managed to keep you safe. Our future queen."

The way she said that ... it rubbed me the wrong way, hearing her justify her role in perpetuating my life's lie.

The same burning hit my chest as before, the buildup of rage that swarmed me when I laid eyes on Baz's witch Scarlet, and again before hitting Sasha. Dallas' warning came to mind and I suppressed it. I couldn't let that part of me rise whenever I got upset. I had to learn to keep a lid on it.

I did stand, though, still hating myself a little for ever having trusted her. It made me feel like I had no real sense of *who* to trust. They'd all put on this elaborate act and for what? To protect me? To protect the secrets of the supernatural? To protect whoever brought me back or how they believed my existence played into their future?

"How am I being punished?" I asked coldly, staring at the wall instead of Alice.

She was quiet for a moment, but then tried to smooth things over. "Evangeline, I know you're upset, but you have to understand, we—"

"I'd like to know what my punishment is so I can go, please." I felt the sting of tears, but my pride wouldn't let them fall. Not here. Not in front of her.

Alice exhaled heavily and glanced down at a sheet of paper before her. "We're revoking your topside privileges for the week."

A frustrated sigh puffed from my nostrils. "What's that even mean?"

"Topside," she repeated. "It's what we call the protected plot of land above the facility. Starting today, you and your peers were supposed to be allowed one hour outside in small groups to get some fresh air, but now you won't be allowed."

"So, I'm a prisoner here. That's what you're saying." I chewed the side of my lip, still unable to look at her.

"No, but if you violate the rules again, I assure you we have cells several floors down." Her voice went cold and it was clear she felt no remorse for conning me into trusting her years ago. No guilt for feeding into the big lie.

"Can I go now?" My tone was just as frosty as hers.

She hesitated a moment and then leaned back in her seat, crossing one leg over the other. "Of course."

I was out of there the next second. The sight of Kas waiting beside the door startled me. He said nothing, just led the way back to the training room. I had to sit it out on the bleachers for the rest of the session, watching the others who seemed far more natural at all this than I believed I ever would be. Sasha was nowhere in sight, so I figured she'd been taken to the infirmary to see about her nose.

I was fuming and sad and hurt and confused all at the same time. *What was the point of all this? The point of me being here ... being alive?*

I just didn't understand.

And now, I knew of several prominent figures in my life who'd been strategically placed there at each stage—as a young child, preteen, teen—had been fully aware of what was going on.

And someone with all the answers had appointed them; someone I believed couldn't be trusted.

Someone with their own agenda.

CHAPTER 12

Liam

There was no easy way to go about this. The heightened uncertainty left me anxious.

These were delicate circumstances. Evangeline's heart was on the line. With her truth just a few floors above, I wasn't sure she was ready to receive it. However, I made her a promise, said I'd always tell her the truth no matter what. That's what she wanted and I would honor my word.

However, I was starting to wish there was another way.

I wandered inside her thoughts. Although I couldn't see through her eyes like she could mine, it was still convenient having ties to her once again. Earlier, when trying to explain how this came to be, I knew the moment the reality of our bond strengthening startled her. But it was true. She wouldn't always be able to deny what she felt. It was powerful, overwhelming at times.

I knew because I felt it, too.

"*Can you meet me?*" I asked when I felt us connect.

"*Sure. Everything okay?*"

I hoped this wasn't a lie. "*Yeah. Everything's fine.*"

"*Where?*"

This wasn't a conversation we could have out in the open. "*My room. As soon as you can.*"

"*Be there in a few.*"

The tie severed and I continued to pace, trying to get the words together. In the two minutes it took for her to knock, I still hadn't come up with anything.

Time was up.

Seven o'clock—that's when Elise would be expecting me to bring Evangeline and it was already well past six-thirty. I waited until the last possible minute to break the news to her, but only because I knew there was a chance she'd take it hard.

And the last thing I ever wanted to do was hurt her. Even if doing so was out of my control.

She smiled despite her rough day. The details of it were still a mystery, but from what I gathered, she had a run in with someone and both faced consequences. As badly as I wanted to, I didn't get involved.

She was beautiful tonight, just like all the others. Her damp hair hung past her shoulders in tight spirals. Before now, I'd only ever seen her wear it straight and ... the sight of her like this overwhelmed me. It was like we'd gone back in time and I was staring at the *old* Evangeline.

The one who belonged to me.

"Come in," I exhaled, stepping aside. She walked past wearing a loose-fitting t-shirt and black shorts that stopped midthigh. I locked us in and smothered the fire she triggered inside me. A fire no one else could ever put out. A fire that had nothing to do with my dragon and everything to do with being a man in the presence of a beautiful woman. One I just so happened to be in love with.

She looked around the room, not realizing I was undressing her with my eyes.

"Wow. It's so much more spacious than mine," she said with a smile. "And you've got a sitting area."

I glanced that way, toward the makeshift living room, and wrangled in my thoughts.

"You're welcome to have a seat." I gestured toward the couch and when her dark eyes caught mine, I began to dread this even more.

"Thanks," she said quietly.

I waited until she was settled before dropping down into the chair across from her. To stall, I inquired about the altercation first.

"So, you're picking fights now?" I asked with a smile.

She grinned and I hoped it meant she was in a better mood than earlier.

"No, but, according to my instructor, we dragons are totally capable of living up to our reputation. You know, the whole *'loose cannon'* thing."

I nodded when a laugh slipped out. "Indeed. Learning to control it is essential, but it isn't always easy," I explained. "You didn't shift, did you?"

With a sigh, she shook her head. "No, it didn't get that far. I was just tired of her knocking me around like some ragdoll."

"What'd you do? Push her?"

When Evangeline bit the side of her lip, I knew I guessed wrong. "Not exactly. I um, kinda elbowed her in the nose."

My lips pressed into a thin line as I fought the urge to laugh again. "You ... wow. Just zero to sixty, huh?"

Her light-brown cheeks tinted red when she shrugged. "It felt like the right thing to do at the time."

And I was sure it did. "We'll work on it," I promised. "What else did you learn today?"

She found the question funny. "What am I, a kindergartner?"

I suppose I was a bit overprotective. Until I knew she could hold her own, I probably wouldn't change. Maybe not even then—side effect of losing her once already.

"Sorry. Just thought I'd ask."

It looked like she felt bad when I apologized.

"No, I don't mind. I just ... it's sweet that you care," she said, quietly blinking before she looked away. "I ended up sitting out the rest of the session as part of my punishment."

"*Part* of your punishment?"

She nodded. "Apparently, I'm not allowed to go topside for a week."

I heard the term used a few times today among other instructors and monitors.

Across from me, Evangeline was quiet. Too quiet for her to only be upset about not getting to participate in this facility's idea of glorified recess.

"Something wrong?"

She glanced up and sighed when I pulled her from her thoughts. "I just ... I found out some disturbing news today. Although, it really shouldn't have surprised me. Things have been sucking a lot lately. Seems to be the default setting of my life—sucky."

I leaned forward, elbows on knees as I focused, intending to listen to whatever she'd share next. Her mouth moved to speak, but no words came. While I should've been wondering what it was she hesitated to say, instead, I stared at her lips. My mind wandered back to a time she didn't remember and, therefore, felt like I dreamt it.

Beautiful didn't even *begin* to describe her. Then. Now. From head to toe, top to bottom, inside and out ... exquisite. I knew this to be a fact because I spent a great deal of my existence mesmerized by her.

Even when she was gone.

The measure of my restraint was an illusion. I was as weak as *any* man in the presence of the only woman he's ever loved. From dawn 'til dusk, the only thing I've ever wanted more than my next breath was her. Only *I* knew what a thin line I walked—holding back from touching her whenever she passed—her hand, hair, face. Keeping my distance was nothing short of a miracle. There was once a time she *welcomed* the idea of the closeness between us. Now, she seemed hellbent on resisting it.

The thoughts evaporated when her voice broke the silence.

"Ran into someone I knew today," she began, immediately piquing my interest. "I used to see a counsellor in Chicago. My parents made me go after finding out I was adopted. But, apparently, she was one in a long list of *watchers* someone placed in my path to make sure I didn't, inadvertently, spill any information to the outside world."

She stopped and it wasn't lost on me that she looked more distant than usual. Her body was here, but her mind was someplace else.

Maybe *several* places.

I was aware that watchers existed, but their missions were never clear. They were most often lycans, but sometimes dragons who'd been put in a specific place to keep tabs on a specific individual.

There was no doubt in my mind that the person who'd appointed these watchers was none other than Elise. And the timing of it all couldn't have been worse. I was hoping to soften Evangeline up to the idea of meeting her mother, hearing her out, but I was almost positive my job had just gotten a whole lot harder.

"Sometimes, it's like I matter and *don't* matter all at the same time," she uttered in a daze. "Someone's gone through a lot of trouble to monitor my life, but thought little enough of me to leave me out in the cold." Her eyes glazed over as she stared at nothing in particular.

How was I supposed to go about telling her that this mysterious *someone* she spoke of was now here in the flesh and hoping to meet her, explain some things to her?

"Evangeline, listen," I began. At the sound of my voice, a glassy, brown stare came my way. Her expression was solemn, but sweet as she waited for me to go on.

"I, um..."

I couldn't do it. The words simply would not leave my mouth. I couldn't add to the heap of pain and confusion she'd already experienced today.

"What is it?" she asked. There was a vulnerability in her voice that made me hyper-vigilant to protect her. Even more so than usual. However, as she watched me with innocent eyes, I recalled the promise she asked of me. One that came at the height of her being tired of the lies others had told; tired of being kept in the dark. What she requested was that I never become one of those people.

Now, what felt impossible to say a moment ago, felt impossible to keep in.

She tipped her chin up when I stood, turning her head as I rounded the coffee table between my seat and the couch where she rested. I sat on the cushion beside her and she drew in a sharp breath like the close proximity made her uncomfortable. But I wouldn't move. With what I had to share, I needed her to know and *feel* she wasn't alone.

I reached for her hand and she didn't pull away despite the war I was well aware my touch always seemed to spur within her; the conflict that made her eyes wander away from mine every time. It was all a sign that some part of her felt for me. Whether she would ever admit that, I wasn't sure.

With incredible uncertainty, I divulged the information I held. Not because it was the easy thing to do or even because I thought now was the best time. I did it because I gave her my word and had never broken a single promise made between us.

"I don't know how to say this." After the first sentence left my mouth, Evangeline's gaze was on me again and I noted how she breathed differently—erratic, like she was anticipating the many places a statement like that could go.

"I recognized someone yesterday. One of the staff members."

Evangeline's lips pressed together like she was stopping herself from interjecting.

"What is it?" I had to ask. Did the look mean she already knew? Maybe her mother's face was familiar somehow?

A deep breath and a nod came before the answer to my question. "I saw you watching her," she explained, her voice sounding quieter than usual, like she wasn't sure it was okay to admit that she noticed. "It was kinda obvious you two had history."

History was one way of looking at it, so I confirmed. "We did. A very long time ago."

Evangeline nodded again and there was a look I couldn't place.

"I went up to her office this morning," I explained. "She was already expecting me. We got to catch up a little bit, but she wants to meet for dinner, but first, I just—"

"Stop," she interjected, shaking her head just before forcing a tight smile. "I really, *really* appreciate you caring enough to tell me this yourself, but you don't ... you don't owe me any kind of explanation," she stammered. "Who you decide to have dinner with or ... *whatever* ... it's your business. Really, it is." She was trying to be so delicate with her words, but had clearly misunderstood.

My brow tensed with confusion and I smiled a bit. "Um ... *what?*"

Her shoulders rose and fell when she let out a breath. "I'm saying it's cool if you, you know, wanna start seeing her." I was too dumbstruck to reply. "I mean, I know you and I had something before, and I know we both ... *feel* things sometimes still, but ... that doesn't mean you can't live your life."

There were so many flaws in that statement, in her way of thinking, I didn't even know where to begin. If she truly knew the extent of our bond, if she really understood how deep our connection ran, the commitment between us ...

The grip I had on her hand tightened and I felt the gentle pulse of her racing heart where our fingers were locked.

"Evangeline ... tens of thousands of moons have risen since I lost you," I shared. "And, with each one of them, my last thought before closing my eyes to sleep ... has always been you. No one else."

She stared for several seconds, the brown centers of her eyes warming more and more until finally blinking.

"I thought ... weren't you trying to say—"

"There's only ever been you," I reiterated, cutting her off.

Her eyes narrowed and it looked like a laugh was on the verge of slipping out.

"You expect me to believe you've been alone for hundreds of years, pining over me like in some fairytale?" A smile ghosted on her lips and my heart thundered inside my chest at the sight of it.

I held her gaze and shed some light on my truth.

"When you've experienced love as pure and *raw* as I have ... you know better than to try recreating it. If it's ever lost, if that love is ever stolen from you, the only choice you really have is to pray the loss doesn't eat you alive."

It felt like my chest might explode when her lips parted and, for that split second, her defenses were down. So, while she was open and vulnerable, I allowed myself to be, too.

"I'm aware that I might be waiting for you in vain," I admitted, "but ... that choice to wait, that decision to not bother searching for a replacement, it's something no one can take away from me. Not even you."

Her teeth sank into her bottom lip as my confession lingered between us.

"I..."

Words escaped her and I hoped she knew I hadn't said these things to make her swoon or to cloud her head. I said them because that was my reality. She was my life.

I still had her hand and hadn't forgotten what I needed to tell her.

"I do have history with the woman, but not the kind you were thinking." Her brow lifted when I stopped there, and it felt cruel not to just come out with it, but equally cruel to just drop the truth into her lap and expect her to cope. "The dinner invite wasn't just for me, Evangeline."

Now her expression reflected the confusion I fully expected.

"It was for *both* of us," I went on. "That woman, Elise, she's ... your mother."

Evie

The room swirled around me.

Those words.

They didn't make sense. I didn't have a mother; not one with the same blood as mine coursing through her veins.

Mine was ... she was dead.

My hand felt hot against my forehead when I pressed it there, squeezing my eyes shut. I recalled the woman's features. How I'd missed the resemblance was beyond me. She didn't look anywhere near old enough to have a daughter my age, but that wasn't a surprise. I just couldn't wrap my mind around this.

"Evangeline," Liam said sweetly. "Say something."

What was I *supposed* to say? "I don't understand. I thought—"

"So did I," he cut in. "And she thought the same about me, following the war. I don't have all the answers yet, but I thought dinner might be a good time for *both* of us to ask our questions."

I stammered a bit and then got the words out. "Did she know who I was when she saw me, or not until you told her?" I asked.

Liam's expression dimmed a bit and the glimmer of hope behind his eyes faded completely. "I think you might have misunderstood."

My eyes narrowed. "Misunderstood what?"

I was more aware of my hand in his because he squeezed it gently. And this time, when he spoke again, I felt a shift from budding excitement and nervousness to anger.

"She's the one who brought you here. The one who brought you *back*."

"She ... what?"

This wasn't adding up. All this time, I imagined the culprit to be someone who cared very little for me. Someone who saw me as a means to an end, the answer to the Sovereign having absolute reign. But, then again, who's to say these things weren't still true. Maybe this woman, Elise, was all these things and more. Who's to say this wasn't *exactly* her agenda?

My face felt tense and my eyes burned. If she was the one who

155

brought me here, that meant she was also the manipulator who put the watchers in my life, the one who moved me from Chicago to Seaton Falls, the one who, despite knowing exactly where I was at all times ... let me believe I didn't belong anywhere.

A sudden burst of heat in my gut made me think I'd go up in flames. The last few years of my life had been filled with so much hurt and rejection. All because I was the girl who came from nowhere. Only, that wasn't entirely true. I *did* come from somewhere, from *someone*, but that someone decided to play puppet master from behind the curtain.

I loved my adoptive mom and dad with everything in me, but I couldn't lie and say a huge part of me didn't long to know my *real* parents when I found out they existed. And this woman, whoever she was, stole that from me. She created this void in my life and then stood back while it grew and grew until it hollowed me out. And to top it all off, her summoning us all here to this facility was, inadvertently, the reason Baz ordered the witches to make my parents forget me.

So much of what had been taken from me, was taken from me by her hand.

I shook my head before speaking.

"I won't meet her." Getting to my feet, I explained why. "She doesn't get to siphon all the important things out of my life, one at a time, and then expect me to suddenly be on her schedule. That's nice that she wants to talk to me, nice that she wants to tell me everything ... *now*. But where was all that when it counted?"

Where was the explanation and the lifting of the veil when I thought I was going crazy? When I started dreaming about a guy I'd never met, but felt completely drawn to? Where was that when I had to leave all my friends behind and start over?

I was a pawn to her.

The thought of being moved around on someone's chess board had always been in the back of my mind, despite not knowing the full scale of her plan. Only now, I had a face to put with the hurt.

I swiped at tears with my arm as Liam stood too, holding me in place so I couldn't escape.

"You know I'm always on your side, right?"

The question was frustratingly simple, and I sighed instead of answering.

"So, you also know I'll support whatever decision you make, but ... all the answers you've been waiting for? The ones even *I* can't give?" he added. "She's got them, Evangeline. *All* of them."

There were, admittedly, a million things I wanted to know, but I didn't like what it'd cost me to get them—peace of mind mostly.

I shook my head again. "No. She's been controlling me all this time without me knowing it, but this is the one thing she can't make me do."

I cleared more tears from my cheeks and stared over Liam's shoulder while he stared at *me*. A few seconds after putting my foot down, he nodded.

"Then that's all there is to it."

I was glad he didn't try to talk me into it because I was holding so much in. If he pushed, I would have fallen apart and that was something I preferred to do in the privacy of my own room.

"Goodnight," I said in parting, turning my back on him so I could rush back down the hall before the waterworks started.

And start they did. Flowing uncontrollably for so long I lost track of time. Beth didn't question me for too long and Liam didn't try to pop into my thoughts to check on me. I appreciated both of them for allowing me the privacy neither, technically, had to uphold.

One too many bubbles had been burst in the last forty-eight hours and, more and more, I was beginning to see the logic behind Nick's decision to separate. Things just kept piling up and what kind of relationship would we have had in the midst of it?

We were kind of a mess. Or at least, I was. For now, things were best this way.

I was getting somewhat used to the world falling apart around me.

CHAPTER 13

Nick

Sweat covered me from head to toe as I stood in the mirror, dazed. The last thing I remembered was going to sleep, and now my hands and feet were covered with dirt and grass and I couldn't even remember walking into the bathroom just now. It was like I laid on the pillow and woke up here, staring at myself as my eyes transitioned back to their usual shade from an odd yellow.

My hands shook as I washed them, racking my brain for even a *hint* of how I'd lost time. That's what it felt like; losing time. It happened before, on the first night I spent at my grandfather's estate when I escaped there to be alone. Stress—that's what I thought it was; from fighting the mutts, from finding out the true nature of what I am. I was awake that time, though, staring at old photographs one second, sitting on the porch, trying to catch my breath the next.

When I finally went home, I thought of telling Richie about it, but the last thing I needed was one more person looking at me like I was a freak.

Well ... a freak among other freaks. Even with other lycans, I was the odd man out. While most felt a sense of comradery, I was still on my own, finding myself, deciding whether I could even be trusted.

I needed to know I wouldn't become the very thing Liam said I would. If you asked me whether I thought it was possible a couple weeks ago, I would've said with certainty that it wasn't. But as I stared at dirt rinsing down the drain, as I acknowledged that I was clearly not always in control of myself ... I considered it a real possibility.

I showered and got dressed before the other guys were even awake. I sat on the edge of my bed, still trying to get my bearings as they laughed and joked about how much worse our new uniforms were than the ones issued by Seaton Prep. Normally, I would've been right with them, but my head wasn't here.

I tried to clear my thoughts as we walked. The way the schedule worked here was kind of confusing. They separated us into two large groups, each made up of around five-hundred-plus shifters. For the first two weeks, my group was broken down into even smaller segments of no more than fifty. We focused on basic training—self-defense and the essentials for survival—while the others participated in the informational sessions, complete with supernatural history courses. At the end of the day, there were traditional, high school classes so we wouldn't fall behind.

The combat training was kind of cool, but I couldn't say the same for our next module. The only good thing about it was that we were on a constant, two-week rotation between the two. Meaning, I wouldn't have to suffer through it long if it sucked.

Behind me, Lucas complained to Chris again. This time, it was something about Beth and a new guy he'd seen her hanging around once or twice. He still hadn't let go of the idea that she'd one day see him in the same way he sees *her*. I was *this* close to telling him to give it a rest and move on, but that would've been the frustration talking.

And it also would've made me a hypocrite because I was, technically, still harboring feelings for a girl I couldn't have either.

Yes, I was the one who broke things off with Evie, but only because, from my perspective, I finally saw the forest for the trees. We were both changing, especially me. If she knew I was losing time, if she knew the growing darkness I felt inside me—the way it flowed through my veins all day, every day—she would've come to the same conclusion:

We were better off apart.

For now. Maybe forever.

Even if the distance killed me inside.

We hadn't spoken in two weeks despite seeing each other daily. Whether in passing as we headed from one session to the next, or spotting one another across the dining hall, but no words had been exchanged. I made sure of that. I needed to keep her away for her own good, plus ... there was more.

Way deep down, in the pit of my stomach, I felt a swell of anger brewing toward her. It was a seed that'd been planted when I first observed her around Liam. It'd only grown since then. There was half of me that missed what we had, missed the closeness. And there was another side of me that wanted nothing to do with her.

Maybe even wished we never met.

I couldn't be sure these ill feelings were my own, normal ... or if these were signs that the Liberator within me was growing stronger, controlling more of my thoughts than I realized.

Whenever our eyes locked, I half suspected she was aware of the struggle going on inside me. That I was half terrified I'd hurt her; that I was half afraid I wouldn't always care if I did. For now, my conscience was intact and I couldn't even imagine it, but as the light within me seemed to dim at record speed, I couldn't say how long I could keep the real me locked away.

I ran so hot and cold these days. There was very little room for in between. Very little success filtering my words and actions toward others. More and more, I did and said the first things that came to mind, bypassing the usual sensors and triggers that prevent most from making mistakes. I seemed to just ... rush full-steam ahead. Meaning, there was the potential to make messes of things I had every intention of handling with grace.

Roz flanked the guys and I from the right, jogging to catch up. "Hey."

My brow lifted, but I couldn't fake a smile when I returned the greeting.

She glanced behind us where Lucas and Chris discussed a small party we were having in our room tonight. Realizing they weren't paying us any attention, she spoke in a quiet voice. "I've been looking into the rings."

I turned her way, feeling a jolt in the center of my chest as those words sunk in. "Really?"

She smiled even bigger. "Really. Some of the stories surrounding them are conflicting, but the most common one is that they belonged to fallen soldiers of some old-school, supernatural war. It's unclear which war it was, who the soldiers were exactly, or why they might be important, but at least we have a lead."

"Thank you. Best news I heard all week."

Roz's cheeks tinted red when she nodded. "You're welcome. And I also remember you saying there were either six or seven. According to what I read, there were seven in existence, but there's no record of where they are present day."

I envisioned my grandfather's hand-drawn picture, recalling the description he gave of the silver rings with dark stones set in the center. Nothing Roz shared explained why these items were impor-tant to him, but I had a feeling it went beyond just wanting to add to his collection of weird artifacts and memorabilia. His obsession with these rings, specifically, went deeper.

My thoughts were scrambled when we rounded the corner and, right there, at the door of the lecture hall, stood my weakness—tall, beautiful ... frustrating. Being apart didn't lessen my attraction to her.

If anything, it made all the good things about her more desirable. Possibly because she felt so far away now, unattainable.

Roz stopped talking when she realized I was no longer listening. In my peripheral, I saw her eyes follow mine toward Evie.

A faint sigh left her mouth. "Still with me?" she asked, snapping her fingers in front of my face until my attention was hers again. "I'm thinking we need to examine your grandfather's journals a little more closely. Are you cool with me taking a look at them with you?"

"Uh, yeah. Sure," was all I could get out, suddenly distracted when Evie's eyes wandered to mine. Apparently, we were headed into the same class.

Not awkward at all.

Roz took another deep breath. "I guess I'll just ... talk to you about it later. When you're a little more focused," she concluded. The next second, she stormed off toward the lecture hall we'd all be stuck in for the next couple hours.

As she passed Evie, the two exchanged a tense look, followed by equally tense smiles, but then I had Evie's eyes again.

'You should say something,' I thought. 'Anything to make having this class together less uncomfortable.'

The idea was stupid, but I started giving in almost immediately. It was like I couldn't make myself be reasonable these days, acting on impulse. She probably didn't want to see me, let alone talk to me after how things had been lately, but still, despite myself, I put one foot in front of the other, leaving Lucas and Chris behind. When I was close enough, I gave a stiff smile. She smiled back and I imagined it was only to be polite.

"Hi," I exhaled, searching for words to say beyond that.

"Hi," she echoed. Her lips pursed together tightly right after and I knew any further conversation would have to come from me.

"So ... how've you been adjusting here?"

After a moment of thought, she shrugged. Her answer was vague and I couldn't help but to wonder if it was so short because, like I expected, she didn't really want to speak.

"It is what it is."

I nodded as body after body passed us by, filling the room.

"Listen, I—"

"I think I—"

We both spoke at the same time and when she smiled about it, my body responded in a way I wasn't expecting—my heart leapt.

"You first," she offered.

Keep your head clear, man.

"I was just gonna say I owe you an apology. I didn't intend to hurt or embarrass you with the run-in the three of us had in the dining hall." I couldn't even make myself say Liam's name out loud. "When I went to my room, when I cooled off, I thought about things. I meant to handle it differently when I finally saw him, your *friend*, face-to-face. I should have just laid low until my anger was in check."

Although, I wasn't even sure such a thing was possible at this point.

She lowered her head, confirming I'd been right to assume I made her feel those things and much more. I really did mean to be more careful, more collected, it just...

"Apology accepted," she said back, forgiving me much quicker than expected. "But only if you accept mine, too."

I wasn't expecting that either.

"You were right. With everything we both have going on ..." She paused and her eyes slipped to the floor. There was so much feeling behind them, I felt it, too. "We should probably focus on that for now," she went on, adding, "Not each other."

I hadn't noticed it until now, but there was a heaviness about her. Like she was carrying the weight of the world on her shoulders. It'd become natural for me to want to share whatever her load was, but I was also sure she wouldn't open up to me. One of our downfalls was not letting one another in completely. Still, I felt compelled to offer.

"Look, I know we're not where we used to be, but ... if you ever need to talk, you can—"

Her brow quirked when she met my gaze again.

"That's probably not a good idea," she interjected, the abrupt words startling me a bit. Maybe even upsetting me, if I'm being honest. "Sharing our thoughts and feelings, communicating ... we were never good at that. So, now that we're trying to focus on finding and fixing *ourselves* and not our relationship ... I think it's best not to blur those lines again."

A smile ghosted on her lips, one I suspected she only gave to soften the blow of what she just said.

It didn't help.

The lightweight rejection stung. No, she wasn't being malicious, but the declaration to *'not blur those lines'* brought with them a sudden awareness. Like, maybe she saw the clarity in my logic, agreed we were better off apart.

Before this conversation, some small part of me held on to the idea that she might maintain her stance from the other night. Then, she rejected the idea of putting space between us, believing we could work through our issues while continuing to move forward together. But now, she seemed to have had a revelation during our time apart.

I offered a weak smile, doing all I could to shove my ego back down where it belonged.

"Sure. I, uh ... I suppose we should just settle for a truce then."

"You only call a truce when someone's your enemy." She smiled again. "And you're not my enemy, Nick." I stared into the face of the girl who made me feel so many things it was frustrating.

I wanted her.

Feared her because no one else had ever had such a hold on me.

Loved her.

"Friends?" she asked hopefully, offering her hand, contrasting my last thought.

I shook it, appreciating the idea, but feeling the emptiness it caused to echo inside my heart. I didn't just want to be her friend, but even *that* was probably more than I should have accepted. Distance was the best thing for us.

I should have turned down the suggestion, shouldn't have even approached her to begin with. However, I took her hand and shook it, putting her at risk yet again with the uttering of one simple word.

"Friends."

She was just about to step into the lecture hall when I stopped her, and I have no idea what made me do it. This stupid hot and cold compulsion again, I guess. Her wrist was looped in my fingers and, reluctantly, her gaze met mine.

"Yeah?"

Her heart was beating so fast it nearly distracted me from what I wanted to ask.

"Since we're kinda okay now ... the guys and I are having a few people over to our room later tonight. We're just hanging out or whatever, but you're welcome to stop by if you want to." I spoke in a rush, knowing I should have just let her walk away. "I think Beth might be coming, too," I added, sweetening the deal as if I didn't know what a terrible idea this was.

There was a long pause that made a lot of thoughts and emotions fly through me.

Fear that she'd say no.

Then, fear that she'd say yes.

Anger toward myself for even asking.

Rage that it was taking her so long to answer either way because, on some level, I wondered if the only reason she hesitated was because of Liam. Because she was taking his feelings into account.

I tasted blood when I bit down into my cheek to keep calm. She seemed to be going back and forth between her options and, just as I was about to tell her to forget it, she nodded.

"Okay, count me in."

I breathed a little easier and the rage slowly melted away.

The slack grip I had on her wrist loosened even more when I let her continue inside, following close behind. I spotted Roz and the guys and was headed over to take a seat with them when the sight of our instructor made my feet stop moving.

Liam stood front and center, arms locked tight across his chest as he watched the seats fill. The fury that kept rising inside me went from a manageable simmer to a full-on boil in a matter of seconds.

My hatred for him hadn't subsided. Not even a little. It had actually more than doubled since the first time we met, causing me to lose sleep several nights as I imagined how the time between him and Evie was spent. On more than one occasion, I just stared at the ceiling, wondering if I'd pushed her closer to him. Chances are, my absence had given him all the room he needed to wedge his way deeper into her life. Even more so than he already had.

I dropped down into the seat between Chris and Roz and tried to keep my cool. Easier said than done.

Evie peered at me from down our row and the look of worry on her face made it clear that, at least on some level, she wasn't so sure what I was capable of now either. The run-in I nearly had with Liam a couple weeks ago proved that I couldn't have cared less what position he held here at the facility. Instructor or not, even with the threat of punishment looming ... I would've still gone after him had she not stopped me.

There was just something about him that made me see red. Yes, it was mostly that I knew some part of Evie was connected to him, but it was also that cocky expression he always wore. Like there was always a challenge waiting to be thrown at me just to see if I'd stand my ground. Like he knew something I didn't.

Like I was the odd man out when it came to Evie.

And what maybe bothered me most of all was that he could have been right.

"Hey, you all right?" I glanced over at Chris when he asked. He pointed to my hand where I'd gripped and smashed the corner of the small, half-desk hinged the side of my chair.

I loosened my hand and nodded, suddenly aware of a few other sets of eyes on me, too. "Yeah, I'm cool."

Chris stared for a moment before hesitantly looking away.

The room was full now. All one-hundred-plus seats had bodies in them and the only sound to be heard was Liam's steps as he moved

RACHEL JONAS

toward the door to close it. On his way back toward the center where he stood before, his eyes drifted toward Evie ... and then to me.

He was *definitely* challenging me. I hadn't imagined it. Or maybe it was a threat—a warning to keep my distance from her.

I didn't look away and neither did he. It was Chris who caught it and leaned in to whispered to calm me down.

"Chill, man. I know you don't like this dude and I get it, but you have to let that go for now. We're stuck in here for two hours a day for the next two weeks," he reminded me. "Find a way to deal with it."

Sometime last week, I ended up telling him and Lucas every-thing. Well, *almost* everything—the part concerning Evie and I breaking up, but I'd only confuse them with talk of being the Liber-ator and how she fit into that. They were aware, however, of what role Liam played. Not willing to give up Evie's secret—that she'd lived before—I had to explain it in terms of Liam being an ex, someone who resurfaced from her past. They were on my side, of course, but Chris was right. I couldn't get out of this session, so I'd have to find a way to deal.

The first step was being the one to end the stare-down between us. It didn't mean he intimidated me. It meant I was trying to get through this without hurting him.

Not long after my eyes left him and focused elsewhere, he went on about his business.

"I'll start by addressing the elephant in the room. I'm sure it's been strange sitting in classrooms and training under shifters who don't look any older than *you* do. So, this will be one of the many things we'll go over during the course of the two weeks you're here with me. And anything we *don't* cover this time, we'll get to in the next module." He smiled a bit and, behind me, two girls started whispering.

"I didn't catch a single word he said. Did you?" one asked quietly.

"Nope," the other whispered. "I was completely blinded by his hotness." They laughed quietly, but I wasn't amused.

The guy was average at best. To me, he looked like a barbarian in need of a haircut and a shave. If I didn't know any better, I would've thought someone let him in by accident.

"I'll mostly focus on our history—that of both lycans *and* dragons. I'm sure many of you have already realized there's an underlying tension that exists between the two, and one of this facility's goals is to eliminate it. Especially seeing as how, much of it is the result of misguided prejudices, skewed eyewitness accounts, and greatly exaggerated rumors. As a dragon, myself, I can attest to the fact that there *is* an element of unpredictability that exists within my species, but I've also known lycans who operate somewhat erratically as well."

He looked at me and I felt my nostrils flare as air rushed in and out of my lungs.

He scanned the class again as he slowly paced from one end of the room to the other. "One of the main things we've been advised to stress to you all is the power of self-control. That'll go a long way as you come into the knowledge of your abilities."

He stopped at the center of the room and, before speaking again, he smiled a bit, rubbing his hand over the scruff on his chin.

"I'm gonna level with you guys; I'm not a teacher, nor have I ever had the desire to be one," he shared. "Actually, based on some choices I made back in the day, I'm pretty sure I have no business whatsoever being given the power to influence our younger generations."

Others in the room laughed at his admission—mostly girls giggling, probably hoping to stand out and catch his attention.

"But I came here for a couple different reasons," he went on. "As a secondary assignment to my *priority,* I was asked to share what I know with all of you. I wasn't chosen to focus on history because I'm an avid reader or some scholar who's made it his life's work to study the wars our ancestors fought—some against each other, some within our own races. I was chosen to stand before you today because ... I *fought* in many of those wars."

Several around the room began to whisper and several others raised their hands. Liam called on a kid off to my left and she stood to ask her question.

"But ... there hasn't been a war in over five hundred years and most were futile, ending with many on *both* sides dead."

Liam nodded. "Five-hundred-fifty-seven years to be exact." His response prompted the girl to slowly take her seat before he finished his thought. "And by that time, I was already pushing three-hundred-fifty."

There was more whispering. Even Chris and Lucas shared a look. I think we were all under the impression that mostly only The Sovereign's closest allies, members of the Council, High Council, and the Elders were that far up in age.

"And to address the second part of your statement regarding both sides being diminished quite a bit, you're right." He paused, but continued to pace as he watched the floor beneath his feet. "While I was lucky enough to come through it unscathed, the last war was definitely a loss for those of us trying to maintain order."

He looked up again. "Does anyone know the name of that particular battle?"

Only two hands went up and I was surprised to see *that* many. But what *didn't* surprise me was that Beth was one of them. He pointed to her.

"*The Lunar War*—the single, bloodiest war in lycan history, fought in a single night beneath the light of a full moon," she answered, but, from the look on her face, she seemed to be confused. "I don't understand, though. That battle had nothing to do with dragons."

Liam's expression shifted, bordering on dark. "You're right. It had absolutely nothing to do with dragons ... but it did, however, have *everything* to do with my family."

"So ... if you fought for the side of the losing lycan kingdom, that means you had ties to Bahir Dar?" she asked as her whole face lit up, putting the rest of us to shame with her knowledge.

Liam gave a weak smile. "I see you've done your homework."

She smiled back, but not in the flirtatious way the other girls had. There was a sense of admiration in her eyes. "I read."

He laughed again. "Well, while we're on the topic, it's important that we understand *why* the Bahir Dar Kingdom fell that day."

Beth's hand went up again, although Liam wasn't asking anyone to answer for him. Looking like her knowledge on the subject had impressed him quite a bit, he called on her anyway.

"It was simple. They were outnumbered by the Sovereign's army."

Liam nodded, but it was clear from his expression he had something to add.

"Yes and no. Yes, we were outnumbered, but not just based on the size of the Sovereign's army," he explained. "In the weeks leading up to the battle, he planned his attack on us carefully. And by *planned,* I mean ... he allowed his soldiers to go out into the town and turn as many humans into mutts as possible—a sacrifice *our* king was never willing to make, which we all supported one-hundred-percent," he shared. "...Even knowing the odds weren't likely in our favor."

You could have heard a pin drop.

"The man all lycans have been forced to revere as their king has *never* had any sort of concern for life—human, lycan, or otherwise. The only thing he cares about now, and has *ever* cared about, is the building up of his kingdom and himself."

The room was silent for several seconds, but Beth spoke again. This time, she seemed reluctant.

"I've heard stories about a dragon who was taken in by King Noah of Bahir Dar. He was mentioned several times in the books my parents have given me over the years, although his story is pretty vague. But ... I was just wondering if the dragon he took in ... was that ... you?" she finally asked. "I mean, your age and experiences seem to fit, so ... I just thought ... maybe—"

Liam smiled, but didn't lift his eyes from the floor. "This dragon, did he have a name?"

Beth shrugged. "He was always just referred to by some Latin phrase I had to Google the meaning of." She went on to reveal what she'd learned to the rest of the class. "He was referred to as *The Reaper.*"

His smile faded some, but I think it shocked us all when he nodded, owning up to it when Beth identified him. She stared at Liam like she just realized she was in the company of a celebrity. Sort of like she idolized him as she mouthed three words:

"No freakin' way."

"That nickname was given during some dark days in my life," Liam shared. "I didn't think I had much to live for, so, all of a sudden, *every* cause became one worth dying for." He paused and I noted how his eyes shifted to Evie for a brief second. Right after, he masked what I guessed was sadness with another laugh. "So, my apologies to the few dragons in the room. I'm pretty sure my past behavior had something to do with others thinking we're all savages."

Quiet laughter ricocheted off the walls.

Beside me, Roz's pen was about to start a fire on the sheet of paper she'd nearly filled from top to bottom with notes. She jotted down keywords I was sure she planned to dive into later. Among them: *Reaper.*

It wasn't until seeing it in written form that I recalled seeing it written *before.* My brow tensed as I fought to remember where. And then it hit me.

My grandfather's notes. The context escaped me, but I was sure he mentioned it.

"But all the wars we've engaged in over the centuries, all the tearing down and rebuilding, is exactly what brings us here today."

Liam stopped pacing for a moment to scan the crowd. "While most of us, myself included, are having a hard time understanding the actions of the clans at the moment, I think this is their version of taking a stand. Granted, we're still in the early stages with many across the planet simply refusing to pay the tariff, but don't be deceived. You'd be surprised how many wars began because one side *'wakes up'* and suddenly sees the big picture, realizes that, if something isn't done, future generations such as yourselves are damned to a fate worse than those who came before you."

I listened as intently as everyone else. Whether I liked him or not, he seemed to know more than any of us did about what was going on. More than even my brothers had been able to explain.

"The tariff serves a dual purpose," he went on. "The most obvious thing it accomplishes is that it builds the Sovereign's kingdom, but not the lycan race as a whole. Monetarily speaking, clans around the world have poured their hard-earned money at his feet for centuries. And clans have also played a major part in fortifying his defense system. Once a year, young shifters are delivered to his doorstep. Three from each clan."

No one said a word. Before shifting, none of us had any clue why certain ones not much older than us would seem to drop off the face of the planet. We were always told they enlisted in the army, but ... we didn't realize until recently which army they were serving.

"But there's something deeper that's instilled in the lycan race every time that tariff is paid," Liam continued. "It keeps your people bound—physically and, more importantly, mentally. The message the Sovereign is sending every time he collects is that he's in control and all of you ... are powerless."

Roz's pen stopped moving and she zoned out as she stared at Liam. His words seemed to be hitting home.

"The man is a master manipulator," Liam added. "I have to give him that. No one has perfected the art quite like him. He's learned to spread fear like a cancer, one that grows unchecked." He paced toward the fake window to his right again. "Have any of you wondered why the generation before you thought it better to keep you all in the dark concerning your true nature?"

Several around the room nodded and mumbled responses.

"The answer is simple and complex at the same time: your generation would be much easier to control, and far more useful to him, if you were all in these superhero bodies, with the mental capacity of a grilled cheese sandwich."

The others laughed and Liam smiled.

"Sounds funny, but it's the truth. It's easier to control those who have no real sense of where they're going. No sense of identity. In essence, you can mold them to be whoever, or whatever, you want them to be. That was his plan. He intended to raise a generation of mindless followers who had no recollection of their ancestors' strength, of the battles they fought and won, of the sacrifices they made."

I hated that his logic stuck with me. Our parents had been fooled into thinking our lives would be easier, more peaceful, if we were kept ignorant and then taught to uphold the Sovereign's laws without question. Without revolt.

Until someone had a change of heart and stopped complying.

Thank God they woke up.

It was clear the Sovereign hoped to raise up a generation of robots who would, in turn, raise *future* robots, and change the order of things altogether.

"Remember those rumors and exaggerations I mentioned when we first got started?" Liam asked, cutting into my thoughts. "Many of those were started by the Sovereign himself. His intentions were to focus all of the lycan races' fear and animosity toward one, common factor. Doing so would enable him to spur a false sense of unity against a common enemy. All the while, blinding your people to the fact that *he* was their greatest adversary. And that's where we get to the eventual conflict between lycans and dragons. It was merely a diversion that was, yes, steeped in some semblance of truth—i.e. the rage I mentioned before—but mostly, it was a divisive tactic, not much different than a politician pushing his own agenda. Raging war against the dragons was a campaign of sorts and, from it, a new day dawned."

Liam took a breath and smiled when he surveyed the room.

"You all look incredibly overwhelmed, so we'll pause here and I'll take questions so I can clear up any confusion before moving ahead."

Beth's hand shot up first and Roz's right after. He called on Beth.

"How does the Sovereign get the young shifters he collects to willingly submit to his militia?"

"Good question. He sires them."

Beth frowned. "I've heard that's possible, but have no clue what the process is. I know mutts are sired when bitten, but how's it done with those who were *born* lycans?"

"They're put on a very strict diet." He paused to smile, probably knowing what he'd say next would turn our stomachs. "For a week straight, the only substance they're offered is the Sovereign's blood. And, because there are so many of them, it'd be impossible for him to provide it fresh for them all day every day. So ... it's *old* blood. Blood that's been stored up over time."

A collective wave of nausea swept the crowd with the occasional "Eew," whined by the girls.

"Appetizing, right?" Liam joked. "But that's the only way. After a week, they're totally transformed and ready to do his bidding."

"That's disgusting. Sorry I asked," Beth mumbled.

Liam pointed toward Roz. "You had something to add?"

She smiled and, at the sight of it, I had this strange sense of her fraternizing with the enemy.

"Um, yes, I do. Was it the Sovereign's tactics that diminished the dragons' numbers so greatly? I mean, it's no secret there don't seem to be many of you. Or ... is that a misunderstanding?"

Liam shook his head. "Unfortunately, no, it's not a misunderstanding. And, yes, you're right. There were many efforts to '*eliminate*' the imagined threat we posed, so it wasn't uncommon for entire villages of dragons to fall victim to surprise, blitzkrieg attacks in the middle of the night, leveling them to the ground. The heads and wings of my people were kept as trophies or sometimes gifts delivered to the Sovereign as a show of loyalty and solidarity."

"Wings?" My head whipped to the right at the sound of Evie's voice. She seemed confused. "I didn't realize that was even ... a *thing*."

It wasn't lost on me how Liam's expression, his *tone,* softened when he addressed her.

"It's more of a latent ability," he explained, "but flying is one of our races many conveniences."

She still seemed confused. "So ... why can't we see them. Are they invisible?"

"In a sense, yes. The only time they can be seen, touched, is in our shifted form and, even then, only if we decide to spread them."

I'd seen Liam in battle before, when we faced the mutts. It would have been so easy for him to leave the scene or even use flight to his advantage, but he never did. He fought on the ground like the rest of us and, without having to wonder '*why*' for too long, I figured it out.

Because of Evie...

She was clearly just learning how to tap into who she really was, just like the rest of us, so there wasn't a doubt in my mind that he stayed on the ground to protect her. Apparently, his own wellbeing meant very little to him compared to hers.

My stomach turned at the thought of him caring that much about the girl I wanted to myself. Just like that, I was right back where I started when first walking through the door of this lecture hall.

Angry.

Frustrated.

Evie settled down again and Liam moved on. "Are there any other questions?" he asked.

When no one raised their hands, he continued, sharing more about the history of both supernatural races and I tried to focus. It was difficult, though. Because, every time his eyes would drift toward Evie, every time she was paying attention and caught his gaze ... her heart.

It raced like crazy.

He got to her, in ways I was beginning to think I never could. If what she said was true, if they really were '*tethered*' in the past, what chance did I stand present day?

Should I even be thinking like that right now, considering?

176

In my mind, I held a small hope that our separation might be temporary, an opportunity for us to both grow and figure things out. But what if we never quite got around to having our second chance? What if me being what I am prevented that? What if the deep-rooted connection she had with *him*, the man I glared at while he lectured from the front of the room, made that impossible?

It was now more real to me than before; the fact that Liam stood a very good chance of winning Evie's heart.

And it *also* became very real that, despite how strongly I felt for her ... there didn't seem to be much I could do to stop that from happening.

CHAPTER 14

Nick

"You're pretty quiet for a guy getting ready to throw a party."

I looked up to find Roz staring as she opened a bag of chips to set on the dresser. We didn't have bowls to pour all the snacks into and couldn't exactly go to the dining hall and ask to borrow any, seeing as how we didn't have anyone's permission to have guests over. So, this was us making do.

"Not looking forward to it anymore?" she added.

There was no straight answer to that. "Just thinking."

Chris, Lucas, and Theo took a trip down to the vending machines with two empty duffle bags to fill with drinks before people started showing up. So, for now, it was just Roz and I. Calling this a *party* was the wrong term. Mostly, it was just a chance for those of us who came in from Seaton Falls to get together and restore some sense of normalcy. I was sure I wasn't the only one feeling overwhelmed by all the new faces to go along with our new surroundings. So, tonight, it'd just be members of the Seaton Falls clan.

Roz set out a bag of popcorn and I wasn't surprised when she started asking more questions.

"Thinking about ... *her?* About having to be in the same class, I mean?" She wouldn't look at me, which was strange. Her behavior was borderline timid when the question left her mouth, and Roz Chadwick was never timid.

"I noticed you seemed uncomfortable through the session today," she went on.

I got started shoving all the boxes the guys and I still had to unpack into the closet for now, just so they were out of the way.

"That's part of it," I admitted, deciding to tell the whole truth because I trusted her with it. "That and the fact that I can't pretend to love who our instructor is for this module."

Roz could be incredibly callous about, well, *everything,* but she was one of the most honest and trustworthy people I knew. Turned out the pesky girl I was once constantly trying to get rid of was quickly becoming one of the best friends I ever lucked up on by accident.

"I hate the guy," I admitted, gritting my teeth as I envisioned Liam. "And, yeah, it's gonna suck a little having to sit there, listening to his voice for two hours a day."

"And I'm sure listening to all the girls going on and on about him isn't helping either." Roz grinned before glancing up to find me glaring at her. "It was just a joke. Chillax."

The explicit comments from the ones who sat behind me were hard to forget. By the end of class, I'm sure both needed a cold shower and a cigarette. My next thought was one I kept to myself...

Did Evie look at him that way, too?

Did she see in him what the other girls did?

I hated that I even cared. Hated that it mattered.

"If you ask me, he's kind of overrated," Roz said in her usual, uninterested monotone. She casually scrolled through the music on my phone before settling on a song and placing it aside.

"I mean, yeah, he's nice to look at, but he's a bit too much of a brute for my taste," she added. "Take what Beth brought up, for instance. The whole '*Reaper*' thing. I haven't had a chance to look into it yet, but sounds to me like this guy has gallons of blood on his hands from the lives he's taken. I'm talking like ... *thousands* of lives." She held her hands out and stared at them as she spoke, as if imagining warm, red liquid covering her own.

I zoned out listening to her speak, not realizing I'd completely stopped shifting boxes. We didn't really have time for standing still, so I went back to multitasking.

"I get that war is necessary sometimes, but you're not supposed to *enjoy* killing people. Not even if they deserve it," she went on, pushing her long, dark hair behind her shoulders. "If you ask me, when someone crosses that line and actually gets off on the kill, that's when they become a monster."

Monster ... that word rung in my ears.

"Don't get me wrong," she added, "the dude's past is like a goldmine to a researcher like myself. I'd jump at the opportunity to sit down and pick his brain for hours, but that's about the extent of any type of allure he has in my eyes."

A huge grin made all her teeth visible. Happened every time she had something witty to say.

"Whoever wants him for his body can have it. All I want is a conversation."

Something about her tone left me without a doubt that these were her true feelings. She wasn't just saying this because she knew I hated him, wasn't just humoring me for the heck of it. Protecting my ego had never been high enough on her list of priorities for that to have even been a possibility. Actually, she'd made it a point to knock me down a peg a time or two when she thought I was full of myself, so there was that.

Of all the things I liked and respected about Roz, at the top of that list was the fact that she was one of few people who saw beyond a person's outer shell and straight through to the heart.

"Which brings me to my next point," she blurted.

I peered up. "*What* next point?"

She smiled again, but this one was kind of reserved, like she was unsure about going on.

"Well, you and I have a ton of questions, right? Questions we've been trying to find answers to for weeks now, and I was just thinking … why don't we bring them to *him*?" she suggested, quickly amending her statement. "Well, *I'll* bring them to him. He seemed pretty cool about letting us ask him stuff at the end of class. Maybe I'll ask a few of the most pressing ones the next time he opens the floor." She shrugged while struggling with another bag. "He could be a shortcut to the info we're after."

As much as I hated to admit it, Roz was right. We could definitely use Liam's help, but there needed to be boundaries.

"He can't know about the rings my grandfather was looking for," I blurted. "We can keep looking into that on our own for now."

I didn't want a conversation about them to lead to how we came to know they existed—the journals. Those were far too personal to have just anyone thumbing through the pages. For now, I only trusted Roz with that.

She shrugged again. "Whatever you're comfortable with."

"And questions about me being … whatever I am," I added. "Those are off limits, too, seeing as how I'm the only one that exists."

Roz's eyes found mine and softened. "Agreed."

I wasn't completely comfortable with the idea, but it could give us too much of a lead to dismiss her suggestion.

We went on with setting up, but the room was eerily quiet now, other than the low hum of the music she selected. Her usual, endless stream of questions had ceased.

"*Now* who's being quiet?" I asked with a smile to lighten the suddenly heavy mood.

She took a deep breath before plopping down on the edge of my bed. Her eyes were trained on the closed door that led to the hallway and it took her a moment to speak. Seemed like that kept happening lately.

"So, I saw how upset you were after talking to Evie and it got me to thinking."

I focused on the raw nerves still exposed between Evie and I and stopped with the boxes for a moment, bracing my shoulder against the wall. "What about it?"

Roz's lips pressed into a tight line while I waited for her to finish.

She blew out a breath and blinked before looking at me. "We're friends, right?"

I chuckled. "Uh oh. That's never a good place to start."

She loosened up and smiled faintly. "Just ... answer the question."

I checked out her stiff posture when I nodded. "Yeah, we're friends."

Her cheeks tinted red. "Good. Because friends can be honest with one another, right? Even when what they have to say is, technically, not their business?"

I nodded again. "Sure."

She hesitated like before and, as she agonized about sharing, I questioned whether I should have given her the okay.

"Just seems to me that, if being around someone makes you so ... *un-you*, why not keep your distance? You broke things off, so you've got a free pass to ignore this girl when your paths cross. So, why not take advantage of that? Why not avoid the awkward conversations and the sick feeling I'm sure you have in your gut afterward?" she asked. "I only mention it because it sucks a little seeing a friend, one who's a pretty decent guy about seventy-eight-percent of the time, getting upset over a situation that should be water under the bridge."

Hearing what Evie and I once had being referred to as '*water under the bridge*' was a little sobering, but I couldn't argue with Roz's wording. Evie and I were over.

Something else Roz said hit me about ten seconds late and I

chuckled. "Wait ... I'm only a decent guy seventy-eight-percent of the time?"

She shrugged and I wasn't surprised she didn't sugarcoat her response. "It's touch and go when you're stressed, but the more I get to know you, the less I want to throat-punch you when you snap at me."

The chuckle turned into a full-on laugh.

"I've come to learn that you're just kinda intense," she reasoned. "Which isn't necessarily a bad thing, it just takes some getting used to."

Her words trailed off and she didn't look away when I thought she would have. Instead, she blinked at me with a look behind her eyes I couldn't quite place. And then, just like that, it was gone.

"So, yeah. That's pretty much all I had to say."

I didn't respond for a while, giving her suggestion some thought. Truthfully, I think I'd given her the wrong impression, somehow leading her to believe this break up—or whatever you call it when two people aren't actually in a relationship—was easier on me than it was. It was heart-wrenching, to be honest.

"So, in your opinion, I should just cut ties altogether?"

Roz took a deep breath and then went on to give an answer I wasn't expecting. "That's not really my call," she reasoned. "I'm not the one who had feelings for her, so that's something only you can decide. I guess I'm just thinking that, if I were you, I'd try to avoid the pain. And if being around her, seeing her, brought me pain ... I'd steer clear."

She had a point. It was sort of insane to keep revisiting my source of agony. However, it was a little too late to avoid Evie completely, seeing as how she was coming tonight. Now I felt obligated to give Roz a heads up, knowing she'd probably think I was crazy. Weak.

"You're a few hours too late with your advice," I blurted, realizing I was actually stalling to tell her what I'd done. I couldn't really explain what I was feeling, but I believe I didn't want to ... disappoint her maybe?

"One of the things Evie and I discussed in the hall this morning was her coming tonight."

Roz's expressions were usually pretty vague, giving very little of what she was thinking or feeling away. However, when I shared that I extended an invitation to Evie, her eyes nearly doubled in size. She was at a loss for words. Twice, her mouth opened and, both times, it snapped shut again.

"You think I'm an idiot, don't you?"

I was completely okay with her saying yes, because she'd be right.

She blinked hard, chewing her bottom lip before answering.

"No, not an idiot; you're just really hung up on her, I guess," she rambled, sounding casual, but ... not. All at the same time. "I guess I just didn't realize you were still so on the fence. When you told me everything, I was under the impression you'd already made up your mind to let go."

Gravity caused her body to shift when I sat beside her on the edge of my bed.

"My mind *is* made up," I shared, keeping my eyes trained on the striped pattern on Chris's bed beside mine. Doing so gave me something else to focus on besides Roz's blank stare. It was time to come clean about the other reason I let Evie go. It wasn't all just because we needed to find ourselves, wasn't all because of Liam.

"My feelings for her haven't changed," I shared. "The cause of the distance is about one-fourth the stuff I already told you."

"And the other three-fourths?"

The word *monster* crept into my head again, hearing it spoken in Roz's voice, and I hesitated. I usually didn't hold back from telling her things like this, but for some reason, I did tonight.

"Fear," I breathed.

She was silent, watching me.

"I'm scared of hurting her," I confessed. "Because I don't trust myself anymore."

I could see her shoulders rise with each breath she took, watching me with so much intensity I felt it. I knew I was being cryptic and it wasn't until this moment that I realized Evie wasn't the only person I didn't want to think I was some bloodthirsty beast.

I didn't want Roz to think it either.

"There's something I haven't told you."

The start of my confession made her stare intensify. Throughout this whole thing, we'd been honest with one another, minus a few minor trust issues in the very beginning. But, since then, the air had been clear.

Until now.

I hadn't shared the revelation Liam gave the night with the mutts. The term *'Liberator'* Roz knew, but she had no clue what it meant for me. However, I believed the time had come to bring her up to speed.

"I know what I am." The words were a struggle to get out. Yet, there they were, hovering in the air between Roz and I, waiting for her inquisitive side to kick in.

"You're a lycan." There was the slightest hint of hesitation in her tone when adding, "Like me."

I wanted so badly to agree, to pretend there was nothing more to it; however, I needed to be real with her right now. There weren't many people I had that privilege with, so I wouldn't taint our friendship by thinking she couldn't handle this.

"Yes, I'm a lycan, but I'm more than that."

Intrigue and concern marked her expression.

"More than that ... *how?*"

Liam's explanation was engraved in my mind, so I knew exactly how to break this down, but that didn't make it any easier.

"I've figured out what it means to be the Liberator. Or rather, I've figured out how legend says it'll affect my future. And Evie's," I added, causing Roz to tilt her head when I guessed confusion set in.

"Evie? What's any of this got to do with her?"

Air surged from my lungs when I exhaled sharply. "Everything."

The silence that entered the room was stifling.

"The legend says I'm supposed to kill her," I blurted, thinking I'd feel better once I did.

I was wrong.

"Why ... *her*? Why not *anyone?*"

I shrugged, having no earthly idea what the connection was.

Beside me, Roz clasped her hands together tightly in her lap. She was uncharacteristically quiet, so I took this time to help her understand.

"I hear her heartbeat," I admitted. "*Only* hers. All the time when she's close enough. That's part of it."

A flash of Liam's furious expression flickered inside my head as I recalled him explaining this very thing.

"It's so I can always find her, kind of like a beacon. So she can't hide. So she can't get away."

This sounded terrible, sadistic, but it was real. No, I didn't want to think or talk about it either, but thinking and talking was the only way to find a solution.

"Now you see why I asked if there's a way to fix me."

Roz took a moment to answer. "There's nothing wrong with you; therefore, there's nothing to fix."

I smiled at her attempt to make me feel better, but I think we both knew that wasn't true. There was something *very* wrong with me.

"I couldn't live with myself if I hurt someone, Roz."

Her gaze was compassionate when it met mine. "Then we'll have to make sure that doesn't happen. I won't stop looking until I find some way to control it."

I nodded and felt like a load had been lifted off me.

"Is there anything else?" she asked. "Anything I might need to know that could help?"

I thought about that for a second. "Well, I'm not sure how useful this will be, but I've been losing time." The words left my mouth in a rush because I knew the only way I'd get them out was to force them.

In my peripheral, I saw Roz's head tilt again and I knew that was the moment her brain flooded with questions.

"What do you mean '*losing time*'?"

"As in, sometimes I wake up from these ... trances, I guess, and I'm not where I last remember and have no recollection how I got there."

She looked away again, taking a breath before asking something else. "How much time are we talking?"

I shrugged. "I don't always know. Sometimes it happens while I'm awake and it's almost like I freakin' teleport from one room to another. That's how seamless it is. Once, while at my grandfather's place, I was in the living room sitting on the couch. Then, the next thing I knew, I was in the kitchen sitting at the table," I shared, despite feeling incredibly hesitant. "The only time I can actually say how long it's been is when it happens after I've gone to bed. Like last night ... I laid down around eleven, then woke up, standing in the bathroom mirror at around four—covered in dirt and grass, no memory of going topside or coming back."

I turned toward Roz now, just needing to see her face, needing to be certain she wasn't judging me.

Wasn't afraid of me.

I found neither of those things there—judgment, fear. Only curiosity, which I was okay with.

"What do you think is causing it all of a sudden?"

I shrugged. "I don't know exactly, but the thought crossed my mind that it's part of my natural evolution. Something that goes along with being the Liberator. For all I know, it's while I'm in one of these blackouts that I'll be capable of hurting Evie. It's not like I could stop myself."

Roz took another deep breath. She sat there, silent just like I was, proof that she was just as perplexed.

"We'll work on figuring it out," was the only conclusion she could offer short of making promises we both knew she couldn't keep.

I raked my fingertips down my scalp when I sighed. "You probably think I'm an idiot for having her over, considering what's been happening, don't you? Because I should be pushing her away, not trying to ... keep her close."

Roz, generally speaking, struck me as a very black and white thinker, leaving very little room for gray areas. But, lately, she'd surprised me a time or two. Like she did with her next answer.

"I think we all behave strangely when we care about someone. It can be subtle things that are just slightly out of character, things no one notices but us," she shared. "But you'll let go when you're ready."

A warm smile passed my way and some of the ice melted from her personality along with it.

I smiled back. "Thanks."

She pushed off my bed and nodded before getting back to work setting up. "No problem. That's what friends are for."

CHAPTER 15

Evie

H istorically speaking, today was supposed to be special.

However, it'd been anything but that.

I stood at Nick's door, waiting to be let in, feeling my stomach twist and turn with each passing second. The main reason being that I knew I shouldn't have come. The wounds were still too fresh, and if I was being honest, it was too soon to try being *just friends*. We were more than that in the very recent past and I wasn't really in the mood to pretend.

But I told him I'd come, so here I was.

My stomach did another somersault when the door unlatched. This time, it had nothing to do with having to pretend with Nick for the twenty or thirty minutes I intended to hang around. The sudden anxiety was because Liam could now, potentially, access my thoughts. And, although he still hadn't tapped into my sight yet, it'd be easy to figure out exactly where I was, or at least who I was with. If that happened, without a doubt, he'd think I lost my mind. He was on a quest to protect me and, to him, Nick was my biggest threat.

But I knew better.

The only person on the planet as focused on protecting me as *he* was, was Nick.

The door pulled open and I had one of those *'speak of the devil'* moments. Before me, deep blue eyes scanned me from head to toe, focusing on my exposed arms and midriff where my tank didn't cover skin.

Nick smiled. "You came."

"I did, but I'm not staying long," I added, smiling back. Luckily, he didn't question why. "And Beth's on her way. We ran into Errol outside our room and she stopped to chat, so..."

He chuckled a bit. "Don't say that too loud. Lucas has been all over that situation."

I stepped inside and laughed as Nick shut the door behind me. "Really? He's noticed they've been hanging out?"

"Are you kidding? I don't think Beth's sneezed once since middle school without Lucas noticing."

It was sweet that he cared so much for her, but sad she didn't seem to feel the same. She and Errol were getting kind of close, so it might have been a good time for Lucas to come to terms with that.

"Well, if it doesn't work out with *her,* hopefully he finds someone else." That was the most I could disclose without saying too much.

The faint smile on Nick's face told me we were thinking along the same lines.

"Have a seat," he offered, gesturing with his hand.

There was an empty chair beside the dresser and I took it. So far, it was just the two of us and Roz. She hadn't spoken since I walked in, seemingly too preoccupied with her phone. However, seeing as how we had zero service in the facility, it couldn't have been anything but a game. In other words, her indifference toward me seemed intentional.

"Hey, Roz," I called out, smiling dimly when she peered up and gave a weak one of her own. One of us had to be the bigger person, I guessed.

"Hey," was all she said back, and the chill attached to it solidified a fleeting theory I had about her from the beginning. At the time, I thought I might have been mistaken, overthinking things in the way I sometimes do, but I'd seen the way she was around Nick. How she always treated me like I was interrupting something, like I was in her way. How she shut down when I was around.

She liked him. As more than a friend. Nick might not have picked up on it yet because guys are sometimes late with these things, but, from one girl to another, I saw it plain as day.

She'd gone back to her phone screen right after the halfhearted greeting and I pretended not to notice. Three bodies burst through the door, out of breath, laughing as they cradled duffle bags against their chests like they carried small children.

"Did someone see you?" Nick asked.

Lucas shook his head. "Only a couple kids, but we bribed them with free pop, so we're all clear."

One by one, colorful bottles were taken from the bags and arranged on the desk against the far wall.

The space was a little smaller than Beth's and mine, and there were more beds—two single and a bunk bed to accommodate all four of the guys. It was neat at the moment, but that was most likely only because they were expecting company today. There were snacks everywhere, though. Like, a *ton*.

"You guys scored all this stuff from the vending machines?" I asked.

Nick shook his head. "Only the drinks. The snacks have been flowing in daily from our parents. Turns out, if you complain enough about feeling like you're in prison, it tugs on their heart strings and it's pretty easy to get whatever you want."

"Like a new laptop for gaming," Chris interjected with a grin, pointing at the one resting on his nightstand.

I scanned it all—the snacks, the gadgets.

"Have yours been sending you a bunch of stuff?"

Nick's question made a breath hitch in my throat. "Uh ... no. They haven't sent anything."

He dismissed my response with a casual shrug before going on. "Between the four of us, feels like that phone never stops ringing." He pointed at the one mounted on the wall near the door.

The landlines and a shaky wi-fi connection were our only links to the outside world. The staff had separate internet access with a much stronger signal, but we weren't allowed to use it.

"It's mostly *Chris's* mom who calls, but she sends a ton of care packages, so I'm not complaining about that," he added.

I forced a smile, trying to ignore how all this talk of phone calls and care packages made my heart ache, but ignoring it was impossible. Especially considering the date. Yeah, today, more than usual, it stung that the one time me and Beth's landline rung was when *her* parents called to check in on her.

Not mine.

Outside this facility, everyone had someone they were connected to, someone who thought about them throughout the day, someone who missed them.

But not me.

"Sounds like you all have a pretty sweet setup," I said with a fake grin.

Nick grabbed me a drink and smiled. "It works out."

A knock at the door abruptly ended the conversation and I was glad for it. Beth walked in looking like an ad in a magazine for teen girls. Her cheeks were tinged red and I had a feeling Errol had something to do with that. Right after her, a few others arrived—boys from our football team back home, some of Beth's teammates, too. Within ten minutes, there was hardly even room to stand.

While, to most, the party was just getting started, I couldn't wait to leave. I felt boxed in and it had nothing to do with all the bodies in the room. Mostly, the clutter was inside my head. Nick hadn't left my side since I arrived and I was very much aware of Roz taking note of that, too. When I leaned in and cupped my hand around his ear to make sure he heard me over the music, my eyes locked with Roz's. She hurried to look away, but not quick enough that I didn't see her.

"I'm gonna take off."

There were clear signs of disappointment in Nick's expression when he turned toward me—tension in his brow, a waning smile. However, he didn't press, which I appreciated. Hopefully, he understood this wasn't easy for me, even if he didn't know the difficulty went beyond our breakup. He had no idea I was currently estranged from my parents and being here was a loud, blaring reminder of the separation.

"Okay, well ... I'm glad you stopped in."

I nodded as we stood and then walked toward the door. When we got there, there was an awkward moment where I don't think either of us knew whether to hug, shake hands, or just part ways.

I thought a handshake seemed like a happy medium, so I settled on that. He didn't seem put off by it.

"Do you need me to walk you to your room?"

"No, you should stay here," I smiled. "You can't leave your own party."

The look on his face told me he wouldn't have minded if I wanted him to.

"I guess I'll see you in class tomorrow, then."

I nodded. "Cool. Thanks again for the invite."

I stepped out then, feeling like I'd suffocate if I didn't. As I put distance between myself and the crowd, I was aware of Nick's eyes on me until I rounded the corner. The second I was out of his line of sight, I breathed deep, letting the weight of loneliness fall on me like a bag of sand I'd been carrying above my head all day. And this moment felt like I finally got to rest my arms.

I was sad.

I was lost.

I was broken.

And I didn't feel like pretending I was okay all the time. Truth be told, I was anything *but* okay. And the salt in the wound was the fact that my birth mother, a woman I thought only existed in a past life that felt more like a dream than reality, was within walking distance.

Only, she was no dream. As far as I was concerned, she was responsible for this entire nightmare, right down to the pain of losing my parents, albeit a temporary arrangement. The fact still remained that, for the time being, I had no family, widening the void that already existed within me.

I was about halfway to my room when the burning started. It was my hands, they were on fire, but it wasn't supposed to hurt—hadn't since the first time I shifted. Panic struck much like it had that unforgettable night in the woods, deepening as the flames spread up my arms to my elbows. And also like that night in the woods, I felt a tug toward Liam. The first time, I didn't realize that was where I was being led, but tonight it was clear as I bypassed my own door and didn't stop until I reached his.

I wanted to scream out, begging him to answer; wanted to yell for him to hurry as my heart raced. I held my hands before me, completely useless as they blazed. Seconds before I kicked the door to let him know I needed him, he snatched it open, shirtless, buttoning a pair of jeans because, apparently, when he was alone, clothing was always optional.

At the sight of my body going up in flames, he didn't say a word, just let me rush inside, and then he locked up behind me. There was always this look of anguish on his face whenever I was in trouble, and it was there now.

"I don't ... I don't know what happened. I was walking and ... it just started and ... I don't ..." My entire body shook as I burned. The sting wasn't as intense as if I'd touched the stove or let a match burn down to my skin, but I felt it enough that it made my heartrate climb.

I wasn't sure what I expected Liam to do, but I knew he was the only one who could fix this, the only one who could ever save me from myself.

"Stop talking," he asserted when I started rambling again. My lips stopped moving right away when his hands settled on my waist. At the first tug, I realized he intended to bring me closer and stopped him.

"You can't!" I protested. "I'll burn you! The flames are different ... I can feel it."

And see it.

Instead of the brilliant orange and white I'd seen before, these were a peculiar shade of turquoise. While the average person would have heeded my warning, Liam kept his eyes trained on mine, silently acknowledging the risk.

It also became crystal clear he didn't care as he brought me into his arms anyway.

We stood chest to chest as my body fit to his, like pieces of a puzzle—the soft lines of my own forming against the hard lines of his in an embrace. His skin sizzled and the sound of it caused me to lean away, glancing where my arms rested around his shoulders, where my cheek pressed to his neck. The flesh had burned away, leaving the edges of blackened wounds trimmed in glowing, turquoise embers to match my flames.

I was ... hurting him.

I wouldn't have known had I not heard the sizzle, had I not seen the evidence for myself, because he didn't make a sound, didn't pull away.

"Liam, I—"

The words, "Trust me, Evangeline," touched my ears and I heard the strain in them, confirming that this was at least as painful for him as I guessed it was. And yet ... he kept me close.

My eyes searched his, wondering what on Earth would make a man put himself through this. I imagined the burn to be sheer torture, and yet he seemed content to endure it. That's when a word pierced my flesh like an arrow, shooting straight from his heart into mine.

Love.

That's what made him do it.

That's what made it seem so easy.

He loved me.

I'd never heard him utter the phrase, but there was no denying that I felt it.

His jaw gritted and I fought against the action that felt natural—the urge to release him, to free him of the torture I brought unintentionally. Instead, I leaned in again and, feeling a sudden rush of calmness, I closed my eyes, letting him take it away.

We stayed that way, holding one another, for more than a minute. And, when my lids lifted again, the flames were gone completely. Staring at his sun-kissed complexion, it had already begun to heal. Tattered, charred skin faded in small sections and, eventually, there was no evidence at all.

My eyes traced the outline of his jaw and then his lips as we kept one another close, panting from the rush of adrenaline as smoke dissipated into the air around us. When it cleared, I saw him differently than before. The change wasn't physical. I'd simply never seen strength like his. It went beyond bravery, went beyond ego and testosterone. Liam was just an incredible, extraordinary being.

'Kiss him.'

The voice that filled my head was mine, but ... *not*.

The feeling that came along with it was urgent. It was the dragon within me. More than usual, that part of who I am was desperate for him, like I needed to get closer; as close as humanly possible.

Close in ways I'd never gotten close to any other guy before.

Ever.

The impulse came on so strongly it startled me. I took my hands off him, leaving his back to cool where they were once planted. My eyes never left his, though. His prominent brow hooded his stare, making his natural expression so intense—a constant reminder of the fierce warrior he was, and still is. The sweet demeanor I knew to exist within him was, I believed, something only I could see. Maybe that was the way he wanted it. Maybe that was the way it was supposed to be. To the rest of the world, old and new, he was a force to be reckoned with, a force to be feared.

198

The Reaper.

But with me, he was loyal, and gentle, and caring, and ... all those things worked against me as that small voice whispered again.

'He's the only thing that matters. The only thing that's ever mattered.'

I took a deep breath and ignored the words as they fluttered into my thoughts, praying the heat lingering between Liam and I would evaporate like the turquoise-tinted smoke a moment ago.

The couch was nearby, but I didn't sit. Instead, I stood with my arms crossed in front of my torso, looking everywhere but at him.

"What ... was that?" I mumbled sheepishly. "The flames; they were different. *Felt* different."

I held myself tight while waiting for an answer. It was the only thing I could do to keep from reaching for him.

"It's a trait you inherited," he explained. "Only the original dragon and her descendants have ever burned that way."

"But why the strange color? Is it some kind of a phase? Is something wrong with me?"

Liam let his back rest against the wall as his arms folded over his bare chest, drawing my eyes there when he spoke again.

"No, there's nothing wrong with you. When you burn turquoise, you're more powerful and you're burning at a higher temp." His expression didn't change when he went on. "Typically, for the rest of our species to take the life of another dragon, we have to break the neck, remove or pierce the heart, but ... for the original, for descendants, it's a little different."

My eyes narrowed when he added more. "Along with the added strength that comes with the turquoise flames, is the ability to burn other dragons to death. It's not the point of them, but more of a side effect."

I swallowed a surge of air when I inhaled deeply. "So, I ... could've killed you just now?" I stared, finding it hard to believe he'd stood there and let me cling to him, knowing what I could've done.

I had zero control over myself and wouldn't have been able to stop if it got out of hand.

"Liam, why would you ... why wouldn't you stop me. I—"

"Because you won't hurt me," he interjected.

"But I *did* hurt you." I recalled the burns I left behind on his skin before they healed.

He shrugged and it was so casual. Like he had this inexplicable belief that no harm would come to him by my hand.

"I guess I just trust you. Like you trust me," he reasoned.

And I did trust him. More than I trusted myself lately.

I glanced back toward Liam when he moved to the couch. "Would you like to sit?"

My gaze landed there, in the spot beside him, and my steps were reluctant as I moved closer. He had no clue how I was struggling physically just being in the same room with him. I was, literally, aching to get closer, knowing I couldn't let that happen.

I was stiff and uncomfortable when I sat with an empty cushion between us.

"What happened tonight?"

If I'd been eating or drinking, the question would've made me choke for sure. I couldn't tell him where I'd been. Not because he'd be jealous, but because he'd be angry. Nick was the last person he wanted me around and I'd gone right into the lion's den. But I was able to leave that part out because my issue went beyond being in Nick's room tonight.

"I guess I was just thinking too much, and ... I don't know," I added with a shrug. "I'm a little tired of feeling invisible."

Liam leaned forward, letting his elbows rest on his knees as he watched the floor. For a split second, I thought I might've hurt his feelings, might've made him feel like having him here wasn't enough, then I remembered who I was talking to—a man who knew me inside and out. I had to trust he knew this was about my parents.

"Today's my birthday," I shared. "Well, according to you, it's not my *real* birthday, but it's the day I've been celebrating these past eighteen years."

It was Liam who revealed that the date reflected on my birth certificate was inaccurate, that Nick and I had to have come into existence simultaneously—the night of the super harvest moon in September. However, November 10th was the day I was accustomed to celebrating.

Only, this year, no one remembered.

Because no one who knew remembered *me*.

"I'm sorry," Liam said solemnly. "I had no idea."

I waved him off with a casual smile. "How could you have? It's fine."

My eyes followed him when he stood from the couch, headed for his dresser. He took a bag from the top drawer. When he came back and handed it over, I eyed him.

"I didn't know today was important, but I still thought of you."

My smile grew a little bigger. Not because I had any kind of expectations for what was inside, but because he thought of me *at all*.

Peering into the bag, I laughed. "Candy!"

He smiled. "Yeah, we've got all the good stuff a few floors up in one of the staff lounges. I figured I'd stock you up."

It was so strange that he knew something so trivial about me, that I had a penchant for sweets, but it was nice to feel like someone did, in fact, know me.

Nice to be reminded that I hadn't disappeared.

The smile on his face warmed a bit. I stared while his eyes wandered toward mine, only after leaving my lips. When he came back with the bag, neither of us had been mindful of the space I intentionally left between us before. It was nonexistent now and I felt it.

Felt him.

His heat.

His soul.

A large hand came toward me slowly, and despite knowing I

should have, I didn't pull away. It rested on the side of my neck. Liam's thumb stroked the tender flesh behind my ear and it felt like all the air had left the room when he spoke.

"I know having me around will never make up for not having your parents, but ... you're not alone," he breathed. "Not here. Not anywhere."

Like always, he got to me. So much so, I had to look away, accidentally turning my face into his hand where my lips brushed his palm. The contact made my eyes drift closed as his fingers slipped further back, into my hair. He didn't pull me closer, but I wasn't sure I wouldn't have let him if he tried.

I was so on fire for him. Something about his touch always made me feel beautiful and complete without him having to say anything. I didn't think such a thing was possible before finding him.

"You're tense," he observed. "I was always pretty good at helping you relieve stress when you needed to. I can still do that *now* if you're open to it."

Liam's husky voice made my eyes pop open when those words sent my thoughts stampeding in one direction, and one direction only —toward the gutter. His expression was surprisingly calm and collected. Meanwhile, I felt myself starting to sweat along my hairline.

"I um ... I don't think we ... Maybe ..." I stood midsentence, moving toward the door as heat crept up my legs and back. I seemed to always be running from him, from the things he made me feel.

"I'm gonna go," I blurted.

Liam stood, too, but when a deep line creased at the center of his brow, I got the impression my sudden attempt to flee confused him.

"Did I say something wrong?"

I paused, hating myself when my feet stopped moving. I should've been halfway to my room by now. I exhaled sharply and let my eyes fall closed while I wrestled with two warring arguments contending inside me. One telling me to run away from there as quickly as I could. The other urging me to stick around and see what happened next.

I couldn't, though.

We couldn't.

"If we ... you know ... it would blur too many lines," I said in a rush. "I just think that, for now, we have too many other things we need to focus on."

I finished speaking and expected to open my eyes to find disappointment on Liam's face.

Not a smile as he rubbed the back of his neck, trying to keep from laughing.

"I, uh ... was thinking more along the lines of us meeting early to spar. I thought we might kill two birds with one stone—get some moves under your belt, and also let you blow off some steam," he explained, making me wish there was a black hole for me to jump into at the moment. Anything to save me the embarrassment of putting my big, stupid foot in my mouth.

Of course he hadn't meant ... *that.*

I covered my face with both hands and there was no point in trying to pretend I wasn't embarrassed. "Oh my gosh ... I thought you meant ... Oh my gosh."

The sound of Liam laughing while I stared at the insides of my eyelids nearly killed me.

"I need to point out that you didn't seem totally against the idea, though," he joked, barely getting the words out as he chuckled.

"Oh my gosh," I mumbled into my palms again. "You weren't clear and ... you're a guy, so ... I just assumed you meant ... *that,* but ... clearly, you didn't. I'm ... oh my gosh. I'm so sorry."

I felt like such an idiot for thinking he'd be anything but a perfect gentleman.

His fingers looped around my wrists and slowly pulled my hands away from my face. I couldn't look at him, but felt him staring right through me.

"Don't apologize," he insisted. "If it makes you feel any better, right after the words left my mouth, that's exactly where my mind went, too, so ... "

I smiled big, and probably blushed a bunch, too, hearing him admit that.

"If *both* our minds are a little dirty, there's nothing to be embarrassed about," he added.

His stare persisted and I finally gave in to meet his gaze, feeling heat spread across my face again when I did. Happened every time.

"It's not a big deal," he smiled. "So, you'll meet me in the morning?"

I took a deep breath, considering the offer—the *real* offer—and then nodded. I definitely needed the one-on-one time before our next combat module began in a couple weeks.

"Okay, yeah," I replied, chewing the side of my lip to keep from grinning again as he continued to hold my wrists. "I'll meet you."

It was impossible to deny the relief I felt when giving in to him. His smile broadened and he sealed the deal. "Four a.m."

CHAPTER 16

Evie

I did my best to move around our room without waking Beth, but when a headful of messy, blonde hair lifted from her pillow, it meant I failed.

"I'm so sorry," I whispered.

It was, literally, not even the crack of dawn yet, but I was due to meet Liam in less than ten minutes. That would give us an hour for him to show me whatever he could before I needed to be back here for another shower. Then, we *both* had to get to his class.

Beth rubbed her eyes and sat up instead of turning back over like I would have. "Where the heck are *you* sneaking off to?"

I wasn't sneaking, per se, but I definitely hadn't planned on getting caught. I even hoped to get back to our room before she woke up. Specifically, to avoid this question.

My lack of a timely answer earned me a suspicious glare from Beth's half-opened eyes. I had to say something.

"Uh, just kind of a tutoring thing," I stammered, tying one black sneaker before moving on to the other.

"A tutoring thing?" The question was dripping with sarcasm and I knew I hadn't convinced her that my leaving out this early was innocent.

Although it was.

Completely.

When she smiled and leaned against her headboard, I wasn't expecting her to say what left her mouth next.

"Yeah, right. You're meeting Nick, aren't you? He looked kinda sad when you left the party early last night."

I stood from the bed and slipped the elastic band from around my wrist to pull my hair up.

"Um ... no. It really is a tutoring thing," I said quietly. "I'm getting some training before we move on to the next combat module." I did my best to make that sound as uninteresting as possible. Deep down, in the part of my psyche I couldn't control, I didn't want Beth to tag along.

I wanted it to just be Liam and I.

Being here ate up a lot of our time. I had responsibilities and so did he. That shouldn't have felt like such an inconvenience, but ... it did. If I was being honest, I was looking forward to this morning for many reasons, but one of them was definitely just that I wanted to hang out with him.

When it was just us, he was softer. He had so many stories and details about my past, I could listen to him talk all day and never get bored or tired of hearing his voice.

My thoughts snagged on that confession—the fact that I liked hearing him speak, the fact that I found the depth and confidence mesmerizing at times.

Beth was quiet. Too quiet.

"Is this '*tutoring thing*' with Liam?" she asked.

I wished I could have seen her face through the darkness, but I purposely kept most of the lights off. The only one keeping me from tripping over my own feet was the dim glow from the closet.

Was she wearing one of those judgey, parent faces right now?

I wasn't sure what to say, so I went with the truth.

"Yeah. Actually, it is."

She was quiet for a bit, but then asked a follow-up question that made her suspicion a little clearer.

"If it's combat training, shouldn't you be meeting with Dallas, Kas, or Martinez?" There was a long pause. "I thought Liam's specialty was history."

I didn't say a word, just continued to braid the ponytail I just secured.

"Relax," Beth said with a laugh as she plopped back down on her pillow. "I'm just giving you a hard time."

I let out the breath I'd been holding in.

Tiptoeing around Beth had been so difficult. Liam and I weren't anything certain or solid other than friends, but I'll be the first to admit our connection was strangely deep and hard to understand. I was sure people, other than me, had to have noticed it.

But I was extra careful around Beth, and that sucked. Not only was she incredibly observant, she was also the best friend I'd made since moving to Seaton Falls. And what complicated the situation more was the fact that she and Nick were friends long before I came onto the scene.

In other words, I had no idea where her loyalty lie.

I was sure the answer to that question was now, and would always be: both. However, I couldn't expect her to understand this thing with Liam.

He was nothing to me and ... *everything.*

He was, literally, the only thing my soul couldn't seem to stop wanting no matter how hard I fought against it.

"How long ago did you know him?" she asked, catching me off guard with the somewhat invasive question. No, it wouldn't have been under *normal* circumstances, but ours were anything but normal.

"We, uh ... not long before I moved here," I lied. She didn't leave me much of a choice.

Beth knew Liam's age—his *real* age—because he revealed it to us in class. But I also knew she was more knowledgeable than many of the others, myself included. Age, within our races, was relative. Still, even if she was making allowances for that, she didn't need to. His age, in comparison to mine, wasn't strange. My soul had been around for nearly nine-hundred years just like his. He was old, but so was I.

A reality I still hadn't wrapped my head around.

"So, I take it you and Nick are really over?"

I swallowed the hurt that rose in my throat when she brought him up again. "Honestly? I don't know what to think anymore. Things just got *really* complicated, *really* quickly."

At the risk of her thinking the only complication was Liam, I kept my mouth shut. I hadn't gone into detail about what Nick was, or what any of that meant for me. Partly, because that was for him to share when he was ready. Partly, because I didn't want to talk about it. With how close we had become, I never would've guessed we'd be so distant, basically living under the same roof.

Ironic.

When I didn't add more, Beth sighed and I turned her way as her bed creaked a little. She was sitting up again, but I couldn't make out her expression. Only her silhouette against the light coming from the closet.

"You know you don't have to be all cryptic with me, right?"

I played dumb. "I know. There's just nothing to tell."

It was clear my response pissed her off a little because she sighed again, and I imagined her rolling her eyes this time.

"It's just ... I know you and Nick were friends first and—"

"Dude, stop," she cut in. "Yeah, Nick and I are cool, but it's mostly because we've known each other all our lives and support each other when it comes to sports, but we're *all* supportive in that way."

I listened, but didn't say anything yet. Maybe still feeling a bit skeptical.

"In case you haven't noticed, you're kinda one of my favorite people, so I'm gonna need you to loosen up," she said with a chuckle. "Nick's a decent guy, but you're one of the best friends I've got, Evie."

Her words hit me right in the heart. We clicked from day one, but I was sure I clung to her more than she clung to me. She had family and friends and teammates, but apparently, she counted me among those she cared about as well.

Hearing her say this would have meant a lot under *any* circumstances, but considering the current state of my life, I needed to hear it.

"So, we agree it's time you stop walking on eggshells around me, right?"

"Agreed."

I nodded, feeling like a load had been lifted off me with this unexpected conversation. Beth didn't know all I'd lost, but she had definitely made my time here a lot less lonely than it would've been.

I checked the time. Liam was probably already waiting in the hall.

"Ok, I'm out. Get some sleep. Sorry again for waking you," I said in a rush as I slipped my ID tag around my neck.

Her head hit the pillow with a thud. "No worries, but I'm gonna hold a grudge for last night until your *grandkids* have grandkids," she said with a laugh.

With my hand on the door, I turned toward her, unsure of what she meant. "Because I left the party early?"

She yawned, so I had to wait for an answer. "No. For talking my freakin' ear off in your sleep."

Hearing that, I temporarily forgot I was running late.

"Wait, I was talking? What the heck did I say?" I laughed, but was honestly nervous I might've mumbled something stupid or embarrassing.

"Couldn't tell you," she sighed, getting situated beneath her comforter. "I don't speak French."

I thought I misheard her. "French?"

"Sounded like it to me. I mean, I only completed one semester of it a couple years ago, but I'm pretty sure." She got quiet, but then laughed. "You went on so long and I couldn't wake you, so I got my phone out and recorded some of it. Partly because I knew you wouldn't believe me, but mostly it was for future blackmail opportunities," she joked.

"But I don't ... speak French."

She was quiet and so was I.

I took my phone from my back pocket. It would have been easiest to ask her to send the recording right to me, but the lack of service we had here made that impossible.

"Play it for me. Maybe if I record it, someone can translate."

And by 'someone', I meant Liam. He mentioned moving around a lot and I had to imagine that meant he also picked up a few languages along the way. With any luck, French was one of them.

Beth groaned when she had to get up again. Her phone glowed in her hand when she unlocked the screen and walked toward me with heavy, sleep-deprived steps. She held her cell to mine and I was speechless as we both listened to my voice flowing from her speaker.

Fear hummed inside me. It felt like that uncomfortable, low frequency vibration that creeps over your skin when entering a room where a television has been left on. To hear yourself speaking a language you've never been taught, it was beyond unnerving. If I didn't need to take this to Liam, I would've asked Beth to turn it off.

"See?" she said when it finally ended. "French."

There was no denying she was right, but I had no clue how to explain it. Over the years, I'd taken Spanish, but even when it came to that, I hadn't advanced past the basics.

I mumbled a distracted, "Thanks," and purposely left before she could start asking questions.

Elise, my mother, came from a small village in France. It was likely that I was fluent in my past, but what did it mean that parts of that life, bits and pieces of who I used to be, were beginning to bleed through into my *current* life?

I thought again about the bluish-green flames that sent me running to Liam last night. The ones he explained were a latent ability most dragons didn't possess. That, too, seemed like a sign I was changing.

When I emerged from my room and laid eyes on Liam where he leaned against the opposite wall, I nearly jumped out of my skin. I was expecting him, but I was still stuck on the conversation I just had with Beth. I quickly traded the tense expression I wore for a smile. I'd tell him about the recording later. Not now.

"Been waiting long?" I asked, feeling myself warm up to him almost as soon as I put the other thoughts aside.

The smile he returned was more natural than my own. He pushed away from the wall and we fell into a slow, even-paced stroll toward the gym before he answered.

"Well, if you're asking if I've been standing outside your door long, the answer is no. However, if you were to ask *in general*," he teased, "I'd have a very different answer."

A gentle flutter in my stomach made me wish I hadn't asked. From the corner of my eye, I looked him over—a pair of the dark cargo pants and black boots all staff wore, but he'd decided against the logoed t-shirt they issued. Instead, a gray, ribbed tank that hugged the ridges of his chest and crags of his abdomen tightly.

The exposed ink on his arms reminded me of the first night I visited him in my dreams on purpose. I still remembered the meanings of each. Next, my eyes settled on the two leather bands on his wrist. They were latched with a peculiar knot and I couldn't remember a time I'd seen him without them. Not even before we technically met.

Back when he was simply some random guy I dreamed about.

Back before I knew he was significant.

Important.

"Feeling okay?"

The question had me nodding profusely to cover my tracks. I needed him to see me as nothing but brave this morning as we went to spar. If he knew my mind was in a thousand different places he'd make me talk about it and I didn't want that right now.

"Yes! Perfect," I added with a smile. "You?"

He seemed to buy the act. "No complaints. I've been trying to figure out where we should start. There's a lot of ground to cover."

I laughed. "Especially seeing as how I have the self-defense skills of a gnat."

He laughed, too, but he shook his head in disagreement. "You've just gotta learn. It'll come more naturally than you think it will. Mostly, I've been trying to decide if our focus needs to be on combat or the abilities you possess in your shifted form."

I had a preference, so I voiced it. "I need to know how to shift on my own."

The last time I turned completely was the night we stood against the mutts. And, then, the only way I managed to turn was with a bit of ... *help* from Liam.

That kiss, the only one ever shared between us, made me breathe heavier every time I thought about it.

"Then, it's settled," he replied. "We'll focus on that and then move on to something else next time."

I nearly grinned when he said that. *Next time.* It meant we'd be doing this more often than just today, and I liked the sound of it.

We were quite a ways from our quarters in the Gold Sector and almost to the gym. Rounding the corner, I think Liam and I were *both* shocked to see Mei, the monitor who occupied the room beside mine, coming toward us. It was early, but, apparently, some of the staff walked the halls at this hour, probably to make sure no one got out of line.

Mei's eyes flickered toward me when the three of us stopped. However, it was Liam she focused on before speaking. "Good morning."

He seemed way more relaxed than she did. "Morning."

Mei's face twitched as she took in Liam's nonchalant attitude, leaving me with the distinct impression she believed she *'caught'* us.

Like, he and I weren't supposed to be walking around the facility right now. I *also* believed she thought Liam was getting ready to make an excuse for why we were together at this hour. Instead, all he did was respond to her greeting.

"Well, *you* two are certainly up early," she said with a forced grin. "Shouldn't you still be asleep, young lady?" That part was addressed to me.

"I ... well, we ..."

"We're headed to the gym," Liam cut in, saving me from myself. "We know each other from before, so I offered to help her with a few things."

He seemed irritated having to explain. I had a feeling that, had it not been for *me* still being in the position of having to answer to these people, Liam would've ignored her prying altogether.

Mei only seemed slightly less suspicious, but honestly, it wouldn't have been her business if there *was* more to whatever Liam and I were up to. This wasn't a school by any traditional means; therefore, traditional rules didn't apply. The evergreen nature of shifters made the concept of age less black and white than with humans. And, if her issue was that I, a student, was going to be alone with Liam, an instructor, then that wouldn't hold up either.

Yes, he'd gotten roped into sharing his knowledge with the young shifters here, but he always made it very clear to me, and everyone else, his main focus and priority was me.

I tried to ignore the way pride seemed to swell in my chest when I acknowledged this. There was something about knowing he, this fear-less warrior from the past, this man who went full-on machine when it came to battle, was so in tune with me. I breathed deep to dispel the buzz that followed.

"Well, have a good one," Liam said dismissively, making it clear he cared very little what she thought as he placed his hand at the small of my back. When we passed Mei, I was sure her eyes were glued to that very spot, assuming whatever she wanted about the nature of me and Liam's relationship.

We came to the gym and I stood quietly while Liam unlocked it with the swipe of a card. His looked different from those the other instructors carried. Most were white with a blue *'Damascus Facility'* logo in the center. His, solid black with a silver logo.

The dark space came to life with the flip of a switch and then the door closed behind us. Our steps echoed against the hard surfaces of the walls and floor without there being extra bodies around to absorb some of the sound. Liam had me stretch and I did so while watching him unroll the large, blue mat in the center.

He was hard *not* to watch.

His hair was down today, and I came so close to telling him I prefer it that way, but who was I to say such a thing? To have a preference? Why was I even thinking like that? Today was about honing my skills, or rather, *finding* my skills. Seeing as how I had none.

Get focused, girl.

My mind needed to be less fixated on what a beautiful work of man-art Liam was, and more on how to, you know, not die. Should things actually get as bad as we've been told they could in the near future, I'm guessing not dying would be a useful skill.

I'd loosened up and was back on my feet. I met Liam in the center of the mat and did everything I could to ignore the twisting and turning in my gut. The last thing I wanted to do was embarrass myself in front of him, but this was the only way I'd learn—letting him see how clumsy and awkward I was.

"Okay, we'll start by closing our eyes," he instructed.

His lids lowered and then mine.

"Breathe deep and focus on the sound of it."

Several surges of air filled my lungs and I pushed them out slowly. With each one, I made myself set aside all I was carrying—the sadness, the fear, the anxiety. There was no place for any of it here. Not if I stood a chance at getting this right.

"Keep your hands at your sides," he said next. I wiggled my fingers. "There's a pulse of energy in your hands. It's always there. It's subtle enough to ignore when you want to, but you should feel it."

A slight thrumming in my palms made me nod. "I do."

"Good. That's where your energy is centered. It's why most of us, when we experience the initial shift, our hands catch first. It was like that for your mother, too, when she turned the children in Ars-en-Ré."

At mention of Elise, I lost a bit of focus. I didn't want to think about her. Actually, I'd gone out of my way not to let her occupy space inside my head, because she didn't deserve it.

Releasing another deep breath, I pushed Liam's reference aside, letting it drop off with everything else.

"Let that sensation spread through your fingertips, up your arm..."

A bright glow penetrated my eyelids and I opened them. "Oh snap! I freakin' did it!"

Smiling, Liam opened his eyes, too.

I couldn't believe it worked. I half expected today to be a complete failure, but I managed to get it right on the first try.

"Good. Now see if you can get it to stretch to your shoulders, but stop there."

I stared at the base of the flames where they rose from my skin, and somehow willed them to go further. A huge grin had my cheeks aching as I watched them do exactly *what* I wanted, *when* I wanted.

A far cry from the random outbursts I experienced in the recent past.

i.e. last night.

"Can I go further?" I asked, sounding like a kid asking her parent for permission to ride her bike all the way around the block.

Liam laughed. "Of course. If you're comfortable."

Warmth moved over my skin and the flames followed. My chest, my neck, until I was completely covered. My clothes were intact this time, too, which was no small feat.

"Now, see if you can extinguish them on your own," were his next instructions.

That part was a bit trickier. He noticed I had trouble and smiled again. "Just… relax. That's the first step."

I recalled how safe and comfortable I felt when he held me last night. That had been the key to putting the flames out then, and was essential now, too.

"Let yourself remember the control you just exuded to ignite. Remember, you commanded them to move from one part of your body to the next. Because they *are* you," he added. Those words resonated with me and put things into perspective.

I could control them because they *were* me.

My face was the first thing to cool, then my neck, shoulders and chest. Everything else followed, leaving only my hands to burn a few seconds longer. Traces of smoke thinned and disappeared and all that was left behind was the huge grin on my face.

"Very cool," I beamed.

Liam nodded. "I can honestly say it never gets old."

I imagined that to be true. I felt alive and free in ways I didn't otherwise. I felt like, when I shifted, I was myself. More *'me'* than any other time, and I remembered Liam once stating that my shifted form was my true form.

"So, when do I get to fly?" I asked.

The question made him laugh, but I didn't see anything funny. "Baby steps."

There was a twinge of disappointment when he shot down the idea, but I guessed it was kind of soon to trust myself hundreds of feet in the air. It'd be my luck to get distracted by something shiny on the ground and plummet back to Earth.

"But maybe you can fly with *me* one day in the meantime." I blinked when he offered. "It might not be as exhilarating as attempting it on your own, but it'll at least give you a feel for what it's like being up there."

I tried to imagine it.

"I mean, if you're comfortable being carried, that is," he added with a chuckle. "I'd put you on my back, but, you know ... wings."

It wasn't lost on me how I got all topsy-turvy on the inside when he did the slightest things. This time, it was the boyish grin he gave. The one that made his eyes crinkle in the corners, warming the hardened glare that usually resided there. Sometimes, he was just too much to handle and it was usually with little to no effort. Like now.

"It'd be fun," I answered, distracted by the imagery of him holding me close while we rose above the tall trees I'd seen topside.

I had to look away from him. "Can you help me with the combat stuff now?"

He seemed just as distracted when he nodded. I stretched my neck again, needing to regain focus.

Liam set his feet apart and crouched, lowering his center of gravity like a football player bracing himself as his opponent charged toward him.

"Come at me."

The words caught me off guard. I was expecting to be taught how to throw a punch, not how to throw myself at a brick wall. That'd always been my perception of him. Not only because of his size. He just seemed impenetrable. Solid. Indestructible.

Loose, dark waves that curled slightly at the ends swept his shoulders. He stared expectantly and one corner of his mouth tugged up with a smile. "Ready whenever you are."

I sucked in a breath, trying to shift my mindset. Running into his arms *this* time had nothing to do with how part of me always wanted to be in them. This was a training exercise and I had to make that sink in. Once it did, I darted toward him. His expression stayed calm and even because, at half his size, I wasn't any kind of threat.

I got about a foot away and was snatched right off my feet by my waist. I breathed wildly as he held me against him—my back to his chest and stomach as I dangled in the air. If I'd been a guy, it would've been humiliating how easily he overpowered me, but ... as a girl ... it was only frustrating.

He set me down. "Again."

With a huff and both hands on my waist, I faced him. "Why? I'm never gonna get you down on this mat," I reasoned.

Not that I minded the trying part all that much.

"Not as long as you *think* you can't," he countered.

We stood there, locked in a stare-down until I gave in. "Fine."

I went back to my post and Liam took his stance. I focused on that energy source he brought to my attention a moment ago, the one that pulsated in my hands. Drawing from that, I clenched my fists and rocketed toward him. I had plans to shove my shoulder against his chest, but instead of tackling him to the mat, the room turned upside down. After a moment of disorientation, I realize I'd been captured again. This time, he tossed me over his shoulder and held me there. If I'd been an actual opponent, I was positive he would've dropped me on my back, but the one thing I knew he'd never do was hurt me.

With his arm locked behind my knees, I hung over his back. It dawned on me as I stared at my braid swinging above my head ... he was laughing.

The sound of it burned through the frustration.

"Glad I can amuse you." The words came out strained due to there being a huge shoulder pressed into my abdomen.

"You'll get the hang of it," he promised.

I wasn't so sure.

Two large hands were placed on my back as he crouched to the ground, setting my feet on the mat. Next, those same hands rested on my hips as he made sure I was steady before backing away. His tattoos were glistening and I gave myself points for at least making him break a sweat. Lord knows I didn't accomplish much else.

"Let's sit while you catch your breath," he suggested and, seeing as how I was winded from failure, I didn't object.

We stepped up onto the bleachers and propped our feet on the row just below us. Like always, he sat close and I was starting to get used to it. I hardly remembered the time when he felt like a stranger. It was more like we were old friends who lost touch for a while, but had recently reconnected. I guess that was almost accurate, only, I knew we were once much more than friends.

I stared at his hands—elbows on knees, fingers loosely interlaced. *Love. Lost. Never. Dies.*

The tattoos between his digits used to be a mystery to me, but I was now positive they spoke of the bond we once shared before my first life was taken.

Our love was what never died.

My eyes trailed past the compass with veins and tendons beneath it that made the ink seem to come alive on his skin. My gaze settled on the leather bands on his wrist again. Without thinking, I reached to touch them. His head shifted there the second my fingertips made contact.

"Are these important to you?" I asked, recalling how they'd always been a part of my visions of him, although I never thought to ask if they meant anything.

When he didn't answer right away, I looked at his face, catching a fleeting glimpse of sadness before he quickly hid it away.

"They're ... yeah. You could say they're important."

My eyes drifted back to the bands when he went quiet. They were worn with age, but not tattered. He still didn't offer much more of an explanation than that.

"Were they a gift?" was my next thought.

He shook his head, again not offering much of a response other than, "They're Hercules knots." A half-smile surfaced. "And, yes, they're as ancient as they look."

I smiled back although he wasn't watching. His eyes were glued to the bands and I left him alone about them. If he didn't want to discuss it, I wouldn't make him.

"There's something I want to run past you," I blurted, suddenly remembering Beth's recording on my phone. I found it and pressed play, not bothering to explain first. His brow pulled together as he concentrated on the words.

My words, despite the fact that I'd never spoken French in my entire life.

The phone went silent again and I lowered it, trying to breathe easy while waiting for an interpretation. Assuming he could even give one. I wasn't sure whether I'd said anything embarrassing or maybe it was just nonsense.

"Do you understand it?" I asked, shoving fear aside. Liam took a moment to nod, but when he did, my heart leapt with intrigue.

"Some of it was muffled," he began, "but the part I *did* hear might seem kind of strange to you."

My brow tensed. "Strange why? What'd I say?"

His serious expression faded, and one corner of his mouth tugged upward. "You were chastising your brother, Josiah, for doing something reckless. I distinctly heard the words '*idiot*' and '*chalice*' in there."

My face went blank. The words sounded so elegant, although I didn't understand them, but ... *that's* what I was mumbling? I was sure my face was bright red because it felt hotter than the surface of the sun. I should have just kept it to myself.

"Do you actually remember that day?" There was hope in Liam's eyes when he asked, but all I felt was confusion.

"Remember *what* day?"

He smiled a bit and a peaceful look came over him. I soon recognized it as nostalgia. It contrasted the shock that rocked me when it became clear the random babble I muttered in my sleep was an actual reference.

"Your parents hosted foreign dignitaries all the time," he started.

"One Emperor, in particular, managed to get on Josiah's bad side one time too many during his visit. So, Josiah retaliated," he added. "... By urinating in the guy's wine before it was taken to the dinner table." Liam let out a laugh. One I imagined paled in comparison to the one he let out that day.

"When you overheard him telling Caleb and Ivan about it, you ripped into him pretty good, telling him how foolish and reckless he'd been. But he promptly reminded you that we're, technically, at the top of the food chain and there wasn't much a human could do to punish him. In other words, you lost the argument."

Staring at the floor while I listened, I eventually smiled. "They sound like a lot of trouble." I tried to imagine what it was like not growing up an only child, having brothers.

"And a lot of fun," I added.

"You're right on both accounts."

Talking about them in my sleep was a big deal to me. It meant I had memories of my family locked away somewhere in there. They may have been buried deep, but they were there, and I don't know, maybe I'd be able to access them one day.

Memories also meant the family Liam spoke of truly existed. They weren't just characters created to fulfill this longing I had, a longing to know I came from someplace. Not that I thought it before, but now ... they felt real.

And not just to him.

They were real to *me*.

Another revelation this brought with it was that I, beyond the shadow of a doubt, was exactly who Liam said I was, who I felt I'd been all along. Not some carbon copy of the Evangeline he once knew and loved, reborn as Evie—broken and missing pieces. I was still the one and only, just different due to circumstance.

"Thank you," I said quietly, still trying to wrap my head around it. "Do you think it means something? That things are beginning to come back to me—speaking French, dreaming of my brothers? That I had those weird-colored flames last night?"

He breathed deep before answering. "I think several factors are forcing you to remember."

That made sense. There was a long list of stressors at play in my life lately. From Baz and his witches stealing me from my parents' memory, the terrible turn of events with Nick, to the looming threat of a war no one could predict the magnitude of, *and* ... being stuck in this facility.

"Mostly, I think it's because you're avoiding your mother." At Liam's words, I turned to stare at him. "I'm not pressing," he quickly amended. "Just trying to help you understand."

My first instinct was to get defensive, to blurt out all the reasons I had for keeping my distance from that woman, but then I remembered how well Liam knew me. There was no need to defend my position because, if I had to guess, he'd practically read my thoughts. Besides, not once had he tried forcing me into anything. Never. Not even that first day I ran into him on Handler Street and he let me walk away. That had probably been one of the hardest things he'd ever done. So, I knew his intent wasn't to persuade me now.

"Why do you think that's causing it?" I asked, deciding not to dismiss his idea just because he brought up Elise's name.

"It's your dragon," he stated. "That side of you has already found a way to reach out to *me*—getting inside my head while you sleep, making you go up in flames because it's figured out that'll send you running to me every time..."

I didn't breathe while listening to him explain it all, breaking my behavior down in such a precise way. Ways I hadn't fully accepted until this very minute.

"If I had to guess," he went on, "I think you also, subconsciously, want to see your mother. Deep down, beneath all the anger and frustration, part of you longs for her."

I was lost in thought when he went on.

"I think that's why you were speaking French, *her* native tongue, instead of your own—Amharic."

My eyes lifted to him again. It was becoming harder and harder to refute his logic. No matter how badly I wished I could. I didn't want to need her for anything—emotionally or otherwise.

But I couldn't pretend there wasn't truth to the things Liam pointed out.

"Has she asked to speak with me again?" There was a chance she could've been angry. After all, I refused to meet with her when I was first invited. However, to my surprise, Liam shrugged.

"Wouldn't know. Haven't spoken to her since she asked us to come up for dinner."

I frowned, confused when he revealed that he hadn't gone up without me that night. Confused he made no attempt to communicate *period*. With him believing she was deceased for years, with the loss I knew he must've experienced after grieving her, seeing her again had to have felt like nothing short of a miracle.

And yet...

"Why?" The question tumbled from my mouth while I studied his face.

Greenish-brown eyes eventually found their way to mine and their usual certainty was no surprise, but his explanation was a completely different story.

"Because we're in this together, Evangeline. All the way," he added. "We'll *both* go to her when you're ready. We can ask our questions then and deal with whatever comes next. *Together*."

Daily, he found new ways to amaze me with his thoughtfulness and loyalty. If I hadn't known already that he wasn't from this era, I wouldn't be able to deny it now. People like him simply don't exist in today's world. Liam proved to me over and over again that he's a rare breed. One of a kind.

My arms were around his neck before I could stop myself and I wasn't even sure what made me hug him. Maybe it was a combination of everything. Maybe it was because I was always his priority and ... I kind of needed to be that to someone right now.

Needed to feel like I was at the top of someone's list, someone's main concern instead of an afterthought.

Disposable.

There was a fleeting thought of Nick that followed this particular word and I shoved it, and him, out of my head. I wouldn't allow either to steal this moment. Not when I needed it so badly.

Needed *Liam* and his unconditional ... *everything* ... so badly.

Large arms encircled me and, despite the power they held within them, he was only ever gentle when holding me, squeezing to bring me closer.

No words were exchanged between us, but who needed words with someone capable of reaching deeply enough to commune with your soul?

That's what he did. That was us—two beings whose souls managed to seek one another and connect despite how crazy and messed up the world was. For the first time ever, I listened to that quiet voice in the back of my mind instead of silencing it. It said this was okay, latching on to him, holding on for dear life.

Yes, today that voice won, and there was no trace of regret within me. The only thing I felt was a sense of being exactly where I belonged.

CHAPTER 17

Nick

The pep talk I gave myself on the way to class made it significantly easier to sit through another one of Liam's sessions. There was no stare-down between us; no animosity. He ignored me like I mostly ignored him—only choosing not to tune his voice out because I couldn't afford to.

Being exhausted may have helped some. I stayed up way too late, but hanging out with friends from Seaton Falls was much-needed. They felt the same way. It was evident when I looked at the clock and realized it was past two a.m. Several still lingered in our room like we didn't have to be up in a few hours. It was worth it, though. It gave us a chance to reconnect and remind ourselves that *everything* hadn't changed. We were still us. We still had each other.

Well … *most* of us still had each other.

Evie left so abruptly I barely felt like I saw her. She came, sat for maybe thirty minutes, and then left. I knew she didn't feel quite connected to our clan because she had no roots in Seaton Falls, but I guess I let myself believe she was one of us. But really, she wasn't. Her journey was adjacent to ours, but the two didn't quite converge.

I was beginning to see that now.

As she sat, watching Liam pace and talk, I watched from several seats away. She was still beautiful, yeah, but ... different than before. The distance was easily felt, but hard to accept. Our connection was growing colder by the minute and I knew the biggest hurdle between us was me.

What I am.

It made moving forward together nearly impossible and there was nothing I could do to change it.

At least, that's how things stood for now, unless Roz and I were able to come up with a solution.

The lesson continued and I tore my gaze from Evie, keeping my eyes glued to the note pad where I jotted down whatever bits and pieces stood out from the lecture. In the seat beside me, Roz did the same. I guess some of her habits were starting to rub off on me.

There were about twenty minutes left and the words I knew Roz had been waiting to hear were finally spoken:

"Any questions?"

At the sound of Liam's voice, her hand shot into the air, but so did about fifteen others. There was no denying how engaged we all were, seeing as how he had the answers we sought. After being buried in secrets, most were thirsty to understand the bigger picture. And he gave us that.

Perspective.

A huge grin came over his face when he saw how many wanted more info.

"What's your question?" he asked, gesturing toward a kid seated in the back row.

The second I turned to see who he called on, Lucas shifted in his seat, doing little to conceal his frustration. Or maybe he just couldn't. It was Errol, the one Beth seemed to be into. Even now, she'd turned almost completely to stare at him, hanging on his every word. The guy had her full attention and there was the unmistakable gleam of infatuation in her eyes. I knew it because it was the same look Lucas tended to have when looking at *her*.

"I've noticed a pattern," Errol began, twirling a pen in his fingers while he gathered his thoughts. "Based on what I've seen, based on some of the stuff you've told us, all clans keep witches around?"

Liam nodded, confirming.

"So, I get what the lycans get out of the deal—access to magic, intel, the power to manipulate people and the elements through spells, but ... what about the witches? What do they get out of it? My first thought was protection, but with some of the stories you've told, I'm guessing they don't need us for that either," he observed.

And he was right about that. The witches seemed to be able to hold their own, so his question had me curious now, too.

Liam stopped in front of his desk, leaning back against it as he gave an answer I don't think any of us expected. Heads tilted and questions were whispered when he said one word: "Immortality."

He gave us a moment to settle down before explaining.

"Strange, right? That witches are, seemingly, all-powerful, but haven't found a way to live forever without the aid of a lycan."

He stayed propped against the desk and crossed one foot over the other. "But it's true. Nature has checks and balances even within the supernatural world. Each species has their weaknesses, their Achilles heel. For witches, there's not a single spell or charm they can cast that will grant them eternal life, thus leaving them bound and at the mercy of the one supernatural race that can—lycans. It's created somewhat of a codependent relationship between the two, but it's worked for centuries."

"It's kind of like the mutualism between clownfish and sea anemones," a girl on the far-left side chimed in. We all turned to face her. "Both offer the other something they need, something they wouldn't have on their own—magic, immortality.

"In a nutshell." Liam smiled a bit. "Thanks for the analogy."

After that, he turned back to Errol when asked, "How's it done? The whole ... immortality thing? Is it just that the witches feed off the lycan's energy and simply being in close proximity makes it possible in some way?"

The grin Liam bore grew darker and I understood why when he answered. He seemed to get a kick out of grossing us out.

"Yes and no," he said first. "They *do* feed off lycan energy, but ... *literally*." Chatter picked up around the room as several added their two cents.

"Once a witch reaches the age referred to as '*the natural end*', at roughly one-hundred years, they take up a new diet, consisting of a few small drops of lycan blood every seventy-two hours or so. It extends their lives indefinitely. As long as their supply doesn't run out, of course."

"Does drinking the blood sire the witches to the lycans?"

I didn't see which kid asked this time. Someone near the door.

Liam shook his head. "No, not in the supernatural sense, but they may as well be," he explained. "That craving for immortality has made most witches as loyal to their clan as those born into it. That can be as helpful as it is dangerous."

I hadn't met *our* clan's witch counterparts, but I'd heard of them. There were many, but three the Elders kept closest according to Roz. She saw them at the last Council meeting—the one I missed—but she jotted their names down in one of her notebooks. They came up once when we were researching together—Lilith, Marin, and Scarlet.

Liam moved on to the next person who had their hand raised. "Yes?"

The thin girl pushed a pair of red frames up her nose. With my keen vision, I could clearly see there were no actual lenses in them. Now that we shifted, I was sure her eyes were just as sharp as mine, which made me guess she only wore them because she'd been accustomed to doing so. Even Roz had ditched hers.

Not sure why, but it made me smile. I guess it was just funny seeing all the crazy nuances that made us each so different despite our huge, glaring similarity—being shifters.

"My mom would kill me if she knew I was telling you all this, but ... she's old. Like, *really* freakin' old," the girl shared, her voice carrying a thick, quirky, southern drawl. The quiet laughter that hummed through the room when she spoke about her mother forced her to pause for a moment.

"She hailed from Germany circa 1520, hopped around most of her life to avoid having to age up, but then settled in Georgia when she met my father. They decided to have my brother and I, so that changed things," she shared before getting to the interesting part.

"Well, Mom called last night while I was finishing the reading assignment for today's session and she asked what we'd been learning. I told her, but I also told her about *you*."

At the girl's words, Liam's brow quirked. He must have been curious what was said right along with the rest of us.

"When I mentioned the name *Reaper,* she told me to, first, extend her gratitude for your bravery and alliance with the lycans, but ... she also told me to ask you to share something with me, with the entire class."

Liam smirked as his arms folded over his chest. "Okay, I'll bite. What's the question?"

The girl's cheeks reddened as she gathered her thoughts and Liam stared her way. *Most* of the chicks here reacted to him just like this.

"She said to ask you about the *other* royals? Said it's rumored that King Noah of Bahir Dar bore children with the original dragon?" Her voice quaked with uncertainty. Like she wasn't positive her mother knew what she was talking about. Like she'd die if Liam said her mother was mistaken.

But he didn't do that. The look on his face made the silence that accompanied it even more mysterious.

"... Yeah." He paused after stammering for a moment, slowly

rubbing a hand down his face. There was a look there I couldn't place, but, in general, he seemed uncomfortable.

"So, it's true?" the girl asked.

Liam nodded.

"My mom said there's no record of where the original dragon came from, how she came to be, and also that it's been mostly erased from history that these children even existed."

Again, Liam gave a nod, but I didn't miss the solemnity in his expression. "It's all true. The Sovereign was careful to alter historical accounts in his favor as much as possible. I imagine it took a great deal of resources and violence to be so thorough."

So many questions, all of them at once, came flying at him. However, one in particular stood out above the rest—another from the girl.

He heard it.

I heard it.

"So, is it also true you were once in love with their only daughter?"

The room was dead silent again.

The girl in the red frames shied away from Liam's hard stare, maybe thinking she said something wrong.

"Well ... 'in love' wasn't the exact term my mom used," Red Frames backtracked. "She called it *tethered* and ... I wasn't really sure what that meant and just ... *assumed...*"

Silence.

Except one sound: Evie's heart pounding like an entire drumline.

But, unlike I normally would have, I didn't turn toward her. Instead, my vision narrowed into a tunnel and it was like I was alone in that room. Several scenes and incidents from the last couple months came flooding in at once, fitting into what I now knew to be their rightful place. They created a picture I hadn't even realized existed.

Tethered.

That was the word Evie used to explain her connection to Liam, which meant ... *she* was the daughter of the king. The one Red Frames just mentioned.

Evie breathed wildly while gripping the edge of her desk, afraid to move. She, too, was a hybrid—born of a lycan and a dragon—but I had no idea she was ... *royalty?*

But the evidence was all there, in black and white, and it changed *everything*. If her real father was alive somewhere, it meant the Sovereign was not the sole ruler. If the other king *wasn't* alive, it meant ...

It meant Evie was, technically, queen.

If it hadn't been for the dread on Liam's face and the insane thrumming of Evie's heart, I might've believed my conclusion was wrong. However, it looked like they *both* wanted to take off running and never look back. Maybe they did. Because if their impression of the Sovereign was in line with my own, Evie's very existence was a death sentence for her.

In a moment of unspeakable clarity ... a thought occurred to me. Maybe this was all related to me, too. Maybe my being the Liberator was somehow connected, was somehow more than a fluke.

For now, Evie's secret was likely only obvious to me, but *Liam* had clearly been outed.

The class sat waiting for an answer to the million-dollar question: whether he'd been tethered to one of the royals, a family everyone but me believed to all be long-dead. I knew of at least one who was alive and well.

"It's true I was once linked to the princess, but ... as I'm sure you've all guessed, that family no longer exists," he lied. "The Sovereign made certain he had no rival, made sure there was no one alive to contest the throne, so ... case closed."

His explanation died there. It came as no surprise to me that he shut the Q&A session down right after. Roz was among those disappointed by not having her questions answered. But judging by the page full of notes she jotted down in the last five minutes *alone,* she'd have enough to get her through at least a week of research.

There was a ton of speculation buzzing when we were dismissed. Several were questioning how abruptly Liam killed the conversation after being asked about the other original lycan. Some thought it was just still too hard for him to discuss, losing someone he cared about. Others thought there might be more to it than that.

I knew the truth.

Or *most* of it anyway: at least one heir to the fallen kingdom still existed, and her life depended on that information remaining secret.

Apparently, I wasn't the *only* possible, future threat Evie needed to look out for. There was undeniable tension in my gut. It accompanied the need to protect her. That hadn't left despite our relationship tanking.

I packed up my things and was aware of her doing the same further down the row, only much slower. She was distracted and peered up at Liam frequently. His eyes, full of concern, hadn't left her either.

"I have to make a quick stop in my room. See you at lunch?" The sound of Roz's voice pulled my gaze from Evie.

"Uh ... I was actually thinking about skipping it today. I've had a bit of a headache since I got up, so I'm gonna see if a nap helps."

She smiled. "I guess that can happen when you hit the sheets at three and get up at six."

I nodded, pretending to be casual as I kept an eye on Evie. She stood from her seat and was heading for the door. At the risk of Roz seeing me scramble to chase after her, I excused myself, taking quick steps in Evie's direction. I made it to her just as she exited.

"Hey, mind if we talk a sec?"

She still seemed a bit shifty after the conversation in class took a turn, but she faked it pretty well—making eye contact, smiling politely.

"Sure, what's up?"

My mind went kind of blank and all I could think about was who she was—royalty. When I didn't speak right away, she seemed to guess as much. It was confirmed when she gently took my arm,

232

leading me further away from where bodies continued to pour out of our last class.

Those big, brown eyes that had been my undoing since day one, peered up at me, and now that it was just us, I saw the fear she'd tried to conceal in them. A question flew from her mouth and her forthrightness caught me by surprise.

"You won't say anything, will you?"

I wasn't so much surprised that she figured I knew her truth, but ... more so by the fact that she didn't trust me to keep her secret. I wasn't sure what to make of that, her thinking it was necessary to ask.

I felt the tension in my brow when I answered. "Of *course* not. I, honestly, wasn't even going to bring it up."

And I wasn't. Mostly, I just wanted to make sure she was okay. With what just happened in class, with her leaving my room so abruptly last night.

Both arms crossed her chest and she glanced around, completely missing the fact that I was offended. But I was. Deeply. Had we fallen that far already? Did she consider me such an outsider that I was no longer trustworthy?

Instead of letting her see she'd wounded me, I went on with my original reason for stopping her, trying to ignore yet another subtle reminder of where we now stood in each other's lives.

"I just wanted to make sure you were okay. You left kinda quick last night, so..."

When I had her full attention again, her expression softened. I wasn't sure what was on her heart, but when her answer came, I knew she held back. Another sign of how her trust in me had waned.

"I just wasn't feeling like myself," was her response. "Guess I felt a little out of place. It wasn't anything you did," she explained. "I think it's just ... *me*."

She blinked a few times and I got the distinct impression she was working up to something. And when she opened her mouth again, I was sure that had been the case.

"I don't know if it's a good idea for us to hang out like that." After getting the words out, her chest heaved with deep breaths. She fidgeted with her nails while staring, waiting for me to respond. Maybe nervous about what I'd say.

My ego took another blow, but I was careful not to let her see that either. It was starting to feel like I was foolish to let my guard down around her. Without even trying, she kept stabbing me right in the heart.

Over and over again.

Those inflictions were sometimes small and subtle—like how that warmth that used to be in her eyes when she looked at me was now gone. And other times, they were more damaging. Like today.

Like now.

"I really thought we could make the 'friends' thing work, but … we were both probably kidding ourselves." A dim, humorless smile touched her lips when she finished speaking and I looked away.

"I didn't think it would come to this," she added. "I wanted to believe it wouldn't be so hard."

While she made it seem as though that last part was only about us, it felt a lot heavier than that. When she didn't elaborate, it reminded me of how closed off she'd always been, reminded me I was never as much inside that inner circle of hers as I thought. Verbally putting space between us when I first arrived was merely a formality. The longer I observed her from a distance, the clearer it became:

She *never* belonged to me.

I was foolish to think otherwise.

"Understood," I blurted, squaring my shoulders. "It is what it is."

She winced a bit when I said that. "This doesn't make us enemies, Nick."

While I agreed, I also knew it meant we weren't exactly friends either. Despite our efforts to prove otherwise.

"It's cool," I added, wishing I really was as okay with this as I tried to pretend. "And don't worry; I won't tell anyone what I know."

This time, it looked like she had at least *some* confidence in me when she gave a solemn nod. "I appreciate it."

It still stung that she needed to hear me say it.

"Well, I uh ... I guess I'll see you around," she said quietly.

A chill settled on my heart and spread to my head, worsening the headache that had already set up shop there. When she walked away, I let her, keeping to myself how I never meant for this break to be so permanent. So official.

As quickly as things with us had come together ... they had now completely fallen apart.

CHAPTER 18

Nick

Thanks to the pain in my head, I sat out the last half of today's training. It also forced me to turn down an invite from some of the guys to hang out in the gym, shooting hoops since it was Friday and we didn't have to be up early tomorrow.

And now, I was wondering if that splitting headache was the reason I was, again, standing in the middle of my room covered in filth. I'd lost three hours this time.

When I last looked at the clock, it was a quarter to seven. Now? Half past ten.

It felt like my head was broken, like time was slipping through the cracks. Dark, damp soil covered my hands and feet just like before, but I still had no recollection of being anywhere but this room.

I was losing it.

Breathing wildly as I tried to contain the mounting rage and frustration, I hurried to the bathroom before any of my roommates came back, asking questions when they saw the state I was in.

What's wrong with me?

Am I going crazy?

Am I becoming what I feared I would?

Brown-tinted water rinsed down the drain as my skin went back to its usual shade. I stared at nothing. Lost, wondering if, one day, I'd black out like this and the *real* me wouldn't ever return, leaving the beast inside to wreak havoc on the world.

On Evie.

I braced the edge of the sink and squeezed my eyes shut. I couldn't afford to think like this, like I was already defeated. I had to fight what I felt growing inside me.

Had to.

But something else was also clear to me now, whether I liked it or not; she was right to put the final nail in the coffin today. It wasn't good for her to be around me.

An urgent knock at the door had me quickly drying my hands and feet before going to answer. Through the peephole, I saw Roz standing on the other side, so distraught she was literally wringing her hands.

I pulled the door open and didn't expect to be ambushed with a hug, followed by the huge sigh of relief she breathed into my ear.

"Thank God, you're okay."

With her still hanging around my neck, I frowned. *What was she talking about?* The last time I saw her was in class. Was she freaking out because I told her about the headache?

When I didn't speak, her grip loosened and, slowly, she pulled away, staring with bewilderment and suspicion in her eyes.

"You ... don't remember, do you?"

My brow quirked. "Remember what?"

She settled on her heels again and reached back to shut my door, closing us off from the rest of the world. Her bottom lip clamped between her teeth while she studied my face. I had no clue what she was thinking, but I wished she'd just tell me what I missed.

With all the time I was losing, I was kind of desperate for that.

"We passed each other in the hallway a few hours ago," she started. "I was ... I was surprised to see you up walking around because I knew you weren't feeling well. So, I stopped to ask if the headache had passed, but ... you just kept walking. Didn't stop. Didn't speak," she added. "So, I followed you."

She followed me. Maybe that meant she could tell me where I'd been, what I do when my consciousness goes on hiatus.

"You went to the elevator and I got on with you, but I didn't know what happened to you after that." The look of bewilderment returned to her face and I felt it, too.

"You didn't get off with me? Didn't keep following me wherever I was headed?" The words came out kind of harsh, but my frustration wasn't with her. It was with myself.

Her dark hair shifted when she shook her head. "For starters," she went on, "...I was afraid to."

My head tilted at those words. So many feelings came at me at once, I couldn't keep them all straight. Mostly, I was angry with what dwelled inside of me, but the next contender was guilt. I felt terrible for whatever I'd done—even if it wasn't actually *me*— that scared Roz off.

"I've never seen you like that," she went on. "The way you looked at me; it was like ... you were dead inside. Like you could have ripped me to pieces without thinking twice about it."

My back fell against the wall behind me.

"It shook me to the point that I almost didn't come here," she shared, "but I needed to know you were okay, so ... I came anyway."

And I was glad she did.

She stood in front of me with so much fear and uncertainty. I could feel it, could see it in her posture as she fidgeted with her nails, unable to keep still.

And yet, she showed up. Right when I needed someone.

Despite my initial thought—that I should shut the rest of the world out and deal with this on my own—having her here made me realize I didn't want to be alone. I needed someone who understood me, someone who knew what was happening to me and, right now, Roz was the only one who consistently came through.

The only one I could trust.

"I'm sorry," I sighed. "For snapping just now, for scaring you earlier. I—"

"It's okay," she interjected. "I'm just glad you're here."

I nodded, knowing she meant that.

"And, for the record, I didn't stop following you because I was afraid," she shared, only leaving me to guess the real reason for a moment. "I stopped because you opened the ceiling tile on top of the elevator and climbed up the shaft. I *couldn't* follow you."

Of *course* that was the only thing that stopped her. I should have guessed it was something like that. It wasn't like her to get rattled to the point that she stopped pursuing the truth. She was the bravest person I knew. Hands down.

Which was why she dared to come to my room just now.

My hand sought hers and I was surprised how much the contact soothed my racing thoughts. She squeezed my fingers between hers.

"I don't know what's going on with me." It was tough admitting I was powerless, but there was no getting around it.

I was spiraling.

"There have to be answers out there somewhere. There was a Liberator before you," she said with a sense of optimism I didn't share. "There has to be some sort of documentation of him other than what we've already found. For all we know, there's a way to stop the blackouts. A way to—"

"Reverse this curse altogether?"

That slipped out.

I didn't mean to keep creating hope where I knew none existed, and Roz hadn't stumbled across anything yet. But maybe I said it because I was desperate not to become a monster. From the way things had been going, I was already on the fast track headed to that exact destination.

Roz's eyes softened, and it wasn't pity that filled them. It was sympathy. She nodded. "Yeah ... maybe there is."

I turned away from her again, but kept her hand.

"I'll keep looking," she promised. "We'll figure this out."

It wasn't lost on me how she always made *my* problems *her* problems. There was once a time I resented her persistence and the way she couldn't seem to let go when she had a lead.

But now, in the thick of things, I knew to thank my lucky stars she stuck around.

Liam

The line at the vending machine was longer than usual, but, from what I'd seen so far, it was like that *every* Friday night. The kids were out and about later than usual because there were no sessions until Monday. So, with very little to do to keep themselves occupied down here, they hit the junk food pretty hard and just hung out.

I hadn't been gone more than five minutes, but returned to find that Elise had let herself into my room. My first thought was that news of how today's class discussion went had somehow reached her.

I'd been on edge ever since. How was it that a well-meaning kid in weird glasses nearly threw a wrench in the entire plan to keep Evangeline safe? It became even clearer that I could never stop being vigilant in my effort to protect her. It'd also made me second-guess my role here as an instructor. It seemed that these kids' parents were finally sharing their knowledge with them willingly and I couldn't risk another connection being made.

Not with there being so much on the line.

Elise sat on the couch, patiently waiting. Seeing her was, of course, a surprise, but not an unwelcomed one. However, it didn't take long to pick up on the emotion bleeding through her expression, one I hated seeing there.

Guilt.

Yes, I was certain that, in part, it was due to the fact that she'd come into my room without permission, but I guessed the larger component was the rift between she and Evangeline.

A rift *she* was responsible for.

I latched the door and she offered a dim smile as she clasped both hands in her lap. "You look well."

I set down my drink and smiled back while taking the seat across from her. "I am."

I was sure she knew that would be my response. Her daughter had always been the only thing I needed to consider myself okay. And despite the way we started—with Evangeline resisting the pull we *both* felt every step of the way—I'd begun to see progress.

"Sorry for just dropping in," she sighed. "I would've waited in the hall, but I've tried to maintain a low profile around here. When my staff catch me roaming about, they tend to swarm me with questions that aren't really my concern. Needless to say, I try to stay to myself, doing my part to keep things running smoothly in the background."

Which begged the question: what was so important that she'd come all the way down here when she could have simply picked up the phone and called? The ill-timed question I'd been asked earlier came to mind again. That had to be it.

"You've been ... distant," she said, pretending it didn't bother her that I'd stayed away, although I knew that wasn't true.

For so long, she thought I hadn't survived the war, and I thought the same of her. As someone she regarded like a son, I was sure she expected we'd be making better use of our time here, reconnecting after so much time had been lost.

But I couldn't do that.

Getting close to Elise again, *now*—with Evangeline feeling so disconnected, so alone—would have only made her feel like even more of an outcast. And, with all she'd lost recently, I wouldn't be the cause of more pain. If she needed time to wrap her head around meeting her mom, then I'd learn to be content waiting with her.

Even if it meant keeping the only mother *I'd* ever known out of my life a little while longer.

"How is she?" Elise asked, unable to even utter Evangeline's name.

I nodded. "Seems to be adjusting well. Considering." That one word was so loaded.

Considering she just found out she isn't human.

Considering she just lost what little family she had.

Considering she just found out even *more* of her life was a lie.

...Considering.

Elise lowered her head as if she heard every thought that just went through mine. "Well ... I'm sure she has you to thank for that."

I didn't' respond.

"And the Liberator? He's been behaving?"

A rush of air left my lungs at the mention of Nick. Evangeline and I hadn't discussed him much lately, but I did notice she had a lot of free time. Since arriving here, she seemed less distracted. I could only guess things between them had changed to some degree, but I hadn't asked. *Wouldn't.* There was no point. In my book, Nick was inconsequential; a blip on the screen that would, eventually, weed itself out.

Besides, in the past, Evangeline never had much tolerance for the insecurities of boys. She preferred her men to *act* like men.

I gave Elise the only answer I had. "He seems to be. He's pretty quiet in class, but there haven't been any disturbances."

"Other than the first day in the dining hall."

It didn't surprise me she'd heard about that.

"Mei," she revealed.

Figures.

"She's one of many sets of eyes I have down here," she shared. "Which is probably why she thought it was worth mentioning that she'd seen you and Evangeline out in the halls pretty early."

I smiled and glanced up at Elise. "So, you came down here to chastise me for spending time with your daughter?"

"Of *course* not," she said quickly, softening her expression.

There were so many reasons she and I both knew that was unnecessary. I was the last person *anyone*—herself included—had the right to keep away from Evangeline.

"I only wanted to caution you that your interaction with her hadn't gone unnoticed."

"Well, how about this; next time someone has an issue with anything they see going on between Evangeline and I, you tell them to come talk to me about it. Deal?"

Anger rose in me quickly and I struggled to suppress it. It was hard enough pretending to be okay with the distance between us; I wouldn't put up with people posing a threat to what little progress I made.

Instead of taking offense to my harsh tone, Elise smiled. "It's good to see time hasn't dulled your love for her."

And it never would.

"Which is why I thought I owed you this visit," she went on.

My brow tensed. "Meaning?"

"I'm putting an end to topside privileges."

Silence hung in the air around us. An unsettled feeling came over me and I knew already that this one, vague sentence was getting ready to lead to a whole pile of bad.

Call it a hunch.

I'd never been one to panic, but had experienced it more times than I could count since having Evangeline back. She was my one and only weakness. Because I couldn't always keep her at my side, I felt like part of me was under the threat of constant danger, unprotected.

I'd already lost her once and knew I'd never survive it twice.

The tether linking us sent a beacon that shot from me, headed straight for Evangeline. Like a flare. At that very moment, there was no doubt she felt a mirroring tug in the center of her chest. It's the same one I feel whenever she's under duress. It wasn't something either of us could control, so there was no stopping it. It was a matter of minutes, maybe seconds, before she'd come knocking, unable to explain the burning need within her to make sure I was okay.

I knew the feeling well because I experienced it often myself.

"For the past week or so, while monitoring topside security footage ... one of our guards reported several sightings of *'an eerie shadow moving amongst the trees',*" she quoted, her native dialect hanging on each syllable.

"And you're just now telling me?" Another jolt shot from me. "I should've been watching her more closely. What if it's mutts?" I rambled. "If they're here, it means *he* knows we're here."

Elise stretched her hands my way, hoping to calm me. "I won't say it's impossible, but it goes without saying that I took the greatest measures one can think of to ensure this facility was safe. We both know I wouldn't have dreamed of bringing Evangeline here if that weren't true."

I was on my feet now, pacing as I tried to think of something else the guard may have seen. However, if there was even a remote possibility the shadow was a mutt, this facility was no longer suitable for Evangeline, and I'd have no choice but to move her.

The risk of exposure was too great.

Elise stood, too. "Liam, I know I'm asking a lot, but be reasonable. Think with your head," she said calmly. "Not your heart."

Her words halted me and she had my attention.

"If you leave here, if you take her away, where would you go? Back to Seaton Falls where the Sovereign is *sure* to find her? Out into the world to be stalked and hunted down like we know those ... those *things* are capable of doing?" She paused and a gentle hand rested on my shoulder. "Or would you rather have her here, surrounded by shifters, old and young, willing to lay down our lives for the cause."

Our.

She didn't say *your* or *they...* she said *our.* Meaning, she was willing to lay down her life for this cause, too.

"Even if there *is* something out there," she reasoned, "this is still the safest place in the world for Evangeline right now."

I hated that she was right, that our best option *still* wasn't good enough.

"Who knows we're here?" I asked, switching over to a more logical train of thought per Elise's request. "The money to fund this place had to come from somewhere."

She shook her head. "That's a dead end. Damascus, and other facilities like it, were mostly funded with money the clans have been syphoning from the tariff."

I looked up, suddenly understanding part of the bigger picture. The clans stole what the Sovereign thought was rightfully his and had taken the future into their own hands by building these places around the world, in secret, right under his nose.

This facility was a physical manifestation of an ongoing revolution, the first step toward independence. And if there was one thing I knew about independence it's that, historically speaking, it always comes at a great price. For any nation—of land or people—to earn it, that price was always bloodshed.

"And what didn't come from *that* was donated by benefactors, families of some of the children here, most of which are housed right in this sector of the residential quarters," she added, explaining why certain young shifters were on the receiving end of special treatment. Their families were, in a sense, cofounders of this place.

The investors wouldn't have been the threat. Not with their own children here.

It was hard to make any of my theories stick, because with so many pieces of the puzzle missing, it would be easy to overlook possible vulnerabilities.

"Is it possible that, whoever helped you bring Evangeline back may have given you up? Could they have told him what you're doing? Could—"

Elise shook her head as she interrupted, speaking with certainty. "No. I brought her back with Hilda's help, and you and I both know she's trustworthy. The last person on this planet she'd think to help is the Sovereign."

My brow twitched. I hadn't seen Hilda in ages. "She's still around?"

Elise nodded and there was the undeniable hint of a smile. "She is, and she's as strong as ever. And if you want to question her yourself, perhaps I can convince her to visit in the coming months. I'm sure she wouldn't mind." Her smile widened. "She hasn't forgotten how vigilant you've always been on Evangeline's behalf."

Actually, I was pretty sure *no one* who'd been around during that time had forgotten. More than once, I'd severed the limbs of those who dared to disrespect her. And for the ones brave enough to put her life in danger ... I preferred to rip out their throats, robbing them of their last breath as I watched their eyes go dim. I wanted to be certain mine was the last face they saw before death.

I liked to think I was less of a hothead now, more rational, but deep down I knew that was a lie.

"Arrange it, please," I replied, not ashamed in the least that I'd just made plans to interrogate an aging witch. One who was, technically, Evangeline's aunt by way of her father, and her mother's oldest confidante. That didn't matter. No one would slip through the cracks on my watch.

The knock at the door only caught *Elise* by surprise. I was fully expecting it.

"Perhaps I should go," she offered, probably knowing there was only one person who'd be coming to my room.

"It's too late for that. Just ... stay." I braced myself for whatever Evangeline's reaction would be when she realized who I had inside.

Large brown eyes locked with mine across the threshold. She breathed hard and fast, like she ran here. From the gym or dining hall, I guessed. That's where most were hanging out tonight.

"I felt ... something. Is everything okay?"

Pursing my lips together when I didn't have an explanation, I simply stepped back and let her see inside my room, let her see her mother.

I promised not to keep things from her.

The look of concern on Evangeline's face faded quickly, being replaced by anger, frustration.

"I misunderstood, I guess. I thought you were in danger," she mumbled. "I'll just come back later."

"No," Elise spoke up, causing Evangeline to pause mid-step. "I showed up unannounced, uninvited; if anyone should leave, it's me." She stood and Evangeline's gaze slipped to the ground to avoid eye contact. I also noted that she didn't disagree with Elise's rationale.

I understood her on levels I don't think she even fully understood *herself* yet. No, her memory wasn't intact, but, to the core, she was the same person today she was hundreds of years ago. This small reminder is what prompted me to act quickly, gently taking her wrist as I coaxed her inside before either could get in their own way again. If that happened, they'd miss this opportunity to move forward, to fix things between them.

Elise was notoriously self-sacrificing and would bypass this chance to restore what was broken with her daughter just to avoid conflict.

Evangeline was a walking bundle of emotions all the time, and she avoided torrents where feelings flowed freely, for no other reason than to protect herself from drowning in them.

So, today, I had to be the voice of reason. Had to intervene or there might not be another opportunity to get these two in the same room.

"I was just leaving. I should—"

"What are you doing? I'm—"

"Just ... sit," I interjected, cutting them both off, adding a softly spoken, "Please."

To my surprise, both complied without me having to beg.

I faced Evangeline, worried she'd look at this as an ambush when, really, my main concern was her safety. I'd been perfectly content waiting out the separation between them, but knowing there might be mutts in the area, she needed to be aware as well. While I respected her feelings, this was the worst time to have a breakdown in communication.

Despite how she felt about Elise.

With the shadow of war infringing upon us all, we'd need each other.

All of us.

CHAPTER 19

Evie

My initial thought when I saw Elise inside Liam's room was that coming here was a mistake.

I wondered if the jolt I felt in my chest had been a false alarm. It was the reason I sprinted full-speed from the other side of the facility. I'm sure Beth still sat in the dining hall, staring at a half-played *Scrabble* board, thinking I'd lost my mind when I jumped up and took off without explanation. But with what Liam said next as I stood before him, I knew the reason he panicked; knew the reason his dragon had sent out a distress signal to mine.

"There's a possible security issue. A guard spotted something in the woods, and the word '*mutts*' has been tossed around," he shared.

I peered up—worried, confused.

"There hasn't been a definitive sighting, but this is a matter we're all taking very seriously." At the sound of Elise's voice, my gaze stayed locked on Liam. I couldn't look at her. *Wouldn't.*

"What does this mean?" I asked, directing my question to Liam, of course.

He hesitated a moment when I ignored Elise's empty words. Her promises and reassurance meant nothing to me. I only wanted to hear from him right now. The one person in this room I trusted.

"It means we have to be careful," Liam replied. "To start, no one's allowed to go topside. We need to maintain a low profile. It also means we have to be careful on the *inside* as well. I'm not convinced someone didn't give up our location."

When Elise shifted on the couch, I glanced that way for a moment. Her lips were pursed tightly and I got the impression she had a rebuttal to Liam's theory, but decided to hold her tongue. Maybe because tension in the room was already so high.

"Elise disagrees," Liam added, confirming what I already guessed. "She's made it clear she went to great lengths to ensure this place was safe, but I think that actually *strengthens* my argument. If this facility is so hard for the outside world to locate, if it *is* mutts that have been spotted, someone had to have led them here. And who's to say that '*someone*' isn't on the inside?"

My heart raced, but I was careful to keep it together in front of Elise. I hadn't forgotten the terrifying incident we recently had outside Liam's house in Seaton Falls. Needless to say, I was in no rush to face that again. And on top of it all, I now felt the need to watch everyone I passed, wondering if they were spies, wondering if they knew who I was, knew who I used to be.

It became clear I hadn't hidden the fear spreading within me all that well when Elise addressed me again.

"Please don't be afraid, Evangeline. The last thing in the world I want is for you to feel unsafe here. If I have to, I'll place my most trusted guard right outside your door," she offered.

I couldn't look at her when I spoke. "I don't want to draw even more attention to myself than I already have," I mumbled. To me, placing me in this sleeping sector was obvious enough.

There was a long, awkward pause and I felt both sets of eyes on me. There was an entire herd of elephants in the room and I knew the silence wouldn't hold. The only question was: who would break it first? Elise or Liam?

"Evangeline, I know how difficult being here has been for you, but I'd be grateful if you'd give me the chance to explain."

When those words left Elise's mouth, water immediately began to pool in my eyes. I'd been fighting it since the moment I walked in, because being around her was like staring at a flashing, red billboard, reminding me of every hurtful thing I'd ever gone through. In her presence, it was like no time had passed at all.

The pain hadn't dulled. It was overwhelming and torturous. She had no idea what she cost me.

Through a blurred, watery gaze, my eyes finally settled on her. I mean *really* settled on her, taking in her features, ones that were undeniably similar to mine. Our most notable difference being complexion—mine a shade or two deeper than Liam's, hers like untouched porcelain. The expression she wore was soft and kind, but I knew the heart that lie within her was cold and calculated. It had to be.

"Do you really think *that's* what's difficult for me? The fact that I'm stuck in this place?" I blurted, feeling the first hint of warm tears slipping down my cheeks.

Liam, who'd been standing between us, slowly stepped aside, lowering his head as the incoming storm, one that had been brewing within me for years, finally reached shore. Because I'd gotten to know him so well, because I knew his nature drove him to protect me, I was sure not intervening killed him inside. Especially when he glanced over and noticed I began to cry.

"I didn't mean to make light of what you've been through," Elise backpedaled. "I was stating the *opposite,* actually; that I know you've had it rough."

Blood rushed through my veins.

"Don't do that," I hissed, tightening my fists at my sides. "Having people watch me all my life doesn't mean you know me."

Her shoulders rose and fell with a deep breath, but she said nothing.

"You cost me *everything*," I forced out. "A normal life, my family."

"I didn't make this world what it is, Evangeline," she countered. "I didn't create the evil that's pushed us *all* to make sacrifices."

Sacrifices. Who was she to tell me about sacrifices?

I shook my head, lifting my eyes toward the ceiling when this got to be too much.

"I'm *dying* to hear what you've lost in all this." The words left my mouth drenched in cynicism and I didn't care enough to consider Elise's feelings.

"You, Evangeline. This undertaking, this ... *huge mission*," she blurted. "It cost me you."

My eyes slammed shut and so many words came to mind. Words I wanted to throw at her like daggers.

Liar.

Manipulator.

Coward.

I was supposed to think she hadn't taken the easy way out by watching me spiral all these years? Struggling to find my place? Struggling to figure out why I always felt different from everyone else? It made it worse to know she'd had people watching and reporting my every move to her all these years. Every difficulty, every traumatic incident, she knew about it and yet, she never did anything to fix it.

She sat idly by like I was some science experiment, watching as life drowned me.

"Evangeline, there's so much you don't know. So much you probably wouldn't understand, but I'm sitting here, willing to tell you what I can," she said, not bothering to hide the blatant plea embedded within the words. "Just tell me what you need from me and—"

"Why am I here?" I blurted. The question was distorted by my sobs and breathy words, but she understood. I saw in her eyes that she did. I wasn't asking why I was brought to this facility; those reasons were mostly clear.

But what *wasn't* clear was her reason for restarting my life.

"Why bring me back and then leave me?" I choked out. "You knew I was different. You knew I wouldn't understand when things started changing. Why would you send me out into the world alone, instead of protecting me?"

The room was eerily quiet and I felt empty inside, unloading these questions on her. For so long, I'd been holding these things in with nowhere to direct them. But now, I had a living, breathing target. The one who'd brought it all on.

Elise's posture changed and some of the guilt and shame seemed to fade. Her eyes locked with mine and I detected that same stifling confidence I tended to only see in *Liam's* eyes. But tonight, it was in *hers*.

Maybe, although she wasn't his biological mother, this was a trait he inherited from her.

"You're here because we *need* you, Evangeline."

Hearing Elise admit that, Liam's head lifted. He'd been so quiet and still while she and I spoke, it was almost like he wasn't even here until now.

"And, while I'm sure this won't make much sense to you," she went on, "giving you up was the hardest and *easiest* thing I've ever done."

My brow quirked at Elise's strange wording.

"Keeping you would have been as good as sentencing you to death myself." She blinked, and to my surprise, her glassy eyes shimmered with tears. However, she was too poised to let them fall.

"You were always a special child. For more reasons than I can explain. But your father and I weren't the only ones who knew that," she added. "When I brought you back, I had no choice but to hide you. I was very selective about who adopted you, and Todd and Rebecca turned out to be as stellar a choice as I knew they would be."

She paused and I took advantage of the break, needing a moment to comprehend all of this. Hearing that my parents had been studied and ... *chosen* for me?

"I handed you—the only important thing I had left in this world— over to them, because they were among the few, genuinely good-natured people I found. I gave you to them, Evangeline, because, despite the fact that they're only human, they were far more capable of protecting you than I was," she admitted. "If the Sovereign knew I was still alive, the lives of everyone I love or care about would be in danger. By some small miracle, he has no idea that I, a dragon, have infiltrated the lycan High Council. Those who share my vision have secretly elevated me to one of the highest-ranking positions of the organization. For that, he'd have me, most of the Council members, and the Elders killed without question."

Her eyes flitted up toward mine and I felt what she said next. Right in my chest.

"To a man like that, all life is expendable, Evangeline. And I couldn't justify putting the same target on your back that I've willingly put on my own for the cause."

I couldn't move an inch as I listened.

"Yes, I watched you grow from a distance, mostly through the eyes and reports of others, but don't think for a single moment it didn't kill me over and over and over again, having to stay in the background."

The pools in her eyes filled a little more.

"Several times, I nearly intervened," she shared. "It took every-thing in me not to go to your home in the middle of the night, deter-mined to take my little girl while she slept. But ... each time, I reminded myself of the pain I felt when I lost you before," she added. "So, if staying away was going to keep you alive, I was steadfastly willing to suffer so you could live."

I hated that she chipped away at the hardness of my heart.

"You said you brought me back because you need me. Why?" I forced out, doing all I could to maintain the same, clipped tone I'd

back because you need me. Why?" I forced out, doing all I could to maintain the same, clipped tone I'd spoken to her in before. She couldn't know I was softening. Not yet. Not until my questions had been answered and I'd had time to process it all.

Elise lowered her head, maybe knowing her answer wouldn't go over well with Liam.

"There are certain things I'm not allowed to reveal right now. The Council has strict stipulations, and not sharing all the details of the plan is one of them. They, too, risked a lot letting me bring you back, Evangeline, and as much as I want to divulge it all despite the oath I've taken, I simply cannot."

"With all due respect, Elise," Liam cut in, "you'll have to do better than that. I understand there's a '*plan*' and you and the Council have the bigger picture in mind, but—"

She offered Liam a dim smile from where she sat. "You can relax. I would never put Evangeline in harm's way. Not for *anything*," she added. "But I truly cannot say more than I already have."

He stared at her and frustration clearly marked his expression.

The emptiness inside me grew as Elise's explanation settled into my thoughts. At first, I didn't understand where the feeling came from, but then, out of nowhere, it hit me. In all she said, not once did she mention that I'd been brought back because she *wanted* me here. It sounded like, to her, I was nothing more than a means to an end; some sort of resource she needed as a contribution to her '*cause*'.

I was set to keep my thoughts to myself, but then remembered the only one who'd suffer from holding it in was me. For so long, I had questions about my past. Now, I had the chance to ask them, so I'd bare it all in the name of self-healing.

"Why now?" I blurted. "I've been gone for centuries. Why bring me back now instead of *years* ago?" My breaths came quick and shallow. "Just because you need me?"

I put myself in her shoes, tried to imagine having the power to bring back a loved one, or even give my parents their memory back whenever I felt like it. It would've taken an act of God to stop me, but not Elise. If I was hearing her right, she *chose* to wait until now. Chose to go on without me. Until I was of some use to her.

Her head lowered and I wasn't sure what the answer would be. Seeing that she hesitated was more nerve-wracking than I cared to admit. However, before she could answer, Liam cut in with a theory of his own.

"Was it because bringing *her* back would also mean another Liberator would be born?"

Elise lifted her eyes to meet Liam's and it surprised me when she shook her head. I honestly thought he might have been on to something.

"As dreadful as that curse is," she answered, "not even *that* would have been enough to keep me from bringing you back straight away, Evangeline."

When she addressed me, I can't explain why, but my heart leapt. I quickly quenched the feeling, though. For all I knew, this was a mind game—her way of making me think she actually cared.

Liam and I stood there, waiting for an explanation, and in the end, all Elise offered was a cryptic riddle, making it clear we had, once again, wandered into the territory of what was off limits to discuss.

"In short," she sighed. "It's a matter of Newton's third law coming into play. It's true what they say: for every action, there is, indeed, always a *reaction*. And let's just say the potential fallout has grave enough consequences that I waited centuries, until things were dire enough to warrant bringing you back." She flashed a dismal smile that never reached her eyes, eventually letting her solemn gaze slip to the floor.

The explanation did nothing but make me ten times more paranoid than I already was. What could have been so bad that it weighed this heavily on Elise's decision?

"How'd you do it?" Liam asked, taking the words right out of my mouth.

Elise crossed one leg over the other, searching for the right words.

"Well, like I explained before, I had a close friend's assistance," she explained. "I was only allowed to enlist the help of one witch, so that meant the magic we had at our disposal was *half* of what we actually needed. The full spell called for two, which would have enabled us to bring you back fully transitioned, memories and abilities intact. So, with just one witch, we had to adjust the spell, placing your soul back inside *me* and, essentially, starting your life over from the beginning."

I stared at her because I was intrigued. Liam stared at her differently, though; like there was another point he was waiting for her to get to.

She sensed it when her eyes landed on him, and then went on. "But, judging by your expression, I'm guessing that's not the information you were after."

Liam shook his head, and when he spoke, it was hard to miss the pain present in his voice, although I believe he meant to conceal it. "She was *dead*, Elise. Gone. Completely."

There was a hush in the room and I felt it weighing me down like wet sand.

"I'm asking what you had to do to bring her back." There was an undertone of an accusation I don't think Elise missed either.

She held Liam's gaze and the two engaged in a brief stare-down. "I didn't *do* anything, Liam. There was a talisman," she confessed.

Liam's eyes were barely visible through the slits they narrowed to. "*What* talisman?"

Elise blinked at him several times before replying, maybe weighing her words because she noticed, like I did, the instability present in Liam's gaze right now. However, when he finally answered, his expression reverted to the calm, sensible look he wore before. There was actually a bit of shock or confusion there as well.

"Her necklace," Elise asserted.

Naturally, my fingers drifted toward my bare neck. I got the feeling I was the only one who didn't know what necklace she referred to, which may be why she went on to explain.

"It was a gift from your father and I on your twentieth birthday. On the day you first shifted." A smile, one heavily doused in nostalgia, touched her lips. "A week prior, I made a trip to visit my friend, Hilda, with a special request in mind."

Liam stared with both arms folded across his chest while listening.

"She's your father's sister, and one of my dearest friends," Elise added. "She's the one who helped me bring you back, an extremely powerful witch. One not only known in our kingdom, but around the world."

I was surprised to hear that I not only had ties to lycans and dragons, but witches, too. Liam mentioned her name once months ago, but not that we were related.

"I handed her a large, black diamond; the one your necklace's stone was intended to be cut from," Elise explained. "And I asked her to make it ... *more* than just a stone. I asked her to make it a link to your soul so that, if something should ever happen to you..."

Her expression flickered, showing sentiment as her words trailed off, but the look was quickly wrangled in. She seemed more comfortable with her rigid posture and stone-faced countenance, as if she wasn't proud of the decision because it hadn't been one devised from logic, but rather ... emotion.

"It linked Evangeline to the necklace," Liam interjected, trying to understand. "So, when she died, her soul went into the stone?"

Elise nodded. "Yes. Hilda did as I asked and I had several pieces of jewelry made using that stone, actually. One of which being the necklace." Her gaze shifted to Liam next. "And your love for her did the rest."

At those words, I saw his brow twitch.

"After the Liberator took her, you kept searching. You didn't stop looking for her until you were sure she was gone; didn't stop until you found the one piece of her that always has and always *will* belong to you."

I held my breath as she finished her thought.

"You found her soul."

Liam lowered his head, maybe recalling all he'd been through that day. The day he'd only spoken of once in my presence.

The day I died.

He mentioned that all he'd been able to recover were some of my belongings—a necklace and a bracelet.

"You may not have realized it then, but you *did* save her life, Liam," Elise said through strained, broken syllables. "He didn't steal all of her from us that night."

Liam said nothing.

"Not everyone has realized this yet, but we're in the middle of a revolution. One in which a shift in power has begun to take place, one where eyes are being opened, one where the *real* enemy is being revealed," she stated. "I didn't just set out to establish these facilities around the world because our young shifters need to learn who they are and where they came from. I shared my vision because ... it's high time we mend the rift between lycans and dragons and unite to defeat our common oppressor."

It went without saying that the common oppressor she spoke of was Sebastian, the Sovereign, ruler of the lycan race, menace to supernatural beings worldwide regardless of species.

I was a ball of confusion. I'd come into this room feeling justified in my hatred toward Elise. I believed I had her figured out, believed I was the only one broken. But now, I saw this plight from a different angle.

Hers.

I saw through the eyes of a mother who'd made a string of tough decisions with no chance of a favorable outcome.

I saw through the eyes of the queen of the dragons, a woman who loved and bore children with one of two lycan kings. The existence of my siblings and I was proof our species could thrive together.

Regardless of what my stance had been mere minutes before, the overall picture had changed. And one of those things I came to understand was that the strength Liam spoke of when referring to Elise, was no myth. She was poised and graceful. Just as one would expect a queen to be.

While I seemed to be a key component, I now saw the forest for the trees. This, regardless how painful, how personal, was not all about me. My feelings, my struggle, were secondary to the cause—one I couldn't help but to sympathize with.

Maybe because I'd come from Elise, I'd inherited her sense of duty as well.

The things I endured were, in a sense, my contribution, my sacrifice for the greater good. Liam had made them, and it wasn't until now that I realized Elise had made them, too. Giving me to my parents was hers.

I hadn't been tossed aside and forgotten by her.

I hadn't been discarded.

In Elise's own way, giving me up was an expression of her love. Even if the aftermath was sometimes hard to accept. My eyes were now open and I summed it all up with three impressively elegant words when I addressed her:

"I get it."

She smiled and it was the warmest I'd seen her give so far. "You have no idea how happy I am to hear you say that. All I've ever wanted is for you to understand."

She stood and after a single step, stopped abruptly. Both her hands clasped in front of her and it was strange seeing such a confident woman wearing such an uncertain expression. Her eyes flitted toward Liam as he stood off to the side. He pursed his lips as we slid into awkward silence.

However, he and I had our own way around that.

"I think she wants to hug you," he said, speaking in our unconventional way, via our thoughts.

When I glanced at Elise again, completely unaware of the internal prompt Liam had just given, she seemed so vulnerable. In some ways, broken. I, again, put myself in her shoes, wondering how it would feel to go this long without family, only to be staring into the face of a child I bore twice, not knowing if it was okay to embrace her.

It didn't take me long to decide to do what she hadn't found the courage to.

Hugging her was like I'd been snatched out of the present and hurled back in time. She was so ... familiar. Even her scent—lilac. Initially, I'd taken this step for her, but, now that she held me tight to her, I realized I needed it just as badly.

The sense of belonging I'd only ever felt in Liam's arms washed over me now, too.

Soft sobs rose from her chest and neither of us rushed to let go.

"I'm so sorry about Todd and Rebecca. If there was anything I could do to change what's been done to them, done to *you,* I would."

I leaned away from her, but only to ask a question. "What about Hilda? You mentioned how powerful she is? I know one witch's magic can't be undone by another, but ... is there a way?"

Before she even had the chance to answer, I knew what she'd say from the look in her eyes. It was the same one I'd gotten from Liam when asking a similar question.

"If that were possible, I would have taken care of it already. But you have my word, when the time is right, I'll see to it that Scarlet and her sisters cooperate fully."

My heart sank a little lower than it already had as I was reminded of my parents' fate. It didn't lessen the blow knowing it was temporary. But this was all about sacrifices, right? Giving up the things you love, stepping out of your comfort zone for the greater good?

For now, I'd just have to accept that they were out of my life for a while and find comfort in knowing that, one day, I'd have them back.

CHAPTER 20

Two months later...

Evie

Back home in Michigan, I was certain Mom and Dad were putting up their tree while *'It's a Wonderful Life'* played on the living room television.

How did I know this?

Because it was our family tradition to put our tree up exactly one week before Christmas while watching Mom's favorite movie of the season. According to Beth's update from home, they had roughly four inches of snow, meanwhile, here in Louisiana?

Just rain. Lots and lots of rain.

...Not that any of us were actually allowed to go topside and see it for ourselves.

The first couple weeks of lockdown were more annoying than inconvenient, but then week three came. Hundreds of moody

265

teenagers all confined to one space, even a space as large as this facility, was like a whole new kind of hell. Mood swings had become the norm, a few minor fights broke out almost daily, and the drama only increased when news about having to stay put for Thanksgiving began to circulate. Needless to say, enough hell was raised that the staff made special arrangements for busses to transport most of us home for Christmas.

Most of us, meaning those with someplace to go.

I was among those staying behind.

Come nightfall, myself and a handful of students and monitors would be all that remained. Down here, it'd feel like being the last people on Earth, I was sure. My only comfort was knowing Liam would be around to lessen the loneliness.

And Elise, too.

I was still in the 'warming up' phase with her, despite several weeks passing. According to Liam, I was even hard to get close to in my first life, so my reluctance with Elise hadn't taken him by surprise.

But when it came to softening up toward *him*, there was definitely progress.

From the outside looking in, I'm sure it still seemed like I kept him locked out. In some ways, I suppose I did, but only while I got used to the new me. That's what it felt like—being reborn for a *third* time as I found my way back to things that felt familiar, including him. Despite my seeming distant and guarded, there was a very different story being told within me.

Liam wasn't as far on the outside as he may have thought. In fact, he was the most trusted person in my life.

Hands down.

Small, festive, artificial trees lined the hallway and I struggled not to kick each one over as I passed by, imagining myself punting them clean to the other side of Gold Sector. Would've been so freakin' fun to watch them soar. Their glowing, white lights, red bows, and mini pinecones were yet another reminder that Christmas was right around the corner and I wouldn't be celebrating with my parents.

Hardly anyone lingered in the dining hall when I passed through. Most had been in their rooms the last hour or two, packing for their soon-coming departure. I, on the other hand, was headed to the gym —a sparring session I purposely scheduled for this time. I didn't want to sit around watching Beth prepare for her trip home. Not only did she get frequent phone calls from her parents, checking in, but now she was on her way to see them, too. Yeah, that made me a bit of a hater, but I was too deep in my feelings to care.

It was easy to convince her I was okay. She'd gotten used to my weekly sparring sessions with Liam, so she didn't question it when I gave her a quick goodbye hug before leaving. She'd be long gone when I got back and I'd have our room to myself to sulk in silence.

I was nearly to the gym and felt Liam already. I'd learned to recognize the tingling in the center of my chest as one of many supernatural alerts that existed between us. This one simply meant he was close.

Waiting.

After several weeks of getting tossed around, gently swept off my feet and onto my back, I was beginning to find my mojo. Now, not only did I keep showing up because I enjoyed the time we got to hang out together; I showed up because I was starting to retain some of what he taught me.

Shifting on my own was so simple I couldn't understand why it'd ever been an issue. He also talked me through how to *'burn blue'*—the not-so-creative term my brothers had coined centuries ago for the strange flames only the original dragon and her descendants could achieve. I was a long way from holding my own in combat, but, thanks to Liam, I was getting close.

I even *felt* stronger. Physically. Emotionally. There was something empowering about knowing how to wield even a few of my supernatural abilities. It made me feel untouchable some days. I wasn't foolish enough to think it was more than an illusion, but it was my brain's way of faking it 'til I made it, I guess.

'Think you're untouchable and you'll be untouchable.'

So far, it was working.

I burst through the doors of the gym with a smile, ready to pretend I could kick Liam's butt, knowing I wasn't really any match for him. Tightening my ponytail as I approached, he smiled back.

I didn't miss how his eyes slipped from mine, deliberately scanning my figure. There was no shame or embarrassment when he stared. The look brought with it a feeling. It was like I could hear his thoughts loud and clear, how he believed I was his to look at whenever he desired to do so. The intensity of it breathed heat across my cheeks and I was sure they were red now.

He'd done that a lot lately, stared in that unapologetic way. I guessed it had something to do with the walls between us coming down. Or he may have felt comfortable checking me out because ... I'd also gotten caught looking at him in the same way on more than one occasion.

Sue me.

I couldn't help myself, though. With all the time we spent together, it was hard not getting sucked in. Not only was he more than easy to look at, he was sweet and fun, and just ... everything I needed him to be. Genuinely. As time passed, I felt less uncomfortable with how much he was starting to mean to me. By this point, it'd just become fact:

I needed him.

"Ready?" he asked behind a perfect grin of soft lips and white teeth.

I nodded and adjusted the hem of my tank top over the waistband of my shorts.

"I was *born* ready," I joked.

He laughed and gestured for me to come closer. I did, stopping about a foot away from him. His hands dwarfed mine when he took them, lifted them into the air and formed both into fists. When he let go, his brow quirked and I was given my first order.

"Hit me."

My expression went from blank to an incredulous smile. "As in ... with my fist?"

He nodded. "Don't hold back."

I'd learned to question him less over these past weeks. Mostly because his methods always yielded favorable results. Because of him, I was making progress. So, with that in mind, I squared my shoulders and swung to hit my target—his bicep.

He didn't even flinch, glancing down at the spot where my knuckles made contact. Then, his eyes were on me again and I could tell by the look he gave I'd done something wrong.

"What?"

He was trying to hold in a laugh and I watched as he took my fists again, re-forming both, starting with untucking my thumbs from inside them.

"Like this," he said gently. I was sure that, if I'd been anyone else, he would've lost patience a long time ago. But whenever he gave me instructions or corrected me in some way, he was always under-standing.

We both knew I had no clue what I was doing, but he had the advantage of recalling a time when I did. The challenge was getting me back there.

I studied how he repositioned my arms, with my elbows close to my body, fists guarding my face while I was in resting position.

"Again," he insisted. "And this time, aim for my face."

The power I'd let fill my limbs drained immediately. Not that I thought I could do a whole lot of damage, I didn't even want to try. When my posture shifted, Liam questioned me with his stare.

"I'm not gonna hit you in the face."

Now he was smiling. "Evangeline, this mug has been slapped, punched, kicked, and stomped more times than I can count." At his words, I studied the perfection standing before me, finding it hard to imagine it'd ever undergone the violence I was sure it endured over the years. Supernatural healing had, clearly, been at work.

"Once, decades ago, a lycan even took a rock to my jaw," he went on. How he was laughing about this, I would never understand, but he was. "Trust me, I can take one of your punches."

At first, I thought I mistook the undertone of an insult, but then he full-on laughed at me, adding, "You know ... assuming you can land it."

Holding in a smile of my own, I decided to give him what he wanted. The energy I let dissipate a moment ago returned. I blew out a breath through my mouth and then fired quickly, aiming for the left side of his face with a right hook.

He ducked, of course, but he seemed proud that I took the shot.

"Good. Now this time, when you release, keep your swing tighter. That way, if you miss again, you're not wasting energy trying to recoil."

I took the stance he showed me and went at him. I missed again, but his advice about recoiling stuck with me and I felt the difference.

"Much better." He paused to make a minor adjustment to my wrist and then looked me in my eyes. "Again."

We went back and forth like this for at least ten minutes; long enough that I worked up a sweat. He just had that glowy-sheen thing going on, making his exposed arms glisten like he'd been oiled up for a photoshoot. He was such a distraction.

The best kind.

"Again," he beckoned.

I was aware of my shoulders feeling fatigued, but pushed past it. That was the only way to build up endurance and stamina. I kept at it, swinging and missing over and over again until, finally, frustration caught up with me.

I stepped back, bracing my palms on my knees, struggling to catch my breath. "I need a break."

I stared at the blue mat, and then Liam's boot-clad feet when they came into view. He stood there a moment, watching me as I heaved and panted, feeling like I was inches from death.

"What are you doing?"

I didn't understand the question at first because I thought it should have been clear. I was giving up. No, not for good, but definitely for today. My emotions were running high and I wasn't as good at ignoring them as I thought. It got to me that I'd be stuck here; got to me that I'd miss out on spending the holiday with my family. It wasn't fair.

"I just ... I can't do this today," I sighed. "There's too much going on and I'm having a hard time concentrating."

Pity, coddling ... those were things I expected to get when Liam spoke; those were things I believed I needed. However, when he opened his mouth, I got neither.

"Stand up."

My heart skipped a beat at the sound of his voice. It was hard and stern, unlike I'd ever heard it when addressing me. Still, despite being startled, I did as I was told, straightening my posture when my gaze met his. He stared and I braced myself for whatever he'd say next, feeling he was unpredictable in this moment.

"You're not tired," he asserted, walking a slow circle around me as my eyes followed until they couldn't anymore. "The problem is you don't believe you're capable."

With each breath moving my shoulders up and down rapidly, I listened to every word that left his mouth.

"You don't believe you can; therefore, your body keeps capping you at what it believes to be your limit," he went on. "You've got to learn to push past that, learn that you're more than this."

My breathing slowed and I caught sight of him in my peripheral when he came back around. He stopped in front of me and a hard stare came my way. The rims of his nostrils flared, and then a tug in the center of my chest alerted me when his presence had awakened my dragon. That side of me loved this side of *him*—the harsh, abrasiveness that tripped every physiological alarm inside my body. It fed something primal within me.

With a quick burst of energy that started in his hands, Liam's entire body went up in flames and he didn't move. My breathing picked up again, but this time it wasn't fatigue.

It was adrenaline.

His eyes burned white as he captured me with a look. He was beautiful this way, in his true form, the outlines of his formidable frame still visible beneath the glow of bright orange flames. I never forgot his explanation of how our flesh was merely a container for what lie within.

My body shuddered when he took a step closer. So close a flame or two kissed my skin, the heat warming me, but never burning. I didn't turn away when he asked a question that continued to ring inside my head several seconds later.

"Do you believe in what you are?"

I couldn't put my finger on what about the question made me sad, but it was impossible to deny the way my heart lurched when asked.

Lately, although I thought I'd begun to come into my own, I was still painfully aware of not fully realizing my potential. It wasn't that I didn't want to, I thought it was simply that I didn't know *how* to. But now ... after Liam made me think deeper, I wondered if there was more to it.

Yes, I'd seen my body catch fire and not be consumed.

Yes, I felt stronger.

Yes, I believed in my connection to Liam, but ... maybe I didn't quite believe in *myself*.

Liam didn't back down. He held his ground despite the single tear that fell from my eye.

"I want to," I stammered.

He came even closer and I wondered if it was to force me into letting him see the truth, everything I tried to hide behind a smile and false confidence.

"Then what are you afraid of?" He couldn't have known this, but that may have been the hardest question anyone had ever asked me. That list was long and seemed to grow and change every day.

"Life. Losing more than I've already lost. Failure. Being—"

"Wrong answer."

I blinked, staring when he cut me off. My eyes slipped away from him so I could think harder, deeper.

"I'm afraid of not living up to—"

I was again interrupted by his deep voice and a sternly spoken, "Wrong answer."

A breath hitched in my throat when I faced him again. I wasn't sure what he wanted me to say. These things were true and I had nothing else to offer. Frustration brought on more tears and he remained unaffected by them.

"The next time I, or anyone else, asks you what you're afraid of, you give one answer and one answer only." He paused and I was panting again when he leaned in, letting the words caress my skin just like his flames.

"Nothing," he breathed. "You. Fear. Nothing."

My hands tingled when my dragon had the inkling to reach for him. *Physical* me was emotional and ready to cave, but *she* was strong and detached from every outside influence that wasn't Liam.

"You're ready for this, Evangeline," he uttered with a kinder tone. "You're ready and the only thing stopping you is you."

Deep down in a place I rarely focused much attention, I knew he was right. Slowly but surely, that feeling became contagious. The rest of me started believing it, too.

"So, are you gonna try again or are you giving up?"

The easy thing to do would have been to walk away, to leave him and his lofty expectations right there on that mat, but he inspired me to abandon 'easy'.

He seemed to take note of the determination I felt beaming through my expression and nodded, going back to his original position a couple feet away. As he walked, his flames dimmed and eventually burned out. Our eyes locked, and with one look, I was encouraged to give it my all.

That turned out to be just the push I needed, seeing that he believed I could get this right.

My fist breezed through the air and, finally, connected with the left side of Liam's chin. Upon impact, I drew back, covering my mouth with a gasp.

"Oh my gosh! I'm so sorry!"

"Don't be," he reasoned, smiling as he worked his jaw. "You got it exactly right."

I hadn't moved my hands, biting my lips behind them. It shouldn't have surprised me that he took so little time to recover, heading across the mat almost the next second. There, he lowered into stance as he braced himself.

"Now come at me."

I didn't think. Thinking tripped me up every time. Thinking made me second-guess myself and hesitate and there was no time for either in the heat of combat. So, I emptied my lungs and filled them with air again before launching toward him. I was suddenly so much faster, felt the power in my thighs as I moved in his direction; in my biceps as they pumped, propelling me. And this time, when I made it to Liam, I wasn't scooped up and lightly manhandled like usual.

Nope. *This* time ... I *moved* him.

It wasn't far—only a few inches—but I knocked him off balance when my shoulder slammed the center of his chest. A strong set of hands caught my waist to steady us both. His lengthy fingers slipped beneath the material of my shirt, unintentionally pushing it up a bit. The warmth of his skin on mine jarred me out of my thoughts, making me forget to celebrate this small victory. Instead, my heart raced.

"Nice," Liam crooned, seeming far less rattled than I was by the contact. "Next time, dip lower and lift upward when you lean in to take me down."

His hands left me and I reminded myself to close my mouth as I nodded. "Okay."

He glanced toward the mounted clock and seemed surprised we'd already been here an hour. "I think that's good for today. We should probably head back so we can shower before dinner."

The last thing on my mind was food, but I kept that to myself, nodding again. "Sure. Sounds good."

He smiled and we stopped at the bleachers where two towels and two bottles of water were waiting for us. One of each was placed in my hand and I thanked him. In every way, he was more prepared than I was, thinking one step ahead.

We walked the tinsel-decorated halls and they were quiet, completely empty, meaning everyone was gone and all that remained were those of us who'd be holed up here alone for the next two weeks. We reached my door and I must not have hid my thoughts as well as I meant to. Liam gripped my chin lightly to get my attention and he had it. Totally.

"It won't always be like this. You won't always have to miss them."

It was comforting to hear. A little reassurance goes a long way.

"Baz will see to it that his witches keep their word," he added. "You're kind of his new main priority." The smile he gave when he finished speaking made me warm all over.

I was brought into his arms and had to admit that, secretly, I wanted to be in them since laying eyes on him in the gym. I lacked the courage to embrace him on my own today, but didn't shy away from hugging him back when he initiated. My face fit into the crook of his neck just right and I stayed there, with my fingers resting at the nape of his neck, with his solid arms gripping me, with so many unspoken words hanging in the air. Holding him made home seem a little less far away.

Against my wishes, he let go and I saw a question in his eyes before he even asked.

"Elise had an idea and I've put off telling you because I know you've had a hard time lately." He seemed to search my face for any indication that it was okay to continue. When I nodded, he went on. "She wants us to join her for Christmas dinner. It'd be lowkey and completely depends on if you're ready or not, but ... she hopes you'll come."

My heart lurched at the idea of fully acknowledging that Christmas was right around the corner. I'd actually planned to spend most of the break in my room reading, or doing *anything* to forget what time of year it was. But now Liam was asking me to face it head on.

I stared, blinking several times before that pleading look in his eyes inspired me to nod. From the bottom of my heart, I didn't want to go, but I knew that if *I* didn't, neither would he.

"Okay," I finally breathed. "I guess it wouldn't hurt."

A reserved smile melted away the otherwise stern expression he always wore. "You know you don't have to," he added, "but I'm glad you agreed."

I smiled back. "Why's that?"

Broad shoulders lifted into the air when he shrugged. "Because I worry about you."

That wasn't the answer I expected. I guess I thought he'd say something more along the lines of how he was looking forward to hanging out. But worry? Didn't see that coming. I knew he was concerned for me physically, but I got the impression that wasn't what he meant.

I thought I was managing pretty well, but apparently, he disagreed.

"You're sad. A lot," he explained as one corner of his mouth tugged up again. "And when you're not, you're in a daze. So, like I said, I worry."

It was nice that he cared.

"I think this'll be good for you, though," he added. "Good for *both* of us."

He was right. Everything he said was spot on. So, if it'd make him feel better to see me take part in this whole ... *celebration* thing, I'd do it.

It was time to part ways, time to head to our own spaces to shower before heading to the dining hall where we'd eat with the others who'd been left behind. But it wasn't lost on me how, as Liam took a few steps toward his room, my hand lingered in his until I *had* to let go. It was *me* who held on.

"See you in thirty?" he called out, walking backwards while watching me.

All I could do was nod as my keycard rested between my fingers.

With the way I'd grown to feel about him lately, he could see me whenever.

CHAPTER 21

Nick

K yle, Ben, and Richie stood in the driveway, all with arms crossed over their chests as Dad and I pulled up. Two of the three seemed anxious for me to step out of the car; Richie never was one to show much emotion. The second I opened the door and my feet touched pavement, they left it again when Kyle lifted me off the ground in a bear hug.

"The prodigal pup has returned," he teased, setting me down again. His wide grin let me know I'd been missed while I was away.

Hoisting my duffle bag higher on my shoulder, I accepted a hard pat on the back from Richie. "Feels good to be home."

And it did. I mean, yeah, it was cold and I never did like the snow much, but there really was no place like home. I missed eating meals that didn't taste like fridge, sleeping in my own bed. Don't get me wrong, sharing a room with the guys was fine, but I had a newfound appreciation for privacy. For the next two weeks, I'd get to enjoy my own space again until inevitably being shipped back to Damascus.

Ushering me toward the house, my brothers bombarded me with a bunch of questions, ones I'd just answered for my dad when he picked me up from the bus.

"What's it like there?"

"Where is it?"

"Does it seem safe?"

"What do you do all day?"

I answered them one at a time, but not until we were inside where it was warm.

"It's secluded. Someplace in Louisiana, but none of us quite know where," I explained. "It's *incredibly* safe. They've got us hidden underground and there are monitors roaming the halls twenty-four/seven. And our day is mostly structured like it was here at Seaton Prep. We can grab breakfast in the dining hall if we're up early enough, then there's either training or lectures until lunch, then the last half of the day is academics—the stuff we'd be learning in a regular classroom."

Ben nodded, but I could tell he was bothered by something I said.

"Wow … they really took you guys far out, didn't they?" He paused and the expressions on my brothers' faces made it clear this was something they discussed before—at least as a suspicion. Until now, no one knew exactly where we'd been taken.

"Would've been nice for them to keep you all closer in case you're ever in danger. At least we'd be able to get to you," Kyle chimed in, adding his two cents.

"Well, it's like I said, things seem safe, so…"

"Still isn't right." The mumbled rebuttal came from my father. "Yeah, you kids are members of the clan, but I'm sick of that taking precedence over the fact that you're *our* kids."

Beside me, Richie lowered his head.

The sound of soft footsteps ended our conversation as well as any further objection to our clan's way of handling the issue. Mom seemed oblivious to how silent the rest of us were when she joined us in the foyer. Her arms went around my neck, squeezing me tight as she fawned over me like mom's do—looking me over like I'd just returned from war. She smelled like cinnamon and vanilla—remnants of whatever dessert she was prepping. Dad mentioned she'd been in the kitchen all day, getting dinner ready for my return.

When she finally backed away, there were tears in her eyes. "I'm so happy they brought you home. Thanksgiving without you was bad enough, but I would've launched an attack against the Elders myself if they kept you away for Christmas, too."

I set my duffle bag down beside the door, realizing my family had no intention of allowing me passage to my room any time soon.

"Mom, I'm fine," I assured her when she did another pass of her fingers through my hair.

She completely ignored me and asked, "Are they feeding you well?" which prompted all my brothers to laugh.

Richie took me by the shoulders and shook them. "Ma, this kid doesn't look like he's missed any meals. Relax."

"But I, on the other hand, haven't eaten since breakfast," Kyle cut in. "So, can we grub now?"

Mom passed him a look before a smile broke free. "Wash your hands and help me fix the table."

Kyle just about ran to the kitchen sink to take Mom up on her offer while the rest of us shifted to the dining room. Within minutes, an entire spread was laid out on the table. A meal fit for a king. I tossed down three full plates and a big heap of apple pie before finally feeling full enough to back away from the table. My brothers were no better. We quickly reduced the feast to nothing more than scraps that could all fit in one Tupperware container. We each helped clear the dishes and then hung out in the living room to let our food settle.

Mom seemed to be working her way up to a point all through dinner. She'd asked about my friends, even Roz, but never Evie. I got the feeling she wanted to, but maybe wasn't sure I'd answer. Or maybe she didn't know if she *wanted* the answer.

It was no secret she never approved of us seeing one another, although I didn't fully understand why until it was explained at the facility. The long-standing feud between the lycan and dragon shifter races was mostly based on one side's prejudices against the other. Dragons had been deemed unpredictable and untrustworthy by my people and, therefore, my mother wanted me to have nothing to do with her. While, no, Evie being part dragon had nothing to do with us ending things, I suppose my mother had gotten her wish.

For nearly two months now, the girl I once clumsily admitted to being in love with, hadn't said more than 'hi' and 'bye' to me. We were, more or less, ships passing in the night. Our worlds were separate, but converged when our schedules made it unavoidable. Every time, she'd give a shy smile like she didn't know me anymore, and then we'd wave. And every time, it killed me a little on the inside.

And now, as I sat with my feet propped up on an ottoman, my mother finally got up the nerve to butt in.

"I'm assuming you and Evie have gotten closer? With all the time I'm sure you're spending together, I mean." She smiled, but it was forced and uncomfortable to look at.

My brothers, through phone calls made while I was away, were aware of my status with Evie. Ben cleared his throat when Mom asked and I felt his eyes on me without glancing that way.

"Then you'd be assuming wrong," I answered.

My gaze drifted out the window toward Evie's house. According to Beth, she'd be visiting family in Florida for the holidays, which accounted for her not being on the bus with us coming home. Seemed strange she wouldn't take this opportunity to be with her mom and dad, but for all I knew, they'd be heading south to join her, enjoying the sunshine, escaping the cold.

A surprised, "Oh!" from Mom did little to hide how pleased she was to hear that things had ended. Maybe pleased was the wrong word.

Relieved.

She sounded relieved.

"Was it ... mutual?" she asked next.

Deciding now wasn't the time to get into the details, I sat straight and scooted to the edge of my seat on the sofa. "Nope. Wasn't mutual," was all I said.

"You're leaving?" Mom asked in a huff. "I didn't mean to pry. It's just that ... I worry. That's all."

And I got that, but I needed to be alone for a bit. It'd been a while since I had the luxury. Being stuck on that loud, crowded bus for nearly twenty-hours—with food and bathroom breaks, plus two driver changes—made finding peace and quiet even more necessary.

"You just got in," she insisted, sounding a bit insulted by me running off so soon. "I won't ask questions about her if it makes you uncomfortable."

I stretched once I was on my feet. "It's not anything you said," I lied. "I just need to shower and get some rest."

Her eyes stayed trained on me for a moment and, finally, she gave in. "Okay."

I flashed her a reassuring smile and leaned down to kiss her forehead as I passed by. All five sets of eyes were on me as I made my way toward the stairs after grabbing my bag from the foyer.

Stepping into my room after months of being away was one of the best feelings in the world. Everything was exactly like I left it. Moving to the closet, I tossed my bag inside. My old Seaton Prep Uniforms hung neatly and I stared at them. It seemed like a lifetime ago that things were normal. So far, my senior year had gone nothing like I imagined it would and there were no signs things would change.

As I stood eyeing the pieces, symbolic of the life I'd left behind, my phone buzzed in my pocket with a text.

'My dad's excitement to see me was overshadowed by exhaustion,' Roz typed. 'He's been working the last two days with little to no sleep.'

'Sux.'

'Totally :(We're grabbing breakfast in the morning, so he's making *up for it. How's your fam? Did they roll out the red carpet for the returning prince?'*

I smiled at the term that once felt more like an insult, mostly because, back then, she meant it as one.

'Funny. Nope, just the expected line of questioning.' I didn't need to explain what that meant. She knew how my mom felt about Evie, knew there would be speculation when we went away together.

'Only 'cause they care,' Roz countered.

'Now you sound like my mom.'

'Ouch lol. Just saying. At least yours stayed awake long enough to get ten words out. My dad hugged me, told me he missed me, then it was lights out for him.'

'Better than having to pretend you're too tired to socialize. Now I'm stuck up here in my room.'

There was a pause in conversation and I stepped into the bathroom to turn on the shower, pulling my shirt over my head. When it hit the floor, I took note of red scratches on my shoulder and chest—scratches I didn't recall getting, which meant they came from one of my blackouts.

They'd gotten more frequent and, as a result, I didn't sleep well anymore. I found myself trying to stay awake, thinking I'd be able to stop this from happening somehow. I'd gotten used to the dark circles under my eyes that came along with it, but I knew my mother would never let it slide. Hence the reason I made sure to get some rest the few days leading up to this trip.

But this led to another concern—sleeping *here*. I couldn't guarantee I wouldn't have another episode. Couldn't guarantee I wouldn't get up in the middle of the night and freak my parents out.

Or worse.

Truth was, I had no idea what I was capable of anymore; no idea what I was becoming beyond the name I'd been given. More and more I leaned toward sneaking off to my grandfather's estate at night, returning by morning before anyone noticed I'd gone missing.

Still hadn't ruled it out as a possibility.

Water pelted the shower floor as I finished undressing. The second I turned to step in, Roz messaged again.

'Wanna hang? Maybe we can scour your grandfather's place tonight.'

It was like she read my mind. His place would've been off limits with anyone else, but I trusted her.

I eyed the message, remembering how heartbroken my mother seemed a moment ago when I excused myself to come upstairs. Getting out of the house would be next to impossible. But I had reasons to do so beyond Roz's innate curiosity rubbing off on me.

At this point, it was more of a safety precaution.

'I can't get a car. Meet me outside the gate in an hour?'

I could practically feel Roz's excitement through the phone when she replied. *'Yep! Bring his journals if you have them; I'll bring my laptop. Don't guess Gramps's place has wi-fi?'*

Sometimes, she was too ridiculous not to laugh at. *'Seeing as how no one lives there, we're lucky there's even heat and electricity.'*

'This is true. I guess beggers can't be choosey. Later.'

I set my phone down and, while showering, devised a plan to get past my mom.

Fully dressed, I rejoined my family in the living room. Just like when I left after Mom questioned me about Evie, they all stared now, but for different reasons.

But that was the plan.

I took the time to style my hair, then searched for a pair of dark jeans to match a button-down Dad gave me on my birthday. I sprayed on cologne and waited for someone to ask.

"Where do you think *you're* going?"

Of course, Mom was the curious one.

"Uh ... on a date, actually." Somehow, despite lying through my teeth, I got the words out smoothly. "Sorry. I know I just got home, but ... I hoped you wouldn't mind."

Mom blinked hard and fast. "Oh! Uh ... with who?"

She pretended to be cool with it, pretended not to be bothered by the fact that I was up to hanging out with a girl, but wasn't up to hang out with *them*.

"Officer Chadwick's daughter. Roz," I answered, knowing full-well our meetup was a far cry from a date. If anything, we'd be nerding out while going through boxes and boxes of relics in my grandfather's study. However, in all honesty, that sounded like a blast.

"That cool?" I added.

There was no mistaking the relief on my mother's face. It was like, as long as I wasn't seeing Evie, she was fine with *whoever* I dated.

"Roz seems like a nice girl."

I nodded with a smile, able to tell the truth when I answered this time. "She is."

"Need the car?" Dad offered, shocking me.

"Uh ... I didn't realize you'd let me take it, so she's picking me up at the gate." I glanced at the large clock mounted above the fireplace. "Actually, I need to get going. Don't wait up," I called out as I turned, knowing I had no intentions of returning before dawn. My bag was packed by the door just in case I needed anything, but I'd be spending the night in my grandfather's king-size bed tonight and maybe *every* night while here in town.

It was for my family's own good.

Just like we discussed, Roz was waiting at my neighborhood's entrance with the engine running. The air was brisk, but I didn't get as cold as I would have months ago, before turning. She smiled when I opened the door and tossed my bag into the backseat. There was a look she gave and I didn't understand it at first, but in true Roz fashion, she spoke her mind the very next second.

"Am I dropping you off somewhere? I thought we were going to your grandfather's," she joked, glancing down at the cartoony pajama pants and t-shirt she wore beneath a heavy jacket with a fur-trimmed hood.

"Had to convince my parents I was going on a date tonight in order to get out of the house without too much resistance. I knew my mom wouldn't put up a fight since she's desperate for me to get over Evie, so I played on that."

Roz nodded as we headed up the hill after I pointed that way.

"Ah, I see," she replied, falling silent for a moment before saying more. "Who'd you tell her you were seeing?"

I chuckled a bit and expected her to laugh, too, when I answered. "You."

But she didn't. Instead, there was this distant look on her face as she kept her thoughts to herself. When it seemed I was the only one amused, my smile faded some.

After a few awkward seconds, Roz was back in all her sarcastic splendor. "So ... do you *always* wear this much cologne when you go on dates? Or are you just trying to kill *me,* specifically?"

Despite the insult being at my expense, I laughed, rolling down the window.

"Sorry, I guess I went overboard trying to be convincing. Had to make it believable."

She fanned her hand in front of her face. "Well, if believability is measured in cologne sprays ... I'd say you could probably convince the entire state of Michigan, because ... *whew!*"

"I get it, I get it," I smiled. "I'll change when we get there. Make a left here."

She followed my directions, all while hanging her head out the driver's side window for fresh air. The side streets hadn't been plowed, so we crept along. Then, eventually, the many silhouetted peeks of my grandfather's pitched roof came into view. The house was massive, but I knew it like the back of my hand despite his passing before I was even born. My family spent a lot of time here during the summer when I was coming up. My brothers and I spent many nights running the halls of his home, finding new places to hide, new things to explore. I always believed it made my father feel close to my grandfather in some way. Like, he was still here with us.

A high, iron fence surrounded the property. When we came to the gate, instead of getting out in the cold to key in the access code myself, I recited the digits to Roz. She blinked large, doe-like eyes at me first, and then pressed in the numbers I gave her. My parents would probably kill me if they knew I shared something so personal, but I had zero hesitation whatsoever. Roz had long-since convinced me she was trustworthy.

The long stretch of blacktop lined with trees dating back hundreds of years marked our path. At the end, Roz killed the engine and gazed through the windshield.

"Holy over-compensation, Batman. This house is ginormous," she said while gazing up at the three-story structure before us. The stone façade gave it the appearance of a medieval castle that'd been dropped right here in the woods.

I opened the passenger-side door and reached back to grab my bag from the backseat. Roz followed, gawking at the house as we took the walkway to the front door. I dug my keys out of my pocket and turned the lock, quickly rushing toward the keypad on the wall to disable the alarm. As soon as Roz turned the deadbolt and secured us inside, I reset it.

Warm, yellow light filled the massive foyer at the flick of a switch. The source? A crystal chandelier hanging above. There were no cobwebs or dust to speak of. We had Mom to thank for that. Once every other month, she and local, hired help came in and cleaned this place from top to bottom. So, to an outsider, it'd be easy to falsely believe the house was still occupied. The home my father grew up in had become somewhat of a museum of our family's history. Only, it wasn't until recently that I discovered the secrets it held.

"The study's this way." My voice brought Roz's attention to me, interrupting her scan of our surroundings. The elaborate tapestries and dramatic staircases at either side of the entrance were a lot to take in.

"How did I not know this place was out here?" she asked wide-eyed.

I shrugged. "Guess he liked his privacy. If you want something to stay secret bad enough, you find a way to keep it secret."

"Ain't that the truth," she chuckled. "Lead the way."

We headed toward the room where my grandfather housed his most prized possessions. Imported runners lined the long corridors that led us toward the house's east wing. I flipped switches that lit our path, bringing life to the dark silhouettes of statues and oversized furniture. Rich, oak paneling covered the walls, making this place feel like a palace in the middle of the woods.

At the door to the study, Roz watched intently as I tipped a large, gold vase and pulled a skeleton key from beneath it. There was one hidden outside several of the locked rooms. My father used to keep them all on a large keyring, but got tired of having to scramble for the right one. Eventually, he wised up and just left each one near the door it belonged to.

Iron hinges creaked when I turned the knob and pushed. The smell of cedar and cigar smoke still clung to the walls even now, two decades after my grandfather's passing. It seemed to stay in the fabric of the chairs and thick curtains no matter how Mom tried to get rid of it. None of us really minded it, though. In a way, it seemed fitting that my grandfather's favorite room still smelled the way it did the last time he'd been here.

"Jackpot." Roz's voice echoed off the two-story, floor-to-ceiling bookcases that lined the walls. Cutting right beneath the top shelf, a brass bar with a wheeled ladder attached.

"I, officially, grant you carte blanche," I announced. "Feel free to rummage through whatever. We just have to leave everything the way we found it."

"Aye aye, captain," she saluted before taking quick steps toward the ladder like I fully expected her to. Meanwhile, I moved toward the desk.

When I hid out here those few days, I came across a small key tucked away inside the nightstand drawer of the master bedroom. I tried it everywhere I could think of at the time—the safe hidden beneath the rug and floorboards in the pantry, a curio cabinet on the landing headed to the third floor, a chest beneath the basement stairs, but it didn't work. Now, as I fished it from my pocket, I had hopes I wouldn't be disappointed tonight.

And I wasn't.

The room was eerily quiet when the lock turned and clicked. It was stiff, a sign it hadn't been opened in years. Curious as to what I discovered, Roz took slow steps down from the ladder.

"Find something interesting already?"

Shrugging, I pulled the top drawer open and laid eyes on a stack of old folders. Aged, yellowing pages stuck out the sides of most, but one lie on top that had been neatly put together. I slid it out and placed it on the desk as Roz approached from my right. Eager to see what was inside, I undid the black string tied around a fastener on the top flap.

Legal documents. Contracts bearing many signatures, but only one I recognized.

"Who the heck is Carmine LiCausi?" Roz asked.

"My grandfather." I knew seeing his last name had thrown her, so I explained. "He insisted that both, his son *and* his wife, not take on his surname. So, while I'm technically a LiCausi by blood, per my grandfather's request, no one will ever know that."

Until now, of course. Until her.

"Heavy stuff," Roz remarked. "Makes you wonder what he was hiding, or who he was hiding from."

I said nothing as I stared at his careful penmanship, wondering what secrets the man took with him to his grave.

"What's this?"

Roz pulled yet another document from the drawer and the bold letters on top stood out to us both.

Project Damascus.

My brow tensed as I stared at the sheet she placed before me. It was the original plan drafted by the Council.

"Damascus," Roz sighed. "Suppose it makes sense to call it that. The city was fought over for millennia. In a way, *we're* kind of like

Damascus—property everyone wants to lay claim to. Our parents. The Clan," she explained, adding, "The Sovereign."

There was a solemn moment where neither of us said a word. Lifting the top page, I read the one attached beneath it. A receipt for his pledge, stating the dollar amount he contributed to the cause.

"Looks like he was a benefactor." I had no idea these facilities dated back so far. Large donations such as his must have been what got the ball rolling. Later developments were likely funded by what was syphoned from the tariff.

"With all the zeroes in this figure, I'm surprised this didn't fund the entire project!" Roz countered. "Not that I couldn't tell from this house, but your grandfather was *loaded*."

There was no arguing with her on that point. "He was incredibly old," I explained. "My father made it clear he made good use of his time, learning to trade stock, investing in the right companies. I guess it just paid off."

"I'd say so."

I scanned the sheet again. "Do you think this is significant?"

Roz stared at it, too. "Not the document itself, but the fact that this project has been in the works for so long. Even listening to our parents talk about the facility, it sounds like new news to them. However, this seems to point toward Damascus, and other places like it, being on the minds of the Council much longer than we thought."

I nodded. "Makes you wonder what's gone on in the past, or what they've been anticipating, that made them act decades before anyone else even knew there'd be an upset among the clans."

When I set the papers down, one word left Roz's mouth and I couldn't have agreed with it more: "Shady."

"Super."

I kept things in a neat pile to be returned to their rightful places when we finished. Roz continued to rummage in the deep drawer and my attention went to a large, yellow envelope when she pulled it free.

The address on the outside was to *my* home, and the name

printed in ragged handwriting was my father's. There was something thick and bulky inside. I stared when Roz removed it with a cheeky grin on her face.

"Look familiar?" she asked, propping her hip against the edge of the desk.

I couldn't blink, staring at a brown, leather-bound book. One that matched the four journals I'd guarded with my life since discovering them several months ago.

"Did you know there were others?" Roz asked.

Shaking my head, I reached for it. "No, I thought I had them all."

Beneath the dim lamp perched on the desk, I began thumbing through pages. The others were packed with info, references I had yet to decode.

"Slow down so we don't miss anything."

I peered up at Roz, feeling my heart race with impatience. "You expect me to read this whole thing, page by page?"

Her brow shot up, implying this was *exactly* what she expected.

"If your grandfather took the time to write it, we should take our time, too. Skipping around versus a thorough scan could make all the difference in the world, Nick."

She was right, but I didn't *like* that she was right.

A deep breath puffed from my mouth. "Fine. We'll read through it."

Satisfied with the win, Roz smiled before taking the seat on the other side of the desk. The journals I'd already gone through were beside her in my duffle bag, so I invited her to check them out while I jumped into the newest. It was interesting to read more about his life, but I'd come across nothing useful after thirty minutes.

"Can I skim yet?" I asked, sounding like a kid asking to be let out of timeout. Roz grinned and I guessed she might've thought the same thing.

"What's the matter? Not your ideal date?" she teased, reminding me I was supposed to change into more comfortable clothes when we got here. My one-track mind made it easy to forget. All I seemed to think about these days was learning more about what I am ... so I could find a way to undo it.

"Be back." Roz only glanced up for a second when I leaned in to take my bag.

"Hurry. This place kinda gives me the creeps."

With a laugh, I left her and headed for the stairs. I climbed them with ease, but there were enough of them that a *normal* person might have gotten winded. At the end of a long, bridge-like hallway that crossed the great room, was my grandfather's suite. Instead of rushing to change, I sat on the edge of the bed for a moment, checking my phone because it was kind of a reflex.

A text from Lucas.

Two from Chris.

An empty feeling hit me right in the gut when I made the mistake of acknowledging that I wished there'd been one from someone else. But that was stupid to even think it. She hadn't spoken to me in months.

And I still hadn't quite gotten over it.

Pathetic, right? To be pining over a girl I'd barely gotten to know, and had officially been apart from longer than we were together? I knew it didn't make sense that I still cared, but try telling that to my heart.

When sulking got old, I changed into the shorts and tee I packed, rejoining Roz in the study. She was right where I left her, engrossed in the journal. If it hadn't been for the question she asked, I might've thought she didn't even notice I was back.

"How'd your grandfather die?"

I paused while lowering into my seat. "Uh ... not really sure. I was always told he had some kind of accident while traveling abroad. Not sure my dad even knows much more than that."

Roz's brow was tense as she concentrated.

"Why'd you ask?" As soon as the question left my mouth, I realized the journal from the drawer wasn't where I left it. Glancing up, I saw that Roz had set the other aside to see what info might be in the new one.

Her eyes never left the page, but there was a look on her face I couldn't place. "Because ... I know I said not to, but ... I skimmed a little."

The confession made me smile as I got comfortable in my seat. "If you found something good, I think I can forgive you."

I expected a smart comeback, the usual Rozalind Chadwick witticism, but ... nothing. Just a blank stare when she finally peered up.

"What is it?"

She blinked and I could tell she didn't want to answer. "He thought he was being followed."

"Followed, as in ... ?"

"As in, there's entry after entry where he mentions someone tracking him, being paranoid to the point of watching the shadows," she explained.

I leaned back, trying to see if there were pieces I'd missed, things that should have connected.

"Were they mutts? The Sovereign?" When Roz didn't answer, my gaze leveled on her again. "Did he give a name?"

Seeming nervous all of a sudden, fidgeting with the corner of the journal. Like she was afraid to speak.

"Roz, is there a name?"

Her eyes flitted back down to the page once before lifting to meet mine again. And, when they did, one word slipped off her lips. At the sound of it, my entire world shifted on its axis.

"Reaper."

CHAPTER 22

Nick

I t was all here. In black and white. The truth, or at least part of it.

That name ... *Reaper*. There was no doubt who my grandfather spoke of. A moment of disbelief prompted Roz to bring the journal around where I could see it for myself. We turned the page and the plot thickened.

"My people are not slaves to the moon, we are one with it," I recited, following the neat handwriting across a worn page. *"But, unlike the others, I have not had the fortune of only basking in her light. To me, she reveals her other side, one where darkness always prevails. It is on that bleak, sunless hemisphere where her true nature lie deep in the shadows, hidden where no lycan has ever wandered. None but me. This burden belongs to no one else.*

I, alone, walk the dark side of the moon."

My heart raced a mile a minute as his words sunk in, as I related to them in ways I hadn't expected. It was like he'd written my thoughts. I lived with the knowledge that I wasn't like other lycans. He felt that, too.

I knew what this all sounded like—he and I were one and the same—but it couldn't have been true.

"I've spent a lifetime hoping to atone for my sins," I read on. *"One, in particular, I fear may never be forgiven. Guilt haunts me as relentlessly as the Reaper. I understand the cause of his pursuit, but I can only hope time has changed him as much as it has me. If we meet again and that change has not come about, I shall accept my end and welcome it with peace and dignity."*

A small hand came down on my shoulder. Had it not been for the contact, I might've forgotten I wasn't here alone. As Roz read alongside me, I believed she reached the same conclusion I did, bringing the story full-circle.

"Innocent blood has only covered my hands once, and I swore to myself, never again. Although no one would believe it, I hadn't acted of my own will the night I pried the beautiful hybrid from the arms of her lover; the night I ripped her body, and his heart, to shreds. The driving force being ... the dark side of myself. The hidden part that, in times past, controlled me more than I was able to control it. Had I known the nightmares, the dark thoughts, losing track of time, were all precursors to that moment, I might have done more to prevent it. Even if the only viable recourse had been to exchange my life for hers."

Nightmares. Dark thoughts. Losing track of time.

It was almost as if I'd written this entry myself. My mind reeled. So many things began to make sense. So many things clicked, but I still needed to say it out loud.

"He was the first Liberator," I panted.

With Roz being the smartest person I knew, I was sure she figured this out long before I said it, but I needed to speak the words.

"He was the Liberator." Confessing it for a second time left me just as breathless as the first, knowing he'd been responsible for taking

Evie's life in the past, knowing Liam—*the Reaper*—was likely responsible for ending *his* in return. A twisted tale of poetic justice.

"I need air."

Roz followed close behind when I rushed from the study, headed
toward the double doors at the end of the hallway. I burst out onto
the patio shrouded by bushes. My breath crystalized in the brisk air
when I exhaled, but I hardly noticed the chill. My eyes scanned the
snow-covered landscape while my thoughts raced.

"He couldn't fight it. He lost control just like *I'll* lose control one
day," I huffed, feeling like my lungs might explode. "I can't ... I can't
let—"

My face warmed when Roz placed her hands at either side of it,
holding my cheeks.

"Breathe, Nick." She was so calm. "We'll fix this. I won't stop
until I find a way."

Drawing in a breath, I had an epiphany. "You need to go. I can't
be trusted. Not around *anyone*. You're in danger just standing here
talking to me."

"No." The response came so swiftly, without hesitation. "And
you're an idiot for even suggesting it. Friends don't bail on friends.
No matter what," she added.

Her hands fell away when I began to pace. "Roz, now is probably
the dumbest time for you to be so freakin' stubborn. I'm doing this for
your own good."

"Because you think you're some monster?" she cut in. "Well,
that's where we have an issue. I'm having a hard time believing that
part." She folded both arms across her chest. "I don't think we were
listening to the same passage being read from that journal a second
ago."

My brow tensed when my feet stopped. I stared her down,
finding it hard to understand why she wasn't getting it. My grandfather had just admitted to shedding innocent blood, *Evie's* blood, and I
was on the exact same path.

Roz's gaze shifted back toward the French doors we'd just exited through. Her eyes were locked on the open door of the study, visible through the segmented panes of glass.

"The man who wrote that piece was remorseful, Nick. He wasn't a villain. There was real feeling in those words and, if he could, I think he'd take it back and there's nothing you could say to convince me otherwise."

"What if it'd been your dad?" The question brought disturbing visuals with it and I was sure the same held true for Roz. No, it wasn't pleasant picturing Officer Chadwick mangled and bloody, but that was the point. Would Roz be so callous if we were discussing the life of someone she loved?

A solemn look indicated the moment my question hit home. She stared off into the distance for a while and I wondered if she was beginning to understand my plight. Whether the last Liberator had taken one life or a thousand, it still mattered.

Blinking, her lips parted and I was all ears.

"When I was about eight, I had this super weird obsession with Legos," she shared with a smile. "I swear I asked for new ones to add to my collection like, every week. It got so bad that, when my birthday and Christmas came around, Legos were the only thing on my list. I didn't want anything else."

Shoving both hands in my pockets, I watched the range of emotion cross her face. Her mouth was still curved into a smile, but the expression never quite reached her eyes.

"Well, one week, I decided to start building this huge, elaborate island. Right in the middle of my room. It was insane," she chuckled. It faded almost as quickly as it came. "I sketched the whole thing out before I started building just to make sure I didn't leave anything out. My dad used to keep tarp stored in the garage and, after going on and on about how it was the perfect shade of blue for the water around the island, he caved and let me take one of the smaller ones."

A shimmer in the corner of her eye caught my attention. She was tearing up. Right away, I regretted saying whatever I said that made her decide to share this story. It sucked seeing people I cared about cry, but it would've been rude to interrupt.

"So, anyway, I got the tarp spread. It took me two whole weeks to build the island just right and all that was left was to add the finishing touch. A pirate ship," she sighed. "I planned the whole thing out. All I needed was some sort of box to tape a sail to and I'd be done. And I knew just where to find one."

When a tear moved down her cheek, she caught it with the sleeve of her shirt. The very next second, she sniffled and straightened her posture, pretending to be unaffected. But she was. Despite trying to play tough all the time, Roz was all heart and, at the moment, hers was exposed to me. I had a feeling she didn't let that happen with just anyone.

"My dad kept one in the top of his closet," she went on. "It was a pretty, tin box with bright blue and turquoise flowers painted over a yellow background. I thought about it while I ate lunch, planning how I'd get it without getting caught. So, as soon as he went out to cut the grass, I listened for the motor and then climbed up to that shelf and took the box."

She wiped her eyes again.

"I emptied it. There were all these old, tattered pieces of paper inside and I walked the canister over to the kitchen trash and poured them right in," she shared. "I didn't even bother looking at them. At that moment, all I saw was my pirate ship. I went back to playing and it wasn't until maybe three weeks later, a month maybe, that I even thought about the papers that'd been inside it. My dad came to my door and I remember staring, wondering why his face was so red." She zoned out, imagining it.

"He asked if I'd seen the tin box he kept in the closet. Thinking nothing of it, I told him I had, and then pointed to the pirate ship I kept on my bookshelf. I knew right away something was wrong.

"I'll never forget the look on his face when he asked what I'd done with the letters inside." Her face went blank and she had my full attention when her eyes met mine. "They were from my mom.

Love notes she'd written him every day for the first year of their marriage. Sometimes, she put them in his lunch, sometimes she'd leave them on the bathroom mirror, but they meant something to him. They were special, and they were all he had left of her, and ... I threw them in the trash like they were nothing."

"But you didn't know."

She shook her head. "You're missing the point."

I didn't respond, just listened.

"I did a really, really terrible thing and, yeah, my dad could've held that against me for the rest of my life because he can never get those memories back. He could've decided my mistake justified his unforgiveness," she added. "But he didn't. Because I was eight and I'm not the same, thoughtless kid I was back then." She met my gaze again. "What kind of hope would *any* of us have if people held us accountable *today* for mistakes we made a lifetime ago?"

The question rendered me silent and I guessed that was her point.

"So, I can admit I'd be a bit more emotionally involved if your grandfather had taken my dad," she confessed, considering my earlier question. "But I can also say with no qualms that I don't believe he was all bad. I don't believe he was the same man when he died." When I looked up, she said more. "He had a conscience. And monsters don't feel."

Snow fell steadily on the wrought-iron railing while we stood face-to-face.

"I'm not going anywhere, Nick," she declared. "You wanna be alone for a while? Fine. I'll sit in the study while you chill and get your head back in the game, but that's as far as I'm going." She stared with her usual defiance before going on. "Or ... you can man up and come back in there with me to see if he wrote anything that might help us."

My mouth was fixed to turn the offer down, but my mind had other plans. Hopefully, her bravery would rub off on me one day, because I was feeling anything *but* brave at the moment.

I caved, agreeing to continue, agreeing not to push her away. She smiled when it became clear she'd won. We moved back inside and settled at the desk again. This time, she brought her chair around and sat beside me. I opened the journal to where we left off and the name *Reaper* was mentioned several more times, bringing my blood to a boil. Liam had already given me a thousand reasons to hate him, but now he'd given me another.

There was no doubt in my mind he'd been responsible for my grandfather's death. All the signs were there.

"Here," Roz piped. She churned through the passages at light speed, meaning she kept getting to the interesting parts before I had the chance. Like now.

I shifted my eyes to where her finger stopped just beneath a word: *Rings*. They seemed to be mentioned in nearly all his later journals.

"Apparently, he hoped to use them as currency of some sort? Or, maybe he wanted to trade them for something?" Roz mumbled, trying to piece it all together.

She scanned a little further and gasped. I sped to the section that drew the reaction from her.

"He intended to use them as bargaining chips," I read further.

"Whatever their significance, he thought Liam might accept them in exchange for something," Roz added, skimming again. "He thought he ..."

Her words trailed off as we must have read the same line, leaving me to finish her sentence.

"He thought Liam would accept them in exchange for sparing our lives if he ever found out we existed. He thought it might save my family."

Roz turned and stared. It struck me, the gravity of my grandfather's quest for these seemingly insignificant pieces of jewelry. And now that I knew how he intended to use them, I wondered what significance they held for Liam.

Why did my grandfather think he'd see the value in them?

"I think we just discovered the reason your grandfather stayed away so much. I think he did it to keep Liam from discovering that he'd settled down, that there were people who meant something to him."

"Also explains why he didn't want my grandmother and father taking his last name."

Roz nodded, but she was distracted from responding when a photograph slipped from between two pages and landed in her lap. She turned it over to read the back.

"And now we have a face to put to Opal's name," she said, examining it further.

I read on. "He had a theory." One that made me sit straighter in my seat so I wouldn't miss the details.

"Like?" Roz leaned to get a better view of the page.

I was dead set against getting my hopes up, but it couldn't be helped. Not when the thing I wanted most might be attainable.

"Witches," I began. "Apparently, he thought there was a way they could break the curse. He was in communication with the coven linked with our clan."

"Does it say how it works? Or if they were successful?"

As badly as I wanted the answer to be yes, I was painfully aware of how close we were to the end of the journal. If there *was* a viable solution, I feared my grandfather's life had been taken before he was able to write about it.

When I shook my head, Roz took a deep breath, placing her hand on mine as she let it out.

"Well at least we know where to turn. Before we leave Seaton Falls, we've gotta find a way to talk to the witches."

I nodded in agreement, feeling a sharp burn in the center of my chest where anger and hatred seemed to always reside these days. They were like two-edges of the same dagger and, this time, the sensation had been brought on at the thought of one name.

Liam.

If he hadn't been blinded by rage, if he had sense enough to see my grandfather was a changed man, I'd have someone to turn to for answers.

But I didn't. There was only me, because that information died with my grandfather.

"Don't sweat it," Roz sighed.

The simplicity of the statement annoyed me beyond words. Maybe because this issue was consuming me and all I wanted was to fix it. To make it right. Maybe because I wished it was that uncomplicated.

"That's easy for you to say, because it's not your life," I snapped.

Right away, I regretted it. She'd done nothing wrong, but frustration got the best of me so easily these days, causing me to think, say, and do things I normally wouldn't. Seemed the littlest things set me off.

Before she could take my tone to heart, I attempted to apologize. "I'm sorry. I'm just—"

"I get it," she cut in, "You're stressed and confused and ... scared," she reasoned.

I nodded, acknowledging all those things were true to some extent.

"But ..." The sound of her voice brought my eyes to her once more when she hesitated. "As a friend, I have to be straight with you." Her eyes deadpanned to mine as she said her piece. "It's getting old."

My brow tensed and I wondered what that meant

She shot me a look. "Your 'tude sucks. I let it slide a lot because I know you're going through things and you haven't been yourself, but ... I'm not your punching bag, Nick."

She was never one for mincing words, so it shouldn't have surprised me that she put me in my place, but it did a little.

However, I knew she was absolutely right.

It was nothing personal. I was pretty sure I'd been short with *everyone* lately, but, because she was around the most, because I'd done a pretty decent job of distancing myself from everyone else, she caught the brunt of it.

"You're right," I admitted. "I'll do better."

Her lips pursed together as she read me, looking through me like only she could do.

"Apology accepted." She didn't dwell on it long, moving on right after. "Should I drive you home now? We can come back tomorrow and see what else there is."

Stretching in my seat, I shook my head. "I know what my grandfather's notes said—that I'm only a threat to Evie—but I don't wanna take my chances. I'm hanging out here tonight, then I'll slip back in the house before my parents get up."

"Cool. Where can I sleep?" Roz asked, glancing from one corner of the room to the next, letting her eyes rest on the brown leather couch near the fireplace.

A laugh slipped out. "Uh ... at home. In your bed. Where you belong," was my answer. "Listen, contrary to how we started off, I'm not as ready for you to die as I was months ago," I joked. "I know you don't believe it's possible and all, but I can't, in good conscience, let you sleep here. What if I—"

"Snore? Talk in your sleep? ... *Fart* ... in your sleep?" she asked with a cheeky grin. "Because that's about as scary as things are gonna get here tonight. You won't hurt me, Nick."

Shaking my head, I pushed again. "I'm not caving on this."

"Neither am I," she countered.

A stare down ensued, ending with Roz plopping down on the couch with an *'I dare you to try to move me'* look on her face. It became abundantly clear that I'd lost.

"Blankets?" she asked.

Shaking my head, I stood from my seat and ventured upstairs to one of several spare rooms. Each had a couple blankets stored in the top of the closet. I grabbed a few and went back to the study where I found Roz attempting to light a fire in the fireplace. She'd taken one of the long matches from the box on top of the mantle and held it beneath the single log she'd placed on the rack.

"You're gonna burn the place down," I teased.

"Not if you help me," she countered, tossing her long, dark hair over her shoulder. Her face had tinted red from frustration, I guessed. I stared while she continued to struggle with the match and, for the first time, I admitted that she was ... *pretty*.

Before, I think there were too many things in the way, clouding my vision. Including the biggest distraction of them all, Evie. But our relationship was in the past and I wasn't as preoccupied these days.

So, yeah ... I saw Roz tonight.

Her dark eyes slipped toward mine and I looked away before she'd realize I was staring.

What the heck am I doing? She's ... a friend. Just a friend.

Clearing my throat, I focused on the fresh match she handed over and took a couple more logs from the cradle on the hearth.

"Let me show you how it's done, woman."

She laughed at the over-the-top display of machismo, which was the only reason I did it.

Despite being upset with me just a short time ago, the mood was already light again. She wasn't one to hold a grudge and I admired that about her, but I sometimes wondered if she was only that way with me. We spent a lot of time together. Like, a *lot*. And it wasn't lost on me that she could've found better things to do. She had friends at Seaton Prep, and yet, she'd chosen to help me work through my issues. Chose to make my quest her own.

Let's just say I was beginning to see her differently than when we first started out.

We got a blaze going and while waiting for the study to warm, we toured the house—the two-story great room, the wine cellar, my grandmother's sewing room. It took us nearly half an hour to do just a brief stop in each room. Making our way back, I turned out the lights, submerging us in darkness until we were back beside the fireplace. Roz settled in on the couch and I took the floor beside her. Sinking deeper beneath a thick, blue blanket, she stared at the ceiling.

"Life's crazy," she sighed. "You couldn't have paid me to believe friendship was in the cards for us."

I laughed, remembering the earlier days very clearly—where we were at one another's throats all the time. "And now here we are, digging into the past of an ancient lycan as a team."

"Yup," she replied. "Perfectly normal stuff. Absolutely nothing out of the ordinary about it."

It was funny, but this *was* our new normal.

"Is it weird that I kinda miss school? Not at Damascus. I'm talking about Seaton Prep. *Regular* school—the unspoken popularity contest, extra credit, science projects, and homecoming floats." She smiled and it was dripping with nostalgia. "I mean, I know our high school experiences were vastly different—with me leaning more toward the socially challenged side, and you being ... well ... *Prince Nick,* but I still miss it."

I hated that she made that distinction, alluding to the fact that I was somehow better than she was.

Or at least that I once *thought* I was better, which was never the case.

"We're not that different."

My words made her laugh. "Oh yeah? How many parties have you been invited to over the last twelve months?"

I gave it some thought and shrugged. "I don't know. I didn't keep count."

"Now, ask me," she countered.

I humored her. "How many?"

"That would be a big fat goose egg, my friend. Nada. Zero."

I was surprised to hear her laugh about it.

"Before I was 'hired' to chauffeur Beth around, the most exciting thing I did on weekends was stay up past midnight." She smiled. "Until some random kid threw himself in front of a moving truck for me, that is."

Our eyes locked at the mention of our first meeting. If you could even call it that.

"Yup, it took a near-death experience to make me realize I had no life. Although, Beth had basically been telling me that very thing for years." Her tone was lighthearted, but I got the feeling she wasn't as nonchalant about their relationship as she pretended to be.

"Have you two *ever* gotten along?"

Before answering, Roz sighed. "You'd think we would've been closer growing up—living in the same town, having only a year and a half between us—but that was just never the case. We're polar opposites," she shared. "And those differences always seemed to be just enough to keep us from being close."

But it was more than just being distant. There was almost an underlying hatred between them. I wanted to press harder, but she asked a question before I got the chance.

"You get along with all your brothers?"

I nodded. "Mostly. When we were younger, we argued over normal things like cheating on video games or wearing each other's clothes, but we've never had any real issues." I chuckled, picturing my siblings. "Even with how different we all are, we managed to stay close."

Roz was thoughtful for a moment and I expected she might say more about her situation with Beth, but instead, she changed the subject.

"Are you okay with everything? I mean, with what we discovered today?"

The details from the journal came rushing at me like a flood, the pieces of a puzzle I hadn't expected to stumble across.

"Not exactly, but I will be."

There was a long stretch of silence. During that time, I thought again about the many ways Liam affected my life. Before tonight, I hadn't realized it reached beyond the thing with Evie. He'd taken the life of a relative, the grandfather I never got to meet, the one person who might have been able to tell me how the heck I'm supposed to control myself.

He robbed me of so many things.

"At least something good came out of this," Roz said, cutting into the fantasy I envisioned, one where I got to do Liam bodily harm.

"What's that?" If there was something good, I'd clearly missed it.

"We know he thought the witches could help," she stated, sounding a heck of a lot more optimistic than I felt. "And I think I know how to contact them."

I turned to face her.

"Give me a few days to gather some items," she smiled. "Before we leave Seaton Falls, we'll have ourselves some answers."

There was no fighting the hope that swelled within me. Maybe, by some small miracle, I wasn't doomed after all.

CHAPTER 23

Evie

Nothing about this holiday season had been typical. And now, tonight, having dinner with Elise, the mother I never knew existed, would make it even more surreal.

Our dealings had been sparse, but at least they were no longer hostile. On the rare occasion that she came out of her office and wandered the halls, I smiled, but didn't make it a point to hold a conversation.

What would I have said anyway?

She was nice enough from what I could tell, but I could admit to not knowing how to relate to her.

Three short knocks at the door made my heart race. Looking over my hair one last time, I placed the brush on the dresser. On my way to answer, I kept thinking I should have put on something nicer than the yoga pants and hoodie I threw on. After all, we were heading up for Christmas dinner at Elise's, but Liam reminded me more than once to dress comfortably. His exact words were: *'wear whatever you'd wear if it was just you and me.'* With him, I didn't have to get dolled up, seeing as how most of our interaction was in the gym, sparring. Still, as I looked myself over, I really, really hoped this was what he had in mind.

Pulling the door toward me, I scanned his attire before saying anything. A pair of stylishly faded and tattered jeans with a t-shirt. It wasn't as *'comfortable'* as my yoga pants, but I guessed it was the male equivalent.

I breathed deep, feeling nervous. I hated it.

"Ready?" he smiled.

Slipping the lanyard with my keycard around my neck, I stepped out into the hall, closing the door behind me.

"Ready."

Liam led the way because I'd never been to Elise's before. I didn't even know which floor or sector she was in. We twisted and turned our way to an elevator I hadn't used before and I guessed it was just for staff.

We stepped on and the doors closed in front of us.

"Relax."

A faint smile rested on Liam's lips when he spoke, and I hated that he knew me so well. I was sure that, to anyone else, I would've pulled off the *'calm and indifferent'* act I was going for, but not him. He had this way of reading me even when I wasn't in the mood to be read. It reminded me of my mom and dad. They always seemed to know what the other was thinking or feeling without having to communicate with words. Standing beside Liam as we watched the numbers above the elevator door change, I couldn't believe I just compared us to my parents—a couple. One that had been married for two decades, no less.

A soft buzz notified us when we reached Elise's floor and so did my phone. I mostly carried it out of habit these days, but a barrage of notifications flooding through made it clear the signal up here was much better than in *my* quarters. A stray glimmer of hope had me checking for text messages or voicemail from my parents, or anyone else I knew, but there were none. Only spam that had piled up in my email and a few others from apps. Nothing significant.

Liam stepped off first and I tucked the disappointment away, pretending not to be affected by the reminder I'd been erased.

Our sector was nearly empty, with most of the other students being home for the holidays. But up here, it was a whole other kind of empty. The quiet was so deafening, leaving me to wonder if she had this entire area to herself.

At the end of a narrow hallway, there was one lonely, silver door with an insane locking mechanism securing it. A camera identical to the one outside my room shifted when Liam and I got close. I imagined Elise's topflight security system had just made her aware of our presence.

Without hesitation, I latched onto Liam's arm.

When he stopped about a foot from the door and didn't knock, I guessed I was right. She already knew we were here and he was familiar with this procedure. He'd come to visit several times since she and I cleared the air. It wasn't lost on me that he waited until then, as if he needed my permission. While, no, it wasn't necessary, it was beyond thoughtful the way he considered my feelings. Even above his own.

After several metallic clicks and clanks, the heavy door opened and Liam and I were greeted by a wide smile.

"Merry Christmas," Elise beamed. The smell of either chicken or turkey, plus all the fixings and dessert, hit me all at once. On cue, my stomach growled.

"Merry Christmas," I echoed, leaning in to return her hug. Liam did the same and then she closed us inside with her.

Aside from having a door that resembled what you'd expect to see on a bank vault, her place was almost homey. Granted, the same stark whites and grays decorating the lower levels were still present here, but there were plants, plush rugs, and bright, colorful pillows to warm the space.

"I hope you two are hungry," she crooned, gesturing for us to have a seat on the couch. "I got a bit excited and went overboard."

"We'll make sure you're not stuck with a bunch of leftovers," Liam assured her. And I'd seen him eat before, so there was no doubt in my mind he meant every word.

He and I sat side-by-side and I was tempted to take his arm again. I knew the nervousness wasn't warranted, but couldn't help it.

On some level, I don't know, I think I was scared of getting let down in some way. Scared Elise would pull the rug out from under me just when I decided to open up to her. As much as I hated admitting it, my heart was sort of fragile these days. For more reasons than one.

Elise emerged from the kitchen carrying a large, silver platter.

"Need help?" Liam offered.

"Sure," she smiled and headed back toward the kitchen. Liam stood and I did, too, thinking it might break the ice to help set the table. When I walked in behind him, Elise and I locked eyes. There was warmth and hope in hers and I found myself praying tonight went well. I really did want this to work out.

"Your hair is different," she commented, eyeing the tight curls I didn't bother straightening after my shower. "It's nice."

Without thinking, she lifted her hand to touch it, but then seemed overly aware of her actions, letting her hand fall to her side instead. I imagined it was strange for her to be so formal around me. This awkwardly stiff interaction with her was all I'd ever known, but that wasn't the case for her. I was sure she and I once shared secrets, laughed and cried together—things I'd only done with Rebecca in this lifetime.

Sadness filled Elise's expression and I knew she'd turn away and go into her shell soon if I didn't say something.

"Seeing it straight took some getting used to for Liam. I prefer it in it's natural, curly state too, but it's more work to manage it throughout the week," I shared.

She smiled when I addressed her. "Well, you're beautiful either way if you ask me. And I'm sure our Liam here feels the same way."

My cheeks warmed when my gaze synched with his, when I noted how his lips curved upward in their usual, devious way after Elise's statement. He turned, but only to take the pan from Elise's hands, not because my stare made him shy. He was *never* shy with me. There was only ever confidence and certainty.

A bowl of corn with a silver serving spoon resting in it was the last thing to carry out. I placed it on the dining room table and then sat when Liam pulled out a chair for me. He took the one to my right and Elise settled in across from us both.

"I hope everything came out okay. It's been a while since I've made such a big meal. Until now, it's usually only me eating here, so..." Her voice trailed off and I hadn't missed that she said *'usually'*, nor had I missed the extra plate she wrapped and set aside in the kitchen.

"I'm sure it'll be perfect," I smiled.

She smiled back and then filled all our glasses from a pitcher.

"So, are either of you looking forward to the next quarter starting?"

Liam and I looked at one another, wondering who should answer first.

"It's been interesting," I replied. "I feel like I'm ready for the next combat module, thanks to Liam."

Elise's gaze volleyed back and forth between he and I. She grinned at us, but there was a little something more hidden beneath it. Hope maybe?

"You two have still been training?"

Liam nodded. "A few times a week. She's getting stronger."

Heat crept up my neck when his attention settled on me. "What he means is, I spend slightly less time on the ground," I joked.

"In Bahir Dar, you had quite the reputation for yourself," Elise chimed in. "Most knew better than to cross you, and it wasn't just because your brothers and Liam hardly left your side," she laughed. "They taught you to defend yourself well."

"I wish I could see them, wish I could remember their faces," I clarified.

Sadness touched Elise's eyes again and I regretted saying so much. "You were their pride and joy. Just as you were to your father and I."

There was a question begging to be asked, but I wasn't sure I should ask it. Liam seemed to notice me warring within myself and gave a discreet nod, encouraging me to speak. He was so much more familiar with Elise than I was, so much more comfortable. With his gentle, silent nudge, I opened my mouth.

"Do you have anything of his? My father's?"

Elise's brow lifted. She seemed surprised I was interested. Surprised, but pleased.

"Of course."

She stood from her seat, leaving her plate untouched as she disappeared in her bedroom for a moment. When she returned, she carried something about the size of a large book in her hands. Only, it was much thinner and, when she brought it closer, I saw a silver frame.

"I managed to keep a few trinkets," she explained. "With the low profile I've been forced to maintain, as well as there being a period of time when I had to stay on the move, I held on to what I could. It's always been important to me that I not forget the past. When you live as long as we do, that can be easier said than done sometimes."

She smiled, but it never reached her eyes.

I held my breath as she handed it over, giving me a glimpse into the eyes of a man I'd never had the pleasure of meeting. The other half of me. My father.

When I first studied the painting, there was a strange sense of familiarity. There was no jarring 'aha' moment. Almost as if his was exactly the face I expected to see. While I saw a lot of myself in Elise's features, I noted a fair amount in his as well.

In the portrait, he wore a kingly robe and crown, but I saw

beyond that. His warm, brown skin creased beside his mouth and I distinctly remembered the curve of his smile. Distinctly remembered the feel of his tightly wound curls as I ran my fingers through them, something I guessed I'd done when I was small. The vivid imagery got to be a bit overwhelming, forcing me to close my eyes when my next breath didn't come so easily.

These memories weren't so much locked inside my mind, they were etched in my being. These people I was once linked to were part of me.

"How did he ... how was ..." I couldn't quite put the question to words, but tried again as I stared at the contours of my father's face as rendered by the artist.

"Liam told me *your* story, how you came to be the original dragon, how you turned many others that same day, but I'm not sure what the process was for lycans. Especially with the women in my father's bloodline being witches. I used to think it was a familial curse, but ..."

Elise shook her head as my sentence trailed off. She sipped from her glass and her gaze went to some distant place when she answered.

"Your father, Noah, was never an ordinary man," she started, the blank stare eventually fading into a thoughtful smile. "In so many ways this is true, but what I mean is ... he was *born* lycan."

That seemed impossible—for the original lycan to be born a shifter to human parents. A quirk in my brow accompanied a question.

"How could that happen?"

My eyes locked with my father's through the portrait as I tried to imagine him as a wolf—large, intimidating, deadly like every other I'd seen.

Elise let out a breath and I listened intently. "You were half right; it was a curse, one placed on *his* father before Noah was even conceived. In the time before shifters, witches were the sole supernatural force, and they weren't shy about wielding their power."

I glanced up toward her. "Did his father do something to cross one?"

Elise was thoughtful for a moment. "I suppose if you were to ask the witch who cursed him, *she* might think so."

Intrigued, my eyes shifted back toward the painting as Elise continued.

"Your grandfather was a religious crusader in his time, one well-spoken of, respected throughout Ethiopia and beyond. He often traveled with a group of Englishmen when they ventured into new lands," she went on. "His work took him to many foreign lands, and his path crossed with many who believed as he did."

When she paused, I glanced up again.

"The Sovereign's father, Luca, was one of his mission's converts in Italy, a man who went on to follow him for many years, went on to become one of his closest friends."

A strange sensation in my chest made my breaths come quicker, more arduous.

"Their journey eventually led full-circle, back to a small village just north of Bahir Dar. There was said to have been a confrontation with a local coven who practiced dark magic. It's believed the men sought to convert them, to make them turn from their ways," Elise explained, the tension in her brow spreading as she continued. "Needless to say, the men were unsuccessful. A curse was placed on your grandfather and Luca, because they were the only two brave enough to enter the coven's camp. The witches declared that the men's firstborn sons would be slaves to the moon. And from their loins, vile, ravenous beasts would forever taint their bloodlines."

Liam and I both sat quietly, although I was sure this was a story he'd heard before.

"But, as I'm sure you've already discovered," Elise added, "magic has its limitations, it's hidden clauses and rules. So, after the men were cursed, the very magic the witches thought they controlled, eventually controlled *them*."

Unsure what she meant, I blinked.

"The day Noah first transitioned, mere months before Sebastian, the witch's curse backfired. Once immortal, they were now slaves to the very beasts they enslaved to the moon; *their* immortality now dependent on the will of the lycans. Needless to say, for a period of time, there was a great dying off among their kind, those older than one hundred years."

I had so much to learn. Luckily, Elise and Liam were more than willing to share their knowledge, answering questions that were probably so basic to most shifters.

"Thank you," I whispered, meaning to speak at full volume, I just couldn't. I was past the point where it all felt surreal. Now, the feelings were just incredibly powerful. Powerful enough to begin filling a void I only recently became aware of.

"I'm not just thanking you for sharing the story," I added, "I appreciate you sharing the portrait as well."

"I wish there was more," Elise said apologetically, gesturing toward the frame I still held.

"No, it's ... it's enough." I handed the portrait back.

In the time it took her to return it to its rightful place, I gathered myself. Beneath the table, Liam gave my hand a gentle squeeze and the feel of it strengthened me like always. Elise rejoined us shortly after and we finished our meal mostly in silence. Not the awkward, uncomfortable kind. The thoughtful, reflective kind.

We cleared the table and cleaned as much as Elise would allow us to. Settling in the living room, the mood was far lighter than when the three of us met at Liam's. Then, I'd been angry and confused, directing my frustration at Elise. But now, I was focused and becoming stronger every day. In every way—emotionally, physically. For the first time in a long time, I believed I had a handle on things. Our time here was winding down. I could feel it. Hopefully, we'd be dismissed before summer. The sooner it was over, the sooner we could all go back to Seaton Falls and return to our normal lives.

The war we'd been warned about seemed to be a false alarm from what I could tell. There hadn't been any threats or reports from the

Seaton Falls clan. While *my* ties to the town were severed, Beth's parents updated her on the regular. Life in Michigan was quiet, and that could only be a good sign.

Unless ... this was just the calm before the storm.

"I'm so happy you agreed to come tonight, Evangeline." I glanced up as Elise smiled at Liam and I. We sat on the couch adjacent from the sleek, white leather chair she perched in. My gaze followed when she leaned to retrieve two small bags from the left side of her chair.

"It wouldn't be Christmas without gifts," she beamed.

My heart squeezed inside my chest. "You didn't have to. I wasn't—"

She waved me off and reached to hand us our presents from across the coffee table. "I insist."

I accepted and thanked her. Liam and I both undid the black, satin ribbons that bound the handles of white giftbags. Inside, black tissue concealed a small, velvet box. Embossed on the lid in silver, foil lettering ... an '*E*'.

Elise sat waiting as I opened it.

"It's yours. From before," she clarified as my fingers ran the length of chain. "After bringing you back, I've kept it safe, hoping I'd be able to return it to you one day."

I didn't expect much to come out of this day, but I was truly moved that she'd held on to something so significant, something tangible linking me to my past life.

A necklace.

"Is this ... is this the one Hilda made? The talisman?"

Elise nodded. "It is, but ..." Her eyes drifted closed for a moment while explaining. "It won't work a second time. The magic that tied you to it severs after one use and such a spell can't be done a second time—on the necklace, on you," she clarified.

While it would have been nice to think it still worked, I was honestly just touched to have it in my possession.

I stood from my seat and Elise's eyes widened when I approached for a hug. "Thank you. This is absolutely perfect."

She held on for a while and I did the same, eventually releasing one another to watch Liam.

He removed a heap of tissue paper from his bag. Reaching inside, he brought his hand back out with something silver between his fingers. A coin was my first guess. Only, it was larger than any I'd ever seen.

I tilted my head to get a better look. Liam said nothing. He simply held the ancient piece while he stared. To me, to *anyone* who didn't understand its significance, it was just a piece of metal with a tree engraved on one side, words etched on the other.

He kept his gaze trained on the gift. "I can't believe you still have this."

A weak smile brightened Elise's expression just a bit.

"What is it?" I asked. I got the sense this moment was far heavier than I realized, but no one had explained what I missed.

"The family emblem," Liam shared. "A gift from your father many, many years ago."

"I tried to gather the most important items," Elise added. "The ones that tell our family's story."

Liam pursed his lips tightly together for a second. "It's perfect." He stood to embrace Elise after returning the piece to his bag.

"I feel terrible," I chimed in. "You're the only one without a gift."

Something I said made Elise laugh.

"Please. Evangeline, having the two of you here with me has been the best gift I could've ever imagined."

The contentment in her gaze told me she meant that and, despite my feelings toward her in month's past, I was glad I hadn't cheated myself out of getting to know her. If life had taught me anything this time around, it's that family might not always come in the form you're expecting or even hoping for. But when you're loved, I mean surrounded with it, *submerged* in it, be grateful.

Today, even though I didn't get to spend the holiday the way I might have wanted, I was grateful.

Because this is *definitely* what love feels like.

CHAPTER 24

Evie

Gravity kept pulling me closer to him. No matter how much I fought it, Liam had a hold on me.

We lingered outside my door long after leaving Elise's. For me, the reason I hadn't moved my feet was because I was in no rush for tonight to end. No rush to be alone. No rush to be without him.

He peered up with a look I might call boyish on someone else, but not him. He was all man, one-hundred-percent of the time. Even now, as a half-smile and a hooded stare threatened to make my knees give way.

"What?" I asked, smiling when I couldn't take it anymore.

He shook his head and his hair lightly swept his shoulders with the motion, tempting me to touch it.

"Nothing," he breathed. "Just dreading the thought of letting you go."

Heat crept up the length of my spine hearing his confession. While I completely agreed, I didn't have even a fraction of his boldness. Tonight had been a good night. I couldn't deny it. Elise was warm and inviting, but I think my favorite part was that I got to spend it with Liam. He made everything better. Not just the bad; the good, too.

My fingers on both hands warmed when his slipped between them, locking his palms against mine. Out of habit, I took a step back, but only because it was still unnerving that he could control me without a single command. My body, my *soul*, preferred to follow his lead more than following my own.

Like now.

He took a step closer to undo the distance I put between us and I should have cared. But didn't. In truth, I *wanted* him to overstep his bounds, wanted him to push me to my limits so I could stop fighting it.

A heated stare burned through me and I couldn't look away. At every turn, he was there. Always protecting me, always putting me first. In that moment, I questioned whether it was possible for love to be contagious. Was it possible for someone to love you so thoroughly, so unselfishly, that it could become infectious?

It didn't come over you like a disease, but there were definitely chills. And fever. I felt both whenever he touched me.

The mass of his chest pressed against mine and a sudden burst of bravery made me look him square in the eyes. I wouldn't turn away until *he* did. With quivering breath, my lips throbbed to the beat of my racing heart in anticipation of his mouth meeting mine. It was coming. I could feel it long before he leaned in and allowed me the privilege of breathing his air.

There were mere inches separating me from what was to come, from what I wanted.

But then ... darkness.

The only sound that filled the hallway was the surge of air I drew in when the lights went out. Whereas Liam stood close for *one* reason; he now did so to protect me.

"What's happening?" My eyes darted in all directions, but there was nothing but the inky blackness you'd expect in a windowless basement.

"I'm not sure, but stay calm."

The next second, his palm went up in flames and he cast light to our left and then right, taking in our surroundings. We were still alone, but it didn't feel that way. Fear crept over my skin. My fingers gripped Liam's bicep because holding on to him never failed to make me feel safe.

As quickly as the darkness came, small, temporary lights spaced along the floorboards began to flicker to life. I guessed a backup generator kicked in. My heart slowed just a bit, but I was still far from settled.

"Stay close."

Following Liam's words, I was led back in the direction we'd just come from a little while ago.

The two staff members we passed on our way seemed just as confused as we were. We stopped in front of the elevator and I panicked, thinking of all the movies I'd seen where scenarios eerily similar to this one didn't end well.

"What if the power goes out again and we get stuck?"

Liam shook his head. "We'll be fine. With the generators on, that won't happen. I just need to get you up to Elise's until I figure out what's going on. Her place is locked down like Fort Knox and she's got a direct link to the security feed. I need to access it," he insisted.

It would've been nice to assume this was a typical blackout, but *nothing* seemed to be typical around here. So, I chose to trust him.

We stepped onto the elevator and I swear I held my breath the whole way up, and then hopped off the second we stopped. Elise's sector was now dimly lit just like all the others, meaning the outage had affected the entire facility.

Once again, she answered long before Liam and I reached her door, clutching the lapel of a black, silk robe tight to her chest.

"Are you both all right?" There was panic heavy in her tone, and when we stepped inside, I think we were both shocked to see she wasn't alone.

It became clear the plate she set aside wasn't for a midnight snack.

Dallas gave a nod, a polite, wordless greeting, but seemed just as surprised to see Liam and I as we were to see him.

It was late. He wore pajama pants and no shirt. The dots weren't hard to connect. He and Elise were, clearly ... a little more than friends.

"We, uh ... didn't mean to interrupt," Liam stammered. "I couldn't think of anyplace else to bring her."

Elise gave a dismissive wave. "Of *course* you were supposed to come to me," she insisted, taking my hand to lead me to the couch. She sat beside me and, like any mother would do, she gave me a thorough onceover, pushing my hair away from my face as that concerned look deepened.

Liam kept his eyes on Dallas. It was no secret that, when it came to me, he had trust issues. He seemed to prefer that I not be around new people because he wasn't sure what they were capable of. He *especially* preferred it that way when my secret was at risk of exposure. Maybe sensing emotions running high, Dallas dismissed himself, retreating to Elise's room while we sorted things out.

"We'll come back when he's gone," Liam declared, making steps toward the door.

"Dallas isn't a threat," Elise assured us, but it'd take more convincing on Liam's part. In his eyes, Dallas was an outsider despite however close he and Elise might have been.

She stood. "Liam ... he's a soldier. In fact, he was one of few dragons to fight in *The Lunar War*. His story is quite similar to yours —a dragon raised primarily by a lycan family," she shared. "He's the reason we were able to recruit so many dragons to this facility. He's a well-respected and honorable man."

"How long have you known him?" Liam's tone was cold and unfeeling, proving he wasn't moved in the least by Elise's spiel.

The question seemed to jar her a bit. "Summer of 1924."

I guessed they'd been together that long—nearly a century. Liam stared, studying her in that deep, penetrating way he has, and I took note of the moment tension seemed to leave his posture.

"He doesn't know yet," Elise assured us. "He doesn't even have a clue who *I* am, or was ... let alone you and Evangeline. However, I've only kept things from him because I vowed it to the Council and out of respect for the two of you. Not because I distrust him."

It was clear her connection with Dallas was deep for her to even *consider* bringing him in on the truth—who I am, who *she* is. Ninety-plus years is a long time to hide your true identity from a person, but I knew this was an example of one of those hard choices, a sacrifice for the cause.

Liam stared and Elise stood her ground, holding her composure until he caved and finally blinked.

"You'd trust him with your life?" he asked, adding, "...With hers?"

Elise didn't hesitate for even a second before nodding and, with that, Liam took her at her word. "Then bring him out."

There was a trace of a smile on her face before going to grab Dallas. In the meantime, Liam took her laptop from the desk and brought it over to the couch. He booted it up and entered Elise's passcode. I wasn't sure when, but she'd clearly allowed him access before now. With his hypervigilance, I shouldn't have been surprised.

The security feed came up and I watched as he maneuvered his way back to the time the blackout occurred. Video showed the entire facility going dark all at once. Liam skipped through the frames from varying angles. Elise and Dallas rejoined us in the living room after several minutes. They were fully dressed now and I imagined, during that time, she'd given him the short version of our story. He didn't seem rattled as he held her hand, unable to hide in his expression how deeply he cared for her.

I turned back toward the screen when Liam stared at something —a shadow on an outside camera, mounted high in a tree, I believed.

"I think we have something." He zoomed in, but the somewhat grainy image was inconclusive.

"I'll assemble a team to do a perimeter check," Dallas offered. "Kas, Martinez, Randall, Mei…"

"And wake David as well," Elise suggested. "While you all do the sweep, he can run a system check to make sure there wasn't a breach to our firewall. For all we know, the blackout could've been a distraction from a more subtle attack."

Dallas gave a quick nod and then rushed from Elise's quarters. She seemed nervous. Right after I noticed, Liam did, too.

"What is it?" he asked. "What aren't you saying? Is it the mutts again?"

She blinked and I knew Liam was right to question her. "There was another security issue, but I've taken care of it and, therefore, didn't see the need in alarming you."

Frustrated, Liam sighed, running a hand through his hair. "I thought we already discussed this. If something happens, you tell me."

At times like these, their mother/son dynamic all but disappeared. When it came to me, my safety, Liam was always the authority figure. Always.

Elise lowered her head when she breathed deep. "Dallas and his crew have been on a special security detail, reporting everything they hear and see."

Liam shook his head before she finished speaking. The rims of his nostrils flared and even if I hadn't seen the ferocity rising in him, I felt it. Right in my chest like always, his dragon signaling mine, waking her.

"Again with the secrets. Maybe it isn't Dallas I shouldn't have trusted."

The accusation stunned Elise, rendering her speechless as she stared at the man she revered as a son.

"The agreement was, when something arises that could potentially threaten Evangeline, I'm to be notified. Why am I just hearing about this now?" he fumed.

"I told you, I've had Dallas on it and—"

"*You* know him," Liam cut in. "I'm not obligated to trust *anyone.*"

The harshly spoken words prompted Elise's mouth to snap shut. Her eyes slipped away from Liam's.

"Show me the footage," he seethed.

Elise swallowed and was slow making her way back to the couch. When she did, she clicked the mouse a few times and typed in a date range before locating the old clip in question. Or rather, a still frame; one that nearly made my heart leap from my chest.

It was ... *Nick.*

She turned the screen toward Liam and he didn't move.

"Of course, he's in Seaton Falls and has nothing to do with this power outage, but he's been slipping out at night. Not every night. It's only been two or three times that we know of," she admitted.

Liam started pacing, but didn't say a word. I was frozen in my seat—from fear, from the rising tension in the room.

"At night, I've had Dallas, Martinez, and Kas rotating shifts, keeping watch with strict orders to notify me if he's seen leaving again," she rambled, trying to plead her case. "With so many eyes on him now, Evangeline hasn't been in any imminent danger."

"That's not your call to make," Liam snapped, halting when his eyes shifted toward Elise. They cut through her like daggers, forcing her to lower her gaze once again.

"This is incredible to me," he went on. "You sit in here, locked up tight behind a steel door capable of surviving nuclear fallout, and yet ... you didn't even think to let me know she might be in danger."

His words struck me deep, sinking in until they hit bone.

"She's your daughter, Elise. She's my..." His words ceased and he never finished that statement, but a look of understanding passed between them.

He stared at her and I was surprised to see it wasn't so much *anger* concealed within the look.

It was hurt.

Frustration.

"Liam," she began. "What you're implying—that I value my own safety more than I value hers—you couldn't be more wrong."

It was clear from his expression that her words now fell on deaf ears.

"Everything I've ever done has been for my family. If it were up to me, Evangeline would have been here with me since the day she arrived at this facility, but I couldn't force my way into her life," she reasoned, glancing toward me right after. "Think about it, if I'd pushed for that, do you think she would've cooperated?"

Her eyes were on Liam again, and I answered the question myself inside my thoughts. No, I wouldn't have allowed her to bully me into staying with her. I was barely even convinced coming for dinner tonight was a good idea. She was right and, even if Liam didn't believe her, I did. My wellbeing mattered to her, but she could only protect me as much as I'd allow.

"Liam." The sound of my voice made him turn. "She's doing the best she can," I stated. "She's working with limited resources, trying to comply with the Council, and I'm sure she's got good reason for keeping this latest incident under wraps."

A gentle smile brightened Elise's expression just a bit. She mouthed a silent '*thank you*' before explaining.

"I know you've been anxious to leave," she said, speaking to Liam this time. "You don't trust this place."

"Can you blame me?"

Elise breathed deep before replying. "I can't, but I hope you'll understand why I can't let that happen. Sure, this facility isn't perfect, but it's better than having the two of you alone and roaming around out there. I know things seem quiet on the Sovereign's end, but you know as well as I do, it's when he's silent that he's most dangerous," she declared. "Mark my words: there *will* be a war, and it's coming sooner than any of us realize."

The grave outlook made my stomach sink.

"I thought that, if I kept this from you, dealt with it on my own, you'd stay," she explained. "*Both* of you."

My heart went out to her, acknowledging how difficult her position was. It had to have been quite the conflict of interest—spearheading a revolution, protecting those you care most about. There was only one thing I could think of to lessen that burden.

"We're not going anywhere," I stated, making the decision for myself instead of leaving it in Liam's hands. Yes, I knew he always acted in my best interest, but I had to stand for what I knew was right. The decision was mine this time. Not his.

Elise's hand warmed mine. The sound of a walkie talkie chirping from the next room prompted her to excuse herself and she left me to deal with whatever aftermath there might be from Liam. His stare lingered although I wouldn't look over at him.

"It's the right thing to do," I said. "She's trying. That doesn't mean she's perfect, but ... she's trying."

It was hard not to sympathize with Elise. Maybe because I, too, understood the fear she must live with whenever she thought of losing Liam and I again.

He didn't have a rebuttal, but I could tell the decision to stay, to wait it out, made him uncomfortable. It was no secret he didn't trust Nick. Now to hear that he'd been sneaking out, it only made him seem that much less stable.

"That was Dallas," Elise announced. "There's no sign of an intruder and, according to David, our security system's been unharmed. The blackout was across the entire county, not just our facility, so I believe we're in the clear."

I breathed a sigh of relief.

"Good," Liam said firmly. "But I think it'd still be best if, just for tonight, Evangeline hung out here."

My head whipped in his direction. He didn't even think to ask what *I* wanted.

"Just as an added precaution," he explained.

Elise nodded. "Agreed." She turned to me, the only one in the room who seemed to remember I had a voice and brain of my own. "Would that be all right with you?" she asked.

It took a moment to answer, feeling my blood heat more and more by the second. Eventually, I gathered myself and was able to nod. "That's fine."

She passed a warm smile my way and then left Liam and I to talk. Her timing was perfect, because I had *plenty* to say.

"I can think for myself sometimes. You don't have to speak for me." The words came out much harsher than I intended for them to, but it couldn't be helped. Maybe my emotions were just running high because the blackout and news about Nick had me a bit freaked out, but I was too old to be pushed around.

By *anyone*.

Liam didn't speak right away. Instead, he seemed to be considering my feelings, which I appreciated. At eighteen, I hadn't done much living, but I'd been through a heck of a lot more than most. It was time I stopped letting my life choices be made *for* me. I understood Liam's intentions were honorable, but I had to draw the line somewhere.

"Forgive me," he said humbly—not even a hint of his ego or pride coming into play. His tone diluted my frustration a bit.

"I know you mean well. I know *most* people mean well, but if I'm ever gonna learn to stand on my own, if I'm ever gonna become who you all seem to think I'll be ... then I need you all to trust my judgment sometimes, too."

Liam breathed deep. "You're absolutely right," he replied. His expression was solemn and I regretted being so abrasive. "I know I've been overbearing," he explained. "It's just that ... I know what it's like to lose you."

My heart sank at the sound of those words. It was never far from my mind that I'd lived a past life, but I had the luxury of forgetting all that came before. Liam did not. He remembered it all—the good, the bad, the ugly. Including the night of my death. I should have been more sensitive to that. Should've handled this delicately.

"I understand. And I'm not saying I don't appreciate you protecting me. It's just that ... I'd like to be included in the plans from now on." My mind ran through all the instances where that opportunity had been stolen from me.

"I think I've earned that," I added.

Liam nodded, agreeing. "Consider it done."

Elise returned with bedding and placed it on the couch. I noted that she brought two pillows because she assumed, like I had, Liam was staying as well. It was kind of automatic. The only time he wasn't at my side was when he had no other choice.

"I'll leave you two, but if you need anything," she said with a smile, "don't hesitate to ask."

I returned the gesture, but stood to hug her as well. She was, perhaps, the most misunderstood person I'd ever met. I, too, used to misinterpret her intentions, but we weren't so different, she and I. I saw that now—how she valued her family, how she wore her heart on her sleeve.

I got it.

"Thanks for letting me stay," I whispered. "And ... for everything else."

Her arms tightened around me and she didn't let go for quite some time. When she did, water pooled in the corners of her eyes, but I only caught a glimpse before she quickly turned to disappear in her bedroom.

Standing in the middle of the rug, I took a breath, feeling thoroughly drained by the day's events. But, for some reason, I smiled. Not even *Christmas* could be normal anymore, and rather than getting bent out of shape about it, I managed to find the humor.

And, all in all, it'd been a good day. Even this power outage proved to be nothing too serious. Dinner with Elise was perfect, and now, I had the chance to spend the rest of my night with Liam—my overprotective, sometimes too macho for his own freakin' good, warrior. He lived up to that title time and time again. Old habits were hard to break, but maybe I didn't want him to. All I wanted was a little room to be an adult.

I reached for a thick blanket and spread it out on the floor, then a couple more to make it softer. It wasn't until I dropped both pillows on top that I even realized what I'd done. Instead of arranging for one of us to sleep on the couch and the other on the floor, I made the pallet big enough for two.

Why was I even surprised? Instead of making a big deal of it, I pulled my hoodie off to sleep in my tank top, and then turned out the light before lying down. Liam did the same, right beside me.

We lie there, staring at the ceiling while a dim nightlight on the wall faintly illuminated the space. Heat from his body warmed the right side of mine and I wanted to get closer. But I was ever conscious of not letting things between us move too fast.

I hadn't forgotten the kiss we almost shared outside my room, though. Had it not been for the lights going out ...

I wanted that moment back. Wanted to recreate the authentic, raw magnetism we allowed to shine through, but here, in Elise's living room, I wanted to be respectful of her quarters.

No funny business.

Not that I had the guts to let anything like that happen anyway.

"I'm sorry again," Liam sighed, stealing my attention. "I smother you," he admitted. He sounded so pitiful, his tone made me laugh.

"It's fine," I smiled. "I shouldn't have come at you as strongly as I did. I mean, I don't take back what I said, but I could've said it differently."

Somehow, my hand ended up in his, resting in the sliver of space between us. My mind was cloudy and I wasn't sure if I'd reached for his, or if it'd been the other way around. Either way, I clung to it, feeling the soft leather band on his wrist against my skin, and despite myself, I inched closer—shoulder to shoulder. His other arm went behind his head and I was so aware of him, of his every move, my breaths came shallow.

"So ... I totally didn't see that coming with Elise and Dallas," I said with a grin, wanting to distract myself from my tendency to over-think things. If I dwelled on the pull, the longing, fear would make me back away.

And I didn't want that.

Liam's fingers squeezed mine just enough to let me know he preferred being close versus apart. Just enough to let me know he wanted this, too.

"You've met him before?" he asked, referring to Dallas.

"Yeah, he's been my combat instructor a few times. Seems cool. Comes across as a hardnose, but he's been nothing but nice to me. He's the one who dealt with that whole ... broken nose incident our first day."

Being reminded, Liam laughed. "How'd I forget about that?"

"Yeah ... not my proudest moment."

"You've come a long way since then," he assured me. "Don't beat yourself up about it. We all have things we'd take back if we could."

I turned to face him in the darkness. "What's your thing?" I asked. "What would you take back if you could?"

It might not have been my business to ask and, maybe to some degree, I was taking advantage of his inability to tell me no. But I wanted to know as much about him as possible. It was somewhat of a hidden obsession, part of that perpetual longing to get completely lost in him. It was a feeling I'd fought since the beginning.

A battle I fought and recently accepted that I'd taken a loss some time ago.

"You love asking the hard questions." I watched him smile in the faint light. "If I had to pick any one thing, I guess it'd be ... the callousness that made me feel like I was someone else for a while."

For a moment, he seemed to disappear to some distant place.

"I was numb and didn't give much thought to my actions, didn't give much thought to the people I hurt, the lives I took."

I drew in a breath and stared at his profile, how the glow outlined unearthly beautiful features—the slant of his nose, the slight downward curve of his bottom lip, the firmness of his jaw.

Without him saying so, I knew the dark stretch of years he spoke of was brought on by my death. It broke him, affected him still. He shared once that he didn't have much to live for, which made every cause seem worth dying for. To hear him say he'd take it all back if he could, was proof he'd grown, proof he'd evolved since those days.

I released his fingers, but continued to hold on, gripping his wrist with one hand and his forearm with the other as I turned onto my side, watching him. The leather band brushed my fingertips and I thought of them again, thought of how he'd only told me what types of knots they were instead of how they were significant to him.

"Hercules knots," I said aloud, prompting him to tilt his face toward mine. "I still don't know what they mean in general," I breathed. "And I'm still dying to know what they mean to *you.*"

He only stared a moment, eventually smiling.

"Let me guess, this is another one of those hard questions," I teased. When he didn't answer right away, I guessed I was right. Instead of forcing him to give up all his secrets at once, I thought it might be more effective to pry them from his hands one by one.

"Did you have them when I was alive?" I asked.

Letting his gaze slip to my lips for a moment, he nodded. "I did." His tone was deep and breathy, making my stomach shudder at the sound of it.

I smiled. "Ok. Hmm ... Was this another one of those things between you and my brothers?"

He blinked and shook his head. "No."

A breath hitched in my throat with the way he looked at me right after. I inhaled deeply to keep him from noticing.

"Is there a reason you have two?"

When he hesitated, I knew I was on to something. He nodded, but didn't say a word.

I felt the air growing thick, felt the heaviness hovering above us. I was compelled to keep pushing, like I needed to have the answer to this one question more than any other I'd asked.

Was it me or did this desperation come from my dragon?

Maybe *she,* that primal side of me, was the one who needed this brought to the light.

"One was mine," I exhaled, feeling my chest constrict when the words left my mouth. It was a statement. Not a question.

This time, he neither confirmed nor denied. He shut down.

"Is that a yes?" I asked.

He stared a moment longer and then turned away again, focusing on the ceiling like before.

I wasn't sure why he seemed weary to continue my game, but I couldn't take it. Remembering how much stronger Elise's signal was than what we had to work with down several floors, I took a chance. When I released Liam's arm and pulled my phone from my pocket, I had his attention again.

"Last chance," I warned with a grin. "Otherwise, you're gonna force me to rely on the internet for an explanation."

"Make sure you really want the answer before you go digging," he replied, making my stomach somersault. He didn't find nearly as much humor in this as I did. That was evident when the words left his mouth without so much as a grin.

He was stone-faced as he went back to staring at the ceiling.

I typed in the letters one at a time, feeling my heart race with each, knowing I was this much closer to an answer. Scrolling past the expected randomness that popped up, I stopped on a site that delved into the symbolism of the knot. The others only explained how to tie one, or it's uses throughout the ages, and other things that were of no use to me. But this one had promise.

I clicked.

I scrolled.

And then ... I stopped.

Words leapt off the screen, filtering through my brain, but not sticking. I held my breath as singular phrases confused me instead of clearing things up.

Union.

Love.

Bound.

And then there was another, one far clearer than the others. I spoke it aloud.

"... *Marriage*."

All sound left the room in a vacuum. My screen went dark and I held the phone to my chest, letting these things, these words, these meanings register. One, above all, stood out, playing on repeat inside my head. Over and over.

In my voice.

In his.

"Actually, for us, a more fitting term is '*mated*'. But I told you; you've got a knack for asking the hard questions," Liam said quietly, cutting into my thoughts, making my head spin more than it already was.

Mated, married ... whatever. It was all the same, and for the first time ever, we both had a complete understanding of our bond. Before now, I thought it was simply that we were tethered—as if that weren't deep enough—but now to know just how connected we were...

"Tell me what you're thinking."

I heard his request, but couldn't form a sentence. So many things made sense now—the way Elise willingly took a backseat when it came to Liam putting his foot down in all instances having to do with my safety. Yes, I was her daughter, but I was his ... *mate, his wife*. It also made sense that Elise had no qualms about me sleeping beside him tonight because, in her mind, in his, this was my rightful place.

This was what my dragon wanted me to remember, what she wanted me to acknowledge, because she wanted him.

"I'm only eighteen." As soon as I said it, I knew how stupid it sounded. Because it was a lie. Regardless of how long I'd been back, I knew I was much, much older than that. It was just a kneejerk reaction to the walls closing in on me.

"I'm not expecting anything, Evangeline."

He said that like he thought I might run off, like this news might make me back away. I wasn't sure *how* I felt, but running didn't cross my mind.

He turned, letting his eyes settle on me. I blinked, focusing through the darkness. My pulse was going a mile a minute and, with it, came a haze of confusion.

Apparently, he saw it all—my minor freak-out.

"For what it's worth, I tried to keep it from you," he explained. "You've had enough on your plate, enough big news to cope with without adding ... this."

Hearing him speak this way about something I was sure he held close to his heart, something sacred that couldn't be diminished by my lack of memory, it made me feel a strange mix of things.

Guilty.

Sad.

Like I was adding to his pain.

My thoughts were turned from within, considering for that brief moment how this must've affected *him,* not just myself. A jolt hit my chest when I put myself in his place. The loneliness, the grief ... he carried it all ... *hid* it all ... to shield me. I'd be foolish to believe for even a second this had been easy for him—seeing me with Nick, how cold I was toward him in the beginning, how I resisted what I felt.

It must have killed him inside.

He could've easily ambushed me with this information months ago, used it to sway me in his direction.

But he didn't. He waited like a gentleman, letting his incredible strength and restraint show through while I found my own way.

Like always, he put me first.

"This isn't what I wanted." His voice trailed off and I held my breath, waiting to hear his thoughts. When he bit into his lip, I knew he didn't intend to go on.

"Tell me," I beckoned softly.

He watched me again, maybe wanting to resist.

"Part of me held out hope," was how he decided to express himself. "I hoped that, eventually, you'd remember and it'd just be natural," he bravely admitted. "I hoped everything would just come back to you and, without needing to be reminded, without needing to be persuaded ... you'd feel it."

I breathed a question, bridling my soul as it reached for him. "Feel what?" My thoughts were already lightyears ahead, anticipating the answer.

I had his eyes again and, with so few words, he made me understand completely.

"...That it was supposed to be forever."

Breathless.

Dizzy.

A deep burn gripped my heart, like a lasso of flames pulling, tugging, roping me into his orbit. My soul circled his until it got to be too much. Unable to keep away any longer, I faced him and leaned in. His breath caressed my skin the instant I stopped being afraid of what would happen if I opened my heart, if I finally let my atmosphere collide into his.

An unfamiliar emotion filled me, making my body vibrate on a foreign wavelength—*his*.

Frustration.

Longing.

Passion.

Our lips moved together and tears welled behind my closed lids. Fueling those tears? Everything. His touch. His love.

My hands slipped behind his neck, knotting in his hair. I got closer, savoring the familiar taste of him on my tongue. I breathed in, releasing doubt as I exhaled.

That conclusion he needed me to reach on my own? That thing he hoped I wouldn't miss? It descended on me like a whirlwind, stealing the air right from my lungs.

I sighed against his soft lips before drawing them between mine again. His fingers gripped the hem of my shirt—tight, like he was afraid to let go. Before I could stop myself, I whispered powerful words against his chin as I floated away in a haze.

Words I hadn't spoken to any other guy, because with any other guy, it hadn't felt right.

"Liam ... I love you."

My body arched toward his and I'd never felt more at home than I did in that moment. He paused, taking his lips away as he held my face. We panted, struggling for air as the heat between us burned it away.

It was not in my plans to share so much, to own my feelings tonight, but they practically leapt straight from my heart to his ears. I'd been in denial for months, rationalizing away what was building within me, telling myself it was too much too soon, but that wasn't true. Because we'd been entangled with one another for ages, lost in a love too powerful to fade.

He smiled against my lips and placed another kiss there.

"Good," he breathed. "Because I'm not going anywhere."

We kissed again and I nearly caught fire from the inside out.

Just like that, the tide had shifted. I allowed my heart to be carried out into open water, uncertain of what would come next, unable to see what lie ahead. But, most of all, I was unable to deny I was in good hands.

The best.

Those of my warrior.

CHAPTER 25

Nick

Beside me, a headful of brown hair rested on my shoulder as we neared the facility. We took back roads once inside Louisiana, an added precaution to ensure none of us could keep track of signs that might say which towns we passed through. Roz dozed somewhere around Magnolia, Mississippi, and I didn't have the heart to wake her when she tipped in my direction. She was exhausted after all we'd squeezed into the last couple days of our two-week trip home to Seaton Falls.

The night at my grandfather's hadn't only changed me, it changed her, too. It gave us a clearer vision of the big picture. It shed light on our role in it as well as the roles of others. Suddenly armed with more information, we set out to get the last few pieces of the puzzle, and a major component was now hidden away inside the bag between my feet.

It started with a conversation between my father and I, and

ended with me now having options ... something I lacked just a week ago.

Among the info my dad shared were the details of my grandfather's final hours in Limerick, Ireland, as stated by the young kid who witnessed everything.

It took place in an alley behind a pub my grandfather visited with Opal, but this was no vacation. Being out of the States served two purposes. For one, it kept *The Reaper's* wrath steered away from the rest of our family, and it was also a stop on Grandfather's hunt for the rings.

Unfortunately, he didn't find them in time.

The kid described a big guy with dark, shoulder-length hair, a low-trimmed beard, and a heavy brow—Liam.

From the first line my father spoke, I knew it was him.

Opal was killed first, and for no other reason than to make my grandfather experience the pain of losing the woman he loved. I guess it was meant to be the final, grandiose gesture before ripping his throat out and standing over him until he bled to death. But Opal died for nothing. Taking her life—that of an innocent woman—was testament to the hollowness in Liam's chest where a heart should have been.

I wasn't the only monster.

Following this talk with my dad, I set out to find our clan's coven. My grandfather's untested theory was all I could think about and time was winding down. This had to be taken care of before returning to the facility where I'd, once again, be on lockdown, cut off from communication from the world. It was my hope that at least one might be willing to help; might be willing to undo the curse nature had placed on me.

And, luckily, I didn't have to wait long for an answer. One by the name of Scarlet was more than eager.

She came to me just like Roz said she would after researching a method for summoning a magic wielder. It required the ash of a long-dead tree and eleven other ingredients that took nearly half the day to gather. I was alone, waiting on my grandfather's property when she came to me.

Despite her being half my size, fear rose in me the moment she manifested, forming out of thin air after a thick, eerie fog rolled in. My breathing deepened and puffed into the chilled air like smoke from a fast-moving train. Her footsteps could be heard before I laid eyes on her—the freshly fallen snow crunching beneath her soles. She emerged from the shadows accompanied by the hollow clatter of naked branches shuddering in the wind. Not too far off in the distance, an owl hooted—the only living thing to be heard for miles.

Illuminated by moonlight, Scarlet approached.

"This had better be good," she hissed with a sickeningly wicked smile.

A black patch covered her left eye, concealing an injury, or worse. But it wasn't just her physical appearance that made my skin crawl— it was her presence in general. Like that of a soulless corpse, hollowed out on the inside.

"I need your help," I stammered, taking two steps back for every one she took toward me.

That smile widened. *"Well, obviously. Otherwise, I wouldn't be standing here, now would I?"* she taunted, keeping her hands hidden inside the dark cloak she wore.

"Why don't we make this easier," she said, her childlike voice contradicting the sense that she'd been here since the world first began. *"Let me take a look for myself."*

Before I had the chance to run or even dodge the pale, slender hand outstretched toward me, she rushed in my direction at lightning speed, the toes of her hidden shoes dragging the snow. Using magic, she took no steps. She was simply several feet away one moment, and then right on me the next.

The second her palm flattened against my forehead I was power- less, paralyzed down to my feet as she stared into me with varying emotions crossing her face. When she finally did let go, something left my body, too. Like she'd taken a piece of me with her.

"*Well, aren't you interesting,*" she smiled, adding, "*And to answer your question ... yes ... I will help you.*"

Confused, I stumbled back, trying to regain the strength she'd stolen a moment ago. "*But I haven't even told you what I need.*"

Her thin lips parted with a grin. "*Trust me ... I know everything I need to know. I can take away the darkness.*"

I froze.

"*But it'll cost you,*" she added. "*And I'll need to collect my payment first.*" There was a haunting chill to her tone, one she tried to mask with another smile. "*Take it or leave it.*"

"*You're not asking me to agree without knowing what you want in return, are you?*"

All traces of humanity drained from her face.

"*No, young Nicholas,*" she hissed, knowing my name despite me never revealing it. There were mere inches between us. "*I'm not ... asking ... you to do anything. These are my terms. Agree or suffer this curse.*"

She was my only option and I knew it. *She* knew it. I had no other choice, no feasible alternatives.

So, reluctantly ... I agreed

Placing my hand in hers, I was brought to my knees when her magic sealed this deal between us. Her icy breath—somehow icier than the December air—grazed my ear when she made clear what offering she expected in exchange for assisting me.

And there was no turning back now.

The bus jerked, pulling me from my thoughts. The memories of meeting Scarlet, of my father's heart-wrenching retelling of my grandfather's death, scurried to the shadows as I came back to the present.

My gaze shifted down toward the bag at my feet again and I thought of what lie inside—the piece that would soon change everything. Scarlet had placed a small, black satchel in my hand before we parted ways and I was given precise instructions on how to use it.

When I was ready, all I had to do was unsheathe it and hold it in my palm. From there, she'd take care of the rest.

There was no snow on the ground here in Louisiana, but it was definitely colder than when we left for Michigan two weeks ago. Pulling up to the decoy house, we were told to stay put until the monitors came topside to escort us down.

I didn't feel like being here. I missed my bed, missed football, even missed a few of my teachers. In short, I missed the way things used to be. It was that longing for times past that made me certain going to Scarlet had been the right thing to do. And to top it all, her methods would fix not one, but *two* of my issues at the same time.

The only problem was that there would be fallout. However, connecting with my grandfather's past, getting to understand him, I was able to keep things in perspective despite who might not understand my actions; despite who might not understand why this was necessary.

...Why it was fair.

I kept the details of my meeting secret from Roz, which she hated, but I knew better than to tell her everything. The less she knew, the less I'd have to worry about her getting in the way, getting hurt. From here on out, I had to see this thing through on my own. There would be time to explain and smooth things out with her later.

"Okay, clear out," the driver announced over the speaker, startling Roz awake.

I waited for her to get her bearings and then grabbed my bag to follow her and the others off the bus. Chris and Lucas had both gotten new shoes for Christmas, so they were sporting them, of course. Beth's hair was half a shade lighter, which meant she'd gotten it done while we were home. Most seemed refreshed, like they needed this break from being within the confines of the facility. Getting to see my family was nice, but it wasn't exactly relaxing. I chilled with my brothers a few nights, dedicating the rest of my time to research and the accompanying legwork.

Several monitors were waiting the moment our feet touched soil.

We were rounded up into groups and the rest of us waited as others were taken inside. I scanned the crowd, searching for a certain girl before catching myself.

That was over.

Completely.

I hiked my bag higher up my shoulders and, as I panned left, my vision snagged on a hard stare. My fists clenched on sight. Seeing Liam made everything I'd learned about him become real. I didn't care what impression he left on Evie; he was a coldhearted killer.

"Come with me, please."

I glanced up at the sound of a heavy, southern drawl. My arm was taken the next second. By Dallas, one of our combat instructors. He didn't explain himself, just requested that I follow him.

Unsure of what was going on, I hesitated. "Something wrong?"

No answer. He simply repeated himself, but this time it was less of a request, more of a command.

I caught Roz's eyes, noted the concern behind them. We had Lucas, Chris, and Beth's attention, too, now.

"Don't make a scene," Dallas said quietly, only loud enough for me to hear. His expression stayed calm, even.

Liam continued to stare, maybe hoping I'd give him a reason to react. Little did he know, nothing would've pleased me more.

Dallas' grip tightened and it didn't surprise me that, when he used force, Roz stayed in step with us.

Dallas paused, sizing Roz up. "Stay put," he ordered.

"No." His gaze landed on me when I protested. "As long as you can promise she won't be in any danger, she's coming."

He scanned us both again, but said nothing as we began to walk—neither confirming or denying.

We veered left, away from the front door. Instead, we took a side entrance I didn't even know existed. Liam, a few feet ahead, led the way. I kept my eyes trained on him, all the while staying aware of Roz, making sure she wasn't being led into a trap alongside me.

A dark, narrow staircase led several floors down as we left behind the ragged façade of the decoy house. Dallas pulled a walkie talkie from his hip and said two words to an unknown person at the other end.

"Open it."

Right after, the sound of a heavy, metal door squeaking on its hinges in the distance. We turned a corner and dim, yellow light filtered from a room. As we neared it, a formidable shadow darkened the doorway. Closer, I recognized Kas, another combat instructor—a tall guy just as intimidating in appearance as Dallas.

He stepped aside, staring down his nose at me as I passed through. And there, inside at the end of a long conference table, sat Evie. Our eyes locked for a long moment and, in those fleeting seconds, I was all too aware of how much had changed between us. Even more since my brief return to Seaton Falls. She was so different —toward me, in general. There was no warmth in the look that passed my way. Only ... indifference. Whatever I meant to her had been eclipsed by Liam's overwhelming shadow. The process of battling her conflicting feelings for us had ended. What remained— little as it may be—was final.

It shouldn't have bothered me that we were no longer close, but it did.

Without a doubt, it did. Especially as I struggled to understand what role she had to play in my being seized as soon as I stepped foot off the bus, brought down to what looked like an interrogation room.

Maybe that's what this was.

"Sit," Dallas mumbled, pointing me toward a seat. Roz took the one beside me. His gaze lifted to Liam before he spoke again. "Kas and I are heading up to get the kids in safely, then we'll be back. Get me on the walkie if things take a turn," he added, glancing at me when he did.

Liam gave a wordless nod, and then it was just the four of us—me, him, Evie, Roz.

A white laptop was turned toward me as he stood with folded arms, staring from across the table. On the screen, four paused videos

—two of the facility's perimeter, one in the entrance of the decoy house, another on an elevator.

Leaning back, I sighed. "What's this about? I'm tired and need to unpack."

Liam said nothing still, but he did move the mouse to the third clip, the one of the decoy house, and he pressed play. And then, within seconds, I understood why I'd been brought here.

The table creaked beneath Liam's weight when he braced his hands against the surface, leaning in.

"Mind telling me what's going on here? No one's had topside privileges for *months*. And yet ... looks like you strolled right on out of here just weeks ago."

I took a deep breath and accidentally glanced at Evie again. Her expression had softened. She was confused, but not angry. No, Liam had the market on angry cornered all on his own.

"Say something before I choke the answer out of you," he seethed through clenched teeth.

"You're not the only shifter in this room," Roz reminded him. A low hum in her throat was clearly the sound of a suppressed growl.

Liam didn't even acknowledge the threat, keeping his eyes trained on me. "Where'd you go?" he asked. "And how'd you do it without triggering the alarms?"

My entire body went rigid, filling with heat as I remembered an item in my possession. Something that would *more* than level the playing field.

It would destroy it.

I stood and turned toward the door, prompting Roz to stand when I took her hand. "We're leaving, and if I were you, I'd think twice about trying to stop us."

Quick steps were the first sign he didn't plan to heed my warning. The next was when the collar of my shirt was grabbed and my back was slammed to the wall. Roz's hand pried from mine with the violent movement.

Evie was on her feet.

My chest rumbled and rage seeped from my bones. Nose to nose, I stared into the eyes of the one person on this planet I hated enough to kill.

"The only way you're leaving here without giving me answers is on hands and knees, vomiting blood after I rip your intestines through your mouth," he spat.

Energy vibrated through my limbs, reaching my fist, already savoring the feel of burying it in his face. Roz cut in, maybe sensing what would've come next if she hadn't.

"He can't give you an answer because he doesn't have one," she said in a rush, desperate.

Liam's eyes narrowed, his brow lowering. "What's she talking about?"

"He … he blacks out," Roz explained.

I turned toward her, wishing she'd stop talking, but knowing she only said so much because she thought it might protect me. But I didn't need protecting.

Slamming my palms against Liam's shoulders, I shoved him away and slipped the bag down my arms. If a fight was going to break out, I was ready for it. I may have even been looking forward to it.

"How long's this been happening?" Evie asked when Liam got beside himself with rage. I saw it in his eyes. I imagined this was similar to the last image my grandfather had seen before death.

My back tensed and I felt the material of my shirt becoming tighter as my body all but begged me to let it shift.

"Since the mutts; the day Maddox was killed," Roz answered, casting a cold look Evie's way. "He's not conscious of what he does when he's like that. This isn't his fault. He's not trying to hurt anyone."

"Just what we need," Liam hissed, "a rogue Liberator."

"With all the lives you've taken, are you really the one to judge? All the blood you've shed?" I questioned.

He laughed, taking a step closer. "And I've been itching to add you to the list." The bulging veins of his hands and wrists began to glow orange as heat waves rose from his skin, distorting the air around him. My inner wolf took notice and responded, forcing my teeth to extend. He took that as a challenge, a *threat*, just like I would have.

Because it was.

"Get help!" Evie screamed. The next second, Roz darted for the door.

A loud clash of thunder ... that's the sound that filled the room when we collided, sending the long table flying to the other side like it weighed nothing.

His face was like stone against my fist when I swung. Instead of the hit taking him down, he smiled, drawing back too quickly to dodge. The blow struck my chest and air wheezed from my lungs. Before I could recover, another to the chin and I staggered back.

My shoulders swelled and the threads of my shirt's seams began to tear as it stretched again. I was shifting, but nowhere near quickly enough. His speed ... it was impossible to get a step ahead of him. He came closer and I raised my arm to block him, but was again one second too late.

The walls of my throat stung when he gripped it, lifting me into the air. I knew all too well that this was his infamous finishing move, ripping the throats of his victims. This was exactly the way my grandfather met his end.

"Liam, stop!" Evie screamed, shaking against the wall as the two of us did our best to make sure only one walked away.

At her words, he squeezed harder, cutting off my air supply completely. A white glow filled his eyes and the fury that came out of him filled the room.

"I should've ended you months ago," he panted, crazy with rage as his fingers sank deeper. I was lowered just enough for the tips of my shoes to scrape the ground, bringing us eye-to-eye. He was unaffected by the grip I had on his wrist as I tried to pry his hand loose.

A sickening smile came before dark words. "Not so hard to remember you're just a boy once you've been put in your place by a man, is it?" he laughed, taunting me for sport.

"Enough, Liam!" Evie called out again—louder, more confident. This time, when her voice hit his ears, he blinked and I could see she got through. There was probably nothing and no one else who could have.

He released me and my body crumpled to the ground as I struggled for breath, coughing, wheezing.

Evie stared, concern heavy behind her eyes as I clutched my chest. To emphasize how little Liam considered me to be a threat, he proceeded to turn his back and walk away, not worried in the least that I might succeed if I retaliated ... which was exactly why I did.

I rushed him with a perfect shot to slam his back with my shoulder, knocking him off balance, proving why it was never smart to get cocky during a fight. He should've been alert, ready. But instead, he was going to her, letting his guard down way too soon.

I quickened my pace, grateful for supernatural speed because it enabled me to get to him without making a sound, without him knowing what was about to hit him. I dropped low, positioning myself with those last few steps and then ... I hit my target, sending a body crashing to the floor.

Only ... it wasn't Liam's.

Evie cried out, writhing on the ground, clutching her arm as her face reddened. Tears were soon to follow, streaking her cheeks. At the last second, she noticed me coming for Liam and intervened, putting *herself* in harm's way to protect him.

"Evie!" Instinct sent me rushing to her. "I didn't mean ... I'm ..." Words failed me. This was all a mistake.

I took a step in her direction, but never got the chance to apologize. An elbow to my temple sent a wave of pain shooting through my skull. Dazed by the blow, I staggered back, clutching chairs and anything else I could grab hold of to keep from falling.

Through blurred vision, I watched as Liam knelt at Evie's side, checking her over with worry overtaking his expression.

But that only lasted a few seconds.

The next, the room quaked beneath his heavy steps as he charged toward me again with Evie struggling to call out from behind. But this time, I knew she wouldn't be able to stop him.

With the hit I'd taken, I couldn't get my bearings straight and wasn't able to get out of his path. I was lifted, nearly touching the ceiling, before being slammed to the table. Pain radiated through my back and limbs as the stone surface cracked beneath me. The room spun and Liam's angry face was all I could make out. My shirt was knotted in his fist, the front of my pant leg in the other. He lifted me again and, just as I was about to be dropped to the tile, a large body swooped in from my left, placing arms beneath my back to catch me.

"Whoa, whoa, whoa!" came a familiar voice.

Dallas.

Liam heaved, sweat coating his face as he kept his eyes locked on me. Nearby, Roz's gaze darted back and forth as fear left her shaken, bewildered.

Dallas took note of all the damage we'd done to the small room, and then of Evie in a heap on the floor. He pointed, sending Liam her way.

"Get her to Elise."

It took Liam's feet a moment to move in response to Dallas' command, because he wanted to finish what we started. But I saw the moment his priorities realigned, the moment tending to Evie became the most important thing.

She winced when he lifted her from the tile to cradle her against his chest. She was hurt and, accident or not, that was on me.

I knew it.

Liam knew it, and would likely never forget.

His cold, hard stare was set on me until he exited.

"I swear, I leave the room for two minutes and all hell breaks loose," Dallas mumbled to himself. "Stand up."

He offered me a hand. I hurt everywhere and probably would for a few hours until my healing mechanism kicked in. The same would happen with Evie, but I was positive whatever damage I'd done to her *body* wasn't what would take a while to heal.

This, hurting her, was what I'd been trying to avoid all this time. And yet ... here we were.

"Come with me," Dallas commanded.

"Where are you taking him?"

He paused and sighed before answering Roz's question. "To a cell where he can't hurt anybody, and nobody can hurt him," he breathed. He knew like I knew, Liam wasn't going to just let this go.

"And if either of you wants to give me trouble, we can do this the hard way," Dallas added. Right after, he tapped his pocket where a taser and the butt of a syringe showed. "Choice is yours."

"But he didn't do anything!" Roz's rationale was falling on deaf ears.

This went beyond the authorities thinking I was a loose cannon, went beyond their sudden lack of trust after seeing the video footage. With what I knew about Evie, with what had inadvertently been revealed in class about her true identity, what I'd just done was no small offense.

Because, technically, she was queen. Even if the rest of the supernatural world wasn't aware yet.

I turned and took Roz's shoulders, forcing her to focus.

"Listen to me," I said as calmly as I could, knowing she was on the verge of losing it. "It'll be fine. This'll blow over in a few hours and I'll come find you."

Empty promises. That was all I had to offer.

She stared, wanting to believe me, but unsure if she should. Eventually, she nodded. Dallas took my arm right after and led me out of the room to the elevator at the end of the hall. Something dawned on me at the last second and I turned to Roz in a rush.

"My bag!" I couldn't leave it behind.

Without hesitation, she doubled back and retrieved it from the room. When she returned, Dallas had just shoved me inside the elevator, getting ready to take me God-knows-where for God-knows-how-long. But wherever it was, Roz wasn't allowed to go. This was where we had to part ways.

"I'll come find you," I promised again.

There wasn't much hope in her eyes, but she nodded, never blinking as the doors of the elevator closed between us. I had no idea what lie ahead for me, but I did know one thing: thanks to Scarlet, I now had leverage.

Soon, the game would change, and for the first time in a long time, I wouldn't be in last place.

CHAPTER 26

Liam

Fewer things wear on the nerves like the sound of a ticking clock in a silent room.

I'd been in this spot for an hour, sitting, waiting. The second Elise emerged from her bedroom where Evangeline rested, I was on my feet.

"How is she?"

The brief hesitation was pure hell. "It's broken in two places, but she'll heal in a few hours."

Broken.

Nodding as I let that sink in—that the bastard managed to break her arm—I came up with a quick plan and took steps toward the door.

"Where are you going?"

An answer flew from my mouth without having to think about it. "To make him pay."

Elise's fingers splayed across my chest when she stepped into my path, blocking me from the door to exit her quarters. But she didn't understand. I needed to make this right. Nick broke Evangeline, now I was gonna break him.

"He's in a cell and Dallas is keeping an eye on him. He won't be able to get to her," she promised. "And, from what Dallas reported, this was all just a huge misunderstanding."

I was shaking my head in protest before she even finished her sentence. "I'm done with all the excuses. Done giving this kid passes when we all know what he really is; all know his mission is to end your daughter's life," I forced out, hating that those words had to leave my mouth.

"Don't you get that? If I end him now, Elise ... I'll spare us both from ever mourning her loss again."

She was silent, staring with wide eyes. I could only hope she was finally considering it, finally seeing the logic in my plan. I'd seen the first Liberator in action—his speed, his strength. I couldn't guarantee that, once Nick fully turned, I'd be able to stop him. Which was why we needed to act now.

It was time to be completely transparent.

"I won't survive losing her again," I confessed.

The first time, I spiraled, leaving a trail of blood and carnage in my wake. I couldn't afford to shoulder more grief. And, being honest, the world couldn't afford for that to happen either.

Elise backed off when she saw I was behaving sensibly ... for now.

"We'll just have to be more vigilant in our efforts to protect her. We'll—"

"What was your plan?" My question ended her babbling. "When you gave her dad that bogus promotion, when you dropped her in that town, in that house beside Nick's ... what was the plan?"

Elise's eyes searched mine for several seconds before having to turn away. She blinked, settling her gaze on the ground while she organized her thoughts to explain. However, instead, she simply said a name.

"Noah."

My brow twitched at the mention of her late husband, our king.

"Before us, no one would have ever thought it possible for our species to coexist. To thrive together, to experience *love* for one another," she sighed. "I knew firsthand how love and respect could triumph over myth."

Breath rushed in and out of my lungs at record speed as I let that sink in. It *sounded* like she was admitting to putting Evangeline in eventual danger based on a hunch.

"You were ... experimenting with your daughter's safety? Her life?"

"Keep your voice down," she whispered, glancing toward the closed door of her bedroom where Evangeline was resting. "I did no such thing."

"Didn't you, though? Intentionally putting her in Nick's path? Hoping for the best?"

"The first time around, we had no idea who the Liberator was, or even that he existed until it was nearly too late," she reasoned. "*This* time, we were able to get out ahead of the situation, position ourselves to ensure he wouldn't go off the rails."

"You know as well as I do, there's no ensuring *anything* when it comes to him. He'll act on instinct alone," I reminded her. "We still don't even know what sets him off! Look what happened today!" I gestured toward the bedroom door. "She's injured because Nick controls himself so well." The sarcasm didn't go unnoticed.

Elise crossed both arms over her chest and took a tone with me I was very familiar with, that of a mother scolding her son. I'd been in that position with her enough times to recognize it.

"From what I saw on the security feed, you were just as much at fault for this incident as *he* was."

My blood ran hot. *Was she serious right now?*

"You had one job," she hissed. "Show him the footage and get him to explain. We discussed nothing about you roughing him up."

"You weren't there," I seethed. "He was losing his head and I just beat him to it."

"The point is, I expect more of you than I do of him. More than I do of *most* people," she added. "We've all got a role to play and, yes, one of yours is to protect her, but you have to stick to protocol in the process."

She had my attention; I heard every word she said, but there was one thing wrong with her statement.

"My *only* purpose is to protect her," I corrected. "I never signed on to be anybody's puppet in whatever this plan is you all concocted. I will always do what's best for Evangeline," I made clear. "Even if what's best for her isn't best for everyone else. Myself included."

"You want him dead and I can't let that happen," she asserted. "I've already told you, I have to act in accordance with what the Council allows and keeping him alive was one such stipulation."

"Yeah, well maybe it's time we say screw the Council and their agenda and start doing what's right for *her*."

Elise didn't answer and it only irritated me more that she had nothing to say.

"What do they have on you that makes you bend to their will so easily?" I stared down on her, remembering how brazen she once was.

Brown eyes that looked so much like Evangeline's peered up at me and she breathed the only answer she had.

"My life," she revealed. "If the Liberator dies, if they can trace it back to me in some way or if evidence even *suggests* that I did nothing to stop it ... they've made it abundantly clear I won't live long to explain myself."

I took a step back, trying to think of a loophole while my head reeled. "I thought you were taken in as a member of the High Council, seated above even the Elders?"

She nodded. "I am ... but, like we've discussed, there are rules, checks and balances. I answer to them and they answer to me. It just so happens that, in their opinion, the Liberator is one of our greatest assets, a secret weapon we may need to employ in the very near future."

"And here we are again, making our plans around the idea that he'll even *be* on a side when all hell breaks loose."

"It's not my call and there's nothing I can do," Elise asserted.

She stared me down and, if I knew her as well as I thought I did, she was only standing firm to mask guilt. She knew I was right, knew we were playing chess with Evangeline's life.

I didn't break my gaze, wanting her to know I still thought this whole game was rigged, and not in our favor.

"Well, I guess we're done here." I dismissed myself whether she was finished speaking or not. Arguing with her was futile and taking my focus from where it really ought to be.

I knocked and then heard Evangeline's voice coming through the door.

"Come in." She sounded weak, like she was in more pain than she wanted any of us to know.

Laying eyes on her I wanted to mangle Nick all over again. There was no need for a sling or cast because she'd be better soon, so she lie there with the arm propped up on a pillow to keep it still.

"I'd ask how you're feeling, but I can see it all over your face."

I hated not being able to do more to help her. Tears pooled in her eyes, but she was trying to be strong, trying to keep them in.

"I'm okay," she forced out through gritted teeth. Elise had given her meds, but that kind of thing was hit or miss with us. With such fast metabolism, they were usually out of our systems before they even had the chance to work.

Which seemed to be the case now.

"This shouldn't have happened."

Shifting to get comfortable, she winced and my fists squeezed tight. The only thing keeping me from going down to that cell was the fact that I didn't want to leave her side.

Otherwise ...

"Have you heard anything about Nick? Where is he? What's gonna happen to him?" She didn't bother trying to conceal her worry for him.

Air rushed from my mouth when I took a seat on the bed, hating that she even cared, but understanding somewhat. They were close once.

"He's in a cell and he's breathing, which is more than he deserves."

She stared at nothing in particular, keeping some of her thoughts to herself.

"Is anyone contacting his family? They check in on him often. They'll worry."

It didn't surprise me that this would concern her—with what she'd been through with her *own* family, it made sense.

"Dallas is working out the details, but I'm sure it'll be handled by the book." Whatever that meant around here. "Can I get you anything? Do anything?" I offered. "I hate seeing you like this."

One corner of her full lips turned up and a small space on my thigh warmed when she placed her hand there. "I'll be healed and ready to kick your butt in the gym by morning."

Somehow, feeling as pissed about all this as I did … she made me smile. That shouldn't have surprised me either.

"I think we'll take it easy for a few days."

Her hair warmed my fingers when I pushed it away from her face, letting my hand settle against her neck. I stared at her often—dazed, silent—yes, because she was beautiful, but mostly because she was my reason for living. Even when she was gone, it was the memory of her that kept my heart beating.

Being careful not to injure her further, I leaned in for a kiss. A surge of tension left me the moment my lips were to hers. No one else could bring peace to my soul like she could.

Pulling back, I watched as her bright eyes fluttered open again. She'd been different since our talk the night we lost power. Before, I was always aware of how she held back, aware of all the things she didn't say for fear of where it might lead. Now, she was open and vulnerable, allowing me to see her heart, allowing me to see I wasn't in love alone.

As if she heard my thoughts, her hand moved from my thigh and soon our fingers were entangled—hers delicate and soft. I loved this side of her, reveled in the fact that I no longer had to live in fear of my strong feelings causing her to run. Discovering that we were linked beyond our tether, finding out that we'd exchanged vows and were bound in the traditional sense as well as the supernatural, it didn't scare her like I expected. No, we hadn't picked up where we left off centuries ago, but with a little time, I was hopeful we'd get there. I had no problem waiting.

"I think you should stay here with Elise tonight. I'll run down and get you something to change into."

Her eyes lowered to the jeans and fitted, black tee she wore, and then she nodded. "Okay, but just pants. I don't feel like struggling to get a shirt over my head."

I landed a kiss on her chin this time before standing to grab a few things from her room. "You got it."

As I stepped away, she held on to my hand until she had to let go.

"Wait," she breathed.

"Something wrong?"

Her long, dark hair fell over her shoulder when she shook her head. "No, but ... can you send Elise back in before you go?"

Working the soft flesh of her bottom lip between her teeth, she peered up at me, blinking. As one who sometimes wore her emotions on the outside, it wasn't lost on me that she was softening toward Elise. Asking her to sit with her was a show of vulnerability—a huge step. Like any girl who'd just had a bad night, she wanted her mom. That was a good sign.

"Sure thing."

This time, I reached the door before she stopped me with another softly spoken, "Wait."

I turned, smiling. "Yeah?"

Her lips parted with a grin. "No special requests this time. Just didn't want you to leave without saying..." She hesitated and I noted how her cheeks reddened as she breathed the rest of her statement. "I love you."

One clumsy syllable followed by another, the words finally tumbled out. She was new to this, owning her feelings, and it showed. I was pretty sure she'd never spoken that phrase to anyone who wasn't family. Until lately.

Until she said them to me.

Being transparent like this made her shy, but she didn't have to be. Not when I was insanely crazy for her. Not when I'd never heard anything sweeter.

Without hesitation, I said it back.

I loved her.

Since the beginning, lightyears beyond forever.

I loved her.

CHAPTER 27

Liam

The moron actually asked for me.

As bad as I wanted him dead ... he thought it'd be smart to request a one-on-one, just the two of us. The call came through to the walkie from Dallas right after retrieving Evangeline's clothes and delivering them to Elise's quarters. I volunteered to make myself scarce for the night to give Evangeline space. She needed time with her mother after the day she had. No, Elise and I weren't exactly seeing eye-to-eye at the moment, but that was between us, completely separate from her relationship with her daughter.

It didn't hurt that it made slipping out easier, without there being a need to explain where I was headed.

I smiled the whole way down to the cells and it grew when Dallas met me at the door, discretely handing over a key. He was the only one on guard and, with a vague nod, I knew he planned to give Nick and I all the privacy we needed. In other words, he'd go far enough away where he wouldn't hear the screams. Far enough away that he'd have full deniability if Elise should find out. It crossed my mind that, maybe, Dallas' thinking aligned with mine.

That maybe he, too, believed Nick ought to be dealt with now, while we were still able to do something about the threat he posed.

But then I remembered Elise's admission. If Dallas had known her life depended on Nick taking his next breath, he would've thought better of handing me this key. I'd behave myself for all parties involved. For now, until we figured something out, I'd have to leave him in one piece.

My steps echoed against cinderblock walls and cemented floors as I walked the narrow passage lined with empty cells. To my knowledge, no one else had been stupid enough to get themselves locked in one of these things.

No one but good ol' Nick.

I stopped when I got to him, staring at the blood-stained shirt he hadn't been allowed to change out of. Our eyes locked from his seat on the edge of a small bed.

I couldn't help but to laugh. A bed that small would never fit someone his size. The Council must've purchased them as a joke, or maybe that was part of the punishment for being dumb enough to get locked in one of these cages.

He stared, but said nothing.

My eyes flickered toward the large clock on the wall. "Something you wanted to say to me? A reason you brought me down here?"

The bed groaned when he relieved it of his weight. He stood there, glaring with a sinister grin. Reaching the bars, he finally spoke. However, I didn't expect these particular words to leave his mouth.

"Does the name Carmine LiCausi mean anything to you?"

White-hot blood surged through my veins just hearing it. My fists and teeth clenched at the same time. Of all the people I'd cut down over the centuries, many with impressive titles and armies at their disposal, and yet ... their names washed away from memory within the day.

But Carmine LiCausi, his was one I'd never forget.

I guessed the pup was trying to rattle me, so I decided not to let him.

"I see you've done a little research on your predecessor." I stepped closer. "Or are you studying his hunting techniques because ... well, let's face it; if you can't beat em', you may as well join em', right?"

When I laughed, a growl rumbled from the other side of the bars.

"Not exactly," he sneered.

If the only reason he'd asked for me was to try getting inside my head, I wouldn't give him the chance.

"We're done here."

I turned to leave, remembering I could've done anything I wanted to him right then. However, when I changed my mind and decided to leave well enough alone, it was because of Elise, and a certain wide-eyed girl with my heart in her hands. She would've wanted me to walk away.

Like I was doing now.

"You slaughtered him," Nick called out, speaking the words to my back. "In an alley. In cold blood," he added.

I faced him again, wondering where he'd gotten all this detailed information.

"And before you took his life, you took the life of the woman he loved. Her name was Opal, and she was innocent," he scoffed. "But you didn't care. Your only concern was to make *him* hurt like he made *you* hurt."

I said nothing. I couldn't. It took everything in me to focus my thoughts on something other than wanting to feel his heart beat its last beat in the palm of my hand.

"He spent most of his life on the run because of you," Nick explained. "Chasing phantoms, chasing some stupid ... *rings*," he added. "Which I'm sure didn't even exist. And it was all because he hoped to change your mind. All because he hoped time had changed you like it had changed him."

When I rushed to the bars, my hands burned as my dragon threatened to burst free.

"*Time* didn't change him," I corrected. "He stopped killing because he'd already done what he came to do. He'd already taken her life," I seethed. "He'd already ripped her limb from limb, leaving me to find ... *pieces* ... of her scattered on the ground like she was an animal!" It was graphic and difficult to say, but he needed to fully understand.

Smoke rolled off my body as I fought to keep my dragon in submission.

"He tore her apart like she was some empty, unloved ... *thing*," I spat, "but she was *everything* to me!"

Particles from the cinderblocks rolled to the ground in small plumes of dust when my voice shook them free.

"Well, I guess you've *never* been big on redemption," Nick went on. "Which explains why you've been ready to take my head off since you first laid eyes on me and realized what I was."

I said nothing because the more I spoke, the angrier I became, listening to him justify that creature's actions. Maybe he wasn't getting it. Maybe seeing Evangeline alive and well present day made it hard for him to fathom her being dead and gone for centuries; made it hard to fathom what it was like for me to miss out on all those years we should've had together. But even considering these things, it was unfathomable to me that he'd talk this way, considering how he felt about Evangeline once. Even if what existed between them was a thing of the past now. Still, it sounded like, tonight, he sympathized with the first Liberator above all others.

He stared a moment before smirking. "You know ... It's kind of ironic that you're the key to me overcoming this curse."

The off-beat threat made my brow tense, but that was when I noticed it, the small object he gripped in his hand—a smooth, dark stone, pulsating red like a beacon.

At the sound of footsteps approaching from behind, I didn't move, noting the stench of witches almost right away. Not all carried the scent, but those who dealt in dark magic eventually took on the aroma of death.

And I smelled it loud and clear.

"Please tell me you weren't that stupid," I breathed.

Nick's shoulders squared. "I'm doing what I have to do."

Doing what he has to do...

Without turning, I knew he'd summoned the Seaton Falls witches. To do what, I wasn't sure yet, but one thing was for sure, if they were here, things were about to go from bad to worse.

"What's your plan?"

At my question, Nick shrugged and I read his posture. He was relaxed, or maybe satisfied was a better word.

"I'm just trying to fix this," was his answer. "Trying to fix *me*."

It became abundantly clear that this—getting me down here—was a setup. One that would, inevitably, end badly for me.

"You know she'll never forgive you, right?" I said, trying to reason with him, knowing his soft spot for Evangeline, assuming some small trace of it remained.

It was true, if he carried out whatever his plan was, she'd never let it go. Even if her physical self didn't fully feel our connection, her dragon did and would stop at nothing to avenge me. There was a good chance her true nature would send her down a path similar to that which I'd traveled myself. If that happened, with her not having the support of family, I couldn't guarantee she wouldn't be a thousand times worse.

To my surprise, my rationale seemed to fall on deaf ears. Like he'd already made peace with the repercussions this plan would have.

"This is about the bigger picture," he explained. "If I don't turn things around now, you and I both know it won't end well for Evie anyway."

My eyes narrowed as I stared at him, practically smelling the naivety oozing from his pores.

"Is that what this is about? They convinced you they can change what you are?" I nearly laughed in his face. "And what? All they asked in return was that you deliver me to them?"

Kid hadn't lived long enough to learn to be careful which witches he trusted. They're self-serving by nature. Giving them the upper hand without actual leverage was never a good look. Once I was dead, then what?

"Ignore the dragon, Nicholas. He'll say anything to spare his life," came a small voice.

I turned, not surprised to be staring into the face of Scarlet. An eye patch marked the punishment the Elder had rained down on her for her insubordination months ago. I could only imagine tonight was yet another example of her disloyalty to the clan that ensured her immortality. And seeing as how I was sure she wouldn't risk this secret visit becoming known to the Elders, I was also sure they didn't intend for me *or* Nick to walk away from this ordeal alive.

Only, he was too stupid to see that.

Keeping my eyes trained on the three who'd just joined the party, I addressed Nick in his cell behind me. "Tell me, dickhead. Who convinced you calling on the devil's handmaids was the answer?"

When he didn't respond right away, I glanced over my shoulder, taking note of his somber expression. "Remember that name I mentioned earlier?" he asked.

I faced him now, but said nothing.

"Well, as luck would have it, this curse isn't exactly random." I listened harder as he explained. "Apparently, it's in our blood. Mine ... *my grandfather's.*"

The room seemed to tilt on its axis when he finished speaking. "Carmine LiCausi was your grandfather?"

Nick's nostrils flared as he breathed deep. "Was. Excellent choice of words, seeing as how you made sure he'd only ever be spoken of in past tense."

The smoke surrounding me thickened as the beast within fought for freedom, fought to be let loose to reap carnage on every soul in this room.

"You have no idea what you've done," were the last words I spoke before the feel of my head being squeezed in a vice brought me to my knees.

"Finally," Scarlet sighed, stepping past me. "I didn't think he'd *ever* shut up."

She went to Nick with that same sick, wicked smile that was always set on her mouth.

Through the pain, I managed to grunt a warning I wasn't sure he'd heed, one I was almost positive the witches wouldn't.

"Call this off, Nick. They're acting against the Elders. When they find out what's happened, when they find out what *you've* done ... you'll be cut down right with them. No questions asked."

Being *'special'* in their eyes, being the Liberator, wouldn't save him from the wrath of the Elders. Defying them would result in a show of power that warned others never to go against them, the Council.

I didn't care what happened to Nick, but I did care how his death would affect those that I loved. If I didn't, I would've taken him out within seconds of Dallas leaving us alone.

"Give it a rest already." Scarlet lifted her eyes to the ceiling while clenching her hand into a tight fist. And when she did, I felt that fist inside my gut, squeezing, twisting.

I yelled out again as blood seeped from my mouth and nose.

With the others flanking her right and left, she stepped closer, leaning in to speak. "You know, you're not so scary," she smiled. "When I was inside your head the day Baz brought us along to unearth all your secrets, I saw nothing but blood and death surrounding you—fear, dread." Her head tilted as she stared. "You caused your fair share of suffering."

My misdeeds were never far from thought. I couldn't take back the things I'd done, nor did I believe I deserved a clean slate. So, if her goal was to make me feel remorse for the lives I'd taken, she'd have to get in line.

"But … you know what I found *most* interesting about your memories?" she asked.

I didn't answer, *couldn't* as blood began to drip from my ears.

"A face," Scarlet sang with a grin. "The face of one victim in particular," she clarified.

I was too woozy to respond, in too much pain to even form words.

Scarlet stood straight again, clasping her hands behind her back as she circled me, continuing to keep me bound and helpless with her magic.

"The woman you killed in the alley the night you exacted revenge on Carmine? The one whose death you used as nothing more than a means of making his final moment that much more excruciating … Do you even remember her name?"

I panted when she let up for just a moment. The question was rhetorical, but I wouldn't have known the answer even if it wasn't.

She leaned in again after coming into view, whispering words that made this all make sense, her reason for targeting me after having seen my past.

"She was our sister."

I turned away from her voice, feeling her breath against my face and neck.

"All she ever wanted was to help Carmine," Scarlet added. "She was trying to undo what'd been done to him and … you killed her because of it. Now, today … you'll have the pleasure of joining the rest of your family," she laughed. "…In hell."

I'd never known physical pain like this. It was the kind that made you pray for death. I was reduced to a heap on the ground when she touched my skull, finishing what she'd come here to do.

It was impossible to hold on to any one thought when every fiber of my being screamed out in agony. But that didn't stop me from finding a morsel of a memory to grasp—a beautiful, angelic face bathed in sunlight beneath her favorite acacia tree. Keeping my mind's eye focused there, my breathing slowed the tiniest bit. Like always, Evangeline brought me peace. Even now, as the room began to dim, as the sound and pain started to fade.

I told her I loved her before I last walked away. There was comfort in that, knowing she'd have that to cling to when I was gone.

Scarlet was right. Everything she said—the circumstances surrounding her sister's death. At that time, I had no regard for *anyone's* life, including my own. But there was no sense in apologizing. It wouldn't bring her sister back. Had I been thinking clearer, someone still would've died that day, but it would have only been Carmine.

His life was one no one could ever convince me deserved to be spared.

I wasn't perfect. Never claimed to be. When I was angered, I was impossible to stop and had done dark things because of it. Evangeline's death was no excuse, but it was true; losing her broke me, took me down a bloody path. Most of the lives I'd taken were the result of the many wars I fought, righting the wrongs of those who thought their riches and might entitled them. But I admit, they weren't always. Sometimes, I lost myself and did unthinkable things. It was those secret acts, the ones I was ashamed of, that made this moment align with my motto concerning justice.

A life for a life.

The things I'd done were the reason I was here.

A sound echoed off the brick walls. It came from the direction of the massive, metal door I'd come through not too long ago. Right away, a pang of guilt hit me, realizing Dallas had returned at about the worst time possible. The witches wouldn't hesitate to cut him down, too, just for interrupting.

If I'd been able, I would've yelled for him to turn back while there was still time, but I was too weak. I struggled, doing all I could to gather enough strength, but it was useless. Scarlet made sure I couldn't give her any trouble. Made sure she'd get revenge for what I'd done to her sister all those years ago.

But then I saw light.

...*Blue* light.

My heart sank, realizing I'd been wrong. The one who walked into the middle of this ambush wasn't Dallas.

It was Evangeline.

This was my fault, her showing up here. I knew it right away. Our tether had, no doubt, brought her. There was no off switch and the incredible pain Scarlet inflicted most likely sent a distress signal straight to her.

"Don't," I managed to sputter.

Not too long ago, I'd given her a speech, one rule she could never break. She was to never put herself in danger for *anyone,* including me. But she'd never been one to follow directions and the evidence was trudging toward me, cloaked in brilliant blue flames.

Her eyes, whited out by the sheer heat bursting within them, were set on me. However, her expression was blank, vacant. Where fear and a sense of self-preservation should've halted her in her tracks, she walked straight into trouble.

Because of me.

Marin was the first she approached. With one quick reach, her throat was in Evangeline's hand, and within seconds, her feet left the ground. I'd all but forgotten about her injury and, from the looks of things, so had she. I found it hard to believe she could've healed that quickly, but the proof was in the power behind the blow she delivered to Lilith's chest with her elbow when she tried to intervene on her sister's behalf. Her cloaked body appeared weightless as it soared through the air. The impact formed a Lilith-shaped crater in the cinderblocks as a crack spread to the ceiling.

Evangeline turned her attention toward Marin's terrified eyes once again. With that vacancy still present behind her gaze, I watched as the love of my life, a forgotten queen, suddenly seemed to remember who she was. Seemed to remember what she was once capable of.

Before I could blink, she reached for the back of Marin's head with the hand not holding her in the air, and the next sound to fill the room was that of a head being turned backwards on its shoulders. Marin's lifeless body slumped to the cement and Evangeline stepped over it with zero regard, as if stepping over a bag of trash.

Lilith stretched a hand toward Evangeline when she charged toward her. The look of shock on Lilith's face was hard to miss when whatever spell she tried to cast failed. These witches were powerful, formidable. And yet, they proved no match for Evangeline in this ruthless state.

"No, no, no!" Lilith cried out as one flame-cloaked hand stretched toward her. With a quick touch to the ends of her hair, she went up in flames as her screams rose to the ceiling.

I'd watched Evangeline struggle to throw a punch for weeks. *Months.* But now, in a matter of seconds, she'd mastered how to control her flames' intensity—leaving one un-singed, consuming another in fire.

My strength was returning, and as I pulled myself up to lean against the closest wall, I watched her—poised, fearless. And that's when I realized her dragon had taken over. It was possible the distress signal that left me was so dire it strengthened her, kind of like a supernatural adrenaline rush.

But I had to wrangle her in.

It was only now that I could think clearly enough to make my way inside her head. She had to be stopped. Two of the three sisters had already met their end and I couldn't let her take out the third—as badly as I would have liked to see that happen. However, my reasons were bigger than revenge.

As it is written, one witch's spell can never be undone by another. Or, in this case, *three* witches. Meaning, if Evangeline couldn't stop, if she took Scarlet's life ... there would be no one left to undo the spell that stole all memory of her from her parents.

Scarlet stepped back when Evangeline's gaze settled on her. I staggered toward them. I had to bring Evangeline to her senses before it was too late.

Before she did something that couldn't be undone.

"Evangeline, don't. The spell," I reminded her through our thoughts. But there was no response.

Lifting a hand, Scarlet tried to use magic to spare her life just like Lilith had done. And, like Lilith, it didn't take.

There was no place left to go. Scarlet's back met the bricked wall and terror filled her eyes. If I had to guess, she regretted underestimating Evangeline. *Most* did. They made the mistake of thinking her slight build and innocent eyes were all there was to her.

Only Elise and I knew better.

From his cage, rapid breaths filled and left Nick's lungs. I couldn't help but to wonder if he now saw the err of his ways. If he now realized he didn't know Evangeline as well as he thought he did. And once she figured out all this was because of him ... things between them would never be the same.

I shifted my attention to Scarlet when she begged for her life once again, just as Evangeline pinned her frail, childlike body to the unforgiving wall. Using only the sole of her bare foot, she held Scarlet there as waves of fear rolled off her body. In that moment, there was nothing sweet and innocent about Evangeline. No. In that moment, she was rabid—wild, feral, feeding off the terror she evoked from her prey.

Scarlet fought to get free, using every ounce of strength within her to escape, but it was all in vain. The cracking of ribs echoed when Evangeline pressed her heel deep. I dragged myself closer, feeling desperation creeping up my spine every step of the way. She wasn't responding when I tried reasoning with her, so the only way was to subdue her.

Assuming I could, considering the state I was in.

"Don't," I panted, but my voice was too weak to be heard over Scarlet's cries.

I stared on, helpless as Evangeline placed both hands at either side of Scarlet's jaw. My heart raced double-time, hoping that by some small miracle I'd be able to stop her, but then ... it became clear.

I failed.

Scarlet's eyes rolled to the back of her head and the distinct sound of bone separating from bone filled the air. And then, in one final, earth-shifting act ... Scarlet's head was pulled free from her body.

The world stopped moving. For me. For Evangeline. Even if she didn't realize it yet.

With her back to me, I watched as her shoulders heaved with the last remnants of fury that flowed through her veins, unsure which aspect of herself was in control. It wasn't until her breathing seemed to slow and her flames began to dim that I knew. Her arms dropped to her sides and the head of the witch who nearly ended my life fell to the ground.

Evangeline didn't move an inch.

I figured she was in shock, suddenly realizing what she'd done, what this meant for her. Suddenly realizing what she'd just given up to save me.

Her parents ... they'd never remember.

Anger filled me to the brim when my eyes darted toward Nick, when I took in that bewildered look on his face. This ill-plotted plan of his had backfired in every way imaginable, and without knowing it, he'd just cost Evangeline everything.

I made it to her just as she collapsed, managing to get my arms around her before she hit the ground. Keeping her against my chest I felt her wildly beating heart.

"I didn't ... I didn't mean to," she stammered, dazed as slick blood clung to her hands. "I don't know what happened, I felt you and I just ... *ran*."

Her eyes drifted shut and when she opened them again, awareness suddenly filled them. She glanced around, taking in the state of this place, and I knew the exact moment the pieces came together.

"What did I ... Liam," she panted when fear set in.

She fought to scramble to her feet, but I held on tight, keeping her with me as reality hit.

Hard.

"Oh, God!" The words ripped from her throat and ricocheted off the walls. It was primal, desperate.

Heartbreaking.

I squeezed her when she began to fall apart right before my eyes. Tears flowed and likely would for hours to come as she came to terms with the repercussions. And, as she dealt with the aftermath of her actions, my gaze fell on Nick again.

Speechless, unaware of the extent of the damage he'd just caused, he stared back. Whoever thought he was worth keeping around would be in for the shock of their lives. Protecting Evangeline, the rightful heir to the lycan throne, was supposed to be priority number one. And that protection wasn't exclusive to her *physical* wellbeing. We needed her functioning with a clear head and heart as well.

But now, despite all our effort to get her through an already trying phase, the work had been undone.

There was no way to tell how long it would take her to recover from this, but the moment the full story was revealed and she discovered the part Nick played in today's event ... I was sure their once strong bond would be severed forever.

CHAPTER 28

Evie

Despair ... it consumed me.
Inside.
Out.
Right down to my soul.

Something was very wrong with me. How could I singlehandedly ruin my own life? My dragon took over and I was fully aware, conscious of my every decision, but ... couldn't stop. In that moment, everything I did seemed perfectly rational. In that moment, all that mattered was saving Liam.

I'd taken three lives just a little over an hour ago. All without a second thought, all without considering they might be redeemable. At the feel of that familiar tug in the center of my chest, I ran straight into danger because he needed me and ...

... that's what love makes you do.

And I loved him so much it hurt.

But there was a cost.

So much slipped through my fingers. Still in shock, I took a seat on Liam's bed, staring at the wall, letting it all sink in. I couldn't go back to my room. There, I'd have to face Beth and questions when she inevitably realized something was wrong. Not to mention, before showering, I was covered in blood from head to toe. All I wanted was this—quiet and Liam.

A warm hand caressed my back through the dark towel I'd been given. He brought me a change of clothes, too, but I hadn't had the presence of mind to get dressed yet. His fingers moved to my shoulders, massaging, pressing gently into my skin where water dripped from my damp hair. His heat soothed me. Deep breath after deep breath, I struggled to accept what I'd done, but ... it simply wouldn't take.

"What's wrong with me? I couldn't stop." Hot tears streaked my face and I ached with regret from head to toe.

"There's absolutely nothing wrong with you," Liam breathed.

I believed *he* believed that, but I knew better. My parents getting their memory of me back was dependent on those particular witches making good on their promise. A promise that couldn't be kept now that they were dead.

My head lowered.

"I lost control," I reasoned, recalling a conversation I had with Dallas on the first day of combat training. He warned me that the rumored rage wasn't myth. That had to be what came over me.

"What am I supposed to do from here?" The question left my mouth, but I didn't expect an answer. Really, I think I just needed to ask it out loud. Needed to acknowledge there *was* no answer and I felt lost.

From here, there was nothing.

"I don't even understand what happened. Why were they here? Did the Sovereign send them? Or Baz? Did he set us up?"

Silence followed my questions and I turned to glance into

Liam's eyes. There, on his face, a solemn expression I didn't quite expect. Granted, he was sad with me, *for* me, but it was more than that.

"What aren't you saying?"

Again, he looked everywhere but at me. Both his hands still braced my shoulders, but they weren't moving.

I turned a bit, facing him. "Was I right? About Baz setting us up?"

My mind reeled, wondering if him sending his witches meant he didn't keep his word. Wondering if it meant something had happened to my parents. Seeing me start to panic, Liam spoke.

"No ... it wasn't him."

My head tilted with a question. "But it was a set up?"

He took his time, but eventually nodded. I racked my brain trying to understand. Who in our circle would do such a thing? Who couldn't be trusted? With how raw and exposed my emotions were, I wanted to kill them. While Scarlet and her sisters' blood was on *my* hands, it was also on this other person's.

"It wasn't meant for you?" was the next part of Liam's statement. I felt my brow tense with a frown before he added, "It was meant for me."

I studied his face and hazel eyes finally locked with mine. And then, a name fell from his lips.

"Nick."

The room seemed to twist and move as things shifted in and out of focus. Blood rushed to my head and I felt faint.

"What? I ... I don't understand? Why would he—"

"Because they conned him into thinking they could cure him," Liam explained. "Because he's incessantly juvenile and naïve. Because all it would've cost him was my life," he rambled before his gaze slipped to the ground. "Or at least, that's all he *thought* it would cost."

My hands ached with a familiar sensation before the centers of my palms began to burn. I clenched them into tight fists as the same flare of rage that filled me earlier threatened to return. I couldn't let that happen again. Last time, blood was shed. This time, I couldn't guarantee it wouldn't be Nick's.

"He was willing to kill you," I muttered, mostly to myself. "Knowing it'd hurt me. Knowing I don't have much ..."

My sentence trailed off and a thought came to mind. Something I'd never thought toward Nick once since meeting him.

He was selfish.

His hatred toward Liam was enough to cancel out any ounce of respect and concern he ever had for me. It was clear and the evidence was splattered on the floor and walls outside his cell. No, he hadn't directly inflicted pain on me, but he cost me my parents today, and nearly cost me Liam as well.

Regardless of how things turned out between us, I would never intentionally hurt him.

Ever.

But he didn't have the same regard for me.

My heart glazed over with ice and I knew I'd never see him the same. Once, he'd been my bright spot, the one who kept me centered ... but now, as I lifted my eyes to another, I knew my heart was sold, and *had* been since the first time I collided with him on the street.

"I'm so sorry," Liam breathed, lost as he searched for a way to make this better. "All I ever wanted was to protect you."

I looked him over, the disappointment behind his eyes. He felt so much, so deeply it spilled over onto me. I took his face in my hands and he met my gaze.

Once I had his attention, I tried to ease his mind. "This isn't on you."

He heard me, but I needed him to believe it. His focus since the moment our paths crossed again was to look after me. At times, I didn't understand it, didn't appreciate it, but I got it now. As everything else fell away, I got it.

My constant hadn't moved.

Yes, today was terrible, one of the worst I'd ever lived through, but it could have been so much worse. I could have suffered a greater loss. Studying Liam's features, I tried to imagine what would have happened if Scarlet and her sisters had succeeded.

If *Nick* had succeeded.

If they'd taken Liam away from me.

He blinked as we got lost in each other, his hazel irises spinning my insides into a cyclone. As if I hadn't already fallen far enough, I fell even further. I needed the hurt to be kissed away and Liam surrendered his lips exactly the way I hoped he would. I was dead on the inside, broken, and desperate to be alive again.

My hands slipped down his arms to his wrists and, at the feel of the leather bracelets resting there—one in its rightful place, the other belonging to me—I was reminded of just how entangled our lives once were. Yes, I was his friend, the one he regarded as his queen. But I was more than that ...

... *we were mated.*

The memory of it had been stolen, but my heart, my *dragon,* couldn't seem to forget. She clung to him.

When my fingers lifted the hem of his shirt, my lips went cold when he abandoned them.

Hoarse, breathless, he asked, "What're you doing?"

I didn't back down. I'd never given myself to another, had never felt like the time or the guy was right, but here with him, there was clarity. This wasn't my emotions running away from me or an action I decided to take in a haze of grief. He was what I wanted.

More was what I wanted.

I sought his lips again, but he was still hesitant, fully aware of my intentions, fully aware of how far I wanted this to go. Warm air moved across my lips when he breathed only inches from them.

I inhaled him and shared what was on my heart. Holding his face, I made it plain.

"Liam ... most men struggle to steal a woman's heart *once* in a lifetime," I explained. "But somehow, you've done the impossible." I smiled and moved my fingers across the shadow of hair shrouding his jaw. "...You made me fall *twice.*"

And tonight, I wanted him to remind me what it meant to fully be his. For the first time ever, with him, with *anyone,* there would be no limits.

I reached to release my towel, untying it from my chest, but just before letting it fall, my hands were covered by his.

"Don't," he breathed, clearly warring within himself when he spoke.

My brow tensed, not understanding why he'd stop me. I knew he loved me, knew he felt the pull, the tension.

"Not like this," he clarified. "Believe me ... I want you, but ... not like this," he said once more.

Confused, I secured the ends of my towel across my chest again, trying to understand. His attention had been focused intently on my figure as I came close to exposing myself. Only now did his eyes come back to mine.

"I think you're beautiful and I love you," he stated, telling me things I already knew. "But when we ... *reconnect* ... I don't want your head or your heart in a million different places."

My hands warmed when he took them. My gaze lowered as every feeling and emotion I tried to drown in him resurfaced.

"You're allowed to grieve," he stated, and I looked to him again, seeing the kindness and restraint of a real man when I did.

He could've let me have my way with him. Right there, right then. Could've taken advantage of my brokenness and the fact that I was at my lowest and most vulnerable right now.

But he didn't.

Because he's good, and honest, and honorable—a few of the many things I loved about him.

His palm moved to my cheek and I leaned into it, already feeling grateful that he stopped me. It wasn't that it wouldn't have been right with him. It was simply that, when it happened, I didn't want the moment to be overshadowed by sadness like it would've been tonight.

"When the time is right, it'll happen, and it'll be incredible," he smiled. "But tonight ... it's okay for you to hurt."

A tear slipped down my cheek as I took him up on that, letting myself feel. Letting myself fully grasp what I'd done; what I'd lost.

Closing the distance between us, I moved into his arms, settling against his chest as the warmth of an embrace tightened around my shoulders. I shouldn't have been surprised that he stopped me. He'd made it his duty to be my protector.

And, apparently, that sometimes even meant protecting me from myself.

Liam

She was warm and perfect beside me where she slept, sharing my bed tonight because she didn't want to be alone. Sleep never came, not for me anyway. Probably because I was still in shock after having turned her down.

It had nothing to do with not wanting her, but had everything to do with not wanting her to regret it all by morning. She was in no frame of mind to make such a life-changing decision. Not after what she'd been through.

I had zero expectations when it came to our progress. That way, if things moved slowly, or didn't move at all, there was no room for disappointment. That was the only thing that got me through tonight —lying beside the woman I love, exercising an inhuman measure of restraint as I struggled not to go back on my word. She needed me, but not in that way. Not tonight.

I traced the bracelet she moved from my wrist to hers right before she drifted off. We'd never been traditional in any sense of the word, so exchanging rings didn't appeal to me *or* her back then. The bracelets were uniquely us, and taking hers back, wearing it, she made it clear she didn't intend to run.

At the risk of waking her, I laced my fingers with hers where they rested on my chest, lifting her hand to kiss the back of it. Her heart beat against my side and I didn't imagine *heaven* could even be so perfect.

This, here with her, was my heaven.

However, the next instant, our little slice of paradise was interrupted by a frantic knock at the door.

Evangeline startled awake, quickly sitting upright in bed, clutching a hand to her chest when the pounding hit the air for a second time.

"Sit tight. I'll see who it is." I moved quickly through the darkness, trudging toward the door.

Squinting when light filtered in from the hallway, my eyes landed on Elise. Hers were wild with concern and the sight of her panicked expression made my heart race.

What now?

"Can I come in?" she asked. Peering over her shoulder as a monitor passed by, making his rounds.

I glanced inside my room where Evangeline climbed out of bed wearing the t-shirt I'd given her before bed.

I stepped back and closed the three of us inside, hitting the switch on a nearby lamp that brought the space to life in the middle of the night.

"I'm sorry to bother you so late, but we've got a problem."

Of course, we did.

"What is it?" I asked, knowing I'd regret this.

Today had been a strange mix of highs and lows. And now, from the way Elise rushed to open and boot her laptop, I knew this was another low. The cycle continued.

"This," she sighed. "Kas got Dallas on the walkie when he found her."

I peered at the camera, staring at one of the combat instructors on the ground with a heavy pipe lying beside her. I could only guess it'd been used to knock her out cold.

But what was even *more* problematic was the empty cell beside her.

My fists clenched at my sides.

"*He* did this?" I barely got the words out, my jaw was so tense.

Elise shook her head. "No. He had help," she replied, rewinding the footage further, pointing toward a still of Roz and Nick escaping.

Hand in hand.

"His accomplice," Elise added.

My gaze moved toward Evangeline as worry spread across her face. I hated seeing it there, but was honestly relieved she wasn't taking this so lightly anymore.

"What's the plan?" I asked, shifting my gaze back toward Elise. "We're gonna need reinforcements to keep an eye on her. Do we even know where he is?"

Elise breathed deep. "All we know is he left the facility. Straight up the elevator shaft like before, but with less finesse," she added. "Meaning, he's conscious of what he's doing this time."

The blood in my veins ran hotter than usual. "Do we have eyes topside?"

Elise nodded. "Dallas assembled a team," she assured me. "If he returns ... we'll know about it, but ... I have a feeling he doesn't intend to come back."

"Not consciously," I corrected. "Who knows what he'll do or where he'll go if he blacks out."

I paced and thought, adding, "There has to be more we can do."

Elise didn't chime in, prompting me to glance her way. She had a thought, but wasn't sharing it.

"What?" I asked, pausing mid-step.

Her gaze flitted toward Evangeline for a moment.

"I've been thinking," Elise began. "Ever since you mentioned earlier that, when she faced the witches ... their magic didn't work on her."

I nodded. "What about it?"

Elise pursed her lips together and, for the fraction of a second, I thought I saw hope in her eyes.

"You've got a plan?" I was ready to hear it. *Whatever* it was.

"Well ... it's half a plan," she began. "If we can get Hilda here, I think Evangeline may be ready. I think she's powerful enough."

My brow tensed. "Powerful enough? In what way and for what purpose?"

I followed Elise's hand when she shoved it inside her pocket, bringing out a tightly closed fist as words left her mouth. Words my brain could hardly register.

"...To bring them back," she replied. "*My boys.*"

Her eyes went to Evangeline again. "I've already explained that Hilda is your father's sister, one of the most powerful witches to ever live," she explained. "That power is inherited, passed down from one generation of women to the next." A kind smile touched her lips. "Meaning ... there's a reason those witches couldn't touch you today, a reason, despite a curse that was placed on me centuries ago ... you were still born."

"Curse?" I'd never heard anything about it.

Elise nodded, breathing deep before she explained. "It was the Sovereign's witches. Shortly after Noah and I fell in love, word traveled quickly, mostly because it was unheard of for a dragon and a lycan to coexist—let alone for the originals to fall in love. One evening before we were married, Noah sent for me. Said he couldn't survive another night without me," she shared with a distant smile. "So, I left with the two guards he sent, but our path was intercepted. It was the Sovereign." A cold look filled Elise's expression.

"He knew he had no one powerful enough to kill me, so he did the next best thing," she explained. "He'd given his witches orders to hex me, damning me to only ever give birth to male children and that they would be sterile, unable to bear children of their own, just to mock me. It ensured that, if we were to ever be killed off ... our bloodline would die with us."

Her gaze lifted toward Evangeline.

"...And then *you* came, defying their magic—a girl child born to a dragon, one who'd been cursed to only ever have sons." She crossed the room and stood before Evangeline, locking eyes with her only daughter. "You're more special than you realize."

Her thin fingers unfolded, finally revealing what she'd removed from her pocket. Six gold rings with smooth, black stones set in their centers—rings that matched one of my own I'd kept locked away for years.

Elise's eyes were alight with hope as she stared into Evangeline's, speaking two words that filled the room with so much uncertainty for the future.

"It's time."

To find out what happens next, get your copy of
HEART OF THE DRAGON, *today!*
https://www.racheljonasauthor.com

Love ARCs, random giveaways, and fun bookish conversation? Come hang out in my Facebook group for readers,
THE SHIFTER LOUNGE!
https://www.facebook.com/groups/141633853243521
Can't wait to chat with you :)
For all feedback and inquiries, email me at author.racheljonas@gmail.com

THE LOST ROYALS SAGA

A NOTE FROM THE AUTHOR

Thank you so much for reading Dark Side of the Moon, *The Lost Royals Saga, Book 2*.

If you have enjoyed entering the world of the Lost Royals, show other readers by leaving a review!
Just visit my website for all available portals where to review the book:
https://www.racheljonasauthor.com

Join my readers' group for more news The Shifter Lounge
https://www.facebook.com/groups/141633853243521
and my Newsletter today!
https://us14.list-manage.com/subscribe?u=
73f44054c9dda516cc713aea7&id=ad3ee37cf1

THE LOST ROYALS SAGA

NEXT IN SERIES

Book Three of *The Lost Royals Saga*
HEART OF THE DRAGON

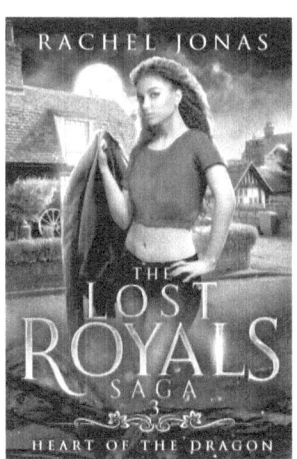

**Even the deadliest dragon warrior has a weakness …
his answers to the name Evangeline.**

Liam suffered the loss of his mate once before, but with forbidden magic, Evie has returned to him. His reputation as "The Reaper" is one he earned ... one kill at a time. So, if there's any warning his enemies should heed, it's that he'll stop at nothing to keep history from repeating itself; will stop at nothing to protect her.

Evie senses the walls rapidly closing in as her role in the revolution becomes clear—a movement in which the supernatural order has begun to shift. All who stand for the cause have made sacrifices, including Evie who's faced several hard truths.

The hardest lesson being one that brought loyalty into question—a single, careless act at the hands of someone she trusted. Someone who nearly cost her everything.

Nick never wanted any of this. As he struggles to understand the nature of his dual identities, he's haunted by the pain and destruction he's caused as his dark side gains strength.

Escaping his cell and running was the only option, but that doesn't mean he'll escape the repercussions.

No one's out of the woods yet. The line between enemies and allies blurs for the Seaton Falls clan amidst rising tension, rumors of a traitor among them ... and the arrival of an uninvited guest.

*Grab your copy of **"Heart of the Dragon"** today!*
https://www.racheljonasauthor.com

THE LOST ROYALS SAGA

NEXT FROM RACHEL JONAS

There's a spinoff of the Lost Royals Saga!
Own the DRAGON FIRE ACADEMY trilogy today!

Four dragon warriors.
A beautiful shifter hybrid.
An island with a dark secret that could bring them all to their knees.

Seriously? Four dragon warriors need to stalk my every move? I get it; they think I'm dangerous, but I'm only on their island to learn. Not to destroy it.

This is another unfortunate side-effect of being the freak who descended from all three supernatural lineages. The bloodthirsty dragons, the destructive wolves, and the disloyal witches. Some believe that, when I transition in a few months, there's a slight, teeny tiny chance I could unleash hell on the supernatural world. Call me crazy, but I'd know if I harbored that kind of power inside me.

... Wouldn't I?

My entire life, all I've wanted was to be normal. Hence the reason I didn't think twice about trading in my crown for a stack of books. I've got three terms on this island to prove the naysayers wrong, including my chaperones—Kai, Ori, Paulo, and Rayen.

These four are gorgeous, but also ominous as heck. Babysitting me has clearly taken their focus off something they've deemed more important. So, now they go out of their way to make my life a living hell, with hopes that I'll give up and leave.

Thanks, guys.

You could cut the tension between us with a knife, but what's weird is I don't hate them all the time. There are even odd moments when I catch them watching me. And not in their usual "wish-you-were-dead" sort of way.

Even if I survive the academy, there's still no guarantee these four and I won't kill each other before graduation.

Grab book 1 now!
https://www.racheljonasauthor.com

THE LOST ROYALS SAGA

ABOUT THE AUTHOR

Rachel Jonas also writes as Nikki Thorne.

Hey, I'm Rachel! Consider this your formal invitation to hang out in my private Facebook group, THE SHIFTER LOUNGE. You'll get fun book convo, exclusive giveaways, and other random acts of nerdiness!

Don't usually talk to strangers? No worries! Allow me to introduce myself. I'm a Michigan native, wife, and mother of three who made a career of indulging the voices inside my head :) With several completed series, and stories in both the paranormal and contemporary YA/NA romance categories, there's something for everyone!

Happy reading!

Don't forget to follow me!

Twitter: @author_R_Jonas
IG: @author.racheljonas
Rachel's Facebook: https://www.facebook.com/authorracheljonas/
Reader Group:
https://www.facebook.com/groups/141633853243521/
Amazon: amzn.to/2BHiLlS
Goodreads:
https://www.goodreads.com/author/show/16788419.Rachel_Jonas
BookBub: https://www.bookbub.com/profile/rachel-jonas
Nikki's Facebook: https://www.facebook.com/nikkithorneauthor/
TikTok: https://www.tiktok.com/@racheljonasauthor